JUDY BLUME

It's Not the End of the World

Then Again, Maybe I Won't

Deenie

DEAN

Dean in association with
Heinemann Young Books

It's Not the End of the World first published in Great
Britain 1979. *Then Again Maybe I Won't* first published in
Great Britain 1979. *Deenie* first published in Great Britain 1980.

This edition published 1991 by Dean,
Michelin House, 81 Fulham Road, London SW3 6RB
Text copyright © 1971, 1972, 1973
Reprinted 1991, 1992

ISBN 0 603 55029 0

Printed in Great Britain by The Bath Press, Avon

Contents

It's Not the End of the World

for John
who married a monkey-face-maker

one

I don't think I'll ever get married. Why should I? All it does
is make you miserable. Just look at Mrs Singer. Last year she
was Miss Pace and everybody loved her. I said I'd absolutely
die if I didn't get her for sixth grade. But I did – and what
happened? She got married over the summer and now she's
a witch!

Then there are my parents. They're always fighting. My
father was late for dinner tonight and when he got home we
were already at the table. Daddy said hello to me and Jeff.
Then he turned to Mom. 'Couldn't you have waited?' he asked
her. 'You knew I was coming home for dinner.'

'Why didn't you call to say you'd be late?' Mom asked.

'It's only twenty after six. I got hung up in traffic.'

'How was I supposed to know that?' Mom asked.

'Never mind!' My father sat down and helped himself to a
slice of meat loaf and some spanish rice. He took a few
mouthfuls before he said, 'This rice is cold.'

'It was hot at six o'clock,' Mom told him.

Me and Jeff kept on eating without saying a word. You could
feel what was going on between my parents. I wasn't hungry
any more.

Then Daddy asked, 'Where's Amy?'

'In the den,' Mom said.

'Did she eat?'

Mom didn't answer.

'I said did she eat her supper?'

'Of course she did,' Mom snapped. 'What do you think I
do – starve her when you're not around?'

My father pushed his plate away and called, 'Amy . . .
Amy . . .'

Amy is six. When she doesn't like what we're having for
dinner she eats a bowl of cereal instead. Then she races into

the den to see her favourite TV show. But when Daddy called her she ran back to the kitchen. She gave him a kiss and said, 'Hi Daddy.'

'How's my girl?'

'Fine.'

'Sit down at the table and drink your milk,' he said.

'First a riddle,' Amy told him.

'Okay, but just one.'

Amy is driving us crazy with her riddles. Ever since she started first grade it's been one riddle after another. And you can't tell her you already know the answer because she doesn't care. She'll keep asking anyway.

'Why did the man put Band-Aids in his refrigerator?' Amy asked.

'I give up,' my father said.

'Because it had cold cuts!' Amy laughed at her joke. She was the only one who did. 'You get it now? *Cold cuts*. The refrigerator had cold cuts! Like bologna ... get it?'

'I get it,' Daddy said. 'That's a very good riddle. Now sit down and drink your milk.'

As Amy sat down she accidentally shook the table and her milk spilled all over the place. Mom jumped up to get the sponge.

'Don't be mad, Mommy. It was an accident,' Amy said.

'Who's mad?' my mother shouted. She mopped up the mess. Then she threw the sponge across the kitchen. It landed on the counter, next to the sink. 'Who's mad?' she hollered again as she ran out of the room and down the hall. I heard a door slam.

My mother's temper is getting worse. Last week she baked a cake. When she served it my father said, 'That's not mocha icing, is it?' And my mother told him, 'Yes, it is.' So Daddy said, 'You know I can't stand mocha. Why didn't you make chocolate?' And Mom said, 'Because I'm sick of chocolate, that's why!'

I love dessert and by then my mouth was really watering.

I wished they would hurry and finish talking about it so I could start eating.

But my father said, 'I'll have to scrape off the icing.'

Mom looked right at Daddy and told him, 'Don't do me any favours!' Then she picked up that beautiful cake, held it high over her head and dropped it. It smashed at my father's feet. The plate broke into a million pieces and the chips flew all around. It was one of our ordinary kitchen plates. I'll bet if it was an antique, my mother never would have dropped it like that.

Later, when nobody was looking, I snitched a piece of cake off the floor. Even though it had fallen apart it was still delicious.

But that was last week. Tonight Mom didn't throw anything but the sponge. As she ran out of the kitchen my father cursed, crumpled up his napkin and got up from the table. Jeff pushed his chair away too, but my father hollered, 'You stay right where you are and finish your dinner!' He grabbed his coat and went out the back door. In a minute I heard the garage door open and the car start.

'You really picked a great time to dump your milk,' Jeff told Amy. He is fourteen and sometimes very moody.

'I didn't do it on purpose,' Amy said. 'You know it was an accident.'

'Well, I hope you're happy,' he told her. 'Because the whole rotten night's ruined for all of us now!' He cursed like my father and Amy started to cry.

'I'm going to my room,' she told us. 'Nobody loves me any more!'

Jeff was the next one to walk out of the kitchen, leaving me there alone. I knew where he was going. To his private hideaway. It's on the third floor and it used to be the spare room. The ceiling is low on one side and the windows are small and up high. I don't see why anybody would want to sleep in there if he didn't have to.

Jeff spent a lot of time decorating it. There's a big sign on

13

the door that says *Jeff's Hideaway/All Who Enter Do So at Their Own Risk*. Then there's a purple light hanging from the ceiling and a million posters all over the walls. It's very messy too. In the fall we had to have the exterminator because of Jeff. He took so many cookies and crackers and cans of soda up there we got bugs. My father was really sore! Jeff doesn't throw his garbage under the bed any more. And he's not supposed to drink soda anyway. It's bad for his zits. My mother calls them pimples and says he's lucky that he's only got one or two.

His zits don't stop the girls from calling though. They call all the time. My father has threatened to limit Jeff's phone conversations to two minutes. Jeff doesn't care. There's only one girl he wants to talk to anyway. That's Mary Louise Rumberger. She's in his formroom. I've only seen her once. She has very nice hair and she smells like Noxzema.

I know what Jeff does up in his room. He lifts weights. Isn't that the dumbest thing? He wants to be on the wrestling team next year. My mother's worried sick because she's afraid he'll get hurt. I wonder if maybe Mary Louise Rumberger likes big muscles?

two

The house was very quiet. I was still sitting at the dinner table, making little designs on my plate with the spanish rice. I thought about clearing away the dishes and even stacking them in the dishwater. But why should I? I didn't start the fight. It wasn't my fault dinner was ruined. I wondered if my mother had something special planned for dessert. I wasn't about to ask her though. She was probably locked up in her bathroom.

I went to the pantry and took down a box of chocolate-chip

cookies. On my way upstairs I scooped up Mew, who was sitting on her favourite chair in the living room.

She is supposed to be the family cat but she loves me best. Probably because she knows I love *her* more than anything in the world. From far away it looks as if Mew's coat is dark grey, but when you get up close you can see that she's really striped – black, grey, a tiny bit of white and even some red here and there. She is also very fat. She wears a collar with bells around her neck. This helps do two things: One is, it warns the birds, which Mew loves to chase. And two is, it keeps her from sneaking up on you. She's very good at sneaking around. Sometimes she hides under our beds and when we walk by she jumps out. That's just her way of playing. Neither my mother or my father is crazy about Mew and her games.

When I got to my room I closed the door with my foot and put Mew down on my bed. I flopped next to her and she stretched out. She likes me to scratch her belly. I ate my cookies and let Mew lick up the crumbs. She has never put out her claws at me. And she doesn't rip up the furniture like other cats do. It's a good thing too, because if she did we wouldn't be able to keep her.

Some people might think Mew is a dumb name for a cat. But when she came to our door two years ago she was just a tiny kitten. She called *mew mew mew* and I gave her a dish of milk. She's been ours ever since. At first we all tried to think up clever names for her. But while we were thinking we got used to calling her Mew. So finally we gave up and agreed that would be her name forever.

She curled up and went to sleep as I sat down at my desk. My desk is very special. It used to be a part of somebody's dining-room set. Mom bought it for five dollars and refinished it herself. She's very good at that. Now it's bright yellow and has small gold handles on every drawer. My friends think it's neat.

I opened my middle drawer and took out my Day Book. My

father gets one in the mail every December and he gives it to me. It has a plain black cover with gold letters that say *Global Insurance Company*. Inside there's a half page for every day in the year. It's not really a diary because it has no lock. It's more of an appointment book, but I don't keep a record of my appointments. If I have to go to the dentist or something like that my mother marks it on her calendar. I'm not interested in writing down that stuff.

I do keep a bunch of rubber bands wrapped around my Day Book just in case anyone happens to be snooping in my desk. They are arranged in a special way that only I understand. I took off all six of them and opened to Thursday, 25 February. At the top of the page I wrote: *Fight – E.N.'s fault.*

E.N. are my mother's initials. They stand for Ellie Newman. Her real name is Eleanor but nobody ever calls her that. My real name is Karen and nobody ever calls me anything else. It's hard to make a nickname out of Karen.

I try to be very fair about my parents' fights. Tonight was definitely my mother's fault. She should have been nicer to Daddy when he came home. She knows he likes to relax with a drink before dinner. And she shouldn't have hollered when Amy spilled her milk. That can happen to anyone.

The time Mom dropped the cake on the floor was my father's fault. He started that one by saying he hates mocha icing. So that night I wrote: *Fight – B.N.'s fault.* My father's name is Bill – well, really William, but that's beside the point.

I put my pencil in my mouth and chewed on it for a while. When I was in first grade we had a contest to see who had the fewest teeth marks on his pencils at the end of the year. I lost. Biting on a pencil helps me think better.

I flipped back through the pages of my Day Book. I always give each day a mark, like on a report card. Practically every day this month has got a C.

My last A+ day was 14 December. That was a really perfect one. First of all, Gary Owens, who is a boy in my class, chose me as his partner in a spelling bee. I hope it wasn't just because I am a good speller. And second of all, Mrs Singer acted practically human. She didn't yell once. But the best thing about that day was the snow. We usually don't get that much snow so early in the season. It started in the morning and didn't stop until dinnertime. As soon as we finished eating, my father and Jeff went outside to shovel the walk. Me and Amy were dying to go out too. Finally Mom said, 'Okay ... if you bundle up good and promise to come inside when you get cold.'

I helped Amy get ready. She has trouble with her boots. I tied up her hood and found her a pair of mittens. Then we went out together.

When Jeff saw us he called, 'How about a snowball fight? Me and Amy against Karen and Dad.'

'Okay,' we called.

Daddy and I hurried around to the side of our house and I made the snowballs for him to throw. Jeff and Amy hid behind the big tree and pretty soon the snow was flying. I think Daddy and I won but it didn't matter because it was such fun. When we got tired of throwing snowballs Amy and me lay down in the snow and made angels. I was moving my arms back and forth to make really good wings. Then I looked up at the sky. There were a million stars. I wanted everything to stay just the way it was – still and beautiful.

When we got up we were both soaked and I was sure Mom would yell at us. But we ran inside and she just laughed and told us we looked like snowmen. After we got into our pyjamas Mom made us hot chocolate with little balls of whipped cream on top. As I drank it I thought, I have never felt so good. Absolutely never!

Later I went up to my room and marked my Day Book A +. I didn't have to chew on my pencil to think it over. 14 December was perfect in every way.

But things have been going downhill since then. I'll bet my father will sleep in the den tonight. He's been doing that more and more. He tells us it's because my mother sits up in bed half the night watching the late show. But my mother says she can't get to sleep because Daddy snores so loud.

I marked Thursday, 25 February C—. Then I put the rubber bands back on my Day Book and went into the bathroom to brush my teeth. Maybe tomorrow will be an A+ day. I hope so.

three

Debbie Bartell has been my best friend since kindergarten. She lives two blocks away. We've only been separated twice in school – in second grade and fifth. This year we're both blessed with Mrs Singer. Debbie has a younger brother the same age as Amy, so we really have a lot in common.

The trouble with Debbie is, she takes a million lessons. I only take piano, on Thursdays. But Debbie is busy five days a week plus Saturday mornings. I know her whole schedule. On Monday she's got piano. On Tuesday it's ballet. On Wednesday, Girl Scouts – on Thursday, ice-skating – on Friday, allergy shots – and art every Saturday morning.

It's all her mother's idea. Mrs Bartell wants her to try out everything. Thank goodness we're Girl Scouts together or I'd never see Debbie after school. I happen to know that Debbie wishes she had more free time to fool around and do nothing, but she doesn't want to hurt her mother's feelings. Now Mrs Bartell has found out the indoor tennis club is giving lessons to kids every Sunday afternoon. Guess what Debbie got for Christmas? A tennis racket!

When I met her at the bus stop this morning Debbie said, 'I don't need my allergy shots today.'

'How come?' I asked. 'It's Friday.'

'My doctor's on vacation. If I start to wheeze my mother's supposed to call some other doctor.'

'Great!' I said. 'What do you want to do after school?'

'I guess I'll come over to your house. Do you think Jeff will be home?'

'No. He's never home on Fridays. You know that. He goes to the Y to swim.'

'Oh,' Debbie said. 'I forgot. Well then . . . we might as well go to the library and get the books for our project.'

Am I wrong to feel that lately Debbie is more interested in my brother than in me? Jeff can't stand her anyway. He calls her Fat-and-Ugly right to her face. She acts like that's some kind of compliment. Maybe because she knows she's not fat *or* ugly. The truth is, she's pretty. I think Gary Owens likes her. He's always tugging at her hair. I wish he'd do that to me!

Our bus came along then and we piled in. Debbie and I always sit in the same seats – the last row on the left. We've been sitting there since I can remember. It's a twenty-minute ride to school, counting the three other stops. This morning Debbie did her maths homework on the way.

I do pretty good in school. I am also supposed to be mature, well adjusted and eager to learn. I saw this written on my permanent record card one day in the fall. Sometimes I don't feel mature, well adjusted and eager to learn. In fact, I think my fifth-grade teacher may have mixed me up with somebody else when she wrote that.

As soon as we got to school Mrs Singer collected our milk money. I didn't know I'd forgotten mine until then. We eat lunch right in our classrooms because there isn't any cafeteria. If you don't bring your milk money on Friday you don't get any milk the following week. Sometimes, if you forget, your teacher will pay for you and you can pay her back on Monday. Mrs Singer doesn't do that. She says it is our responsibility to remember and if we don't, we have to suffer the consequences.

If Mrs Singer hadn't got married I'm sure she would still be nice. Last year whenever I went into her room with a message she was always smiling. But this year, on the very first day of school, she screamed at me in front of the whole class – just because I didn't hear her say we should open our maths books. Is that a reason to scream at a person, even if I wasn't paying attention? I was just excited because it was the first day of school. Couldn't Mrs Singer see that?

This is the first time I have ever forgotten my milk money. Now I will have to bring something from home to drink next week. Warm juice . . . ugh! I could already tell that this was not going to be an A+ day.

four

My father didn't come home for dinner tonight. But that's not unusual. The store is open until nine on Fridays. It's called Newman's Modern Furniture and it's out on the highway. Nothing in our house comes from the store though. That's because my mother loves old stuff. She is an antique nut. Little china babies sleep on every table in our living room. We even have an old potbellied stove, which Mom painted blue. It stands in our front hall and holds fake geraniums.

When Amy asked, 'Where's Daddy?' my mother said, 'Working late.'

On Saturday mornings my father leaves very early, same as during the week, but the rest of us sleep late. He doesn't need an alarm clock to wake him. He gets up automatically. My mother is just the opposite.

It wasn't until Saturday night at about six that I began to wonder what was going on. My parents go out every single Saturday night, rain or shine, all year long. Sometimes they argue before they go – about what they're going to do or who they're going to see – but still they go out together. The only time they stay home is if one of us is really sick.

'What time is Mrs Hedley coming tonight?' I asked, stuffing my second cupcake into my mouth.

'Don't talk with food in your mouth,' Amy said.

'Oh, shut up,' I told her. 'What time, Mom?'

Mrs Hedley has been baby-sitting since I was born. Jeff is getting pretty mad about having her come every week. He thinks he's old enough to stay alone. But my mother says if we stop using Mrs Hedley some other family will grab her.

So Jeff complains but Mrs Hedley still comes. She smells like gingersnaps. I used to like her a lot when I was little. Now I am not too crazy for her. For one thing, I am sick of holding my arms out with her knitting wool stretched across them. She spends Saturday nights making wool balls that must last her the rest of the week.

My mother sat at her kitchen desk reading the newspaper while the three of us had our supper. 'Mrs Hedley's not coming,' she said.

'She's not?'

'No.' Mom kept the newspaper in front of her face.

'How come?' I asked.

'We're not going out tonight.'

'You're not?'

'That's right.'

'How come?'

'We're just not, Karen.'

'Goody,' Amy said. 'Then we can all watch TV together.'

My mother put the paper down and got up to clear away the dishes. 'You can watch whatever you want. I just don't feel like any TV tonight.'

'Are you sick?' I asked.

'No.'

'Then what?'

'It's just that . . . well . . .' Mom stopped talking and looked at us. Then she shook her head and reached for a tissue. 'I'll be upstairs,' she practically whispered.

Amy finished her milk and followed my mother. Jeff took an apple out of the refrigerator, polished it on his shirt and went upstairs too.

I put the dishes in the dishwasher, then marched up to Jeff's room. I knocked. I'm not allowed in without his permission.

'What?' he called.

I had to shout because his record player was on full blast. 'It's me.'

'What?'

'I want to come in.'

'Just a minute,' he yelled. He switched off the music and opened the door.

'I'm scared,' I told him.

'Of what?'

'I don't know. I think something's wrong between Daddy and Mom.'

'Well, it took you long enough to figure that out.'

'I mean *really* wrong, Jeff.'

'Yeah ... so do I.'

'Do you know anything for sure?' I asked.

'I know Dad didn't come home to sleep last night,' Jeff said.

'He didn't?'

'Nope. And I don't think he's coming back either.'

'How can you say that?'

'I can tell by the way Mom's acting. Didn't you hear her at supper? She could hardly get the words out.'

'But that doesn't mean Daddy isn't coming back.'

Jeff shrugged and walked over to his record player. He turned it on and opened a book. He was through talking to me. 'I don't believe you!' I told him. 'You don't know anything!'

Jeff didn't answer. He didn't even look up.

I went to my room and took out my Day Book. I marked

Saturday, 27 February *D*—. I wish something would happen to make my mother and father happy again. On TV everything always turns out all right. Once I saw a show where the parents were separated. Then their little boy was kidnapped and they got together to help the FBI find him. And naturally, when they did, the kid was fine. The mother and father were so glad to see him they decided to make up and everyone lived happily ever after. It was a very nice show.

I'm sure if one of us got kidnapped my mother and father would forget about their fights and everything would work out fine. I think it would be best if Amy was the one, since she's the youngest. And everybody says she's Daddy's favourite. But who'd want to kidnap her? She's such a funny-looking kid, with big rabbit teeth and snarly hair. She is supposed to have inherited her rabbit teeth from Aunt Ruth. My mother says she'll look a lot better after she has had braces. Jeff is the good-looking one. He has a dimple in his chin and his eyes are very blue. Aunt Ruth says it's a shame to waste that face on a boy!

I am in between Amy and Jeff in looks. If I had to describe myself I would say Karen Newman is ordinary looking. I plan to do something about that in a few years. I might wear purple eyeshadow.

My father is always home on Sundays. But I checked the garage early this morning and his car wasn't there. At first I thought, maybe he's been in an accident and he's in the hospital. Maybe he's even dead! Just thinking about it made me feel sick. But he couldn't be dead. My mother would have told us. You can't keep something like that a secret.

So I went into the kitchen and mixed the pancake batter. I do that every Sunday morning. I love to crack the egg into the blender, then watch the tornado inside. Even the time I dropped the eggshell in by mistake Daddy said the pancakes were good. A little crunchy maybe, but very tasty.

We eat Sunday breakfast at ten, but at quarter after there was only me and Jeff and Amy in the kitchen. Maybe the car is at the gas station for a check-up, I thought. And Daddy is upstairs with Mom. He took a taxi home late last night and I didn't hear him come in because I was sound asleep. So naturally he and Mom are staying in bed a little later this morning. They probably were up half the night talking things over. Daddy will have his arm around Mom's shoulder when they come down for breakfast and he'll tell us we're all going into New York for the day.

'Where's Mommy?' Amy asked then.

'Still asleep,' I said.

'Where's Daddy?'

'Stop asking so many questions!' I shouted.

'The one who asks the most questions learns the most,' Amy said.

'Well today you can just learn to keep your big mouth shut!' I told her. Why did she have to interrupt just when I was planning a perfect A+ day?

I could tell Amy was going to cry. She doesn't come right out and do it like other kids. She thinks about it for a while. You can see her face scrunch up before the tears start rolling.

Jeff dug into the Sunday papers and came up with the funnies. I threw a few drops of water on the griddle to make sure it was hot enough. When they sizzle it's ready for cooking. 'Why don't you put out the syrup, Amy?' I said. 'Your pancakes will be ready in a minute.'

'You're mad,' Amy said, sniffling.

'No I'm not.'

'You yelled at me.'

'I didn't mean to. Honest.'

'Well . . . okay then. I'll put out the syrup.' She walked over to the pantry. 'Karen . . .'

'What?'

'Do you know why the boy put his father in the refrigerator?'

24

'Yes.'

'Jeff ... do you?'

'Yeah,' Jeff mumbled.

'Because he wanted cold pop! Get it?' Amy asked. '*Cold pop*, like soda.'

'That's a good riddle,' I said.

'But you already heard it ... right?'

'Right.' I poured the batter on to the grill. I shaped it like Mickey Mouse head. Amy loves it when I make her fancy pancakes. I shouldn't have hollered at her. After all, what does he know?

As soon as I gave Amy and Jeff their pancakes my mother came into the kitchen. 'Good morning,' she said. Her eyes were red and swollen.

'Look what Karen made me,' Amy said, holding up her Mickey Mouse pancake.

Mom said, 'That's beautiful. Be sure to finish it.'

Amy cut off one Mickey Mouse ear, dipped it into the syrup and ate it. 'Where's Daddy?' she asked.

Jeff looked up from his funnies. I think he was just pretending to read them anyway because he didn't laugh once.

'Daddy's busy,' Mom said.

'Doing what?' I asked.

'He's got some things to take care of. Look, you kids finish your breakfast while I go up and get dressed. Aunt Ruth will be over soon.'

She was gone before I had a chance to ask exactly what things Daddy was so busy doing.

I am so afraid Jeff is right!

five

Aunt Ruth is my mother's older sister. She is also my mother's
only living relative besides us, unless you count Mark, my
cousin. But we never see him any more. He lives in Atlanta.
My mother is ten years younger than Aunt Ruth and if you
ask me Aunt Ruth enjoys acting like her mother. She is married
to Uncle Dan, who is six feet five inches tall. When I was little
he would hold me up to touch the ceiling and I thought that
was really exciting. Aunt Ruth and Uncle Dan live in
Maplewood. It takes about ten minutes to get from their house
to ours. I wondered why Aunt Ruth was coming over on a
Sunday morning. She never does.

I was in the bathroom rinsing out my toothbrush when Amy
barged in. 'You're supposed to knock,' I told her.

'Karen ...'

'What?'

'Do you know where Daddy is?'

'You heard Mom,' I said. 'He's busy doing something.'

'I think I know what,' Amy said.

'You do?'

'Yes. I think he's out getting us a puppy and it's supposed to
be a big surprise.'

'Where'd you get that idea?'

'In my head.'

'Oh, Amy ... I don't think that's it at all.' I felt sorry for her
then.

Amy sat down on the toilet.

I went into my room and made the bed. When I finished I sat
sat at my desk and opened my Day Book to Sunday, 28
February. I wrote: *Something is going on. I wish I knew what.*

I put the rubber bands back and took out my English
homework. I nearly jumped right out of my chair when Aunt
Ruth stuck her head in and called, 'Good morning ...'

She has her own key to our house, so she doesn't have to ring the bell or knock. I never even heard her come in. She can be as sneaky as Mew. She should wear bells around her neck.

'You scared me!' I said.

'I'm sorry,' Aunt Ruth told me. 'Where are Jeff and Amy?'

'Jeff's up in his room and Amy's probably in the den watching TV.' You can't pull Amy away from those dumb Sunday-morning shows. She likes the one where the kids throw pies at each other.

'Where's your mother?' Aunt Ruth asked.

'Getting dressed, I think.'

'Well, suppose you tell Jeff and Amy to get ready and I'll tell your mother I'm here.'

'Get ready for what?'

'Didn't your mother tell you?'

'Tell me what?'

'Uncle Dan and I are taking you out to lunch.'

'But we just had breakfast.'

'We're going for a ride in the country, Karen. By the time we get there it will be lunchtime. So get your coat and tell Jeff and Amy to hurry and get ready.'

'Okay,' I said. We never go out to lunch on Sunday. Sometimes we go out for dinner, but *never* lunch. We don't even eat lunch on Sunday. And Aunt Ruth knows it!

'Aunt Ruth . . .' I called as she was leaving my room.

'Yes?'

'Is Mom coming too?'

'Of course.'

'And Daddy?'

'No. He's not coming.'

'Where is he, anyway?'

'He's got some business to take care of,' Aunt Ruth said.

Business? What kind of business would my father do on a Sunday morning? Unless he's selling the store! I'll bet that's it. Didn't he just tell us that sales are way down? So he's going to sell now and get some other kind of job. Jeff is wrong! Mom was upset because this means we'll be very poor. She might have to hock all her antiques. I'll get a job after school, to help out. Maybe I can deliver newspapers.

I ran downstairs and found Amy in the den. She was wearing her underwear. The rest of her clothes were spread out on the floor. I told her to hurry up and get dressed.

Then I went into the laundry room to check Mew's litter box. It was clean and I was glad. I rinsed her bowl and gave her fresh water. I filled her dish up with dried food. I didn't know how long we'd be gone and I wanted to make sure she wouldn't get hungry. She prefers canned cat food but I'm not allowed to leave that in her dish all day.

When I open a *can* of food for Mew I have to hold my nose. It really stinks. So does her litter box sometimes. But I have discovered that if you love someone the way I love Mew, you learn to overlook the disgusting things. And when I hold her close and she purrs at me it's all worth it.

When we were settled in the car Aunt Ruth drove down to her house to pick up Uncle Dan. Then they switched places so Uncle Dan could drive. We rode all the way to Basking Ridge with Jeff, Amy and me in the back of the car. And when Uncle Dan drives he moves the front seat as far back as it goes because of his long legs. Which means whoever is sitting in the back gets squashed.

Aunt Ruth and Uncle Dan talked the whole time. About the weather and what a nice day it was and how it was just perfect for a drive and how all the snow melted since last week and that there is only one month to go until spring. When Aunt Ruth said that, she put her arm around my mother and added, 'Everything will look brighter in the spring, Ellie.'

Jeff leaned close and whispered, 'You see ... what did I tell you?'

'It's not what you think,' I whispered back. I couldn't tell him in front of everyone that what Aunt Ruth meant was that then the store will be sold and Daddy will have a new job.

By the time we got to the restaurant Amy was carsick and she threw up in the parking lot. We are used to that. She does it every time we go for a long ride. She is so experienced she never even messes herself up. And she can eat like a tiger afterwards. She never gets sick on the way home – only going. I wonder why?

The restaurant was called the Red Bull Inn and it had bare wooden floors and paper place mats that looked like lace on each table. I studied the menu. Our waitress recommended the curried shrimp. Jeff, Amy and I ordered hamburgers and french fries. My mother said she'd have an omelet and Aunt Ruth and Uncle Dan said they would try the curried shrimp. The waitress seemed really glad to hear that, as if she had been cooking all day and now at last somebody was going to eat her stuff.

When we were almost through, Mom said, 'I have something to tell you.' She wasn't looking at Aunt Ruth or Uncle Dan. She was looking at me and Jeff and Amy. 'I wanted to tell you before, but I just couldn't. It isn't easy for me to say this and it won't be easy for you to understand ...'

I dropped my fork then. It made a clinking sound when it hit the floor. I bent down to get it.

Uncle Dan said, 'Let it go, Karen. The waitress can bring you another one.'

'Go ahead ... tell us what you were going to say, Mother,' Jeff said.

Mom took a deep breath and said, 'Daddy and I are separating.'

'I knew it!' Jeff said, looking at me.

I felt tears come to my eyes. I told myself, don't start crying now Karen, you jerk. *Not now.* I sniffled and took a long swallow of Coke. I guess I knew it all the time. I was just fooling myself – playing games like Amy.

'What's separating?' Amy asked.

'It means your father isn't going to live at home any more,' Aunt Ruth explained.

'But he has to!' Amy said. 'He's our father.'

'Shush ...' Aunt Ruth told her. 'Everyone can hear.'

'I don't care,' Amy shouted, looking around the restaurant. But there were only a few other customers.

Uncle Dan reached for Amy's hand. 'Sometimes, when a mother and father have problems, they live apart for a while to think things over.'

'Is he coming back?' Jeff asked. 'Or are you getting a divorce?'

'We don't know yet,' Mom told him.

'A divorce!' I said, when I hadn't planned to say anything. 'You wouldn't! You wouldn't get a divorce!' Then I started crying for real and I jumped up from the table and ran throug' the restaurant. I heard Aunt Ruth call, 'Karen ... Karen ... come back here.' But I kept going. I didn't want to hear any more. I went out the front door and stood against the sign that said Red Bull Inn, letting the tears roll down my face.

Soon Aunt Ruth came with my coat. 'Karen,' she said, 'put this on. You'll freeze to death.'

'Go away,' I told her.

Aunt Ruth wrapped the coat around my shoulders. 'Karen ... don't be like that. This is even harder on your mother than it is on you. She's very upset ... if she sees you like this it's going to make her feel even worse.'

You don't argue with Aunt Ruth. She has a habit of not listening to anything she doesn't want to hear. So I put on my coat and Aunt Ruth said, 'Now, that's better.'

We walked through the parking lot to the car. Aunt Ruth kept her arm around me. 'Nothing is settled yet,' she said. 'Your father is home packing his things now. That's why we all went out to lunch. To give him a chance to move.'

'But doesn't he want to see us? Doesn't he care? How can h move out of his own house?'

'Karen ... there are some things that are very hard for children to understand.'

That's what people say when they can't explain something to you. I don't believe it. I can understand anything they can understand. I got into the car but I didn't say anything else. I looked out the side window.

'You have to be the one to help your mother,' Aunt Ruth said. 'She needs you ... more than ever.'

I shook my head and pressed my forehead against the window. Why did Jeff have to be right? Why couldn't it have been something else? If only we could go back a few days and start again maybe things would work out differently.

My mother came out of the restaurant with Amy and Jeff. Mom was carrying an ice-cream cone. 'Here, Karen,' she said. 'I know you like dessert best.'

I tried to smile at Mom because I couldn't say thank you. I knew if I said anything I'd start crying. I didn't want the cone, even though it was coffee, my favourite flavour. But I took it from Mom and licked it anyway.

'Dan will be right out,' Mom told Aunt Ruth. 'He's paying the bill.'

'Shove over, Karen,' Jeff said.

'No, I like it here,' I told him. 'Get in on the other side.'

'I said shove over!' Jeff repeated.

When I didn't, he climbed across me and stepped on my foot. I kicked him as hard as I could. He gave me an elbow in the ribs and my ice cream landed in my lap.

six

What will happen to me if they get divorced? Who will I live with? Where will I go to school? Will my friends laugh? I want

31

a mother and a father and I want them to live together – right here – in this house! I don't care if they fight. I would rather have them fight than be divorced. I'm scared … I'm so scared. I wish somebody would talk to me and tell me it's going to be all right. I miss Daddy already. I hate them both! I wish I was dead.

On Monday morning I didn't get up. My mother came into my room to see what was wrong. 'I'm sick,' I told her. 'I can't go to school.'

Mom sat down on my bed. 'I know how you feel about me and Daddy …'

'It's not that,' I said. 'I wasn't even thinking about you. It's my head and my stomach. I might throw up.'

Mom put her hand on my forehead. 'You don't feel warm.'

'A person can be very sick without a fever,' I said.

'You're right,' she told me. 'I better call Dr Winters.'

'Don't bother,' I said. 'I just want to sleep.'

'Well … okay. But if you get any worse I'll have to call him.'

'If I can just sleep I'll feel better.'

'All right.'

I heard Jeff and Amy getting ready for school. How can they go? How can they face their friends? I heard my mother calling, 'Amy … Amy … hurry up or you'll miss the bus.' Some things never change, I thought.

I stayed in bed all day. My mother made me tea and toast but I wouldn't eat it. Later she tried soup but I wouldn't eat that either. She said if I didn't take something she'd have to call the doctor. So I drank some juice.

Debbie stopped by after school, on the way to her piano lesson. She came upstairs and stood in the doorway of my room.

'Hi,' she said. 'What's wrong?'

'Everything,' I told her. She looked pretty. Her cheeks were all pink from the cold. I wanted to tell her about my mother and father. I wanted to tell her so bad it made my head hurt for real. But I couldn't. Saying it would make it come true.

Debbie sat down on my other bed. 'Your mother said it's not catching so it's all right for me to be in your room.'

'My mother told you it's not catching?' I asked.

'Yes.'

'Well, I'd like to know how she can say that.'

'I don't know,' Debbie said, 'but she did. You look like you've been crying.'

'So? Maybe I have been. Don't you ever cry when you're sick?'

'No,' Debbie said.

'Well, this is an unusual sickness. It makes you cry!'

'Why are you mad at me?' Debbie asked.

'I'm not,' I said. 'I just don't feel like talking. Can't you see ... I'm sick!'

'Want me to make monkey faces for you?'

'No – not today.' Debbie can make very good monkey faces. She can look like a chimpanzee or a gorilla. Usually I crack up when she does them. But I didn't feel like laughing today.

'Will you be back in school tomorrow?' Debbie asked.

'No. I'll be out a long, long time. I may never get better.'

'Oh, come on, Karen! You want me to bring you your books?'

'I've got my English book home.'

'How about maths?'

'No ... I don't want it.'

'Should I tell Mrs Singer what's wrong with you?'

'No. Don't tell her anything!'

Debbie looked at the floor. I turned away from her and faced the wall. After a minute she said, 'Is Jeff home yet?'

'How should I know? I'm in bed. Can't you see that?'

'I was just wondering ... that's all.'

'He doesn't like you anyway, so why don't you just leave him alone.'

'Did he say that?' Debbie asked.

'He doesn't have to. Anyone with eyes can see it. And who did you come here to see anyway . . . me or him?' I was making Debbie feel bad and I was glad. Sometimes I am a mean and rotten person.

Debbie jumped up. 'I came to see *you* and you know it! Whatever's wrong with you I hope it goes away soon because it's making you impossible!' Debbie walked to the door. 'I'm going.'

'So go!' I told her.

'I am.'

Lying to Debbie did not make me feel any better. It made me feel worse.

Later Mom came into my room and told me to put on my bath-robe and come downstairs for dinner.

'I don't want anything to eat,' I said.

'Karen, if you don't get up and come down you can't go to school tomorrow.'

'So?'

'If you don't go to school tomorrow, you won't be able to have dinner with Daddy.'

I sat up. 'He's coming back?'

'No. He's taking you and Jeff and Amy out to eat. He wants to talk to you.'

'Who says I want to talk to him?' I asked.

'Karen . . . don't be like that! Daddy is a wonderful person. He loves you.'

'If he's so wonderful why are you separated?'

'Because we can't get along,' Mom said.

'You could try!' I told her, feeling a lump in my throat.

'We have tried. Now I don't want to talk about it any more.'

I put on my bath-robe and went down for dinner. I wonder if anyone will ever talk about it!

seven

Debbie was really surprised to see me at the bus stop the next morning. 'I thought you were very sick,' she said.

'I was. But I got better.'

'So fast?' she asked.

'Yes. It was one of those twenty-four-hour bugs.'

'Oh.'

'Hey, look, Debbie ... I'm really sorry I acted that way yesterday. It was just that my head was killing me and all ...'

'Forget it,' Debbie said.

'Did I miss much in school?' I asked.

'No. Same old thing. Mrs Singer changed our desks around. I'm next to Gary Owens and Eileen.'

'Where am I?'

'I'm not sure. But I think you're next to the wall on one side.'

'That figures,' I said. 'One more way for Mrs Singer to get me.'

'I really don't think she's out to get you,' Debbie said.

'Ha-ha.'

'I mean it, Karen. You know I can't stand her either, but I don't think she treats you any worse than the rest of us.'

'Well, I do.'

When we got to school I handed Mrs Singer my note from home. It said: *Please excuse Karen's absence on Monday. She wasn't feeling well.*

Mrs Singer said, 'I'm glad you're feeling better, Karen.'

I looked at her. Did she know something? Did my mother call the school and tell them about Daddy moving out? Why else would Mrs Singer act nice all of a sudden? She never says anything when you've been absent. One time Debbie was sick for a couple of weeks and when she came back to school Mrs Singer didn't even smile. So why should she be glad I'm feeling better? If she knows the truth about my parents I will absolutely die.

My father called for us at five that night. He didn't come inside. He just tooted his horn. Amy ran out of the house first. 'Daddy ... Daddy ... Daddy ...' she yelled. Jeff and I followed. We got into the car and said, 'Hi.'

We went to Howard Johnson's on the highway. We sat in a booth in the back room and my father ordered a Martini. You have to sit in that section if you're going to have a drink. It was pretty quiet in the dining room. Maybe because it was so early or maybe because it was Tuesday night. Monday and Wednesday are the Big Fish Fry and Big Chicken Fry nights, where you can eat all you want for $1.98.

I can't remember ever eating out with just Daddy and not Mom too. I think we all felt funny. I know I did. There I was with my own father and it was like I hadn't seen him for ages instead of just a few days. He looked the same. I didn't expect him not to. But I thought there'd be something different about him now. I don't know what. But something that would let people know he didn't live at home any more.

After we ordered, Daddy said, 'I miss you all very much.'

Me and Jeff mumbled that we missed him too.

Then Amy asked, 'Do you miss Mommy?'

My father looked sad and said, 'No, I don't.'

'Are you getting a divorce?' Jeff asked.

'Yes,' my father answered.

'I thought you were just thinking about it,' I said. 'I thought it wasn't definite yet.'

'We're definitely getting a divorce,' he said. 'It's the only way.'

'Do you love somebody else?' Jeff asked. 'Or does Mom?'

I never even thought about that! I couldn't picture my father with another woman or my mother with another man. That was disgusting! How could Jeff even think of such a thing? I took

36

a sip of water and waited for my father to answer.

'No ... no ...' he said. 'It's nothing like that. There's nobody else involved. Your mother and I just don't get along. We can't go on living together. It's making a mess of our lives.'

'Suppose we don't want you to get a divorce?' I said.

'I'm sorry, Karen, but this is between your mother and me.'

'I want to live with you, Daddy!' Amy said.

'Don't be a jerk,' Jeff told Amy. 'The kids always live with the mother.'

'Is that true?' I asked.

'Yes, usually,' Daddy said. 'Unless there's some reason why the mother shouldn't have the children.'

'What about us?' I asked. 'Where will we live?'

'With your mother.'

'But where?'

'Right now you'll stay in the house.'

'But for how long?' I asked.

'Karen ... you're asking me questions I can't answer,' Daddy said. 'We haven't worked out any of the details yet. I'm seeing my lawyer tomorrow. You don't get divorced overnight.'

'How long does it take?' Jeff asked.

'That depends. I guess about six months. Maybe more.'

'Daddy ...' Amy said, 'please come home.'

My father held Amy to him. Then he took off his glasses and started to clean them with his napkin. I think he had tears in his eyes. I didn't feel like eating anything.

After dinner Daddy took us into the motel to see his room. It has two beds and a TV. The bathroom is very small. 'Are you going to live here forever?' I asked.

'No. Just until I find an apartment.'

'Will we still see you?' I said.

'Of course you will. I'm your father and I'll always love you. Divorce has nothing to do with that.'

After a few minutes Jeff said, 'Well ... I've got to get home. I have lots of homework to do.' His voice broke on every word.

Nobody said much on the drive back to our house. When we got there Amy asked Daddy to come in and carry her up to bed like he always does. But Daddy said, 'No, I'm not coming in.'

Tuesday, 2 March
Divorce ... it's the end of the world.

eight

In the middle of the night Amy shook me. I sat straight up in bed. 'What's the matter?' I asked.

'I'm afraid to go to sleep,' she said.

'Why?'

'I'm afraid if I do you'll all be gone in the morning, just like Daddy.'

'That's silly,' I told her.

She threw her arms around me. She was shaking. I held her tight. 'Can I sleep in here with you?' she asked.

'I guess so,' I said. But I really didn't want her to. I wanted to be alone. How could I cry with Amy in my other bed?

As soon as I tucked her in she fell asleep. But I tossed and turned for a long time. I wish I could talk to somebody about my parents. If only Debbie knew – I think I would feel better. I've got to figure out a way to tell her what's happening. She'll be able to cheer me up. Besides making monkey faces, Debbie has a very good sense of humour. I guess that's why everybody likes her. She doesn't even mind laughing at herself. I'm really lucky to have her for a best friend, even though I don't always show it. I am sure just having her know the truth will help.

On Wednesday afternoons Debbie and I walk to Girl Scouts

together. Our troop meets at Willow Grove Church. That's just a few blocks from school. Then either Debbie's mother or mine picks us up. I used to love my Girl Scout uniform. But I am thinking of quitting after this year. So is Debbie. We are both sick of selling cookies and calendars to the same people year after year. If we had a good leader it would be different. But ours is a bore. If I was ever going to be a Girl Scout leader I would think up interesting activities for my group to do. And if they made a lot of noise I wouldn't yell that they give me a headache.

I planned to tell Debbie about my parents while we were walking to our meeting. But by three o'clock I was so mad at Mrs Singer I couldn't think of anything else! Because this afternoon she called me up to her desk to discuss this month's book report. It was due last Monday. I scribbled mine out Sunday night before I went to sleep. I never even read the book. I just copied some stuff off the inside flap of the jacket. I've never done that before, but some kids in my class do it all the time.

Mrs Singer said, 'Did you enjoy the book you read this month, Karen?'

I said, 'It was all right.'

'Your book report wasn't nearly as good as usual.'

'I was very busy,' I told her. 'I had to do it in a hurry.'

'What did you think about the ending?'

'It was all right.'

'Were you surprised by it?'

'A little,' I said. I could tell that Mrs Singer knew I hadn't read the book. Just as the bell rang she handed me my book report. I got a D – my first bad mark in school.

I could feel my face turn red as I walked to the back of the room to get my coat. Debbie waited for me at her desk. I picked up my books and marched out into the hall. Debbie called, 'Goodbye, Mrs Singer,' as she followed me.

Mrs Singer called back, 'Goodbye, girls.'

39

I didn't answer her.

When we were out of the building Debbie asked, 'What's wrong?'

'Nothing!'

'What'd Mrs Singer want to see you for?'

'Don't mention that witch's name! I hate her!'

'What'd she do?'

'Gave me a D on my book report!'

'She did?'

'Yes. There's something about me that Mrs Singer can't stand. This proves it!'

'She hardly ever gives out Ds for book reports,' Debbie said, 'unless she thinks you didn't read the book.'

I glared at Debbie, then I pulled my scarf up around my face. The wind was howling and it was really cold. We hurried along not saying anything for a while.

We only had one more block to go when Debbie said, 'I heard about your parents . . . and I'm sorry.'

'Heard what?' I asked, biting my lip.

'You know.'

'Know what?'

'Oh, come on, Karen. That your parents are getting a divorce.'

Well, there it was. Out in the open. But not the way I'd planned it. *I* was the one who was going to tell Debbie. And *she* was the one who was going to make me feel better. 'Who told you?' I asked.

'Your aunt met my mother in Food Town and she told her.'

'Oh,' I said. I always knew Aunt Ruth had a big mouth. It must have to do with her rabbit teeth. She's just like Amy.

'How come you didn't tell me?' Debbie asked when we got to the church.

'It wasn't definite.' We went inside and jumped around a little to get warm. Then we hung up our coats.

'What's it like?' Debbie asked.

'What do you mean?'

'What's it feel like?'

How could she ask such a dumb question! 'How do you think it feels?' I said, running for the bathroom.

'Hey, Karen ... wait up!' Debbie caught me before I got inside. 'I'm sorry. I didn't know it would be so bad.'

'Well, it is.'

'Are they going to have a fight over you and Jeff and Amy?'

'What kind of fight?'

'You know ... about who gets the kids.'

'No. We stay with our mother.'

'Doesn't your father want you?'

'I don't know. He said we'll live with our mother.' Now I was getting all mixed up. Why did she ask if Daddy wanted us? Did Aunt Ruth know something else? Did she tell Mrs Bartell something that Debbie knows? Oh ... I hate everybody! I must have been crazy to think Debbie could cheer me up.

nine

I have only one grandparent and that's Daddy's father. We call him Garfa because Jeff couldn't say 'Grandpa' when he was a baby. When you are twelve you feel pretty stupid calling somebody Garfa, especially in public. So whenever I talk about him in school or to my friends I say 'my grandfather'. Only Debbie knows he is Garfa.

Garfa started Newman's furniture store when he was young, in the olden days. Daddy took it over thirteen years ago when Grandma died and Garfa retired. I never knew my grandmother but everybody says I look like her. I've seen some pictures though and I don't think there is any resemblance between us at all. But you can't argue about something like that with your family. Once they make up their minds that you look like somebody special, that's it.

Garfa lives in Las Vegas. The dry climate is supposed to be good for his health. But I have heard that he likes gambling. This is not something that the family talks about much. Last year Garfa got married again. His new wife's name is Mattie and she is sixty-five years old. Imagine getting married when you are sixty-five!

Garfa and Mattie visited us over the summer. The only thing wrong with Mattie is she doesn't like cats. She more than doesn't like them – she is terrified of them. So Debbie kept Mew at her house for two whole weeks.

I just found out that Garfa is going to pay us a visit this weekend, but Mattie is staying home in Las Vegas. Daddy called to tell him about the divorce, which is why he is coming.

On Saturday, Garfa came into our house alone. Daddy just dropped him off. The first thing Garfa said after he kissed us and gave us the once-over was, 'Well, Ellie, there hasn't ever been a divorce in our family. Not even way back. When the Newman's get married they get married for keeps. Or until one of them dies.'

My mother didn't say anything. She just shook her head. I didn't think Garfa should discuss the divorce in front of Amy. But of course he didn't know she was so afraid at night.

'Listen, Ellie ... everybody has problems,' Garfa said. 'Even me and Mattie have problems. But we're willing to work them out. That's what you have to do. Work out your problems with Bill.'

'We can't,' my mother said.

'Dammit, Ellie! Don't give me that! Of course you can. That's why I came. I want you and Bill to get away for a little while. All you need is a vacation. And it's on me.'

'Oh, Garfa ...' Mom said. 'Thank you for trying but it's just no use. A vacation isn't going to solve anything. Don't you see ...' Mom ran upstairs.

Later, after Daddy picked up Garfa, my mother drove downtown to get a box of Kentucky Fried Chicken for supper. Daddy can't stand that stuff. Well, now he'll never have to eat it.

I set the table while Mom cut up the salad. I didn't put out our regular paper napkins. I went into the den and came back with some of the cocktail napkins that say *Ellie and Bill*. I folded them up and put one at each place.

My mother called Jeff and Amy for supper. She didn't see the napkins until we were all seated. Then she looked at me and said, 'I don't think this is very funny, Karen.'

'I wasn't trying to be funny,' I said.

'Then why did you use these?'

'Because there isn't going to be any more Ellie and Bill and I thought we might as well use them up now.'

Mom collected the napkins and mashed them into a ball. She got up from the table and threw them away. 'Where's the rest of the box?' she asked me.

'In the den, by the bar.'

'Okay . . . after dinner get it and put it in the garbage.'

'Boy, are you stupid!' Jeff whispered to me.

My mother didn't eat any chicken. I don't think she's been eating anything lately. She is getting very skinny. If she is so miserable without Daddy and he is so miserable away from us then why are they getting divorced? I don't understand.

On Sunday night Daddy took us out to dinner. We went to The Towers Steak House, which is my all-time favourite restaurant. I have never eaten out as much as in the week my parents have been separated.

During dinner Garfa tried to persuade Daddy to take a vacation with Mom. But it didn't work. Daddy said that was out of the question.

I could see how disappointed Garfa was at not being able to get my parents back together, so when we were alone for a minute I said, 'Don't worry, Garfa.' I thought of telling him about that TV show where the little boy got kidnapped. But I

43

didn't. Because those things never happen in real life, do they?

'I can't help it, Karen,' Garfa said. 'I was so sure I'd be able to straighten everything out.'

'Do you think I should try too?' I asked.

Garfa smiled at me. 'It can't hurt.'

Before he flew home to Las Vegas, Garfa told me to keep him posted on whatever was going on. 'You're the most dependable person in this family, Karen. You're just like your Grandmother Newman. And you know something? You look more like her every time I see you.'

'Oh, Garfa!' was all I could think to say.

ten

Petey Mansfield seems to have moved into our house. He is Jeff's new best friend. They're always locked up inside Jeff's hideaway.

I don't know if Petey Mansfield is normal or not. He doesn't talk at all. Sometimes if you ask him a question he'll grunt at you, but otherwise, forget it. How does he manage in school? I wonder. His brother Brian is in my class. He never shuts up. Mrs Singer is always yelling at him. Maybe that's why Petey doesn't talk. Maybe he doesn't ever get a chance.

Eileen Fenster, who is a girl in my class, says Brian Mansfield likes me. She knows because she spends every afternoon calling up boys. She asks them questions such as 'Who do you like in our class?' or 'What do you think of Debbie?' or something like that.

Debbie and I went over to Eileen's a few times. She knows all the boys' phone numbers by heart. The last time I was there she called up Gary Owens and I listened on the upstairs phone.

She said, 'Hi Gary. This is Eileen. Listen, Gary . . . what do you think of Karen?'

And Gary said, 'Karen who?'

Imagine him saying that! How many Karens does he know anyway?

So Eileen said, 'Karen Newman.'

And Gary said, 'Oh, her.'

'Well?' Eileen said.

And then Gary hung up! Why did he go and do that? I'm never going to Eileen's house again.

Aunt Ruth came over tonight. She was full of advice for my mother because tomorrow is Mom's first meeting with Mr Hague, her lawyer.

We were sitting around the kitchen table. Aunt Ruth and Mom were drinking coffee and I was eating a banana. I only like bananas when they are pure yellow, without a spot of brown. That's why I hardly ever eat them.

Aunt Ruth said, 'What are you going to wear tomorrow?'

And Mom said, 'I don't know. What difference does it make?'

Aunt Ruth said, 'You want to make a good impression, don't you? And remember, Ellie, you've got to tell him everything, no matter how hard it is for you.'

'I know,' my mother said. 'Dan told me the same thing.'

'I wish you'd try to eat a little more, Ellie. You don't look well.'

'Oh, Ruth . . .' Mom said.

'I don't want to interfere, Ellie . . . I just wish you'd take better care of yourself.'

Aunt Ruth is right. Suppose my mother gets sick? Then who'll take care of us?

Nobody said anything for a minute. Then Aunt Ruth asked Mom, 'Do you remember Henry Farnum?'

'I think so,' Mom said. 'Is he the accountant?'

'That's the one,' Aunt Ruth said. 'From West Orange. Dan

45

and I ran into him the other day. You know his wife died last year ...'

'No, I didn't know that,' Mom said.

'Yes ... he's been very lonely. He's got a beautiful house and nobody in it. His children are both away at college.'

'He ought to move to an apartment,' Mom said.

I got up and threw my banana skin away.

'I'd like you to meet him, Ellie.'

'Oh, please, Ruth ... don't start in on that.'

I sat back down at the table. Start in on what?

'Look, Ellie ... that's the wrong attitude to take. Here I know a really nice man. He's lonely. So what's wrong with going out to dinner with him? I'm not saying you've got to marry him.'

'Ruth, please! I'm not even divorced yet. I don't want to think about getting married again.'

'Okay. Fine. But a year from now when Henry Farnum is married to somebody else, don't come crying to me. And don't tell me you think Bill is sitting home alone every night!'

'Ruth ... not in front of Karen ... please.'

Aunt Ruth looked at me. Does she know something? Why doesn't she just stay home and mind her own business! I hope my mother never goes out with Mr Henry Farnum or any other man!

On Friday there was no school because of some special teachers' meeting. Debbie and I decided to go ice-skating. There is a pond in the middle of town, next to the library. When the blue circle is up it means the pond is frozen and safe to skate on.

Debbie's mother called for me and drove us downtown. I felt funny because Mrs Bartell knows about my parents. I was scared that she would ask me something and I wouldn't know what to tell her. But she didn't mention one word about the divorce. She talked about keeping warm instead. And how she wanted Debbie to wear a few pairs of underpants instead of just one. 'That's the best way to get a kidney infection,' Mrs Bartell said, 'sitting on that cold ice and getting a chill.'

'I promise I won't sit on the ice,' Debbie said.

I think Mrs Bartell spends a lot of time worrying about diseases. She dropped us off right in front of the library and we walked down the path to the pond. There was already a bunch of kids there. I saw Eileen Fenster right away. She waved.

I love to ice-skate. I learned by myself when I was nine. That year I got my first shoe skates for Christmas. Debbie is always joking about her ice-skating lessons. She says it took her one whole year just to learn to stand up on the ice.

We were already wearing our skates, so all we had to do was to take the covers off the blades and skate away. I don't think Debbie was on the pond for two minutes before she fell down. I pulled her up. She started to laugh. 'Three years of lessons and I still stink!' she said. Then I started to laugh too. Eileen Fenster skated over to see what was so funny and pretty soon we were all standing there laughing. I had forgotten how good it feels to laugh. From now on I am going to concentrate on laughing at least once a day – even more if I can arrange it.

After an hour I could see why Mrs Bartell wanted Debbie to wear lots of underpants. She wound up sitting on the ice more than she was standing on it! I skated out to the middle of the pond to practise my figure eights. When I turned around to look for Debbie I saw her standing on the grass talking to Eileen. I waved and called, 'Hey, Debbie ...' but she didn't notice. What were they talking about that was so important? Were they telling secrets? Was Eileen saying something bad about me? I skated across to them and said, 'What's up?'

As soon as they saw me they stopped talking. Eileen said, 'Oh, nothing. Me and Debbie were just saying it's fun to have a day off from school.'

I knew that wasn't the truth. I could tell from their faces.

After Eileen went home I asked Debbie, 'What were you talking about before?'

'Nothing,' Debbie said. 'Just forget it.'

'I'll bet it was about me.'

'Okay . . . so it was.'

'About me and Gary Owens . . . right?'

'No. About your parents, if you want to hear the truth.'

'My parents?'

'Yes. Eileen just found out they're getting divorced.'

'Oh.' I took my chapstick out of my pocket and rubbed some along my bottom lip.

'You can't keep it a secret,' Debbie said. 'Sooner or later everyone is going to know.'

'I never said it was a secret.'

'Well, anyway . . . that's what we were talking about.'

'What did Eileen say?'

'Oh, she was just asking me if your mother has a lot of money, that's all.'

'Money? What's money got to do with it?'

'I don't know exactly. But Eileen heard her mother say that she hopes your mother has a good lawyer and plenty of money.'

'I think Mrs Fenster should mind her own business,' I said.

'Well, so do I! Come on, now . . . just forget about it.' Debbie made her chimpanzee face. I tried to laugh.

But I spent the rest of the day thinking about what Eileen had said. My mother has no money that I know of, unless Aunt Ruth and Uncle Dan are going to give her some. It's scary to think about my mother with no money to feed us or buy our clothes or anything. Maybe we will eat at Aunt Ruth's every night. And instead of giving all our outgrown clothes to some poor family someone will give their old clothes to us. I've got to talk to somebody about this. Maybe Jeff can explain things to me.

eleven

Trying to get to talk to Jeff is like banging your head against the wall. You just don't get anywhere. I've been tagging along after him for three days now but he says he's very busy and I should get lost. I think Petey Mansfield is a bad influence on him. I would tell that to my mother but suppose she says, 'Why are you so anxious to have a private talk with Jeff?' What can I possibly answer without giving everything away?

I have come up with some information, though. From now on my father will be taking us out to dinner every Wednesday night and we will spend Sunday afternoons with him. This is part of something called a separation agreement. Daddy's lawyer's name is Mr Levinson and he specializes in divorces just like Mr Hague. Their offices are even in the same building in Newark. I wonder if maybe my mother and father will run into each other there.

Divorce is a very complicated thing. I always thought if you wanted one you just got it. But now I know that sometimes you need special reasons and each state has different rules. Uncle Dan explained this to me the other night. When I got into bed I thought of a million questions I should have asked him, like suppose I am sick on a Wednesday and can't go out to eat. Does that mean I don't get to see Daddy at all? I have *got* to talk to Jeff. If it takes me a week I am going to corner him. I will station myself outside the bathroom door when he is inside and I will not move until he comes out. There will be no way he can ignore me.

It didn't take me a week. On the second night, I sat down cross-legged right in front of the locked bathroom door. I listened as Jeff brushed his teeth and took a shower. When he opened the door he was really surprised to find me there waiting. He had a towel wrapped around himself and his hair was all wet.

'What are you doing?' he asked me.

'Waiting to talk to you.'

'I'm busy,' he said.

'I can wait.' I wanted to say, 'Please talk to me – I need somebody so bad.' I felt tears come to my eyes. I think Jeff noticed.

He said, 'Okay ... go up and wait for me in the hideaway. I'll be right there. And here' – he handed me a tissue – 'blow your nose.'

I took it and ran up the stairs. I opened the door to his hideaway and sat down on his bed to wait. There was a picture of Mary Louise Rumberger tacked up on his bulletin board. She was wearing a bathing suit. She's pretty hefty.

When Jeff came up he was wearing a bath-robe and his hair was still wet but he had combed it. 'What's wrong?' he asked.

'Does Mom have any money?' I said.

'What do you mean?'

'I mean does she have any money of her own ... that's not Daddy's.'

'I don't know,' Jeff said. 'I never thought about it. Why?'

'Because if she doesn't, what do you think is going to happen to us?'

'I think they make some kind of deal when they get divorced. Dad pays a certain amount of money to Mom every month. Something like that.'

'Are you sure?' I asked.

'He's not going to let us starve, if that's what you're worried about.'

'You're sure about that?'

'Yes, I'm sure. But if you don't believe me why don't you ask him yourself?'

'That's a very good idea. I think I'll do that. And another thing,' I said.

'Go on ...'

'Well, suppose I get sick and can't go to see him at all?'

'How am I supposed to know about that? You're thinking too much about the divorce.'

'Do you mean you never think about it?'

'Well, sure I do. But we'll probably see more of Dad now than we did before.'

'I don't care,' I said. 'It's not the same as having a father living at home where he belongs!' I started to cry again.

'You just better get used to it, Karen,' Jeff said in a funny voice. 'Because there's nothing you can do about it!'

That's what he thinks! I'm going to get them back together. I told Garfa I'd try, didn't I?

twelve

Friday, 26 March
My life is going from bad to worse!

I found out today that Gary Owens is moving to Houston. His father has been transferred there. I wonder if he will start to like me before he moves? Probably not.

I forgot my milk money again. Mrs Singer wants to know what's wrong with me. I told her nothing. Debbie said her parents bumped into my father at the Chinese restaurant. He was all alone, so the Bartells invited him to join them. Debbie said her mother told her not to tell me this – but my father is very lonely and unhappy. Why did she have to go and tell me?

If one more bad thing happens I just don't know what I am going to do!

My mother went to see Mr Hague today for the second time. And when she came home she had a new haircut, a new dress and a smile on her face. So right away I thought, she's in love. Because I've been thinking a lot about that lately. Jeff says he is positive that Daddy and Mom are not too old for that stuff. I wonder!

Mom was in her room changing into a sweater and a pair of pants. I sat on her bed. 'What's Mr Hague like?'

'Who?' she asked from inside her sweater.

This time I waited until her head was all the way through. 'Mr Hague,' I said. 'What's he like?'

'Oh ... he's very nice. He's going to take care of everything.' She fluffed out her hair.

'Do you want to marry him?'

'Marry who?'

'Mr Hague.'

'For heaven's sake, Karen! I've only seen him twice. And he's already married, with five kids.'

'How do you know that?'

'I saw a picture of his family on his desk.'

'Oh. Then you're not in love?'

'No, I'm not. And what's all this *love* business anyway?'

'I don't know,' I said. 'You seem so happy today.'

'Well, I am. It's a relief to know that soon everything will be settled.'

'Mom ...'

'Yes?'

'Will you tell me *exactly* why you're getting divorced?'

'Oh, Karen! We've been through this before.'

'But there has to be a reason.'

'There isn't any reason.'

'How can there not be a reason? Is it a secret? Is that it? Something I shouldn't know about?'

'No ... no ...'

'Well then ... what?'

'I mean there isn't just one reason. It's not that simple. There are so many reasons. It's just better this way that's all.'

'Does it have anything to do with your antiques?'

'Of course not. Whatever gave you that idea?'

'Oh, I don't know. Because the store sells modern furniture and you like old things.'

Mom laughed a little. 'Daddy likes antiques too. It just happens that his business is selling modern furniture.'

'Well ... does it have to do with the way you cook, then?'

'Oh, Karen!'

'Daddy's always saying you should try more recipes.'

'But people don't get divorced over those things. You're all mixed up, aren't you?'

'I don't know,' I said. 'I guess I am.'

Mom sat down next to me and took my hand. 'I wish it was easier for you to understand. Daddy and I just don't enjoy being together. We don't love each other any more. We love you and Amy and Jeff just the same, but not each other.'

I took my hand away and fiddled with my chain belt.

'You're going to be a lot happier living in a house without constant fighting,' Mom said.

I didn't say anything.

'You are, Karen. You'll see.'

I nodded. If she was so sure, how come I didn't know it?

'Now let's go down to the kitchen and get dinner ready,' Mom said.

We went downstairs together. Mew was on her favourite chair, bathing. She spends more time licking herself clean every day than I spend in the bath tub in a week.

thirteen

On Sunday my father called for us at noon. Mom never comes to the door when she knows Daddy is outside. I don't know how I am going to get them back together when they never even see each other.

We went to visit Daddy's new apartment. He moved this week. The place is called Country Village and it has the kind of streets running through it where you can get lost pretty easy because everything looks the same. There are two swimming pools. One for Country Village East and one for Country Village West. My father's apartment is in West. Each section has four apartments. Daddy's is in building 12, upstairs on the right. It's all fixed up like a magazine picture. Everything is brown-and-white and very modern. The kind of stuff that Newman's Furniture Store sells.

'Well . . . what do you think?' Daddy asked.

'It's terrific!' Jeff said. 'It's a real man's pad. I'd like to live here myself.'

That reminded me of what Debbie said. That Jeff might not want to be the only male in our house.

'Well, son,' Daddy said, 'you can stay here any time you want. That sofa opens up and I've got two rollaway beds in the storage room.' He looked at me and Amy.

'I'll bet you're glad you're in the furniture business, right Daddy?' I asked. 'I mean, suppose you had to go out and *buy* all this stuff!'

'I don't exactly get it free, Karen . . . but I do save a lot,' Daddy said.

'Well, that's good,' I told him.

After we saw the apartment there wasn't much to do. Amy sat down on the floor in front of the TV and Jeff looked through my father's magazines. I went into the kitchen for something to drink. Daddy followed me.

'How's your mother?' he asked.

'She's fine and you should see her, Daddy . . . she looks great. She got a new haircut and—'

Daddy didn't let me finish. He said, 'What kind of soda do you want?'

'I don't care,' I said. He opened a Coke.

'Daddy, are you still going to pay for us?' I asked.

'Pay for what?'

'Oh, you know . . . our clothes and food and stuff like that.'

'Of course I am, Karen. The lawyers will arrange for your support, and alimony for your mother.'

'What's alimony?'

'An amount of money I'll be paying your mother every month.'

So Jeff really knew what he was talking about.

'Anyway,' Daddy said, 'who's been putting all these ideas about money into your head?'

'Nobody,' I said. 'I was just wondering.'

'You're sure no one told you to ask me?'

'Of course I'm sure.' Who did Daddy think would tell me that?

'Because there isn't anything for you to worry about. I want to make sure you understand that.'

'Suppose I get sick on a Wednesday or a Sunday and I can't come out with you. Does that mean I won't see you that day?'

'If you're sick I'll come to see you.'

'You'll come up to my room?'

'Of course.'

'But what if Mom is home.'

'Listen, Karen . . . your mother and I aren't going to go out of our way to see each other. But if there's an emergency we won't let our personal feelings interfere. Now promise me you aren't going to worry about anything.'

'I'll try not to,' I said. But I was already thinking about getting sick next Wednesday so Daddy will have to come home. And once he's there he'll stay for dinner. Especially if I have a fever. How can I get myself a good fever? I wonder.

'There's a girl about your age in the apartment downstairs,' Daddy told me. 'I thought you might like to meet her.'

'Oh . . . I don't know,' I said.

'Her parents are divorced and she lives with her mother. They've been very nice to me since I moved in. I told her you'd be visiting today and she said you should come down. Her name is Val Lewis.'

'Well ...' I said.

'It might be nice for you to have a friend here.'

'Okay ... I guess ... if you think I should ...'

'It's apartment 12-B, on the left. Do you want me to come with you?'

'No. Did you say her name is Val?'

'Yes. Val Lewis.'

'What's she like?'

'Oh ... a little taller than you maybe and ...'

'Not Val,' I said. 'Her mother!'

'Oh. She's a very attractive woman.'

'Better looking than Mom?' I asked.

'In a different way. Why?' Daddy said

'Just wondering,' I told him.

I went downstairs and stood outside apartment 12-B. I wasn't sure if I wanted to meet this girl or not. Finally I rang the bell.

Val answered. 'Oh, hi,' she said. 'I'll bet you're Karen.'

'Yes ... my father told me to come down.'

'Come on in,' Val said.

Daddy was right. She is taller than me. But not much. She has very long black hair and bangs that cover her eyebrows. Her eyes remind me of Mew's. They are the same colour green.

'Excuse the mess,' Val said when I walked into the living room. 'I read the whole *New York Times* every Sunday. From cover to cover. I don't skip an inch!'

'That must take all day,' I said.

'It does. And part of the night too. Let's go into my room.'

I followed Val down the hall. 'My father's only got one bedroom,' I said.

'I know,' Val told me. 'All the apartments on the right have one bedroom and the ones on the left have two.' When we got to Val's room she spread her arms. 'It's small, but it's all

56

mine,' she said, pulling up her bedspread. 'I never make the bed on Sunday,' she explained.

'That's okay,' I said. The bed was up against the wall. There was a pink bulletin board that said *Valerie* on it hanging over the bed. She had a big desk with lots of drawers, plus a rug on the floor shaped like a foot, with toes and everything.

Val pulled her desk chair next to the bed and told me to sit down. 'My mother's asleep,' she said. 'I know she'd like to meet you but she was out very late last night.'

'With my father?' I asked.

'Your father?' Val laughed. 'What gave you that idea?'

'I don't know. I just thought that's what you meant.'

'My mother only goes out with one man. Seymour Chandler. Do you know him?'

'No.'

'He's very rich. My mother wants to marry him. Actually, my mother wants to marry anybody who's very rich.'

'Oh,' I said. I hope my mother won't be like that.

'She and my father have been divorced almost three years. My father lives in San Francisco.'

'Have you been there to visit him?' I asked.

'No ... I haven't seen him since the divorce. He's a runaround and he drinks too much and his cheques are late every month. Once my mother's lawyer had him picked up for nonsupport.'

'My father isn't anything like that,' I said.

'Sometimes the children are the last to know,' Val told me.

'How did you find out about yours?' I asked.

'Oh ... my mother spent the whole first year after the divorce telling me what a bum my father is.'

'My mother keeps saying my father is a great person,' I said.

Val laughed and said, 'Uh-oh! Watch out for that.'

'Why? What do you mean?'

'Because she's not being honest with you, that's what.'

'How do you know?' I asked.

'It says so – right here.' Val reached under her bed and came up with a book. She opened it and read, ' "If your mother never says bad things about your father it's because she thinks that it's better for you not to know about your father's faults. She may think that you can only love a person who is perfect." ' Val closed the book. 'You see?' she said.

'What kind of book is that?' I asked.

'It's called *The Boys and Girls Book About Divorce* and it's just for kids like us. A doctor wrote it. I'm his greatest fan. I used to write to him once a week when I first got his book. He even answered me.'

'Did your mother buy it for you?' I asked.

'No. I read about it in *The New York Times* and saved my allowance until I had enough. It's very expensive. It costs $7.95.'

'For just one book?'

'Yes, but it's worth it. You ought to ask your father to get it for you. Wait a minute and I'll write down all the information.' Val got up and went to her desk. She wrote on a piece of notebook paper, then folded it and gave it to me. I put it in my pocket.

Val put the divorce book back under her bed and came up with another. 'Do you know the facts of life?' she asked.

'Yes,' I said.

'Oh. If you didn't I was going to say I'd be glad to tell you. I have a book about that too. See ...' She showed me the book. It was a lot like the one I read at Debbie's.

'What grade are you in?' Val asked.

'Sixth,' I said.

'I'm in seventh. I was twelve in September.'

'I'm twelve too,' I said. 'We're just a few months apart.'

'In age maybe,' Val said. 'But being in seventh grade makes a big difference. For instance, I wouldn't dream of liking a boy in my class.'

'How come?' I asked, thinking about Gary Owens.

'Seventh-grade boys are babies. I like eighth or ninth-grade boys.'

'My brother's in ninth grade,' I told her.

'Oh ... I didn't know you have a brother.'

'Yes, and a little sister too.'

'Then you're the middle child?'

'Yes.'

'Uh-oh! That's bad,' Val said. 'Middle children have all kinds of problems.'

'Says who?' I asked.

'Everybody knows that. You're not the oldest and you're not the youngest. So you wind up with problems. The divorce will be harder on you than on them. But cheer up! I'm an *only* child. I have lots of problems too.'

'Val ... how do you know so much?' I asked.

'I told you,' she said, 'I read the entire *New York Times* every Sunday!'

fourteen

Compared to Val, Debbie doesn't know anything. I don't think she's ever read *The New York Times*. And what does she know about divorce or alimony or support? Not much, that's for sure. It's funny how things can change all of a sudden. Now I have more in common with Val than with Debbie. Oh, we're still best friends but we don't see that much of each other outside school. Especially since Mrs Bartell has decided Debbie needs dramatic lessons. She's going to get them every Saturday afternoon.

Now that Gary Owens has moved to Houston, Mrs Singer's let me move my desk away from the wall and next to Debbie's. She said if there is any talking or giggling between us she will separate us again. It's too bad that Gary moved away without ever knowing that I've spent four whole months thinking about him. If I ever feel that way about a boy again I won't waste time. I'll let him know right off. At least I think I will.

We are studying about the Vikings this month. They were pretty interesting guys, but very mean. When they went into battle they acted absolutely crazy. They killed everybody, including the women and children. But they were smart too. For instance, they built great ships. We are going to make Viking dioramas. That sounds like fun, for a change.

This afternoon I tried to find out if Petey Mansfield talks. I waited until he and Jeff locked themselves up inside the hideaway. Then I crept up the stairs very quietly and stood outside Jeff's room, holding a glass to the wall. I pressed my ear against the bottom of the glass. Eileen told me this is the best way to try to hear something you're not supposed to.

It works too! First I heard them laughing. But then they switched on the record player and that was the end of it. All I got was an earful of music. If you ask me, Petey Mansfield can talk when he feels like it.

Debbie says if only I like Petey we could have a double wedding. Meaning her and Jeff and me and Petey. I told her, 'Ha-ha! I wouldn't marry Petey Mansfield if he was the last boy on earth.' And anyway, I'm not getting married.

My mother is eating again. She goes around the house singing now. I still wonder if she's in love. I would like to get a look at this Mr Hague because my mother has gone to his office a few more times, and once when I answered the phone it was *him*. Last week Val told me that women getting divorces always fall for their lawyers.

Tonight at dinner Mom gave us some big news. 'I'm going back to college,' she said.

Amy practically spit out her lima beans. 'To college?'

'Yes,' Mom said. 'That way I'll be able to get a better job.'

'A job?' Jeff and I said together.

'Yes.'

'You're really getting a job?' Jeff asked.

'I hope so,' Mom told him.

'Doing what?' I asked. 'Refinishing furniture?'

'No,' Mom said. 'That's what I'd like to do but I have to be more practical right now.'

What kind of job will she get? What can she do? Maybe she'll be a cashier in the supermarket. Or maybe she'll be a cocktail waitress. That's what divorced women on TV always turn out to be – cocktail waitresses. Imagine my mother dressed in a skimpy costume! Suppose Debbie comes over while she's getting into her waitress clothes. Debbie will say, 'Why is your mother dressed up like a Bunny?' And I won't tell her the truth. I'll say, 'She's going to a costume party.' Then Debbie will say, 'Oh. She looks cute.' But I'll know that she looks terrible.

'I don't know what kind of job I'm going to get,' Mom said. 'That's why I'm going back to college. To take a course in typing and shorthand. I've signed up for an evening class at Seton Hall too. In English literature. The term's half over, but I can still learn a lot.'

'English literature!' Jeff said. 'Why?'

'Because I only had one year of college before I got married. I had you when I was just twenty,' she told Jeff. She finished eating her salad. Then she said, 'I think I might like to get my degree. I never really had a chance to find out what I might be able to do.'

'Well, don't let me stop you!' Jeff said. 'I can always go and live with Dad.'

My mother's face turned very red. 'Did he tell you that?'

'He said any time I want to I can stay there.' Jeff stood up. 'At least he's not sorry he had us!' He clomped out of the kitchen and slammed the front door.

Mom pushed her chair away from the table. 'Jeff is wrong,' she told me and Amy. 'You know I'm glad to have you.'

Maybe you are and maybe you're not. Who can tell any more?

Tuesday, 6 April
Can Jeff really move out of our house? That would be awful!
Even though I can't stand him sometimes, I would still miss
him a lot. I like just knowing he's around.

But the next morning Jeff was back and Mom was furious.
She threw our breakfast at us. 'Where were you last night?'
she asked him.

'That's my business,' Jeff said.

'Just who do you think you're talking to?' Mom asked.
'From now on you're not to run out at night without telling
me first. And I want you home by nine thirty during the week.'

'Says who?' Jeff asked.

'Me!' Mom hollered.

'Since when are you the boss?'

'Jeff ... stop it!' Mom said. 'What's got into you?'

By the time Jeff left for school my mother was on the verge
of tears. But when she saw that he had forgotten his lunch she
ran after him calling, 'Jeff ... Jeff ... you forgot your lunch.'

He yelled back, 'Eat it yourself!'

Wednesday, 7 April
I hate Jeff today. He's making everything worse, just when it
was getting better.

fifteen

I have been trying to get sick. I don't wear a sweater when I
should, and two days ago I walked in the rain without my boots
and my feet got soaked. But so far nothing has happened.
Debbie once told me about a girl in her cabin at camp who liked
to stay overnight in the infirmary. She used to rub the end of
the thermometer until it went up to 102°. Then she'd stick

it in her mouth and the nurse would think she was really sick.

This morning I tried doing that but it never went above 94°
– and I rubbed it for ten whole minutes. So I held the tip of
the thermometer next to the light bulb in my desk lamp and it
went up to 105°. I figured I'd walk downstairs like that. Then
my mother would take it out and wouldn't she be surprised
when she saw what a high fever I had!

The only trouble was I didn't know the thermometer would
be so hot. As soon as I put it into my mouth I burned my
tongue something awful! I spit the thermometer out. It fell
on the floor but it didn't break.

I will have to think up a better way to get my mother and
father back together. I can't waste my time trying to get sick.
That could take forever.

I had my piano lesson right before dinner tonight. Mrs Lennard
told me to cut my nails shorter. She says she can hear a
click-click sound when I play. And that from now on Mew
can't sit on top of the piano when I take my lesson. I told her
my cat is very musical and that she always sits on top of the
piano when I practise. Actually, Mew is almost human, but
I didn't say so.

Mrs Lennard looked at me kind of funny. I'll bet she wishes
she was still teaching Jeff and not just me. It's no secret that
he's the one with the talent. But this year he quit piano. I don't
think I play so bad. It's just that my fingers don't always do
what I want them to.

Before Mrs Lennard left she told me to practise the same
songs for next week. She said I wasn't ready for anything new.
I felt like asking her how she would play if her parents were
getting divorced.

As soon as we sat down to dinner Amy said, 'Wendy, my
friend in school, has a Talking Jessie Doll. She brought it in for
Show and Tell. I want one too. The kind with the hair that
grows.'

'Maybe for your birthday,' my mother said.

'My birthday's not until the end of June,' Amy told her.

'Well, that's not so far away,' Mom said.

'Oh, please, Mommy! I can't wait until my birthday!'

'I'm sorry, Amy. But you'll have to.'

'Why?' Amy asked.

'You know Mom doesn't have a lot of money to throw around,' I told Amy. 'Stop being so selfish.'

'I'll bet you Daddy would get it for me.'

'That's enough, Amy!' Mom shouted.

'I *hate* you.' Amy screamed. 'You made Daddy go away just so you could be mean to me!'

My mother reached across the table and smacked Amy. Then she sent her to her room.

'I thought you said there wouldn't be any more fighting once you and Daddy were apart,' I said.

Jeff laughed and got up from the table.

'Try to understand,' Mom told us. 'Won't you please try to understand?' She put her head down right on her plate and started to cry. She got gravy in her hair.

Thursday, 15 April
Sometimes I feel sorry for my mother and other times I hate
her. And besides all that, I didn't laugh once today!

sixteen

Gary Owens wrote our class a letter. Mrs Singer found it in her mailbox in the office. It said:

Dear Mrs Singer and Class 6-108,
Texas is neat. It's warm enough to play baseball even in the
winter. We got a dog. His name is Alexander, like the Great.

We call him Al for short. Most of the kids here are okay except for a few. They call me the new kid. Here's my address in case anybody feels like writing.
Gary Owens
16 Sanders Road
Houston, Texas

Mrs Singer said we should all write to Gary and that would be our English lesson for the day. I wrote:

Dear Gary,
It must be nice to be where it's warm. We made Viking dioramas. Did you learn about the Vikings yet? Your dog Al sounds very nice. I still have my cat Mew, but I like dogs too. By now you're probably not the new kid any more. Well, that's all the news from here.
Your friend,
Karen Newman
(I hope you remember me!)

Mrs Singer made me copy my letter over because I didn't make paragraphs. There are a lot of things I would have told Gary, if only he had liked me before he moved away.

seventeen

My mother got a job! She's going to be the receptionist at the Global Insurance Company in East Orange. She'll probably get to bring home a million Day Books next year. She says this is just a stepping stone – something to get her going until she decides what kind of work she wants to do permanently.

Aunt Ruth and Uncle Dan came over tonight. My mother was in the basement working on an old trunk she picked up at some sale. She's refinishing it and lining the inside with flowered material. It's going to be for Amy's toys, she says. So Aunt Ruth and Uncle Dan went downstairs to see her. So did I. I wanted to hear what my mother had to say because I am almost positive Aunt Ruth doesn't want her to go to work.

'The children need you at home, Ellie,' Aunt Ruth said.

'They're in school all day,' Mom told her. 'They won't even know I'm gone. I'm only working from nine to three and Karen will watch Amy until I get home.'

'Except Wednesdays,' I reminded her. 'Don't forget I have Girl Scouts on Wednesdays.'

'Amy can play at Roger's for half an hour on Wednesdays. I'll be home by three thirty.'

'Suppose one of them gets sick?' Aunt Ruth asked. 'Then what?'

'Mrs Hedley can come. I'll make some kind of arrangement with her. Besides, they don't get sick that often.'

Isn't that the truth? And I've been trying so hard.

'Ellie ...' Uncle Dan said. 'I wish you'd think this over for a while. Are you sure you can handle the responsibility of running a house and keeping a job?'

'Not to mention the children,' Aunt Ruth added.

'I think I can manage,' Mom said. 'At any rate, I'm going to give it a try.'

'What will people at work call you, Mom?' I asked. 'Will you be Mrs Newman or Miss Robinson, like before you were married?'

'I think I'll call myself Miss Newman. I'm used to being Ellie Newman. After all, that's who I've been for fifteen years.' Mom opened another can of shellac and started painting the trunk.

After Aunt Ruth and Uncle Dan went home I asked Mom, 'How come you didn't give in to Aunt Ruth this time?'

And Mom said, 'I don't always give in to Aunt Ruth.'

'Yes you do.'

'That isn't so, Karen.'

'Well I think it is. Every time you go shopping Aunt Ruth tells you what to buy. And when Amy had all those sore throats Aunt Ruth made you go to her doctor.'

'You're wrong,' Mom said. 'I may have listened to Aunt Ruth a lot of times but I don't always do what she thinks is right. And from now on I'm going to be much more careful to make up my own mind about everything.'

'Mom ...'

'Yes?'

'What do you really want to do?'

'I don't know yet. But I'm going to try to find out.'

My mother is grown up. So how come she can't decide what she wants? Does she want to go to work or does she want to go to college? 'I sure hope you find out soon,' I told her.

'It has nothing to do with you, Karen. It isn't going to change your life one way or another.'

'That's what you say!'

'Look ... some day you and Jeff and Amy will grow up and leave home. Then what will I have?'

'You see!' I raised my voice. 'That proves it! All you care about is yourself! You never think about me.'

'That's not so and you know it!' Mom said.

'Oh, yes, it is so! You never ask me what I think or what I feel or what I want ... I wish I was never born!'

I ran upstairs, picked up Mew and took her to my room. I closed my door and put a chair up against it.

Pretty soon my mother knocked on the door and called me. I knew she would. 'Karen ... this is silly. Let me in. I want to talk to you.'

'Go away,' I told her.

'I'll bet anything that Mom will change her mind about her job just like she did about Daddy.

A few days after my mother started her job I had a dental appointment. Mom said from now on she will schedule our appointments later in the day, but just this once Aunt Ruth would pick me up at school and drive me to Dr Harrison's.

I am the only one in my family who has never had a cavity. I don't know if this is because I am a better tooth-brusher or because I was born that way. Whatever the reason, I'm glad.

Dr Harrison sings while he looks at your teeth. He has a terrible voice. He makes up his own words too. Usually they don't make much sense but they always rhyme. When he cleans my teeth I laugh. I can't stand that tickle on my gums. And when I laugh he tells me not to, because I open my mouth too wide.

Today he said that my teeth are in good shape and that I don't have to come back for another six months. But he gave me a fluoride treatment and I almost threw up. I hate fluoride treatments!

When I was through I told the nurse my mother would call to make my next appointment. Aunt Ruth put away her needlepoint and asked me if I would like to stop for a snack on the way home. I said, 'Sure.'

We went to Grunings on the hill. They have the world's most delicious ice cream. Aunt Ruth ordered a hot-fudge sundae with whipped cream and nuts. I guess she's off her diet this week. I ordered two scoops of coffee ice cream. I don't like sundaes. All that goo gets in the way and it makes you very thirsty.

When we were served and I took my first bite of ice cream I remembered that my teeth are very sensitive to cold and hot after a cleaning. The ice cream nearly killed me. I had to mash it all up and then lick it off the spoon so it wouldn't hurt my teeth.

'How are things going at home?' Aunt Ruth asked.

'Okay, I guess. Next week is Mom's and Dad's anniversary.'

'That's right,' Aunt Ruth said. 'I forgot all about it.'

'Are you sending a card?'

'No ... when a couple is getting a divorce they don't want to be reminded of wedding anniversaries.'

I don't agree with that but I didn't tell Aunt Ruth. I think
if we remind Mom and Dad about their anniversary they will
feel very bad about getting a divorce. They will remember how
happy they were when they first met and all that. Then they
will see how silly it is of them not to get along. 'They'll be
married sixteen years,' I told Aunt Ruth.

'That's right. I remember it very well because Mark had the
chicken pox and the wedding was at our house and your
grandfather never had chicken pox so the doctor gave him a
shot. But two weeks later he got it anyway.'

'Garfa had chicken pox?'

'All over him.' Aunt Ruth laughed a little. 'You know …
I haven't thought about that in a long time. Sixteen years ago …
Mark was just a little boy and now he's all grown up.'

'How long have you and Uncle Dan been married?' I asked.

'Twenty-six years.'

'That's really a long time!'

'Yes, it is.'

'Do you ever fight?'

'Sometimes.'

'But then you make up?'

'Either that or we forget about it.'

That's like me and my mother. We have just forgotten about
the fight we had the other night. Neither one of us has
mentioned it. Why couldn't she and Daddy have done that?
'You know something? I don't remember my parents fighting
when I was little.'

'I suppose they got along better then,' Aunt Ruth said. 'It's
only in the last six or seven years that things have been bad.'

'That long?' I couldn't believe it! How could two people
not get along for so many years?

That night I was sitting in the den with Mew on my lap. Her
fur shed all over my sweater. I got up to get her brush, then
settled on the couch again. She doesn't always like me to brush

her. Sometimes she gets mad and tries to bite the brush. Tonight she purred and let me do whatever I wanted.

Mom and Amy were watching TV. Jeff never sits with us any more, except at mealtime. Amy was snuggled up close to Mom, which is really unusual for her. She always used to do that with Daddy. When I am cuddling Mew I never feel bad that my mother or father is paying attention to someone else.

As I brushed Mew's fur I started to think about what Aunt Ruth had said – that my parents haven't got along for six or seven years. And that's when it hit me! If the trouble between Daddy and Mom started that long ago, maybe it had something to do with Amy. That would have been around the time she was born. Maybe they didn't plan to have her. Maybe they only wanted two kids – me and Jeff. But then when Amy was born, Daddy liked her best. Mom was angry that he picked a favourite and she got back at Daddy by making Jeff *her* favourite. So really, if Amy hadn't been born they'd still be very happy.

I wonder if Amy knows about that? Probably not. She is too young to figure out such a thing. If you ask me Val has it all wrong. I might be the middle child, but it looks like I am the only one who is normal. Amy and Jeff have the problems. Poor Amy! No wonder she can't sleep at night. I am lucky to be no one's favourite.

eighteen

On Friday night Mrs Hedley came and Mom went rushing off to her class at Seton Hall. When Mrs Hedley opened her knitting bag and pulled out a pile of yarn I left the room. Amy could help her make wool balls tonight! I had more important things to do.

I went up to the hideaway. The door was open. Jeff was

lying on his bed with his eyes closed. Only his purple light was on. The whole room glowed.

'Hey Jeff ...' I said.

'Yeah?'

'Did you remember that Monday is Mom's and Daddy's anniversary?'

'So?'

'Don't you think we should do something?'

'Are you kidding?'

'No ... I think it would be very nice to have a little party or something.'

Jeff opened his eyes and sat up. 'They're getting divorced, Karen.'

'So?'

'So you don't go around giving parties for people who're getting divorced.'

'Don't you even want to sign my card?'

'You bought a card?' Jeff asked.

'Two,' I said, holding them up.

I bought them yesterday. One for Mom and one for Daddy. They are both the same. There's a picture of two bluebirds and it says *TO A SWELL COUPLE*. I'm going to mail them tomorrow morning because I want to make sure they are delivered on the twenty-sixth, and that's Monday. I'm sure when they remember that it is their sixteenth anniversary they will call their lawyers and cancel the divorce.

'Well,' I said to Jeff, 'You want to sign them or not?'

'You're nuts!' Jeff said. 'You can't send them anniversary cards like there's nothing wrong.'

'Says who?'

'You just can't.'

'Well, I'm going to. Amy's signing them and so am I and I think you should too.'

'That's the dumbest thing I ever heard.'

'This is your last chance to sign,' I told him.

'Forget it!'

'Okay, I will.' I turned and walked out of his room. Let him lie there forever – with his stupid purple light bulb!

When Amy came up to bed I showed her the cards. She liked them a lot. I told her she could sign them and she chose a different colour crayon for every letter in her name. And she didn't just sign *Amy* – she signed *Amy Denise Newman*.

On Saturday morning Mom said I could ask Debbie to sleep over if I wanted because she was going out to dinner with Aunt Ruth and Uncle Dan. 'I don't think we need Mrs Hedley any more,' Mom said. 'Jeff is old enough to be in charge.'

'I thought you said if we give up Mrs Hedley some other family will grab her.'

'They probably will,' Mom said. 'But it's foolish to pay her when we can manage by ourselves.'

Did Mr Hague tell Mom to watch her money? Or doesn't Daddy send enough for a baby sitter?

Debbie came over in time for supper, which we made ourselves. We had hot dogs, potato chips and chocolate pudding for dessert. The only part of the night that wasn't fun was telling Amy that she couldn't sleep in my other bed. She cried and carried on but before Mom left she explained that Amy has her own room and that's where she has to sleep from now on. I don't think Amy ever told Mom that she is afraid we'll be gone in the morning. Maybe I should be the one to tell my mother. I don't know – Amy might not like it if I did. That is supposed to be our secret.

Mom got all dressed up and I couldn't help wondering if just Aunt Ruth and Uncle Dan were taking her to dinner or if maybe Henry Farnum was going along too. And I didn't want to ask her about it in front of Debbie anyway. Mom looked very nice and she smelled delicious. I think she was wearing the perfume Daddy gave to her last Christmas.

At ten o'clock Amy fell asleep in the den and Debbie and I

carried her up to bed. We decided to leave her overhead light on all night. That way she might not get so scared if she woke up suddenly.

At quarter to eleven the phone rang. Debbie and I were in my room. I thought it might be Mom, checking to see how everything was. So I went into my mother's room and picked up the phone, but Jeff beat me to it on the kitchen extension. And it wasn't my mother either. It was Mary Louise Rumberger! I put one hand over the mouthpiece and called to Debbie, 'It's Mary Louise ...'

Debbie came running. We shared the phone and listened. Imagine Mary Louise calling my brother at quarter to eleven at night! And they barely even talked. They just laughed very softly at each other.

I could hardly wait for Monday night. I hoped Daddy would call as soon as he saw his mail. Then he and Mom would talk about the day they got married sixteen years ago and they'd laugh about Garfa catching the chicken pox!

Mom opened her mail as soon as she got home from work. I stood there watching her. After she read my card she did the craziest thing! She started to cry and she took me in her arms. She said, 'Oh, Karen ...' over and over again.

Later Daddy called. Only he didn't call to talk to Mom like I was hoping. He called to talk to me. He said, 'Thanks, Karen ... but from now on you have to remember we don't celebrate our anniversary any more. Try not to think of 26 April as a special day.'

Monday, 26 April
How can I not think about this day? It is special and it will always be special even if I am the only one who knows it!

nineteen

Jeff has a broken toe. He has to wear a sneaker with a big hole cut in it. His toe is bandaged and he pulls an athletic sock over that foot to keep the rest of his toes warm. He broke it himself. He dropped a weight on his foot. Dr Winters says he is lucky he didn't do more damage. He uses a cane to walk around. I wonder what Mary Louise Rumberger thinks of broken toes? She probably feels very sorry for him. She calls him every single night now.

Jeff doesn't talk to any of us. Not to me or Amy or my mother. He is getting just like Petey Mansfield. They can turn themselves off like radios. I am starting to really hate him!

Val invited me to sleep over Saturday night. I asked my mother if I could go. She said, 'I don't even know her, Karen. How can I let you sleep there overnight?'

'Please, Mom! She's very nice. So is her mother.' That was funny because I really don't know Mrs Lewis. I've seen her twice. She says hello, but that's about it. She is the best-looking mother I have ever seen. 'Daddy lives right upstairs,' I told Mom.

'You'll have to call him and see what he thinks,' Mom said.

'Now?'

'Yes, now.'

I picked up the phone and dialled. 'Hello Daddy? This is Karen ... I'm fine ... They're okay too. Daddy, Val wants me to sleep over Saturday night ... Yes, I'm dying to but Mom won't let me unless you say I can. Well, because she doesn't know Val or Mrs Lewis ... Okay, I'll tell her you're going to be home. Thanks a lot, Daddy. I'll see you Saturday. 'Bye.'

After that my mother said I could go.

The next night my father called to invite Jeff and Amy to stay over at his apartment Saturday night. Amy said she couldn't wait, but Jeff told Daddy he already made other plans.

I'll bet they have something to do with Mary Louise.

On Saturday, before I left for Vals, I made my mother promise to take good care of Mew and to feed her *canned* food in the morning. I think Mom would give Mew food from a box if she could get away with it.

I picked Mew up and kissed her goodbye. I am not allowed to kiss her. It has something to do with the possibility of her carrying germs. So I take her into the bathroom with me, lock the door and kiss her as much as I want to.

Later, when Daddy called for us, me and Amy were waiting by the front door. As soon as we were in the car Amy said, 'Jeff doesn't like me any more.'

My father said, 'Oh?'

'And he doesn't like Karen either. He doesn't like anybody. He's so mean! He's almost as mean as Mommy. She won't get me a Talking Jessie Doll. The kind with the hair that grows.'

'Your mother's not mean, Amy,' Daddy said.

'How do you know? You don't live at home.'

'Because I know your mother and if she doesn't think you should have a Talking Jessie Doll right now she must have a good reason.'

'She's always leaving us alone,' Amy said. 'That's mean, isn't it?'

'I can't believe she leaves you alone,' Daddy said.

'She doesn't,' I told him. 'We don't use Mrs Hedley any more, that's all. Jeff is in charge when Mom goes out.'

'That sounds reasonable to me,' Daddy said.

Amy sulked the rest of the way to Daddy's apartment.

twenty

I rang Val's bell. She let me in. I got there in time to meet her mother's boyfriend, Seymour Chandler. He doesn't really look anything like a boyfriend. He looks more like a grandfather to me. His hair is silver and he's kind of fat. But Mrs Lewis looked beautiful. I wouldn't want to have a mother that good looking. I'd spend all my time worrying about how I was going to turn out compared to her. Not that Val is ugly. She's okay. But she doesn't look like her mother.

Val introduced me to Mr Chandler. She said, 'Seymour, this is my friend Karen. Her father lives upstairs. He's getting a divorce.' Then Val told me, 'Seymour's divorced too.'

'That's right,' Seymour said. 'I am. Twice, as a matter of fact.' Then he laughed.

Twice! I never even thought about getting divorced more than once. That must *really* be awful!

'Well, girls . . . Seymour and I are leaving now. You have a nice time,' Mrs Lewis told us. She leaned close to Val and kissed her good night. I noticed that her lips didn't touch Val's face. It was an air-kiss. 'Go to sleep by eleven, Valerie.'

'I will, mother,' Val said. She closed the door behind them and fastened the three extra locks on it.

It must feel funny to see your own mother go out on dates.

'Well . . .' Val said. 'What do you want to do?'

'I don't know. I usually watch TV on Saturday nights.'

'TV ruins your mind,' Val said. 'Let's wash our hair.'

'Mine's not dirty,' I said. 'I just washed it Monday night.'

'Oh, come on, Karen. It'll be fun. Then we can soak in my mother's bubble bath. I always do that on Saturdays. Tell you what . . . I'll wash your hair first, then you can do mine.'

We went into the bathroom, where Val attached a rubber hose to the sink. 'It's like a beauty parlour. You'll enjoy it,' she said.

'Well . . . okay.'

Val fixed up a chair for me and spread a towel under my neck so it wouldn't hurt from leaning back so far. Then she went to work. I have never had such a good shampoo in my life. When I do it myself I don't get out all the soap, because my hair is so thick. But Val got it squeaky clean. She even gave me a cream rinse so I wouldn't get tangles. When that was done she wrapped my head in a big green towel.

Then it was my turn to do Val. I didn't do as good a job on her. I tried, but her hair is awfully long. She had to give me advice. She said, 'Rinse behind my ears now. That's it. Watch it, Karen ... the water's running down my face. Okay ... now the cream rinse. Take two capfuls and rub it in all over. Good ... rub some more in if that's not enough. Okay ... now give me another rinse. Careful ... it's going down my back.'

Val wrapped her head in a towel like mine, then she ran the tub. She poured in three-quarters of a bottle of bubble bath. While the tub was filling we rubbed each other's heads until they were damp. Val gave me a couple of barrettes to pin up my hair so it wouldn't get all wet when I took my bath.

She let the water run almost to the top of the tub and by then the bubbles were so thick you couldn't see through them.

I don't feel funny getting undressed in front of Debbie, because I have known her forever. But I did feel strange in front of Val. She could tell too. She said, 'If you want, I won't look until you're in the tub. You can hide under all the bubbles.' Then she turned around and I took off my clothes, dropped them in a heap on the floor and stepped into the tub. When I did, some of the water ran over the side.

Then Val got undressed and I didn't look, even though she didn't care if I did. More suds overflowed when she got into the tub, but Val didn't pay any attention to that. She said, 'When I grow up I'm going to be a nudist. People would get along better if they didn't wear any clothes. Then they couldn't pretend to be what they're not.'

'But you'd get cold in the winter,' I told her.

'Possibly. Maybe I'll move to a warmer climate.'

That reminded me of Gary Owens. I wonder if there are nudists in Houston?

We soaked in the tub for half an hour. Neither one of us used soap or a washcloth. I guess if you sit in bubble bath all that time you're bound to get clean.

When we finally came out of the tub Val put on her mother's terry robe, which was about four inches too long. It dragged all over the wet bathroom floor. I got into my pyjamas. We both smelled very nice. Then we brushed out each other's hair.

When that was done Val sat down on the closed toilet seat and rubbed some kind of oil all over her legs. 'I have to shave my legs now,' she said.

I don't know anybody who shaves her legs yet. Debbie says she will when she's fourteen or when her legs get hairy, whichever comes first.

Val ran a silver razor over her legs. *Zip zip zip.* She reminded me of my father, shaving his face. I used to love to watch him. He'd always put a dab of shaving cream on my nose when I was little. 'Don't you ever cut yourself?' I asked Val.

'Oh, sure. But nothing serious. I've had lots of practice. I've been shaving since September.'

'Did your mother show you how?'

'Nope. I learned myself. Want me to do yours?'

'No,' I said. 'My mother would kill me. She says the earlier you shave the more you have to keep shaving. And anyway, the hair on my legs is very light. See ...' I held a leg up for Val to look at.

'You're lucky,' she said, inspecting it. 'I'm a very hairy person.'

I noticed that when we were in the tub but I didn't tell Val.

When she was done shaving I helped her clean up the bathroom. She took big handfuls of the suds that were left in the tub and threw them into the toilet. They made a sizzling sound. And even after she flushed three times there were still suds floating around. 'I think I used a little too much bubble bath tonight,' Val said. By then it was almost ten o'clock.

We went into Val's room. She has a trundle bed. It looks like just one bed, but underneath there's another one. It was already pulled out for me. I asked Val where she got the rug that's shaped like a foot and she said she saw an ad for it in *The New York Times* and cut it out to show her mother. Then she got it for her birthday.

'I put my new sheets on your bed,' Val said. 'Do you like them?'

They were pink-and-orange striped. 'They're really nice.' I said.

'I thought you'd approve.' Val snuggled down under her covers.

I'll bet it's lonely for her to spend every Saturday night all by herself. And Mrs Lewis goes out during the week too. No wonder Val hopes Seymour will marry her mother. Then she won't be alone so much.

'Val . . .' I said.

'Yes?'

'I still don't understand why you don't see your father. Couldn't you take a trip to San Francisco?'

'No. I told you before . . . he doesn't care anything about me.'

'How can you say that?' I asked.

'Because it's true.'

'Did your mother tell you?'

'No. That's one thing she won't admit. She says he's just busy.'

'Then you don't know if he really wants to see you or not.'

'Oh, I know all right. I'll show you,' Val said, reaching under her bed. She came up with her divorce book. She opened it and said, 'Listen to this. "Fathers who live close by but do not visit—" '

I interrupted. 'But your father doesn't live close by. He lives in San Francisco.'

'Wait a minute,' Val said. 'I'm not done reading.' She started again. ' "Fathers who live close by but do not visit and fathers who live far away and hardly ever call or write either do not love their children at all, or they love them very little." ' She closed the book, with her finger marking her place, and looked at me.

'It really says that?'

'It does.'

'Do you believe it?'

'Of course I do. It's true. Why should I kid myself?' She opened the book again. 'It says right here, "There is something very wrong with an unloving parent. He deserves pity as well as anger." I've got along without him for three years. I'll get along without him forever! He was never interested in me anyway.'

'What does your mother say ... besides the bad things?'

'That he married her because she was pretty and he wanted to show her off, like a new coat or something. He never really loved her, she says.'

'I think my parents loved each other when they got married. Their wedding pictures look so happy. But my mother says they were too young.'

'How old was she?' Val asked.

'Nineteen.'

'You should never get married that young,' Val said.

'I'm not getting married at all!' I told her.

'I am,' she said.

That surprised me. 'You are?'

'Yes. When I'm twenty-seven and I'm a successful scientist.'

'You're going to be a scientist?' I asked. 'I thought you were going to be a nudist.'

'One thing has nothing to do with the other. I'll be both.'

'What kind are you going to be? Scientist, I mean.'

'I'm not sure. But I'm going to discover something important. I'll be famous and my father will want everyone to know that

I'm his daughter. I'll be very cool about the whole thing. I'll admit that we're related but I won't say anything else.'

'If you get married ... will you ever get divorced?'

'No. Never!'

'Me neither,' I said. 'You know something? I think if my father could see my mother now he'd move back in.'

'Forget it. It'll never work.'

'How do you know?' I asked. 'You never even saw my mother.'

'I'm telling you, Karen. Just forget it.'

'I don't see how you can be so sure,' I said. 'My father's very lonely.'

'But that doesn't mean he and your mother are going to get back together.'

'Well, I still don't see how it can hurt to try.'

'Go ahead,' Val said. 'Try ... you'll see ... you'll be the one who gets hurt.' She put out the light then. 'Good night Karen,' she said.

'Good night Val.' I'll bet she doesn't want my parents to get back together. Just because her father moved to San Francisco and never sees her. But I'm still sure it will work.

twenty-one

When Daddy drove us home on Sunday afternoon he asked me to run into the house and get Jeff. 'I have something to tell all three of you,' he said.

Jeff was playing the piano. I heard the music before I opened the front door. He's been spending a lot of time practising lately. He writes his own songs. Most of them are in a minor key and sound sad. His newest one is called 'Mary Louise ...

81

Please.' Those are the only words. Please what? I wonder. But I wouldn't dream of asking him.

I went inside and said, 'Hey Jeff ... Daddy's out in the car. He wants to talk to you.'

Jeff banged the piano with both hands before he got up and stomped out of the house. I followed him. We both got into the back seat of the car. Amy was up front with Daddy.

My father turned around to face me and Jeff. 'I'm leaving for Las Vegas a week from tomorrow,' he said. 'I'm staying with Garfa for about six weeks and while I'm there I'll get the divorce.'

'You're getting a Nevada divorce?' Jeff asked.

'Yes,' Daddy told him.

'But why?' I said. 'Why can't you just get it right here in New Jersey?'

'Because that would take a long time,' Daddy said. 'At least a year.'

'So?' I asked.

'Well, your mother and I want to get things settled now. This isn't easy for either one of us.'

What's the big hurry? I wondered. Why can't they wait? Why does Daddy have to go away for such a long time? Unless ... unless there's some other woman that he wants to marry! Thinking about that makes me sick. But it is possible. One night last week I called Daddy and there wasn't any answer. Maybe he was out with her then, making plans! Or could Mom be the one who wants the divorce right away? Suppose she wants to marry Henry Farnum! No, that can't be. We'd have met him by now. It's got to be Daddy! I wonder who the woman is? I hate her already. I will never speak to her. Not as long as I live!

That night I helped my mother do the dinner dishes. When we were almost through I said, 'Is Daddy getting married?'

Mom turned off the water and looked at me. 'Where did you ever get that idea?'

'Well, is he?'

'No,' Mom said.

'Are you positive?'

'Yes. The divorce has nothing to do with anyone else. You know that, Karen.'

'How can you be sure Daddy didn't meet somebody last week and now he wants to marry her?'

'I'm sure. That's all. Besides, he'd have told me.'

'Why should he tell you?'

'Just because. I know him. And he'd certainly tell you and Jeff and Amy. He wouldn't just run off and get married.'

'Then why is he in such a hurry to get the divorce?'

'Oh . . .' Mom said. 'So that's it!'

'Well?'

'He's going now because he can get away from the store now. In a few months he might not be able to.'

I thought that over. And I had to admit it makes sense. Maybe things aren't as bad as I thought.

Later I called Val. I said, 'If a person goes to Nevada for a divorce, can he change his mind about it at the last second and tell the judge to forget the whole thing?'

'Who's going to Nevada?' Val asked.

'Nobody special. But just suppose somebody did. Do you think the judge would understand and cancel the divorce?'

'I don't think anybody changes his mind at the last second.'

'But it's possible, isn't it?'

'Karen . . .' Val said.

'What?'

'I know your father's going to Las Vegas to get the divorce.'

'You do?'

'Yes. He told my mother the other day. We're going to take in his mail and newspapers while he's gone.'

'Oh.' No wonder Val tried to discourage me last night. She knew about Daddy all along.

'So why don't you just forget about him changing his mind?' Val said.

'Listen . . . when he gets out there and sees how much he

misses all of us I'll bet you anything he *will* change his mind!'

'Don't count on it.'

'I've got to go now,' I said. 'I've got a ton of homework.'

I hung up the phone and went to my room. Mew was asleep on my bed. I lay down next to her and rubbed my face against her fur. 'I must do something, Mew,' I told her. 'I must do something right away to stop the divorce! There's only one week left.'

twenty-two

I've got to get my mother and father into the same room. My new idea is this: I will ask Mrs Singer if I can bring my Viking diorama home now, instead of at the end of the month. It's in the showcase in the hall, near our classroom. We have a whole Viking display. Everyone stops to look at it. Since my diorama is very fragile, Daddy will have to come into the house to see it. I wouldn't dare bring it out to the car or to his apartment. That's what I'll say anyway. He'll be very proud of me. I made a Viking ship with twelve small Vikings sitting in it. There are pink and purple mountains in the background and I used blue sparkle for the water. Even Mrs Singer said I did an excellent job. I'm glad she noticed.

Once Daddy comes home and sees Mom, everything will work out fine. I just know it. First they'll look at each other and then they'll touch hands. Finally Daddy will kiss her and they'll never fight again. Daddy will call Garfa to cancel his trip to Las Vegas and I will write to tell him how I got them back together. Garfa will write that he knew I'd be able to do it all along. And won't Val be surprised! I'll never tell my parents I planned the whole thing. Let them think it was all an accident.

*

On Monday morning I went up to Mrs Singer's desk and said, 'I'd like to bring my Viking diorama home this week.'

'But Karen,' Mrs Singer said, 'it's in the showcase.'

'I know,' I told her. 'But I have to take it home. So maybe we could put something else in the showcase.'

'Like what?' Mrs Singer asked.

'Oh, I don't know. A picture or a book. Anything.'

'I'd rather that you wait until the end of the month when we change the showcase.'

'I can't Mrs Singer,' I said, raising my voice. 'I need it now!'

'What for?'

'For ... for ...' But I couldn't tell Mrs Singer why I needed it, even though I felt like yelling, 'To keep my parents from getting divorced.'

Instead, I turned around and walked to my desk. As soon as I sat down Debbie leaned over and whispered, 'What's wrong?'

I made a face and shook my head towards Mrs Singer. Then my nose started to run and I knew I was going to cry. So I ran out of the room. I stood in the hall with my forehead pressed against the showcase window. My Viking diorama was in the corner, with a little sign under it that said *Made by Karen Newman*.

Debbie came out into the hallway. 'Are you okay?' she asked.

'I guess.'

'Mrs Singer said I should take you to the nurse's office.'

'I don't need any nurse,' I told her. We walked back to our classroom together.

I got through the rest of the day without doing any work. I made some plans though. If I could find the key to the showcase I could open it and take my diorama. That's not stealing. After all, it does belong to me! Mrs Singer keeps the key to the showcase somewhere in her desk. I'm sure of that.

At two thirty I excused myself to go to the girls' room. I wanted to get a good look at the showcase lock. Maybe I could pick it open with a bobby pin. But when I looked in the window

I saw a big book with a Viking on the cover in the corner where my diorama used to be. I ran back into the classroom and told Mrs Singer, 'It's gone! My diorama is gone. Somebody stole it!'

Everybody in the room started to talk at once, but I didn't care. Mrs Singer shouted, 'Calm down! No talking at all!' Then she reached into her bottom desk drawer and pulled out my diorama. 'Nothing's happened to it, Karen. I took it out of the showcase myself. If it's that important to you, take it home.'

I didn't say anything. I couldn't. I just nodded and took the diorama to my desk. I guess even witches have good days!

Monday, 3 May
I am counting the seconds until Sunday when Daddy calls for us and I get him inside to see my diorama.

twenty-three

My mother, Jeff, Amy and me are getting to be regulars at Howard Johnson's on the highway. We go there every Friday night because of Mom's English literature course.

The Howard Johnson's hostess knows us by now. She tries to give us the same booth every week. My mother likes it because it's not near the kitchen and it's away from the front door. Jeff has to sit on the aisle so he can stick out his foot. Next week the bandage is coming off his toe. If you ask me he likes his cane. It gets him a lot of attention.

Amy and I always order the same supper – hamburgers and french fries. We drink Ho-Jo Cola too. I think that's really Coke, even though the waitress won't admit it. Tonight Jeff ordered fried shrimp.

'You never eat fried shrimp,' my mother said.

'So I'll try it and maybe I'll like it,' he told her.

'I don't think this is the place to try something like that.'

'I feel like fried shrimp!' Jeff said. 'So I ordered it. So now forget about it!'

'Okay,' Mom said. 'It's just that you'll have to eat them whether you like them or not.'

'I said I'll eat them, didn't I?'

'I just want you to be sure.'

'Daddy always takes us out for steak,' Amy said.

'Daddy can afford to,' Mom told her.

This is the first time my mother has ever said anything like that. She looked at Jeff. 'Would you go wash up, please. Your hands are filthy.'

'I washed at home,' Jeff said.

'I'm asking you to go to the men's room and wash again.'

Jeff stood up, grabbed his cane and left the table. When he came back our main course was served. He sat down, picked up one shrimp and nibbled at it. 'Will you quit looking at me,' he said to me and Amy.

I didn't look at anything but my hamburger for the rest of the meal.

When my mother finished her dinner she said, 'Well, Jeff ... how are they?'

'Not great,' he said. 'I didn't know they'd be all breaded like this.'

'I told you,' Mom said.

'Oh, lay off, will you!'

'Jeffrey ...' Mom began.

But Jeff stood up then.

'Sit down,' Mom told him.

'No.'

'I said sit down!'

'No. I said *no*. Are you deaf or something?'

A lot of people were looking at us and my mother was embarrassed. So was I. I hoped we wouldn't see anybody we knew.

Jeff took his cane off the coat hook and walked to the front of the restaurant.

'Where's he going?' Amy asked.

'Out to the car,' Mom said.

'How do you know?' Amy asked.

'Where else would he go?' Mom said.

'You want me to go see?' I asked.

'No,' Mom said. 'We'll have our dessert and when we're through we'll go to the car. Jeff's not going to spoil our dinner.'

We all had ice cream. When we finished my mother gave me the check and the money to pay the cashier while she took Amy to the ladies' room.

But when we went outside to the car Jeff wasn't there.

'Karen ... check inside the restaurant again. He must be in there somewhere. Look in the men's room too.'

'Me?' I said. 'Me ... go into the men's room?'

'Just knock on the door and ask if anybody saw Jeff.'

'Okay,' I said. I went back inside. I checked the counter. He wasn't there. I walked all through the restaurant, pretending I had left something in our booth. I didn't see Jeff anywhere. So I stood in front of the men's room. I didn't knock like my mother told me to do. I couldn't. Suppose somebody came to the door and when they opened it I saw inside? No, I didn't want to look inside the men's room. Even though I've always wondered what it's like in there. Tonight wasn't the right time to find out.

'You want something?' a man asked me.

'No,' I said.

'Then, excuse me, please. I'm trying to get in here.'

'Oh,' I said, jumping away from the door. 'Would you do me a favour?'

'Sure,' he said. 'What is it?'

'Would you see if my brother's in there?'

'What's he look like?'

'He's fourteen and he's got a broken toe.'

'All right. Just a minute,' the man said.

He went inside. I turned my back to the door. He came right away. 'Nobody's in here,' he told me.

'Well, thank you anyway,' I said.

I went back outside and told my mother that Jeff wasn't anywhere in Howard Johnson's, including the men's room. 'Maybe he went home,' I said.

'No. You can't walk from here,' my mother told me. 'There's no way.'

'Well, then, where is he?' I said.

'I don't know,' Mom answered. 'Now stop asking me questions and give me a minute to think.'

'The one who asks the most questions learns the most,' Amy said.

'Oh, shut up,' I whispered.

'Why don't you?'

After a minute my mother said, 'We'll drive home now. Then I'll decide what to do. I can't think here.'

When we got home Mom waited until nine o'clock before she did anything. Then she called Aunt Ruth and Uncle Dan. They came right over. Uncle Dan said the first thing to do was to call the police. But my mother didn't want to. So Uncle Dan said, 'Okay ... but that's what I'd do if he was my son.'

Mom said, 'Let's try the hospitals first.'

So Uncle Dan sat down by the phone in the kitchen and called all the local hospitals. Jeff wasn't in any of them. I guess my mother thought Jeff got run over or something. Otherwise I don't know why she wanted Uncle Dan to call the hospitals.

Aunt Ruth said we should try his friends. So my mother asked me to make a list of all the kids Jeff might go to see. I couldn't decide whose name to put first – Petey Mansfield or Mary Louise Rumberger. I decided that Jeff, being in such a bad mood, would pick Petey. I handed Uncle Dan a list of twelve names. He called every one but none of them had seen Jeff.

'He could be at Bill's,' Uncle Dan said.

'No. How could he have got there?' my mother asked.

'Maybe he hitched,' I said.

'He knows I don't like him to hitch rides,' Mom said.

Maybe he knows it, I thought, but he hitches all the time. I've seen him do it. All the big kids hitch after school.

'And Bill wouldn't have been at the apartment anyway,' Mom said. 'It's Friday night. The store's open late.'

'How about the store?' Aunt Ruth said. 'Maybe he went to see Bill there.'

'Want me to call?' I asked.

'No,' Mom said. 'I don't want Bill to find out about Jeff.' She checked her watch. 'Anyway, Bill must be home by now. The store closes at nine.'

'He's going to have to know, Ellie. He is the boy's father,' Uncle Dan said.

'Would you call him, Dan? I just can't,' Mom told him.

So Uncle Dan called my father and when he hung up he said that Daddy was on his way over.

twenty-four

When my father got to our house I was hoping he would take Mom in his arms and kiss her and tell her not to worry, because everything was going to be all right. Instead he said, 'Did you call the police yet?'

And Mom said, 'Oh, Bill ... do we have to? Why get Jeff mixed up with the police?'

'I suppose you have a better idea?' Daddy asked.

'No,' Mom said. 'I haven't any ideas at all.'

'I'm not surprised,' Daddy said.

Mom looked around. I think she wanted to throw something

at Daddy. But there were too many people in the room. I saw Aunt Ruth raise her eyebrows at Uncle Dan.

My father walked into the kitchen and picked up the phone. He called the police. He told them his son was missing and gave them his name and our address. When he hung up he said, 'They'll be right over.'

We've never had a policeman in our house. The only time I've ever been close to one is on the street. Sergeant Tice got to our house in ten minutes. He was chewing gum and he had a pad and pencil with him, just like on TV. Aunt Ruth showed him into the living room, where we all sat down. He started asking questions right away.

'Name of the missing boy, please.'

'Jeffrey Peter Newman,' Daddy said. 'We call him Jeff.'

Sergeant Tice snapped his gum and wrote that down. 'Age?' he asked next.

'Fourteen,' my mother said. 'He'll be fifteen in August.'

Mew walked into the living room then. I called, 'Psst ... psst ...' and she came to me. She jumped up on my lap, made herself into a fur ball and started purring.

'Do you have a recent snapshot of him?' Sergeant Tice asked.

'I don't know,' my mother said. 'I think we might have one from last summer. Karen ... would you see if you can find one?'

'I don't know where any pictures are,' I told her.

Sergeant Tice said, 'Never mind. Let's get a good description of the boy now. Later, if you can come up with a picture, fine.'

'Well, he's about five foot seven,' Daddy said. 'And he weighs about one-thirty-five.'

'Hair?' Sergeant Tice asked.

'Brown,' Mom said. 'Down to his collar in back and just over his ears in front.'

'What's he wearing?'

'Jeans, a grey sweatshirt and a navy jacket,' Mom said.

'Eyes?'

'They're blue,' I said.

'Complexion?'

'Fair,' Daddy said. 'And he's got a dimple in his chin.'

'And some zits on his face,' Amy added. 'They're pimples if you don't already know.'

My mother looked over at Amy then, as if remembering for the first time that she was in the room. 'Go up to bed now, Amy. It's after ten!'

'No,' Amy said.

'Ruth ... would you take her up and get her into bed?' Mom said.

'No!' Amy yelled. 'I want to stay ... I want to stay and listen.'

Aunt Ruth tried to pick up Amy but Amy kicked so hard Aunt Ruth couldn't get hold of her.

'Daddy ...' Amy cried. 'Don't let her take me away. Daddy ... help!'

That sister of mine can really be impossible. And if you ask me she was doing it on purpose! But Daddy went to her and held her in his arms and stroked her hair and said, 'It's all right, baby. Everything's going to be all right.'

She really acts like a spoiled brat when Daddy is around.

Sergeant Tice cleared his throat to get our attention again. 'Any idea where he might be headed?'

'None,' Mom said. 'We've tried his friends but nobody knows where he is.'

'Any reason you can think of for him running off?'

'He got mad at Mommy!' Amy said. 'Because he didn't like his fried shrimp!'

Sergeant Tice looked at my mother.

'We did have a few words,' she told him. 'He got angry and walked out of the restaurant. Howard Johnson's on the highway.'

Sergeant Tice wrote that down. 'Is he on drugs?'

92

Daddy said, 'Of course not!'

'Are you certain?' Sergeant Tice asked.

'Damn right I'm certain,' Daddy told him, but he was glaring at my mother.

Sergeant Tice closed his notebook and stood up. 'Well ... these kids usually head for New York. We'll see what we can do.'

Mom stood up too. 'That's all?' she asked. 'You'll see? What are we supposed to do in the meantime?'

'Just carry on,' Sergeant Tice said. 'Not much else you can do. He'll probably show up. Most of them do.'

'He's walking with a cane,' I said. 'He's got a broken toe.' I could just picture Jeff on his way to New York. He'd fall down every few miles and he'd be cold and hungry and nobody would help him. Maybe I'll never see him again.

'Well, he can't get very far like that,' Sergeant Tice said. 'I'll be in touch.'

We walked him to the front door. I saw him spit out his gum by our dogwood tree.

Aunt Ruth said she'd make some coffee and Uncle Dan excused himself to go to the bathroom. Daddy carried Amy upstairs and put her to bed. When he came back down he and Mom went into the living room.

Now that the police business is out of the way, they can have a chance to be alone, I thought. They'll see that they belong together. That we're a family. Any minute now Daddy will tell her he's sorry he left.

I stayed in the kitchen with Aunt Ruth and Uncle Dan. I guess they wanted to hear what was going to happen as much as I did.

The first thing Daddy said was, 'I want the truth and I want it now.'

'I have nothing to say to you,' Mom told him.

'You damn well better have something to say! Because I want to know why my son ran away!'

'Your son!' Mom shouted. 'He's my son too ... and don't you forget it!'

'When I left this house he was fine,' Daddy said. 'But you fixed that, didn't you?'

'It's not going to work, I thought. They're just like they were before, only worse.

Mom yelled, 'Did you ever stop to think maybe it was your fault Jeff ran off? You're not exactly a perfect father!'

'Shut up!' Daddy raised his voice too. 'You want everybody to hear us?'

'I don't give a damn who hears! You make me sick!' Mom yelled.

'I'm warning you, Ellie ...'

'Lay a hand on me and I'll have you locked up,' Mom screamed.

Was he going to hit her?

'I wouldn't waste my time,' Daddy shouted.

No, he wasn't going to hit her.

'That's the trouble with you,' Mom hollered. 'You think everything is a waste of time ... me, the kids, the house, everything! The only thing you care about is the store! That goddamned store is your whole life!'

'I never heard you complain when the store got you a new car or this house or a vacation,' Daddy yelled.

'Those aren't the only things in life.'

'Come off it, Ellie.'

'No, I won't! You never looked at me as a person. I have feelings ... I have ideas ... did you ever stop to think about that?'

Amy ran into the kitchen then. She was crying. Uncle Dan picked her up and held her to him.

'Now you listen to me,' Daddy shouted.

'No!' Mom hollered. 'I'm tired of listening to you.'

'And I'm still tired of the whole business. You don't know what you want. You never did. And you never will! Because you never grew up! You're still Ruth's baby!'

Aunt Ruth pressed her lips together so tight they disappeared.

My mother shouted, 'I should have listened to Ruth a long time ago. I should have listened the first time I brought you home. She saw you for what you are. Conceited, selfish—'

'One more word and I'm going to take the kids away from you!'

'Don't you dare threaten me!' Mom screamed.

'I mean it. So help me. I'll have you declared incompetent.'

'You rotten bastard ...'

There was an awful crash in the living room then and I ran in to see what happened. One of Mom's best china babies was on the floor, smashed, like the mocha-icing cake.

'That's how you settle all your problems, isn't it?' Daddy said with a terrible laugh. 'Just like a two-year-old.'

Mom started to cry. She bent down and tried to pick up the pieces of her antique. I think it was the first time she ever broke anything she loved.

Then Daddy backed up and sat down on the chair by the fireplace, right on top of Mew. Mew howled and Daddy jumped. 'Damn cat!'

I shouted, 'You never liked her, did you?' I could see that Daddy thought I was talking about Mom, but really I meant Mew.

I don't know what they started yelling about then but I couldn't stand it any more so I put my hands over my ears and I started to scream. And I screamed and I screamed and I screamed, without stopping to take a breath. I saw Aunt Ruth and Uncle Dan and Amy and my mother and my father, just standing there like idiots, watching me scream, but still I didn't stop. I kept on screaming ... until Daddy slapped me across the face.

And then I cried.

twenty-five

When I opened my eyes it was morning. The first thing I saw
was my Viking diorama sitting on top of the dresser. The
sunlight coming through my window hit the blue sparkles and
made them shine. I threw off my covers and jumped out of bed.
I grabbed the diorama and flung it against the wall. It didn't
break. Two of the Vikings fell out of their ship but the box was
okay. So I stamped on it with both feet until there was nothing
left but a broken shoebox and a lot of blue sparkle all over my
rug. Then I kicked it as hard as I could, again and again.
Stupid, ugly Viking diorama! I hate you!

I got back into bed and pulled the covers over my head.
I was all set to cry, but the tears didn't come this time.

I must have been a crazy person to think that my silly
diorama could work magic. Now I know the truth. My parents
are not going to get back together. And there isn't one single
thing I can do about it! My mother doesn't think Daddy is a
wonderful person. She was feeding me a bunch of lies. Val was
right. Not that Daddy thinks much of Mom either. Well, I'm
through fooling myself.

I rolled over. I wonder where Jeff is. I think he would have
liked the way I screamed last night. I'm sorry he missed it.
I'll bet he wishes he had some of those fried shrimps with him,
breaded or not. He must be hungry by now. I hope he's okay.
I don't want anything bad to happen to him, even though I did
hate him for a while. If he doesn't come home Daddy won't be
able to go to Las Vegas on Monday. Hey, I'll bet that's why
Jeff picked last night to run away! Maybe he knew what he was
doing after all. Except for one thing. He didn't hear them
fighting so he doesn't know that they're hopeless. Poor Jeff!
He ran away for nothing.

The phone rang, but I didn't jump up to answer it as usual.
My mother came into my room. I closed my eyes and pretended
to be asleep.

'Karen . . . are you awake?' Mom asked.

I didn't answer her.

She stood next to me and shook my shoulder a little. 'Karen, your father wants to talk to you.'

This is the first time she's ever called him my *father*. I still didn't answer.

'Karen . . . are you okay?'

I could tell by her voice she was getting upset because I wouldn't open my eyes. So I got out of bed on the side away from where Mom was standing and I said, 'I'm up and fine.' I walked from my room, across the hall, to hers. I picked up the phone. 'Hello.'

'Karen, about last night . . .' Daddy began.

'I don't want to talk about it,' I told him.

So Daddy said, 'Well, I want you to know it was just because we were so upset about Jeff.'

'Sure,' I said.

'And I don't want you to worry about your brother either. Because I've already hired a private detective and he'll certainly find him if the police can't.'

'That's good,' I said.

'Listen, Karen, the only reason I slapped you last night was because you were hysterical. And that's what you have to do when someone's hysterical.'

'That's okay,' I told him. I haven't ever been hysterical before. I wonder if I ever will be again?

'Are you still flying to Las Vegas on Monday?'

'I don't know yet,' Daddy said. 'It all depends on Jeff.'

'If he doesn't come home you're not going?'

'I'm not going anywhere till I know Jeff's okay. My trip can wait a week or two,' Daddy said. 'If you need me for anything I'll be at the store all day.'

'Okay. 'Bye.' I hung up and went back to my room. My mother was making my bed. She looked very tired. When she was done she sat on the edge of the bed and said, 'Karen, about last night . . .'

I told her the same thing I told Daddy. 'I don't want to talk about it.'

But she said, 'I think you should know that it was just because we were so worried about Jeff.'

'Sure,' I said. 'I know.'

'And we didn't really mean any of the things we said.'

'How about Daddy taking us away from you? Can he do that?'

'No, of course not. That was just his way of hurting me. I told you, we didn't mean anything we said last night.'

I didn't believe that. I think they really meant *all* the things they said to each other.

My mother blew her nose. When she was done she asked, 'What happened to your Viking diorama?'

'It broke,' I told her. 'But don't worry about the mess. I'll clean it up.'

'I wasn't even thinking about the mess. I just think it's a shame that it broke. It was beautiful.' Mom stood up and checked her watch. 'It's almost nine o'clock. I've got to run downtown to police headquarters. I found a picture of Jeff for Sergeant Tice.'

'Which one did you find?'

'His school picture,' Mom said, pulling it out of her pocket. She showed it to me.

'That's a nice one,' I said.

Mom nodded. 'Hurry and get dressed now, Karen. I want to go right away.'

'Why can't I stay here and watch Amy?'

'Amy's not home. Aunt Ruth picked her up early this morning.'

'Well, you go ahead and I'll stay here and clean up my room.'

'I don't want to leave you alone,' Mom said.

'But suppose Jeff calls and there's no answer. What will he think?'

'I never thought of that,' Mom said. 'You're right. You

better stay here just in case. I won't be gone long.'

As soon as my mother left the house I went down to the kitchen. I was very thirsty. I felt like drinking a whole giant-sized can of pineapple juice. I gulped down two full glasses, then poured a third and walked into the living room. The smashed china baby was gone, but all the drawers in my mother's antique chest were halfway open and the floor was covered with photos. There were so many of them!

I put my glass on the coffee table, sat down on the floor and picked up a picture. It was of me when I was little. My two front teeth were missing. I was standing next to a huge fish and crying. I remember I was really scared. I thought the fish could bite me. I didn't know it was dead.

There was another picture that showed all of us at a picnic. I must have been about eight. That was the day Jeff's kite got caught in the tree and I fell into the brook.

I found our baby pictures. And one of Daddy and Mom at a costume party. My mother was wearing some dumb-looking Cleopatra wig. She and Daddy were laughing.

I grabbed up the photos and stuffed them back into the drawer. Then I ran upstairs to my room and took my cat bank off the dresser. Jeff gave it to me for my last birthday. He said he knew I'd rather keep my money in a cat than in a pig. I pulled the stopper out of the bottom of the bank and dumped all the money on to my bed. There was $10.49. Good! The divorce book costs $7.95, Val said. So I have enough.

I got dressed, threw my diorama into the garbage and took out the vacuum. There was no other way to get rid of the blue sparkle all over my rug.

When my mother got back from police headquarters I was still vacuuming.

'You didn't have to do that,' Mom said.

'I felt like it,' I told her. 'Did Sergeant Tice find out anything yet?'

'Not yet,' Mom said. 'But he will. Especially now that he has the picture. That should help a lot. Jeff might even be home this afternoon.'

'Sure,' I said.

'You know what I'm going to do?' Mom asked.

'No, what?'

'I'm going to give Jeff's room a good cleaning. The closets and everything.'

Why would she do a silly think like that? Jeff likes his room messy. The messier the better.

Mom took the vacuum. 'I want his room to look really nice when he comes home. You want to help?' she asked me.

'I can't,' I said. 'I have to go over to the shopping centre. I need something for a school project.'

Mom acted like she hardly heard me. 'Be careful' was all she said.

The shopping centre isn't that far from our house. I rode my bike straight to the bookstore. I had the paper with Val's information on it tucked away in my pocketbook. I asked the saleslady for *The Boys and Girls Book About Divorce* by Richard A. Gardner, MD, published by Science House, Inc, illustrated by Alfred Lowenheim, with a foreword by Louise Bates Ames.

She seemed pretty impressed that I knew so much about it. She smiled at me a lot. Then she said, 'I'm sorry, but we don't have that book in stock. We'll have to order it for you.'

Imagine not having such an important book in stock! What is the matter with this bookstore? I asked her how long it would take to get it and she told me *maybe two weeks*. I said I didn't think I could wait that long and she smiled again and told me she'd put a rush on it and it might come through sooner. I had to pay in advance and write down my name, address and phone number. I don't know how I am going to last two whole weeks without that book!

twenty-six

Sunday, 9 May

Dear Garfa
How are you? I hope you're fine. Yesterday I ordered The Boys
and Girls Book About Divorce. *Did you ever hear of it? It's a
very famous book and I need it a lot. I need it because Daddy
and Mom are definitely going to get divorced! I've tried hard
to get them back together. Honest! But nothing works. I have
discovered something important about my mother and father.
When they are apart they're not so bad, but together they are
impossible!*

*Anyway, I hope you understand and won't be too
disappointed, even if this is the first divorce in the history of
the Newman family. Do you want to hear something funny?
When Daddy told us he was flying to Las Vegas to get the
divorce I still didn't believe it would really happen. Now I
believe it! Another thing I think you should know is this – I
don't look like Grandmother Newman at all. I just pretended
to agree with you. I don't look like anyone but ME! I hope
Mattie is fine and that you are having fun.*
Love,
Karen

Maybe I should have mentioned something about Jeff in my
letter but I think that would upset Garfa even more. And I am
hoping that by the time my letter gets to Las Vegas Jeff will be
home.

I folded the letter, put it in its envelope and licked it closed.
I had to sneak an airmail stamp out of my mother's desk. I didn't
want to ask for one because then I would have to explain why
I was writing to Garfa. After breakfast I walked down to the
corner and dropped the letter in the mailbox.

My mother spent all of Sunday morning washing and

ironing Jeff's shirts. If you ask me she was just keeping busy so she wouldn't have to think about all the awful things that might happen to him.

That afternoon Aunt Ruth and Uncle Dan brought Amy home. Then we all sat around in the living room, waiting for something to happen. But nothing did. Uncle Dan called my father a couple of times. Daddy didn't want to leave his apartment in case Jeff decided to go there. Mom called police headquarters once, but Sergeant Tice wasn't in and there weren't any messages for my mother. It was a very gloomy afternoon.

At three thirty the phone rang and I jumped up to answer it.

'Hello, this is Mary Louise Rumberger calling. Is Jeff home?'

At first I didn't answer her. I didn't know what to say.

'Hello . . .' she said again. 'Is anyone there?'

'Yes,' I told her. 'I'm here.'

'May I please speak to Jeff?'

'No . . . he's not in right now,' I said. 'Can I take a message?'

'Who is this?' she asked.

'It's Karen . . . his sister.'

'Oh. Well, tell him I called and ask him to call me back.'

'Okay . . . I'll tell him.'

'What time do you think he'll be home?'

'I don't know,' I said. 'Maybe around five or five thirty.'

I don't know why I said that.

'Okay. Thank you,' Mary Louise said.

'You're welcome.' I hung up the phone and went back into the living room. 'That was Mary Louise Rumberger,' I said. 'She wanted to talk to Jeff.'

'I hope you didn't tell her anything,' Mom said.

'I just told her he wasn't home right now.'

'That was very good thinking, Karen,' Aunt Ruth said.

'Is it a secret that Jeff is lost?' Amy asked.

'Kind of,' Uncle Dan said. 'Can you keep a family secret?'

102

'I guess so,' Amy said.

An hour later Aunt Ruth ordered some pizzas for supper and I went outside to wait for the delivery truck. It was a good excuse to get away from everybody.

I sat down on our front steps. Mew ran out of the bushes and rubbed up against me. I picked her up. Her front paws smelled like mouse. Mew loves springtime. She sleeps a lot during the day and prowls around at night. The Great Grey Hunter, I call her. She brings a mouse or a mole to our door every morning. This doesn't make my mother happy. And to tell the truth, I don't like to be the one to get the shovel and scoop up Mew's catch. I love her a lot and I'm glad she's happy, but I wish she wouldn't bring home so many surprises.

In a little while I saw a girl walking up the street. When she got to our house she turned and came up the driveway. It was Mary Louise Rumberger. I knew it right away. And if I hadn't recognized her face I'd have know her by the Noxzema smell.

She said, 'Hi. I'm Mary Louise.'

I said, 'I know. I'm Karen.'

Then we just looked at each other until Mary Louise said, 'I brought Jeff a book he wants to read.'

'Oh, that's nice,' I said. 'You can leave it with me and I'll give it to him.'

'I'd rather give it to him myself.'

'Jeff isn't here right now,' I said.

'Where is he?' Mary Louise asked.

I knew she'd say that sooner or later. 'He's not home,' I told her.

'I know,' she said. 'You already mentioned that.'

This conversation might last forever, I thought. I'll keep telling her Jeff isn't here and she'll keep saying she knows.

'Well, where is he?' Mary Louise asked again.

'Who?'

'Jeff!'

'Oh, Jeff. He should be back soon.'

'Do you know that somebody called my house Friday night looking for him?'

'Yes,' I said. 'That was my uncle.'

'Why did he call my house? Didn't he know where Jeff was?'

'I guess he thought Jeff was with you. But really he was in New York visiting his friend from camp.' There, that sounded pretty good.

'None of this makes any sense to me,' Mary Louise said.

'It does, if you really think about it,' I told her.

'I didn't know Jeff was going to visit his friend from camp.'

'He doesn't tell you everything, does he?'

'I don't know,' Mary Louise said. 'I thought he would have mentioned something like that. He was supposed to meet me at the Y Saturday night.'

'Oh, well probably he didn't mention it because it was a last-minute thing. He didn't plan to go. He just went.'

'Why didn't you tell me that when I called?'

'I don't know,' I said. 'I guess I forgot.'

'How long will Jeff be gone?' Mary Louise asked.

'Oh, he'll be back any day now.'

'You mean you don't know *exactly* when?'

'Sure I do,' I told her. 'Any day. Soon. This week, I think!' I was getting in deeper and deeper.

Mary Louise shook her head. 'I'm having a party Friday night. Jeff is supposed to be there. If he's not coming back I'm going to cancel my party. Why should I have a party without him?'

'I don't know,' I said. I wished she would stop sniffling like that. I didn't want her to cry.

'You can tell him for me that if he doesn't come home by Friday I never want to see him again!' Mary Louise started down the front walk, holding her book tight against her.

'Hey, Mary Louise ...' I called.

She turned around. 'What?'

'I think he'll come back for your party.'

'I hope you're right,' she said as she walked away.

I hoped so too.

Sunday, 9 May
I am so afraid J.N. is dead!

twenty-seven

Mom didn't go to work on Monday and when I got home from school I found her sound asleep on the living-room couch. I called Aunt Ruth. 'Did you hear anything about Jeff?' I asked.

'No, not a thing.'

'Mom is sleeping. Should I just leave her alone?'

'Yes,' Aunt Ruth said. 'I finally got her to take one of the sleeping pills the doctor prescribed. You know she hasn't slept since Friday.'

'I know it,' I said. 'I can take care of Amy when she comes home. So don't worry.'

'Thanks, Karen. I'll be over with something for supper about five o'clock.'

'Okay. 'Bye.'

I got a blanket from upstairs and covered my mother. I'm worried about her. If anything happens to Mom what will become of me and Amy?

Where is that detective my father hired? And how about Sergeant Tice? What is he doing besides chewing his gum?

I've got to try to find Jeff myself.

On Tuesday I went to the Mansfields' after school. I had to start somewhere and Petey was number one on my list. Brian answered the door.

'Hey, Karen,' Brian said. 'What are you doing here?'

'I came to see Petey,' I told him. 'Is he home yet?'

'Yeah, he's upstairs. What do you want to see him for?'

'It's personal,' I said.

'Oh, yeah?' He started to laugh. 'How personal?'

'Look, Brian, just tell Petey I'm here, will you?'

Brian turned away from me and yelled up the stairs. 'Hey Petey . . . somebody's here to see you about something personal.'

'Very funny,' I told Brian.

'Yeah . . . I'm a riot . . . everybody knows that!'

I wonder if it's true that Brian likes me?

Petey came running down the stairs, but when he saw me he stopped.

'Could I see you alone?' I asked him. 'Outside maybe?'

Brian made a noise then. It sounded like *woohoo!*

Petey nodded at me and we both walked outside. He even shut the front door in Brian's face so he wouldn't be able to hear anything.

'Listen, Petey,' I said. 'If you know anything about my brother you better tell me. Because my mother's really sick about him. I mean it . . . she's sick! And if he's dead . . . if Jeff is dead . . . I want to know it! And I want to know it now!' I put my hands on my hips and waited.

Petey did the craziest thing then. He started to laugh. And that got me mad! 'I don't see anything funny, I said. 'Maybe you think it's funny that my brother could be dead in some alley, but I don't!'

Petey just kept laughing.

'Do you understand me, Petey? Please tell me if you at least understand what I'm saying.'

Petey stopped. 'Jeff's not dead,' he said in this deep voice that surprised me. So he can talk!

'How do you know he's not dead?' I asked.

'I just do, that's all.'

'You tell me where he is, Petey Mansfield!'

'I don't know.'

'Then you don't know if he's dead either, do you?'

'I'm telling you, Karen, he's not dead! Now that's all I'm going to say!'

'Well, if you know that then you know where he is and you can just tell him for me that if my mother has a heart attack or something, it's all his fault. You hear that, Petey? It's all his fault! You just tell him that for me. And if you're lying about Jeff being dead and anything happens to my mother, then it's all *your* fault!'

'You're really something Karen. You know that? You're really something!' Petey said.

I took a good look at him. Maybe he's not so bad. Maybe if he was the last boy on earth I would marry him. That is, if I was going to get married at all, which I am not.

I went home. I wanted to tell Mom not to worry, that Jeff wasn't dead. But I had no proof. So I didn't say anything.

Later that night, after Amy was in bed, I went into the kitchen to get an apple. While I was peeling it the phone rang. I answered. It was Jeff! He said, 'Hello Karen.' Just like that. When I've been worrying he might be dead! *Hello Karen.* Like there was nothing wrong at all. I hollered, 'MOM . . .' and dropped the phone.

'What is it, Karen? What's wrong?' Mom asked.

'It's Jeff,' I said. 'On the phone.'

'Oh, thank God!' Mom said. She picked up the phone. 'Jeff, Jeff where are you? Are you all right? Oh, Jeff please come home . . . yes . . . yes, no questions. I don't care where you've been as long as you come home. Where are you now? Jeff . . . Jeff . . .'

My mother put the receiver back on the hook. 'He hung up,' she said. 'I don't know where he is, but he's coming home.'

'When Mom? Did he say?'

'I don't know. Tonight I think. Karen . . . you go up to bed now.'

'Oh, Mom.'

'Please, Karen! I don't want Jeff to have to face anyone but me tonight. You'll see him tomorrow . . . or whenever he's ready to see you. Okay?'

'Okay . . . if you say so.'

As I went upstairs I heard Mom phone Aunt Ruth. 'Jeff's okay,' she told her. 'He's coming home . . . Oh, Ruth, I can't . . . You call Bill for me.'

I went to my room, took out my Day Book and wrote:

Tuesday, 11 May
J.N. is alive! I heard his voice. He is coming home. M.L.R.
doesn't have to worry. He'll be able to go to her party.

I didn't get into bed. I turned out my light and sat in front of the window. I waited and waited. Finally I saw Jeff come up the walk.

Maybe Petey did know where Jeff was. Maybe he told him to come home. I wouldn't be surprised if that's what happened. Or maybe Petey didn't know a thing. I suppose that's possible too. Jeff could have decided to come home all by himself. I'll probably never know the truth.

I sneaked out into the upstairs hall. With the lights turned off nobody could see me, but I could see down. My mother hugged Jeff for a long time. Then she held him away to get a good look at him. While she was looking he started to cry. Just like a little kid. Imagine Jeff acting like that! They sat down on the bottom step then and my mother held him tight. I always knew she loved him best.

twenty-eight

'Jeff is back!' my mother told me and Amy at breakfast the next morning. 'I'm taking the day off from work.'

'Where is he?' Amy asked.

'In his room . . . asleep,' Mom said.

'Where was he?' Amy asked.

'Wherever he was he's home now. And that's what counts. We aren't going to ask him any questions. I want you both to understand that completely.'

'The one who asks the most questions—' Amy started to say.

But my mother didn't let her finish. 'Never mind about that. No questions!'

'Okay,' Amy said. 'You don't have to yell.'

'I'm not yelling,' Mom told her.

Amy fiddled around with her waffles. We eat them every morning now. They're the frozen kind that you pop in the toaster. I think they're good. We never had them when Daddy lived here. Daddy doesn't trust frozen foods.

That afternoon when I got home from school, I went up to Jeff's hideaway. The door was closed but I heard Jeff grunting, so I knocked.

'Yeah . . .' He sounded out of breath.

'It's me, Karen.'

'Oh.'

'Can I come in?'

'Yeah . . . I guess so.'

I opened the door. Jeff was on the floor doing push-ups.

'Hey . . . your toe is unbandaged!'

'Yeah . . . Mom took me over to Dr Winters. It's fine now.'

'That's good.'

Jeff was counting. 'Eighty-five, eighty-six, eighty-seven . . .' When he got to ninety he stopped and lay flat on his stomach. He was breathing hard.

I sat down on his bed. 'Mary Louise Rumberger was over on Sunday,' I said.

'I know . . . I talked to her before.'

'She wanted to make sure you were coming to her party.'

'I know.'

'Are you?'

'Sure.'

'That's good. Jeff?'

'Yeah ...'

'Did you have fun when you ran away?'

'I didn't run away,' he said.

'Oh. Well, was it fun when you were gone?'

'No.'

'I'm not supposed to ask any questions ... I know that. But I just want to tell you one thing. If you went away because you wanted to stop the divorce, you better forget it. Daddy and Mom had an awful fight Friday night. They yelled and screamed and called each other a lot of names. They're just impossible together.'

'I know that, Karen.'

'Then you didn't run away to stop Daddy from flying to Las Vegas?'

'No,' Jeff said.

'But I was sure you did.'

'Well, I didn't.'

'Oh.'

'Dad was over to see me this morning.'

'He was? Was Mom home?'

'Yeah.'

'Well, what happened?'

'Nothing. She stayed upstairs the whole time.'

'Is Daddy going to Las Vegas?'

'Yeah. Tomorrow.'

'I guess I knew he would,' I said. 'Jeff ...'

'Yeah?'

'I'm glad you came home.'

Jeff turned over and looked up at the ceiling. 'Don't ever run away, Karen. It stinks!'

'I won't. Not ever. I promise.'

110

Wednesday, 12 May
I will never run away. Running away does not solve anything!
Also, I will never tell anyone I went to see Petey Mansfield
yesterday. If J.N. knows, let him tell me.

I have started to mark my days again. I am back to C—. I just
had an awful thought. Suppose there aren't any more A+
days once you get to be twelve? Wouldn't that be something!
To spend the rest of your life looking for an A+ day and not
finding it.

twenty-nine

I got two postcards from Daddy. I wrote him back while
Mrs Singer was giving us her daily lecture on manners. She told
us we haven't had a real sixth-grade day all year. Now isn't that
too much? Here we are getting ready for junior high and she's
telling us we don't act like sixth graders yet!

Debbie says if Mrs Singer sprays hair stuff on herself once
more this year she's going to report her to the principal.
Imagine a teacher spraying herself in front of the class and then
telling *us* we have no manners. I will be so glad to be rid of
her!

This afternoon we had to fill out little green cards for next
year. One question was about parents. You had to check a box
telling if they were deceased or divorced. I checked *divorced*.
I might as well get used to admitting it.

Tonight I found out my mother is going to sell our house!
How can she do such a thing? She says she *has* to put our
house up for sale. It has something to do with the divorce. I
can't believe it.

I asked Mom, 'What about us? Where will we go?'

'I haven't made up my mind yet,' Mom said, 'but I'm thinking about Florida. We might as well move someplace warm as long as we're going to move.'

'Florida! That's about a million miles away,' I said. 'I'll never see Debbie again. Or Val. And what about Daddy?'

'Oh, you could see him during school vacations. It would be fun. But nothing's definite yet. So don't start worrying.'

'I'm not worrying. I just want to know what's going on.'

'Right now the only thing I can tell you for sure is that we're selling the house.'

'Daddy won't let us move to Florida,' I said. 'It's too far away.'

'It's not *that* far,' Mom said. 'You'd be able to write and phone.'

'That's not the same as seeing him!'

'Karen ... I don't want to argue about this,' Mom said. 'I have a lot of thinking to do before I make up my mind.'

'But we *are* going to move?' I said.

'Yes ... but I don't know where.'

'When will you know?'

'By the end of next month I hope,' Mom said.

'You mean we'll move over the summer?'

'Yes. I want everything to be set before school opens in the fall.'

'You mean I might go to a different school?'

'You probably will,' Mom said. 'Even if we wind up in an apartment around here you'll all have to change schools.'

'You mean we might take an apartment near Daddy?' I asked.

'Well, it's a possibility. Or we might take one in New York. I've always wanted to live in the city.'

'But what about your job at Global?' I said.

'It's a temporary job, Karen. I'll get a better one if we move. Or I might go to college full time until I get my degree.'

'But what about Aunt Ruth? How could you leave her?'

112

'That will be good for both of us,' Mom said.

'But ... but ...' I couldn't think of anything else to say.

Later when I got into bed I remembered that Gary Owens said it's warm in Houston. So I went back downstairs. 'Hey Mom ... if we have to move, how about Houston?'

'Houston!' she said, like I was crazy or something. 'Why would we want to move there? That's in Texas.'

'I know it,' I said. 'Somebody from my class moved there. It never gets cold.'

Mom said, 'Look, Karen ... if we move someplace warm it will be California or Florida. But Texas is out of the question. And nothing is settled yet. I told you that before.'

I hope my mother knows what she is doing this time. Suppose we move to Florida and then she decides she doesn't like it. Do we move back to New Jersey or do we try California or what? I have always lived right here on Woods End Road. I love our house. I don't want to move anywhere.

thirty

I got my divorce book!

Debbie is very interested in divorce. Now that I have my book it will be easy to teach her all about it. Even though Debbie says her mother and father are not going to get divorced it can't hurt her to know the facts. This way she will be prepared for anything!

I talked to Val this afternoon. She says maybe my mother will meet a man when we move. I guess it could happen. Suppose she gets married and her new husband doesn't like kids? Suppose he's mean or else very old? There are too many things for me to think about.

113

If I do move away Val promises to keep an eye on my father and let me know if anything important comes up. I think the idea of my leaving has her feeling pretty sad. She's not looking forward to summer at all.

'I'll be around for at least another month,' I told her. 'And maybe my mother will decide to stay near here after all. We might wind up living closer than we do now.'

'Or we might not,' Val said.

'Oh, well . . . even if we don't we can still write and phone and see each other over vacations.'

'That's not the same,' Val told me.

'I know it,' I said. Poor Val. I wish there was a book to make you feel happy when you're not. I would get it for her.

I got a letter from Garfa:

Dear Karen,
I'm sorry that your mother and father are going through with their divorce. But I'm glad you're getting used to the idea. Mattie tells me not to be so upset. I'll try to accept the situation too. Don't blame yourself. You are still my most dependable Karen.

I'm going to buy the divorce book you wrote about. Maybe it will help me understand too. Your father is here and he's fine, but he misses you a lot.
Love,
Garfa

thirty-one

Today the sixth graders were invited to spend a day at the junior high. Debbie and I went together. We toured the whole

114

school and had our lunch in the cafeteria. There was plenty of room for us because all the ninth graders were over at the high school getting their tour. I guess Jeff feels pretty grown up now that he's almost done with junior high.

We met some of the teachers, and the principal made a short speech. He looks fairly young and sounds very nice. I wish I wasn't going to move away.

On the way home from junior high Debbie said, 'I'll really miss you this summer, Karen. I wish we weren't going away on vacation.'

'I'll miss you too,' I told her.

'You're my best friend.'

'You're mine.'

'Do you think you'll have moved by the time I get back?'

'I'm not sure. Nothing's definite yet. You know my mother.'

'Well . . . I hope Jeff doesn't forget about me,' Debbie said. 'My mother always says, "Absence makes the heart grow fonder."'

'Mine says, "Ought of sight – out of mind."'

'Oh, Karen!' We both laughed. Debbie knew I was just teasing.

When we got to my house I said, 'Come on in . . . I want to show you my divorce book.'

'I can't,' Debbie said. 'It's Tuesday – I've got ballet.'

'That's right. How could I forget?'

'Karen . . . I've got something for you.' Debbie reached into her skirt pocket and pulled out two pictures. 'Here—' she said.

I looked at them. They were of Debbie making monkey faces.

'My father took them just for you.'

I will never find another friend like Debbie.

Jeff came out of the house then. 'Hi, Fat-and-Ugly . . . long time no see—' he said. I haven't seen Debbie smile like that in months.

We had Kentucky Fried Chicken for supper. We ate it right

out of the box because Mom is taking us to the movies and we don't want to be late.

While we were eating Amy said, 'Hey, Karen, why did the man put Band-Aids in his refrigerator?' She didn't wait for me to answer. She went right on. 'Because it had cold cuts! Get it? Cold *cuts*!'

'I get it,' I said. Then I laughed. Imagine Amy telling riddles again!

I had a B+ day today.

Then Again, Maybe I Won't

for Dick

Then Again, Maybe I Won't

Who says March is supposed to come in like a lion and go
out like a lamb? That's a lot of bull. All it's done this March
is rain. I'm sick of it.

'Hey Tony . . .' Mrs Gorsky yelled from her upstairs
window.

I pretended not to hear her. I took a *Jersey Journal* out
of my sack and tossed it onto her front porch. *Pow-Pow-Pow*
. got you Mrs Gorsky! Now you can't scream if I don't
put your paper under your doormat.

This time she banged on the top of her window while
she yelled. 'Tony Miglione! I know you can hear me!'

Sure I can. So can the whole neighbourhood.

'Don't you forget to put my paper *under* my doormat!'

I didn't say anything.

'TONY . . .'

Then I turned around and looked up at the window.
'Who, me?'

'Yes . . . you!'

'But it's pouring, Mrs Gorsky,' I called.

'So? You won't melt.'

Maybe I will. Then you'll be in big trouble because my
family will come looking for me and you'll have to tell them
how I melted down to nothing right on your front porch.

I walked away from Mrs Gorsky's house. She was still
banging on her window. Well, let her. I didn't feel like
climbing her porch steps. What's the worst thing she can
do to me? Call my boss . . . that's what. So? He'll understand.
There's no rule that says I've got to put the paper under
her doormat. As long as it doesn't land in the bushes I'm
allowed to throw it from the sidewalk. If this rain ever stops,
I'll go back to doing it her way. Then she'll be satisfied.

I don't know what I'll do about my paper route next year,

when I go to junior high. I don't want to give it up. But Jefferson Junior has an after-school basketball league and I want to play in it. Basketball is my favourite sport. I just wish I was taller. My brother Ralph says I'll probably sprout up at fourteen like he did. I hope I don't have to wait that long. It's important to be tall when you're playing basketball. You're that much closer to the basket. I play at the Y all day Saturday and every Sunday afternoon. Always with the same bunch of guys – Frankie Bollino, Joe Schenk, Joe Rosella and Billy Turner. We call the two Joes, Big Joe and Little Joe. Rosella's the big one.

Maybe my boss will let me deliver later in the afternoon next year. I hope so. I could get around a lot faster if I had a bike I could depend on. But all I've got is Ralph's old one, which doesn't work most of the time. I've been thinking about buying a new bike – a ten-speed Schwinn – bright red. But my father says it's more important tó put my money in the bank for college. He's saving for my education already and I don't even know what I want to be. Suppose I don't want to go to college? My father will be disappointed. He wants me to be a teacher, like Ralph. And we have a State Teachers College right here in Jersey City. That's where Ralph went and where Angie goes now. She's Ralph's wife. They live upstairs. Between the two of them you'd think they invented education.

I wonder how I'll feel going to the school where my brother teaches. Probably I won't get Ralph anyway. At least I hope I don't. It'll be bad enough when the other kids find out my brother's The Wizard of Seventh Grade Social Studies. Suppose they get ideas and ask me to fix it with Ralph for them to get good marks? What will I do then?

Wait a minute. Maybe I can say I'm no relation to Ralph Miglione, the teacher. We just happen to have the same last name. After all, Jersey City is a big place. Not everybody knows my family. Yeah ... that's what I'll say. And I'll warn

Big Joe, Little Joe, Frankie and Billy in advance. They're my best friends. They can keep a secret.

If only the rain would stop.

I can hear my mother saying when I get home, 'Why didn't you wear your rubbers? Why are they just sitting in the closet?'

Four more houses and I'll be done delivering for the day. Good ... I'm starving. I wonder what's for supper. Grandma does all the cooking at home. She's my mother's mother and she's really a great cook. Frankie says he'd rather eat at my house than anywhere.

One thing I really like about Frankie is how he treats Grandma. He acts like there's nothing wrong with her. But Grandma can't talk anymore. She had cancer of the larynx two years ago and they had to operate and remove it. She could learn to talk again through a burping method if she was willing. But she's not willing. She moves her lips a lot, like she's talking, but no sound comes out. If she has something really important to tell us she writes it down – always in Italian, which I can't read.

Once I caught Billy and Little Joe fooling around pretending to be my grandmother. They were waving their arms and moving their lips like Grandma does. When they saw me standing there they stopped.

If I hurry I might get home before my mother. Then I can change my shoes and she won't see how wet they are.

I made it. My mother probably got hung up in traffic somewhere. That happens a lot when the weather's bad. She works in Newark, selling underwear in Ohrbach's. I wonder what it's like watching ladies try on underwear all day? I'd really like to get a look at that!

I took off my shoes in the front hall and hung my raincoat on the hook. My feet were soaked. So were the bottoms of my pants. I sat down on the floor and peeled off my socks.

One had a big hole in it. Angie came flying down the stairs then and almost crashed right into me.

'Tony ... you're absolutely drenched!'

'I know,' I said. 'It's pouring out.'

She started back upstairs. 'I'm going to get a towel to dry off your hair.'

'I can do it myself,' I told her. Angie likes to play mother with me. Sometimes I let her and sometimes I don't. It depends on my mood. My father says Angie has fat legs. I've been looking at her legs a lot lately and I don't think they're too fat. I think they're nice. Maybe some day I'll marry a girl like Angie. Then again, maybe I won't. Maybe I'll never get married.

I went into my room, dried off and changed my clothes. Then I headed for the kitchen. Grandma was tossing a salad. 'I'm home,' I said.

Grandma smiled and offered me an olive. I really like olives. Big Joe says if you eat a lot of them you make out good with the girls when you're older. But that's not why I eat them. I liked them before I ever heard about that. Big Joe knows plenty. He told me and Frankie about wet dreams. I wonder if I'll ever have one?

'What's for supper?' I asked Grandma.

She pointed to the oven.

'Chicken?' I asked.

Grandma shook her head.

'Lamb?'

She shook it again.

'Veal?'

Now Grandma nodded. I play this game with her every night. She likes me to guess what we're having to eat. The only way I can have a conversation with her is if I ask the questions and she answers by moving her head. As far as I know Grandma spends her time doing two things. One is, she cooks. And the other is, she walks to church every single morning. I think she's Father Pissaro's best customer.

When my mother and father got home we all sat down to supper. Ralph and Angie eat with us every night too. I don't think Angie knows how to cook.

Pop told us that starting tomorrow morning he'll be working on an office building downtown. They need a lot of rewiring done. My father's an electrician. He works for a contractor. He's even got his own truck. It says *Vic Miglione* on the door. Under that there's a picture of a telephone book with *you saw it in the yellow pages* written across.

'Is it a big job?' my mother asked.

'Pretty big,' Pop said. 'Should last about four weeks.'

'Well, that's something,' Mom said.

I was just about finished with my veal cutlet when Ralph pushed his plate away and said, 'Angie went to the doctor today. You might as well know ... she's pregnant.'

My mother said, 'Ralph ... Ralph ...' She shook her head.

My father closed his eyes.

Grandma moved her lips very fast.

Angie jumped up and ran to the bathroom.

I know I shouldn't think about Ralph and Angie the way I do. I know I shouldn't think about what you have to do to get somebody pregnant. But sometimes I just can't help it. He and Angie really do those things. Ralph admitted it. All of a sudden it was very quiet. Did they know what I was thinking? I tried a laugh and said, 'What's everybody so gloomy about? They're married!' I meant this to be a joke but nobody got it.

'Tony ... Tony ...' my mother said in her *Ralph ... Ralph* voice. 'You don't understand.'

'Understand what?' I asked.

Ralph explained. 'We don't have much money, Kid. Angie was supposed to teach for a few years to get us started. We can't afford to have a baby.'

'Oh ...' I said.

Angie didn't stay in the bathroom long. She came back to the table and sat down. She didn't look so good but she smiled at me.

'Well, you're going to be an uncle, Tony. How does it feel?'

'Oh fine.' What was I supposed to say?

Then Angie looked at Ralph and started to cry again. My mother stood up and put an arm around her. 'It's all right, Angie. We'll help out. Don't worry.'

'How can I not worry?' Angie asked. 'You and Pop have done so much already. The apartment upstairs and our meals and ...'

My father coughed. 'Listen Angie, you're my family. That baby is going to be my grandson ...'

'How do you know it's a boy?' my mother asked.

'I know. That's all,' my father said.

'I'm sorry,' Angie told us. 'I wanted to teach. I really did.'

'I know ... I know ...' my mother said, as if repeating everything twice meant it wasn't as bad as it sounded.

'At least Angie will be able to finish college and get her degree,' Ralph said.

'That's good.' My father tried to sound happy.

'Maybe I'll give up Ohrbach's and take care of the baby so Angie can teach anyway,' my mother said. 'Let's wait and see.'

While my mother was talking, Grandma got up and came back with her pad and pencil. She wrote a note and handed it to my mother, who translated:

We'll call him Vinnie.

Vinnie was my other brother. He was killed in Vietnam. My mother got tears in her eyes and she and Grandma touched hands.

Why does everybody think babies are such an expense? They're very small and they hardly eat anything. While I was thinking this Angie ran into the bathroom again. If you ask me she was puking.

124

As soon as we got up from the table my father went downstairs. He's got a workshop fixed up in the basement and that's where he spends all his free time. He invents things. I don't understand the stuff he does in his workshop so I don't go down much. Neither does Ralph. Vinnie was the one with the scientific mind. At least that's what my family is always saying.

Tonight, when I go to bed, I might think about Vinnie. I do that sometimes so I won't forget him. Or maybe I'll concentrate on getting good enough to shoot thirty baskets a minute.

In a few weeks the weather changed. It was really spring. I knew because my mother sent my winter jacket to the cleaner. She never does that unless she's sure it's going to stay warm. She says changeable weather is sick weather and that I have to wear a winter jacket until the middle of April, like it or not. What she doesn't know is that as soon as I'm out of sight I take off my jacket and carry it around with me.

Once my father finished the job in the office building he started spending more and more time in his basement workshop. A couple of nights he asked Mom to give him a sandwich for supper and he even ate down there. My mother and Ralph are both working at extra jobs. Mom is staying at the store two nights a week and Ralph is selling shoes after school and Saturdays. Every night the family is so pooped out they fall asleep right after supper. The only good thing about this is I get to watch whatever I please on TV.

One morning in the middle of breakfast, my father came into the kitchen wearing his best suit. He was carrying a small metal box. He didn't sit down at the table. He just grabbed a cup of coffee and said goodbye.

'Where's Pop going?' I asked.

'New York,' my mother said.

'What for?'

'Eat your eggs,' my mother said.

'I am eating them,' I told her. 'What's he all dressed up like that for?'

'Finish your milk too.'

I got the point. She wasn't going to discuss it with me.

My father put on his best suit for the next three days. He left the house carrying that metal box every morning and he didn't come home until late at night.

Whatever Pop's secret was I felt pretty lousy that they didn't let me in on it. I had a few ideas of my own though.

1 My father is a secret agent. The electrician business is a front. His real spy work is done in the basement workshop. And his information is in that box.

2 My father is in trouble with the Jersey City mob. He has to testify at hearings every day. The secrets are locked in that metal box.

3 My father is sick. He has cancer, like Grandma. He has to go to New York for special treatments. His medicine is in the box.

The more I wondered about Pop the more my stomach started to hurt. Last January I had really bad stomach pains and my mother took me to the doctor. He said it was nothing – that I just shouldn't eat so much roughage. I told him I never ate roughage in my whole life. The doctor laughed and said roughage is lettuce and celery and stuff like that. So now instead of eating salad every night I have it only once or twice a week. I still get a lot of stomach aches. But my mother says it's gas. I don't even tell her about them. anymore. I'm afraid she'll come after me with the castor oil.

At the end of my father's third day out my mother worked late and Pop met her in Newark. I was already in bed by the time they came home. I was reading *Great Basketball Heroes of our Times* and figuring if I got good enough I could get an athletic scholarship to some college and my father wouldn't need the money he was saving for my education. He could use it to pay for the baby instead.

When they came into my room to say goodnight my mother asked me to put my book away and listen carefully because she had something very important to tell me.

'What is it?' I asked.

'You see Tony ...' she began. Then she looked at my father and said, 'Oh Vic ... I'm just too excited. You tell him.'

I sat up in bed. This is it! He's going to tell me. At last I'll know the secret. No matter what it is, I won't break down in front of him. I'll tell him it's all right. That I know how these things can happen.

'I've made a deal, Tony,' my father said. 'That is, I think I've made a deal.'

So it's a deal, I thought. He's sold out to protect us. That's why my mother's excited.

'Are you listening, Tony?' my father asked.

'Sure Pop.'

'Well, I'll know more tomorrow when the lawyers talk.'

'What lawyers?'

'Sam Ranken, my lawyer, has to meet with the lawyer for J. W. Fullerbach Electronics,' my father said.

I asked my mother, 'What's he talking about?'

'Tony ... Tony ...'

Here she goes again, I thought.

'Your father's a genius! An absolute genius! Did you know that, Tony?' She gave my father a juicy kiss and kept talking. 'I always knew it ... deep down inside I always knew!'

My father? A genius? What's she talking about now? My father's regular. 'I don't get it,' I said.

'Well, Tony ...' my father began, loosening his tie. 'One of my ideas about electrical cartridges ... one of the things I've been working on downstairs ...'

I interrupted. 'You know I don't understand that stuff, Pop.'

'So listen! Maybe this time you'll understand.'

'Okay ... I'm listening,' I said.

My father told me how he took his idea to Mr J. W. Fullerbach. And how he had to see two assistant secretaries, three regular secretaries and a vice-president before he got to see J. W. Fullerbach himself. But it was worth it because Mr Fullerbach likes the electrical cartridges – and my father – and my father's ideas – and he wants all three.

'You're going to work for him?' I asked.

'We'll see,' my father said.

'You're quitting your job with Mr Dalto?'

'We'll see.'

'Oh.'

'This means money, Tony,' my father said. 'It means Ralph and Angie won't have to worry. Can you understand that?'

'Sure Pop. Sure I understand.' I put my head on the pillow. My mother turned out the light and kissed me on my forehead.

So my father's not a secret agent.

He's not mixed up with the mob.

And he doesn't have cancer.

But what was he talking about? One of his inventions? He really invented something that somebody wants? Is he a genius? And if he is how come it took so long to find out?

My father took the bus to New York every morning for the next week. His regular boss, Mr Dalto, called in the afternoon to find out how Pop was feeling. That's how I knew my father had reported in sick. I didn't give him away though. I said, 'He's getting better, Mr Dalto. Thank you for calling.'

At the end of the week, when Pop came home from New York, he picked me up and swung me around. Now that's something he never does anymore. I'm much too big.

So I yelled, 'Hey, put me down!'

Then my father picked up my mother and swung *her* around, then my grandmother and Angie but not Ralph. Ralph is bigger than my father. While he was swinging us all around like that he laughed and yelled, 'We're going to be rich ... rich!'

My mother hollered, 'Vic! Calm down. You're no kid. Think of your heart!'

So Pop made us all sit down on the couch while he stood up in front of us and told us about his deal.

J. W. Fullerbach Electronics is going to manufacture my father's electrical cartridges. And my father is going to manage the plant that's going to do the manufacturing.

'It's one of the Fullerbach plants in Queens,' my father said. 'But now, thanks to Sam Ranken, it's going to be called the Fullerbach–Miglione Engineering Corporation.'

My mother tried that out for size. 'Fullerbach–Miglione ... Fullerbach–Miglione ...'

And I thought, Fullerbach–Miglione?

'I get stock in Fullerbach Electronics, with options, of course ...' my father said, doing a little dance. 'I tell you ... *we are going to be rich*!'

I don't know anybody rich. Everybody I know is just like me. I wonder what rich is like. It probably means that Ralph and Angie can have a baby every year.

'Angie, let me kiss you!' my father said. 'If it wasn't for that baby you and Ralph are expecting, I'd never have had the guts to try out my electrical cartridges on anybody.'

'Say, Pop,' I said. 'How're you going to get from Jersey City to Queens every day?' That was the part of it I understood.

'I'm not going to, Tony,' my father said.

'You're not?'

'Nope.'

'Well then, what?' I asked.

'I'm going to get from Rosemont to Queens.'
'What's Rosemont?' I asked.
'It's a town in Long Island.'
'You're going to live there?'
'*We're* going to live there!' my father said.
'We are?' I asked.
'That's right!'
'All of us?'
'All of us!'

Goodbye Jersey City, I thought.
Goodbye basketball at the Y.
Goodbye Little Joe and Big Joe.
Goodbye Frankie and Billy.
Goodbye Jersey Journal *paper route.*

'What's the matter, Tony?' my mother asked.
'The Kid's excited,' Ralph said. 'Can't you see ... the Kid's just so excited!'
'And why not?' my mother asked. 'How many kids have a genius for a father!'
I don't cry any more. I'm too old for that baby stuff, which is why I ran for the bathroom and locked myself in. I cried really quiet. Not like Angie who does it so loud everybody knows.

Then Again, Maybe I Won't

We all finished the school year in Jersey City but it wasn't the same for me. Because when the guys talked about Jefferson Junior I knew I wouldn't be there. I didn't tell them we might be moving or about my father's new job. I pretended everything was just fine. Then Pop announced that we had a new house. In Rosemont, just like he promised.

On Sunday afternoon we went for a ride to Long Island. On the way my father said, 'You know, Tony, Mr Fullerbach made all the arrangements for our new house.'

'I know,' I said.

'He says Rosemont's a nice place to live.'

'I know. You already told me.'

'And what a coincidence that Father Pissaro's cousin should be a priest there,' my mother said.

We just found out about Father Pissaro's cousin this morning. After church, Pop told him we were moving to Rosemont and he told us about his cousin. So when Pop said we were going there this afternoon, Father Pissaro said he'd call his cousin and we could stop and say hello.

'I'm telling you, Tony, this family's getting lucky,' Pop said. 'I can feel it!'

It doesn't make me feel lucky to know Father Pissaro's cousin is a priest in Rosemont. It's not that I don't like him. It's just that I don't care one way or the other about his family. I'd feel luckier if my father told me Jimmy Connors or Muhammad Ali lives there.

Pop looked over at me. 'Well, what do you say, Tony? Are we getting lucky?'

A passing car tooted its horn at us then. 'Vic!' my mother shouted. 'Keep your eyes on the road.'

'Who's driving?' my father asked. 'You or me?'

'You ... you ...' Mom told him. 'All I'm saying is just be careful.'

'I'm always careful! Right, Tony?'

'Right, Pop.'

We have the same conversation every time we go someplace in the truck. My father looks at whoever he's talking to, my mother yells, 'Be careful!' and my father tells her he's always careful. Usually this happens once going and at least once coming home.

131

In an hour and a half we got to Rosemont. Pop drove us all around. Rosemont is really something! I think I'd be excited about moving there if only I could take my friends with me.

My father and mother kept smiling at each other. 'Our dream come true, Carmella,' Pop said.

'Oh Vic ... I love it!' my mother told him, squeezing his arm.

Our new house is a big white one with a round driveway right up to the front door. All I could think of was, who's going to cut all that grass? So I said, 'How much land do we have, Pop?'

And my father said, 'Just about an acre.'

'That's a lot of grass.'

'And look how green it is,' my mother said.

'I guess the gardener takes good care of it,' Pop told her. 'And Mr Fullerbach arranged for the same man to work for us.'

Whew – that's a relief. For a minute I thought I'd get stuck cutting it. And if I had to cut all that grass I'd never have time for basketball. That reminds me – now the guys will find out the truth. That I'm moving away. And I feel kind of bad because our team will break up. How can you play with only four guys on a side?

We couldn't go inside our new house because people are still living there. My father said we should be able to move by 20 July. That means I'll have my thirteenth birthday in Rosemont. I wonder what I'll get?

We drove up and down our street a few more times and then went to visit Father Pissaro's cousin. His church is called Saint Joseph's and it's smaller than our church in Jersey City, but a lot more modern. It's made out of brown bricks and the front doors are all glass. The cross doesn't sit on top of the church. It's built right into the front and goes straight up past the roof. There are a lot of tall trees around it and a parking area right behind. My father pulled the truck in there and we got out.

My mother said, 'Wait just a minute, Vic. I want to fix my hair.'

When she was done we walked around to the front of the church and went inside. It was very quiet. Services were over. The priest was expecting us. He came out to greet us right away. He and my father shook hands.

'I'm happy to meet you, Mr Miglione. My cousin called to say you'd be here this afternoon. Welcome to Rosemont.'

'Thank you, Father,' Pop said. 'I'd like you to meet my wife and my youngest son, Tony.'

'Mrs Miglione ... I know you're going to enjoy living in Rosemont.'

'Thank you, Father,' my mother said.

Then he looked at me. 'Well, Tony ... how old are you ... about twelve?'

'Almost thirteen,' I said.

'In junior high?'

'Yes, I'm starting in September.'

'He would be going into eighth grade, Father,' Mom said, 'but he had pneumonia when he was five and the doctor told us not to rush him into school. So he started a year late.'

My mother's always explaining why I'm a little older than the other kids in my class. If you ask me she's worried that people will think I stayed back. I wish she'd stop explaining. I don't think anybody cares.

'We have an active Junior Youth Group here, Tony,' Father Pissaro said. 'I think you'll like our activities. You can join when school starts.'

'Thank you,' I said. I felt funny about calling him Father Pissaro. He doesn't look like his cousin. He's younger and rounder and he has more hair. To keep things straight in my mind I decided to name him Father Pissaro the Second.

On the way back to Jersey City my father told us that

J. W. Fullerbach lives on Long Island too, but much farther out. His chauffeur drives him to work every day.

'Is that how it's going to be for us?' I asked.

'Don't be silly, Tony. We're going to be the same as always. Only we'll have a nice house and a new car,' my father said.

'We're buying a car?' I asked.

'Mr Fullerbach will lease one for us. He does that for all his executives.' My father said *executives* really slow so I wouldn't miss it.

'What kind?' I asked.

'What kind of what?'

'Car. What kind of car will we get?'

'Whatever Mr Fullerbach decides,' my father said.

I found out the next week. It's a dark green hardtop with stereo speakers. The inside smells like new shoes.

Big Joe, Little Joe, Billy and Frankie came over to see it right away. I let them sit in it and they were really impressed. Nobody we know has a hardtop with stereo speakers.

Frankie asked me could he take over my paper route since I was leaving town. I told him sure I'd fix it with my boss.

'My father says your father hit it big at the races,' Big Joe said. 'That's how come you got the car and all.'

'That's not how come,' I said. 'He invented something.' How could Big Joe's father spread a story like that!

'Yeah? What'd he invent?' Little Joe asked.

'Some electrical cartridges,' I told him.

'What's that?' Billy asked.

'It has to do with using lamps in the middle of a room. This way you don't have to plug anything in and you don't need a cord. You just attach an electrical cartridge.'

'You mean it's a kind of battery?'

'No, not exactly.' I hated to admit I didn't really understand it myself.

'Never mind any electrical cartridges,' Billy said. 'My father says your father's hooked up with the mob. They bought him the car.'

'That's a lie!' I yelled. I couldn't believe these guys. I always thought we were great friends. So why were they carrying on like idiots! 'The car is part of the deal. So's the new house,' I explained. 'My father's got a good lawyer. He arranged it. A good lawyer's pretty important when you're making a deal,' I said, like I knew all about it.

'If your father's so smart how come he never invented anything before?' Big Joe asked.

'He did,' I told him. 'But he didn't try to sell any cf his inventions.'

'So how come he did now?' Little Joe asked.

'Because Angie's going to have a kid and we need some money.' I got out of the car and they followed me. I pretended not to care about what they were saying. I told myself the guys just feel bad because I'm moving away. Only Frankie was the same. He told me we'd still be great friends and he'd visit me and I'd visit him and all that.

That night while I was getting ready for bed, Ralph came into my room and said, 'Guess what, Kid?'

'What?'

'Me and Angie are moving to Long Island too.'

'To Rosemont ... with us?'

Ralph laughed a little. 'We'd love to live in Rosemont, Kid, but who can afford it? We got a little apartment in Queens. It's a nice neighbourhood with plenty of young people.'

'Isn't that pretty far from Jefferson Junior?' I asked.

'I won't be teaching at Jefferson Junior next year.'

'You quit?'

'I've applied for a teaching job in Queens. No point hanging around Jersey City if the whole family's going to Long Island. Besides, Pop wants to sell this house and it's time for me and Angie to be on our own.'

'Oh.' I finished buttoning my pyjamas and made a ball out of my dirty clothes.

'Hey Kid ... aren't you glad? Now we'll still be able to see each other all the time.'

'Sure I'm glad,' I said. I didn't tell Ralph I thought he and Angie would stay in Jersey City and I'd come visit them every weekend and maybe play a little basketball at the Y.

We moved on 20 July just like Pop said. The funny thing about moving was, we didn't even need a moving van. And that was what I was looking forward to most. One of those big orange trucks parked outside our house with a dozen men carrying out all our stuff. The reason we didn't need a moving van was we weren't taking anything old with us, except Grandma's pots and pans and my Jefferson Junior High wall pennant. My mother didn't want me to take it.

'It's old,' she said. 'What do you need it for?'

'I like it,' I told her. 'I want to hang it above my bed.'

'You'll get a new one ... from Rosemont Junior High.'

'I want this one anyway. It used to be ...' I almost said, 'Vinnie's.' But I caught myself in time and said, 'Ralph's.' We never talk about Vinnie. Everytime somebody mentions his name Mom starts to cry.

'Oh, all right. If it means so much to you, take it,' she said.

Frankie came over to say goodbye again. He told me he got my paper route and I warned him about Mrs Gorsky. 'You've got to put her paper *under* the doormat or she'll call the boss and report you.'

'Okay,' Frankie said. 'I'll remember.' Then he reached into his pocket and came up with a coin. 'This is for you, Tony,' he said, handing it to me.

'Thanks,' I said, taking it.

'It's from England. It's worth about a dollar.'

'Thanks a lot, Frankie. It's really interesting.' I wished

I had something for him too. I was still holding my Jefferson Junior wall pennant. I unfolded it. 'I was hoping you'd come over this morning because I wanted to give you this.' I handed it to Frankie.

'Hey ... thanks a lot, Tony. That's really nice.'

'It used to be Vinnie's.'

'No kidding! That's really something. I didn't know Vinnie went to Jefferson Junior.'

'Yeah ... he did.'

'I'll hang it over my bed.'

'That's where I had it.'

'Yeah ... I know.'

My mother called me then. 'Tony ... hurry up ... we're ready to go.'

'Well ... see you, Frankie.'

'Yeah ... see you, Tony.'

A few trips in the green hardtop – a few more in the old truck – and Goodbye Jersey City ... Hello Rosemont!

Everything in our Rosemont house is new except the carpeting. The old owners left it in as part of the deal. It's yellow and it's so thick you can lose your shoes in it. My father says my mother bought out Newark, Jersey City and half of New York fixing up the house. But he doesn't mind. He wants her to enjoy herself now that he can afford it.

I have my own room with my own closet and also my own bathroom, which my mother says I'm supposed to keep neat. Grandma has her own bathroom and so do my mother and father. All of these are upstairs. Downstairs I counted two more, which makes a grand total of five bathrooms in one house. In Jersey City we had one. If anybody had an emergency and the bathroom was in use we always ran up to Ralph and Angie's.

My closet has a light in it. I found this out when I opened the closet door. The light went on automatically. When you shut the door it goes out. You don't even have to bother touching a switch or anything. I spent about ten minutes just opening and closing my closet door.

My bedroom is at the opposite side of the house from my mother and father's. Grandma's is in the middle. I have three windows in my room. Two overlook the backyard and one overlooks the side by the garage. I think the reason we have this circular driveway is so you won't get tired walking from the garage to the front door.

From my two back windows I can see my next-door neighbour's yard. It has a big wooden fence all around it. The kind you can't see through at all if you're on the ground. But from my room I can see right over it. That's how I know we might really be rich and my father isn't kidding around. They have a swimming pool! It's rectangular with a statue at one end. There's a diving board and everything!

The thing is, every time I think about us being rich I get scared. I know it's not going to last. I think the money will run out by January. My father used to kid around about if he won the state lottery the money would probably last five months. It's not that I'll mind moving back to Jersey City. It's just that I'll hate to face the guys. Big Joe will probably laugh and tell me he knew it all the time. And then there's Mom and Pop. They'll really be disappointed. They're so excited about living in Rosemont. But there's nothing I can do about it.

Grandma spent the first few days in Rosemont in the kitchen. She opened every cabinet a million times and wrote my mother a whole pad full of notes. Mostly about the stove and oven which she doesn't like because they're electric instead of gas.

My mother kept telling Grandma what a wonderful kitchen it is ... so modern! And how easy it will be for her to cook now. My grandmother kept shaking her head. So my mother talked louder. She always does that when they disagree. She talks loud, as if Grandma's deaf. Only

Grandma's hearing is fine and talking loud doesn't do any good at all.

I found out what happens to garbage in Rosemont. Number one is, we have an automatic disposal built into the sink. All the food scraps go down there and get ground up. Number two is, we have three garbage cans in the ground by the kitchen door. And twice a week the garbage truck comes by and the cans get emptied. Nobody puts their stuff down at the kerb.

The first few mornings we lived there I got up early and rushed outside. So did Grandma. But not for the same reason as me. She walked to Saint Joseph's every day. I wanted to make some friends before school started. That way I won't really be a new kid. I have a whole month to meet the Rosemont guys. That should be plenty of time. I hung around the front of our house waiting for somebody to notice me. It didn't take me long to find out that my new neighbourhood is dead in the summer. I didn't see any kids. Not even little ones.

On my fourth Rosemont morning I met Mrs Hoober, from the swimming pool house. I was walking up and down my driveway counting stones when I saw her open her garage door. I watched her, hoping she would notice me. She did.

'Oh hello,' she said. 'You new?'

'Yes.'

'I'm Mrs Hoober.'

When she said that I noticed she was carrying a pair of brown and white shoes, with spikes.

'What's your name?' she asked me.

'I'm Tony Miglione.'

'Well, hi Tony.' She got into her car and backed it out of the garage. Then she rolled down the window and told me she was on her way to play golf at the country club.

My mother met her later that afternoon and that night she told my father that our next-door neighbour is Diane

Hoober and that Mr Hoober is Vice-President of Amilard
Drugs. And aren't we lucky to be rubbing shoulders with
such people?

Then my mother told me that the reason I haven't
made any friends in four whole days of looking around is
because in Rosemont practically all the kids go away to
camp in the summer. And that Mrs Hoober has two kids
who'll be home the end of August. Mrs Hoober also told
Mom that some families have places at the beach and stay
away from June to September.

Back in Jersey City we'd have thought you were pretty
lucky to get to spend the summer in a place like Rosemont ...
never mind camp and the beach!

A week later I met Mrs Hoober again. She was getting out
of her car with a lot of packages. So I ran over and said,
'Want some help?'

She handed me a big box and said, 'Thanks, Tony.'

I carried it to her front door and then she took it from
me. 'I see you're having a lot of work done on your house.'

'Us?' I asked. 'No, we're not having anything done. It's
perfect the way it is.'

'Well, that's funny. There's a truck parked in your driveway
all the time.'

'Oh ... that's my father's truck. Sometimes he drives
to work when my mother needs the car.'

'It belongs to your father?'

'Sure. It even has his name on the door.'

'Oh ... well, thanks for helping me, Tony.'

'That's okay. Bye Mrs Hoober.'

That night after supper I said, 'You know what, Pop?
Mrs Hoober thought we were having a lot of work done on
our house just because she saw your truck in the driveway.'

My mother looked at my father. 'She asked you about
the truck?' Mom said.

'No. I told her it was Pop's. She didn't ask me anything.'

The next day, my father came home from work driving a new Ford instead of the old truck. He laughed and said, 'What do I need with a truck now?'

My mother said, 'I'm glad you decided that way, Vic. We don't want to start off on the wrong foot here.'

Did he get rid of the truck just because Mrs Hoober thought we were having some work done? That's crazy!

'You know, Tony ... you can't get anywhere without a car when you live out here,' Pop said. 'Your mother can't even get a quart of milk without driving a couple of miles. And the truck isn't so good on the highway. I'll be much more comfortable now.'

Sometimes I get the feeling my father can read my mind.

Along with the new car Pop brought home a regulation basketball net and professional basketball. He put up the basket on the garage and said I should keep in practice because he expects great things from me. As a basketball player or what? I wondered.

I spent the next few days shooting baskets until my mother told me the noise was making her head hurt and that *thump, thump, thump* all day long was too much for anybody's nerves. Would I please try to find something else to do a few hours a day, she asked.

So I watched the Hoobers' swimming pool from my window. Nobody ever used it. What a waste! Life in Rosemont was not exactly what you would call exciting.

On 5 August I was thirteen years old. I knew we were having roast beef for dinner and that Grandma baked me a birthday cake. But nobody asked me what I wanted. So I figured our new house is supposed to be a kind of birthday present. And anyway, I just got my basketball equipment. Still, a birthday's a birthday! In Jersey City I always got something. Usually a shirt, a game and $5.00 to spend any way I wanted.

But if my family wasn't going to mention my thirteenth birthday ... well, neither was I. I'd pretend to be happy without any presents.

That afternoon my father came home from the plant early. He hustled me off with him in the green hardtop. He drove past the Miracle Mile Shopping Centre to the middle of another town called Belmart.

'I have a surprise for you, Tony,' my father said, backing the car into a space.

'What?' I asked. 'Tell me.'

'If I tell you it's not a surprise.' Pop laughed. 'You'll see soon enough anyway. Come on.'

I jumped out of the car and followed my father.

The surprise turned out to be a brand-new red ten-speed Schwinn. Wow! This was my best birthday ever!

After that I rode my bike around every day. I explored every street in Rosemont. I knew all the stores downtown. I found my junior high. I found the football field. I found the park. I wished it was September.

Then Again, Maybe I Won't

Finally Joel Hoober came home from camp. We met right away. It was after supper and my mother was doing the dishes while Grandma sat at the kitchen table shelling pistachio nuts. I was eating them as fast as she was shelling them. My father was dozing in the other room. He doesn't have a basement workshop in our new house. I guess he doesn't need one now that his hobby is his business. When the doorbell rang my mother asked me to get it.

'I'm Joel Hoober,' this boy said, when I opened the front door. He was my height but thinner, with very light hair and an awful lot of it. When mine looks like that my mother tells me it's time to go see the barber.

142

'Are you Tony?' he asked.

I nodded because I had a mouthful of nuts. When I finished chewing and swallowed them I said, 'Come on in.'

My mother came out of the kitchen drying her hands on her apron.

'Mom, this is Joel Hoober,' I said.

Joel offered his hand to my mother. 'How do you do, Mrs Miglione. I'm happy to meet you.' Joel pronounced our name right. Not everybody does. A lot of people say Miglion-ie. But the 'e' on the end is silent.

The doorbell woke up my father. He padded into the hallway in his stocking feet. This time when Joel shook hands he said, 'How do you do, *sir*. Glad to meet you.'

I could tell right away that my mother and father were impressed. None of my friends in Jersey City say *sir*. And we don't shake hands every time we say hello to somebody. Are all the guys in Rosemont like this? I hope not. If they are I may not make any friends here. I wish Frankie lived next door instead of this creep.

'Well, let's not stand here in the hall,' my mother said to Joel. 'Come in ... come in ...'

Now why did she have to go and do that? Doesn't she think I can pick my own friends?

Joel followed my mother into the kitchen. 'You want some pistachio nuts?' she asked him.

'No thanks,' Joel said. He spotted my grandmother. I could tell Grandma was studying him because she looked up and squinted. Joel offered his hand but Grandma didn't bother to shake it. He started his line about how happy he was to meet her and Grandma laughed, which is really unusual for her. When she laughs her mouth opens but no sound comes out.

'My grandmother can't talk,' I told him. 'She has no larynx.'

Joel gave me a funny look but he didn't say anything. We walked back into the front hall.

'Do you play chess?' he asked.

'No, do you?'

'Yeah. It's a good game. Maybe I'll teach you.'

'Okay,' I said, but I didn't mean it.

Then he said, 'Can you come over for a swim tomorrow?'

'Yeah . . . I'd really like that.' I didn't tell him I'd been watching his pool most of the summer wishing somebody would invite me over to use it.

Before he left, Joel shook hands with my father again. 'Glad to have met you, *sir*,' he said. And then to me, 'See you tomorrow, Tony.'

'Okay,' I said, closing the door behind him. I'd already learned that when the air conditioning's on you've got to keep all the doors and windows closed.

'What a nice boy!' my mother said.

'Some manners!' my father added.

I wonder how long Joel would last in Jersey City. About a week, I figure . . . if he was lucky!

I went to the Hoobers' right after lunch the next day. The pool was heated. It was cooler than a bathtub but not really cold. I was mighty glad I know how to swim. I don't do anything fancy and I don't dive, but I do jump off the board and in Hoobers' pool I could swim back and forth twice before running out of breath.

Joel had on this grubby red bathing suit and he has about the knobbiest knees I've ever seen. I felt funny in the new suit my mother bought me this morning. I should have worn my old one.

The chess board was set up on a round umbrella table. Joel seemed really anxious to teach me how to play. I only let him because, after all, it was his swimming pool.

After I was there almost an hour the back door slammed and Joel's sister Lisa came out. She was wearing a bikini and was very suntanned which made her hair look even lighter than Joel's. All I could think of was *Wow!* She was the best looking girl I've ever seen in person anywhere. She has curves all over. I turned away from the chess board so I could keep watching her.

Lisa climbed onto the diving board and did a perfect swan dive into the water. After four laps of the crawl she stuck her head up and spit out some water.

'Hey Joel,' she called. 'Who's your friend? He's cute. Too bad he's not a little older!' Then she laughed and started to swim again.

I could feel the red climb from the back of my neck where it started, to my ears and then my face. Why do girls always say *cute?* That's such a dumb word. It makes me think of rabbits.

The next time Lisa came up from under the water Joel yelled, 'This is Tony Miglione from next door.'

'Hi ...' I called.

But she didn't hear because she was underwater again. I sat back in a lounge chair and watched Lisa swim. She did laps – back and forth, back and forth. Sidestroke, backstroke, butterfly – I got dizzy just watching.

'She's sixteen,' Joel said.

I nodded.

'You want a good laugh? Some day I'll show you her diary. I know where she keeps it.'

I looked away from Lisa. 'No kidding!'

'Yeah,' Joel said. 'It's great.'

Then I remembered how I promised my mother that I would be polite to Mrs Hoober. That I would shake hands and everything, just like Joel. 'Is your mother home?' I asked.

'Nah ... my mother's never home. She plays golf every day unless it rains. Then she shops or plays cards. When she's not on vacation, that is.'

I wondered if that's what my mother was going to do.

'Hey, you want something to eat?' Joel asked.

'Okay.'

Joel shouted at the house. 'Millicent ... hey Millicent! We're hungry.'

'Who's Millicent?' I asked.

'The maid. Only her name isn't really Millicent. She's got some Spanish name that my mother can't pronounce so when she came to work for us my mother renamed her. She didn't even speak English then. She taught me and Lisa to curse in Spanish.'

'No kidding!' Maybe there's hope for me and Joel after all.

'Hey Millicent!' Joel called again.

'What you want?' a voice answered from inside the house.

'You got any cake?'

'I got. You come get.'

'I can't. I'm all wet,' Joel hollered.

'Okay. I bring. But no crumbs by pool or your father kill me.'

'She's scared of my father,' Joel said. 'A lot of people are. Not me of course. I know how to handle him. It's easy. Just stay out of his way.'

Later, as I sat in my lounge chair eating chocolate cake, drinking cold milk and watching Lisa, I thought – this is really the life!

I spent most of Labour Day weekend at the Hoobers' pool. I learned to play a simple game of chess. Joel said he'd teach me more next time. I saw Mr Hoober once. Lisa called him George. She was swimming around when Mr Hoober came out the back door. She called, 'Hi George!'

Joel poked me and smiled with half of his mouth. I wondered how he did that. I mean when he smiles regular a whole row of teeth shows. But this way only one side of his lip goes up. He must have developed it from watching old gangster movies on TV.

Mr Hoober said, 'I don't like the George business, Lisa. That will be enough. Do you hear me?'

Lisa dove under the water and stood on her hands. I watched her wiggle her toes around.

I found out that Mr Hoober plays golf twice on Sundays

and holidays. Once in the morning with the men and once in the afternoon with his wife. And every Sunday night the Hoober family eats supper at the country club. So when Joel and Lisa had to get dressed to go out I went home.

My mother put me through the third degree. Questions – questions – questions. She's driving me nuts! She's a lot more interested in the Hoobers than she is in my father's new job. I can get her really mad if I want to. When she asks me something I answer, 'I don't know.' I've been saying that all weekend. She's about ready to explode.

Ralph and Angie were already at the house for supper. I asked Ralph was he still going to be the world's greatest teacher and he said, 'Sure Kid.' But he didn't sound so enthusiastic. All he talked about was my father's electrical cartridges, which is pretty funny for a guy who isn't scientific.

The night before school started me and Joel made arrangements to ride our bikes together every day.

'Your bike is really neat,' he told me.

'It's just like yours,' I said.

'Yeah, but mine's a year older.'

'Well, it's still the same,' I said.

'Yeah ... I guess so.'

'See you in the morning.'

'Quarter after eight. Don't forget,' Joel said as he walked home.

I told my mother that me and Joel were going to ride to school together.

'I'm so glad you and Joel made friends,' she said. 'He's such a nice boy. With a face like an angel's!'

I don't know what angels *really* look like but I doubt if it's like Joel. Lisa maybe, but not Joel.

I'm kind of glad me and Joel aren't in the same formroom. This way I can get to make some other friends. But there's one thing that bothers me. When you have somebody your age living next door either you wind up great buddies or you don't talk at all. I'm still not sure how it's going to turn out with us.

Junior high isn't as bad as I thought it might be. Once you get used to those bells ringing all the time and going to different rooms for different subjects it's pretty good. You feel a lot older than sixth grade.

Two guys from my formroom are in all my other classes – Marty Endo and Scott Gold. The three of us stick together. That way if we have trouble finding the right classrooms we look stupid as a group instead of three individual stupids.

Joel turned up in my English class, which is the period right before lunch. When the bell rang we went to the cafeteria together. The cafeteria is really neat.

Joel brought his lunch from home. He carried it around with him in a brown bag. But he bought his milk and an apple. I bought the whole school lunch. So did Marty Endo and Scott Gold.

During the first week of school I found out why Joel brings his lunch instead of buying it. He likes some strange sandwiches. Salami, tomato and mayonnaise is his favourite. His second favourite is onion slices on buttered whole wheat bread. Either way you have to keep a safe distance from him after lunch. I think he enjoys breathing hard after he eats – especially on the girls.

One thing I don't like about the cafeteria is the cashiers. They're all ninth graders. You can tell by the way they look and by the way they ignore the seventh graders. To an eighth grader the cashier might say, 'Hi.' But to a seventh grader, nothing! Now that's a real shock after being in sixth grade where you're the boss of the whole school. Next year I plan to treat the new seventh graders the same way.

I joined the Junior Youth Group at church. It meets every Tuesday night from seven to nine. You have to be in seventh or eighth grade to belong. Marty Endo joined too. And a

148

skinny girl named Corky from our formroom. Father Pissaro the Second stopped in during our first meeting to ask how we were getting along. We all said, 'Fine, Father.' Then he smiled and left.

Our Youth Group leader is Ted Gibbons. He's a sophomore at Long Island Community College. He's really tall, wears glasses, and it looks like he's growing a moustache. When he wants our attention he waves his arms around and hollers, 'Simmer down!' Since there are twenty-four of us it takes a long time to get quiet. Ted told us about some of the things we'll be doing this year. The one I like best is, we're going to have our own basketball team.

Corky raised her hand and asked if she could start a cheerleaders club to go along with the basketball team.

Ted said, 'Sure.'

I think Corky looked at me and smiled then. I didn't smile back. I can't stand skinny girls.

All in all me and Marty Endo agreed that Junior Youth Group seems pretty good. Marty's a nice guy. He reminds me of Frankie, only he's really smart in school. He asked me to go to the movies with him next weekend. He said maybe Scott Gold and Joel can come too. I told him that sounded great. Then I remembered I didn't have any spending money. Mom hands me enough for lunch and Ralph brings me all my school supplies, but there's nothing left for extras. In Jersey City I used to keep a little of my paper route money so I never had to ask Pop for a handout. That's what got me thinking maybe I should get a paper route in Rosemont.

So on Sunday night I said, 'I think I'll try to get a new paper route.'

'What are you talking about?' Mom asked. 'You're not getting any paper route!'

'Why not? I've got a great bike.'

'That's crazy,' Mom said. 'Vic ... tell him that's crazy.'

'Do you miss your old job, Tony?' Pop asked. 'Is that it?'

'Not exactly,' I said. 'But I could use the money.'

'Vic ... Tony needs an allowance,' my mother said. 'I don't know why I never thought about it.'

'How much do you need?' Pop asked.

'Whatever Joel gets,' my mother said. 'How much, Tony?'

'I don't know what he gets,' I told her.

'Well, find out,' she said. 'You should get the same.'

'How's ten bucks?' Pop asked.

'You mean a week?' I said.

'Can you manage on that, Tony?' Mom asked.

I laughed. 'Well, yeah ... sure! That's plenty.'

'Good,' Pop said. 'You buy your lunch out of that, but if you need more you come to me. That's what I'm here for.'

'Thanks, Pop.'

'And don't let me hear you talking about a paper route anymore,' my mother added.

Wow! Ten bucks a week. I wonder what Frankie would say?

Every morning when we get to school me and Joel park our bikes in this huge rack. We all have our own locks and keys. I wear my key around my neck on a silver chain so I won't lose it. To tell the truth I don't know how I would manage in Rosemont without my ten-speed bike.

After school on most days I shoot baskets while Joel sits on the grass watching me. He has a stack of paperback books he's working on. What he does is underline certain passages and then paperclip those pages so it's easy to find what he's looking for. He showed me a couple of them one day. They're pretty good. Our gym teacher told us if we start to think about those things we should keep our mind on sports and that will help a lot. He told us about wet dreams too, only he calls them nocturnal emissions. I'm still not sure if I'll ever have one.

When I read Joel's paperbacks I can feel myself get hard. But other times when I'm not even thinking about anything it goes up too. I don't know what to do about that. I mean, if my brain is working right it's supposed to control my whole body. But if I don't have any control over that part of me what good is my brain? It's getting so I don't have anything to say about what goes on. I think that part of me has a mind of its own.

Suppose it decides to go up in school and everybody notices? Or at a Junior Youth Group meeting? What will I do to get it down? I think from now on I'm going to carry a raincoat with me every day. Then, if anything happens I'll have something to put over me in a hurry.

When football season started me and Joel rode our bikes to the high school field every time there was a home game. Lisa is a cheerleader. She wears red boots and a white sweater with a big R on it. I like the way her hair flops around when she's yelling cheers.

Sometimes she talks to us during halftime. It depends on her mood. Other times you'd think we were strangers. One day Lisa really put on the big sister act. She hugged me and Joel together and told the rest of the cheerleaders, 'These are my favourite guys!' I knew it was a big joke between her and her friends but I didn't care. Because she was touching me and it felt good.

Corky goes to every game too. She hangs around Lisa a lot. Joel told me Lisa is teaching Corky how to be a cheerleader. Corky ought to get Lisa to teach her some other things too. Because Corky looks like a fifth grader. You can't even tell if she's a boy or a girl unless she happens to be wearing a skirt, which is practically never. Her hair is cut short and she's really small. She spends a lot of time giggling. I'll bet Lisa never giggled in her whole life!

One afternoon on the way home from the game Joel asked me if I'd go to the store with him. He needed some notebook paper. I said 'Sure Joel.'

We left our bikes up against the side of the store and Joel went straight to the counter where the school supplies were. He bought two packages of wide-ruled three-hole looseleaf paper. He paid the saleslady and took the bag she gave him.

'I'm done,' he said. 'You need anything?'

'No. I've got plenty. Ralph brought me a whole bunch of supplies last week.'

'Okay. Let's go.'

We walked side by side to the front of the store. I couldn' believe it when Joel grabbed three flashlight batteries from a bin and shoved them into his pockets. I saw him do it. He didn't look at me. He didn't even look back to see if anybody in the store noticed. He just kept walking with that funny lopsided smile on his face. I was sure he was kidding around

But when we got on our bikes and started for home and he still didn't say anything I knew he wasn't kidding. Should I say something? I wondered. Like uh ... 'I saw you take those batteries, Joel. Who do you think you're fooling!' Maybe I should have, but I didn't.

We rode home without a word. When we got to my driveway Joel said, 'Why don't you sleep over tonight? That'd be great. I'll show you Lisa's diary and everything. And I've been working on some new books too – real good ones. I'll even let you read them.'

'I don't know, Joel,' I said, very unfriendly.

'Come on, Tony.'

'Maybe,' I said.

Joel went to his house and I went to mine. I locked myself up in my bathroom for about thirty minutes. My stomach hurt bad.

Is taking three batteries worse than cheating in arithmetic? Frankie used to cheat in arithmetic all the time in Jersey City. I never reported him. And how about the telephone booth at the Y? We all used to shake it to make change come out. And when it did I always helped myself like the other guys. Is taking three batteries worse than that? Well, what if it is! What am I supposed to do about it – call the police? I suppose I could. I wouldn't have to give them my name or anything. Or I could tell the man in the store about it. But I don't want to. Really, what I want to do is get a look at Lisa's diary.

If I tell on Joel we'll never be able to be friends. Just when things are looking good and I'm feeling settled. It would be bad news to have to start out all over again.

So I told my mother I was going to sleep over at Joel's.

'Who invited you?' Mom asked.

'Joel did.'

'Is it all right with his mother?'

'How should I know?' Why do I have to get permission for every little thing I do? Isn't it enough to tell her where I'm going? Why does she have to make such a big thing out of it?

But she called Mrs Hoober anyway. The last thing I heard her say before she hung up was, 'Well, I guess it's okay if just the maid is home. After all, Vic and I are right next door.'

I went to Joel's after supper. I got there in time to see his mother and father leave for a dance at the country club and then to see Lisa leave with her date, a senior from Rosemont High who looks like a monkey. I wondered why she was wasting her time on him. I wanted to shout, 'Hey Lisa ... this guy's a creep! Don't go out with him. Stay home with us. You and Joel can watch TV and I'll watch you. Please stay, Lisa ...'

But she didn't She gave the monkey a big smile when he helped her on with her coat. She left without even saying goodbye.

Joel and I were on our own. He explained that Millicent was closed up in her room where she has her own TV. Then he checked his watch and said, 'I have to make a phone call. Come on.'

I followed him upstairs. He said, 'I wish I had my own phone, like Lisa. Then I wouldn't have to go into my parents' bedroom all the time.'

I have never seen a bedroom like Mr and Mrs Hoober's. They have a round bed. It's hard to believe anybody really sleeps on it. It's two steps up from the rest of the room and I thought, if you fall out of bed here you also fall down the stairs. I started to laugh. Besides the bed being round there's a lamp hanging over it. If Mr Hoober sits up in bed does he whack his head on it?

Joel jumped up the two steps and sat down on the edge of the bed. He took the phone off the hook, and dialled. He examined his fingernails while he waited for someone to answer. 'Hello,' he finally said. 'Is Denton F. Buchanan in? Oh ... I'm sorry sir. I'll dial again.'

I wondered who Denton F. Buchanan was.

Joel hung up and tried again. 'Hello. May I please speak to Denton F. Buchanan. What? Wrong number ... the second time? I'm terribly sorry sir.'

He looked up at me and smiled as he dialled again.

'Hey, why don't you check the phone book, Joel,' I suggested.

He dismissed me with a wave of one hand. He got his number. 'Hello ... Denton F. Buchanan please. Yes, I'm sure this is the number he gave me sir. Yes ... well, I do understand. But I have checked with information sir. Certainly. I won't make the same mistake again.'

'Joel,' I said. 'Will you look it up? Who is he anyway?'

'You'll see,' Joel said. 'This is my last phone call.'

He dialled. 'Hello,' he said, disguising his voice. He made it sound very deep, which isn't exactly easy the way his voice changes around from high to low all the time. 'This is Denton F. Buchanan calling. Have there been any calls for me?'

Then he hung up and rolled around on the bed laughing

and holding his sides. 'Isn't that the greatest! That poor guy. He really thought I was serious at first.'

More laughing and rolling around – now tears running down his face. 'Who was he?' I asked.

'Who knows! I just made up the number. I always do that.'

'You were fooling around?' I asked. 'You don't know any Denton F. Buchanan?'

'Of course I don't know any Denton F. Buchanan! I don't know any Manfred T. Oliver either.' Joel sat up. 'That's the other name I like to use. You've got to try it. You've got to hear how funny it is at the other end.'

'Now?' I asked. I really didn't want to call anybody. I think you can get into big trouble for fooling around on the phone. But if I refuse Joel will call me chicken.

'You can't call now,' he said. 'I only make one call a night. The next time you're over you can try it. Okay?'

'Sure,' I said. Whew – now he won't know I'm chicken. 'Listen, what about Lisa's diary?' I didn't want to seem too anxious but after all, that was the main reason I decided to accept Joel's invitation to spend the night.

'Oh yeah. I promised, didn't I. Come on.'

I followed Joel to the opposite end of the upstairs hallway. Lisa's room is right next to Millicent's. Joel held a finger over his lips as we tiptoed past her door. Inside Lisa's room Joel snapped on a light and whispered that he's not allowed in there. It's off-limits.

He shut the door. Lisa's bedroom is all pink and white. Girly looking. Her room faces the side of my house. I looked out her window and saw my room across the way. My shades were up. The light from our upstairs hallway made it easy to see everything. I'd have to be a lot more careful about pulling down my shades from now on. I wouldn't want Lisa to be able to see me. I hope she doesn't know that's my room.

'Psst ... give me a hand with this mattress,' Joel whispered.

'She keeps it under here.'

I held up the mattress while Joel searched. But all he came up with was a note. It said:

too bad snooper
your sister's smarter than you think!!!

'How about that!' Joel said. 'She found out and moved it. Well, never mind. We'll find it. It's got to be in here some place.'

He started searching her dresser drawers, then went to her desk, dressing table and finally to her closet. But he couldn't find it anywhere. I could tell he was embarrassed because he promised he'd show it to me and now he couldn't make good on his promise.

'I'm really sorry,' he said.

'Forget it,' I told him. I didn't want him to think I cared much.

Just as Joel was climbing back down from Lisa's top closet shelf the door opened. It was Millicent. She looked funny. She was wrapped in a plaid blanket and her hair was up in curlers.

'What you doing?' she asked.

'Never mind,' Joel said.

'What never mind! I gonna tell on you, Joel. You no supposed to be in here. This time I gonna tell.'

Joel shook his finger at her. 'Will you listen to that!' he said to me. 'Is she a good one? You tell on me, Millicent. You go ahead. Then I'll tell on you!' Joel shouted.

'What you mean?' Millicent asked.

'You know,' Joel said.

I didn't much like him having a fight with Millicent in front of me. I don't think you're supposed to talk to somebody who works for you like that.

'Oh ... you give me hard time, Joel. But some day God gonna punish you! *You wait.*' Millicent crossed herself and left. I heard her slam the door to her bedroom.

Joel turned out Lisa's light and we went back to his room.
'How do you know she's not going to tell on you?' I asked.

'She wouldn't dare!' Joel laughed. 'She's scared of me!
I caught her trying on my mother's clothes one night. If I
tell my mother she'll lose her job. And she knows it!'

'I'm beginning to change my mind about Joel. He's not
the kind of creep I thought he was when I first met him. He
might last longer than a week in Jersey City after all. But the
more I know about him the more I'm not sure if I want to
be his friend.

Then Again, Maybe I Won't

On 19 October Angie had a baby girl. My father was
disappointed. 'A first baby and it's a girl! There hasn't been
a girl born first in my family for five generations!'

'So what?' my mother said. 'A girl's just as good. Anyway,
I always wanted a daughter. Now I have a granddaughter!'

They named the baby Vincenza, after my brother Vinnie –
just like Grandma planned. But everybody is supposed to
call her Vicki for short. Lucky for her – who'd want to go
through life with a name like Vincenza?

When Angie came home from the hospital we all went
to Queens to visit the new baby. My mother said she was
the most beautiful thing she'd ever seen in her whole life. I
thought the baby looked like a plucked chicken, but I didn't
say so.

Grandma stood over Vicki making funny faces but all
Vicki did was cry. Then the baby-nurse, Mrs Buttfield
told us we'd better not stay long because new mothers and
new babies shouldn't have too much company right away.
She said this like she owned Vicki.

Mrs Buttfield is a present from my mother to Angie. My

mother wants Angie to rest and not have to get up at night with the baby. Privately, I renamed the nurse The Butt. She looks about eighty and I know she doesn't want anybody hanging around.

Ralph pranced through the apartment with a big box of cigars. He even offered one to me.

'Go on Kid, take it. You're an uncle now.'

'What are you crazy?' my mother yelled at Ralph. 'He's thirteen years old. A cigar! You want him to wind up in the hospital?'

My mother didn't have to worry. I wasn't about to smoke one. Cigars stink!

All afternoon I kept thinking, I could be home playing basketball instead of wasting my time in a stuffy apartment in Queens. It's really funny, the way everyone is so excited about a baby that looks like a plucked chicken. Maybe Vicki will get better looking. Then again, maybe she won't. Maybe she will always look like that. I feel sorry for her. But why should I worry? She's not my kid. Right?

When we got ready to go home I told Ralph and Angie that Vicki is really neat and very pretty too. That's what everyone else was saying so I decided to be polite about the whole thing. Sometimes it's better to tell a little lie than to tell the truth and have everybody hate you.

When Angie said goodbye she called me Uncle Tony and she kissed my cheek. I only let her because she just had a baby.

The next Sunday, when Mom and Pop got ready to go to Queens I said, 'I'm staying with Joel this afternoon. We might go to the movies.'

But the Sunday after that when I tried the same thing Mom asked, 'How do you think Ralph and Angie feel that you don't want to see Vicki? Very bad, I'll tell you that. And you're her only uncle too.'

'Oh ... all right. I'll go with you today.'

When we got there The Butt wanted to check my hands

before I even *saw* the baby. Clean hands and runny noses are the big things in Mrs Buttfield's life. I was about to tell her I wasn't interested in touching Vicki and that I was only looking to be polite.

But Ralph said he'd had enough of her and her inspections. So The Butt packed her bags and left. This made Angie cry for a long time and say she didn't know how she was going to manage all by herself.

A week later my mother started the maid business at home.

'I can't run this big house with no help, Vic. I want to enjoy my granddaughter. I don't want to be stuck here all day cleaning the place.'

My father was behind his newspaper and I couldn't tell if he was really listening until he said, 'So get some help, Carmella.' He spoke without taking his cigar out of his mouth.

'You mean it, Vic?' my mother asked.

'Of course I mean it. I wouldn't say it if I didn't mean it, would I?'

The next day my mother drove to an employment agency and came home with our first maid. She was from South America, her name was Gerta, and she spoke only Spanish. I thought about Millicent and wondered if Gerta would teach me to curse in Spanish.

After five days my mother whispered to my father, 'If I look at her wrong she cries. I think she's very lonesome. I hope she'll improve with experience.'

My father said, 'I'm sorry if she's lonesome. But I can't wear my shirts with wrinkles down the front.'

'I can't tell her, Vic. She'll cry.'

'Then I'll tell her,' my father said.

That was the end of Gerta.

The next week my mother came home with Vera. She was from Haiti and spoke only French.

My father said, 'Why can't you get one that talks Italian?'

My mother said, 'Oh Vic!'

But after a few days my mother complained that Vera didn't like to get up in the mornings and my father complained about the way the beds were made.

That was the end of Vera.

Pauline, LaBelle and Florie followed. Grandma took care of them. Even though she can't talk she can just *look* at you and you know what she's thinking. And she wasn't thinking anything good about any of our maids.

Then Maxine arrived. You could tell she was different right away. First, because she interviewed my mother instead of my mother interviewing her. When she saw me she said, 'When I wash the floor nobody walks on it. That includes you. Understand?'

My mother said, 'Tony's a good boy. You won't have any trouble with him.'

'He'll stay out of my way?' Maxine asked.

I thought, who'd want to get in your way?

My mother put her arm around me. 'Of course he'll stay out of your way. Won't you, Tony?'

'Sure, sure,' I said. I wonder if she'll try on my mother's clothes, like Millicent. I don't think so. She's about a foot taller than my mother.

'Well ...' Maxine said, running her finger along the furniture, then inspecting it for dirt, 'I'll try it.'

My mother sighed with relief and later she told us that Maxine has excellent references and we are to do everything possible to keep her happy. This included all new towels for Maxine's bathroom. In her favourite colours – purple and brown.

On Maxine's third day she told my mother that *she* had to be in charge of the kitchen. Not the *old lady*.

My mother said, 'Oh dear! I just don't know about that.'

Maxine tapped her foot at my mother.

'You see,' my mother explained, 'Mama's always done all the cooking.'

Maxine glared.

My mother tried a nervous smile. 'I suppose we could arrange something. I mean, why should Mama work so hard when she doesn't have to?'

I thought, Grandma's going to be furious when she hears about this.

She was furious all right. She stomped to her room, slammed the door and refused to come out. My mother banged on her door and called, 'Please, Mama! You'll take it easy for a change. You'll enjoy it ... I know you will. Just let me explain.'

But Grandma wouldn't open up. Maxine was in charge now and Grandma knew it. There are times when I'd like to throw something at my mother. How can she let Maxine boss her around? Doesn't she care about Grandma? Can't she see how she's hurt her feelings?

The next night my father brought home a colour TV for Grandma's room. Lately, my mother and father seem to think that presents can fix everything. And if you ask me, they think more about Maxine than they do about Grandma.

Every night during dinner my father says, 'Delicious, Maxine!' Of course Maxine stands over him until he says it. After our meal my mother says, 'Thank you very much, Maxine.' Like she's doing us some kind of favour!

When Grandma did the cooking nobody paid much attention to it. And it was better than Maxine's, I'll tell you that. Maybe not as fancy looking, but better tasting. Since Grandma won't eat anything that Maxine cooks my mother fixes her meals separately. Usually Grandma gets a broiled lamb chop for supper – on a tray in her room. Grandma won't come downstairs any more. She never even goes to church.

One night I walked into the kitchen while Maxine was cleaning up. I saw her throw away all the leftovers.

'Well, Mr Big Eyes,' Maxine said. 'What do you want?'

'How come you're throwing all that food away?' I asked.

'Who's going to eat it, do you think?'

I thought, in Jersey City we saved everything – including cold spaghetti! I made up my mind right then to study extra hard. The way my mother and father are throwing money around I figure there won't be anything left by the time I'm ready for college. If I decide to go I'll need a full scholarship!

I bought a small chess set with some of my allowance. Not a fancy one like Joel's, but the pieces are made of wood. I taught my father how to play.

Pop's not as tired out as he used to be. Business at the plant is okay and things are running smoothly. Every night after supper we sit in the den and play a game. Pop says chess is good because it teaches you how to solve problems. He likes it so much he keeps on playing even after I have to go up to my room to do my homework. He has a make-believe opponent he calls Sam. Pop moves the pieces for both of them. Sometimes I think he likes playing with Sam better than me.

We were in the middle of a hot game one night when the doorbell rang. It was Father Pissaro the Second.

'Vic!' my mother called. 'Look who's here.'

Pop stood up. 'Father ... what a surprise!' He looked at my mother as if to say, *Did you invite him without telling me?*

And my mother looked back at him with a *don't ask me* expression on her face.

So I said, 'How come you came to see us, Father?'

'Tony!' my mother said. 'Where are your manners?'

Father Pissaro the Second smiled at me. 'That's all right, Tony. I really came to see your grandmother. I've missed her.'

My mother took a big breath. Then she smiled. 'Oh Father ... that's very nice of you. Mama hasn't been feeling too well.'

'I'm sorry to hear that,' Father Pissaro said. 'Do you think I could see her? I know she'll want to make her confession. She never used to miss a week.'

'Well, Father, that's very thoughtful of you,' my mother

said. 'Would you give me a minute to run upstairs and tell Mama you're here?'

'Take your time, Mrs Miglione,' Father Pissaro said.

I wondered if Grandma would make a fuss. And how does she confess every week when she can't talk? Does she write it all down or what?

'How's the Junior Youth Group going, Tony?' Father Pissaro asked.

'I like it a lot,' I said. 'Ted is really nice.'

'How about a drink, Father?' Pop asked.

'No thank you.'

'Coffee, or tea?' my father said. 'It's no trouble.'

'Thank you Mr Miglione, but I really don't want anything.'

We looked at each other for a while and then my mother called from the top of the stairs. 'You can come up now, Father. Mama would like to see you.'

After she showed Father Pissaro to Grandma's room, my mother came downstairs. 'I hope Mama doesn't tell him anything to embarrass us,' she whispered to my father.

'She has a right to tell him whatever's on her mind,' Pop answered.

'But you know how stubborn Mama can be these days. She might tell him something just to get back at me.'

'For what, Carmella? She's not a prisoner here. She can come out of her room any time she feels like it.'

'Shush . . .' my mother whispered. 'Here he comes.'

That didn't take long, I thought. Did Grandma tell him any family secrets? I studied his face. But I couldn't tell anything from his expression. It was the same as before. Still, I don't think it would be easy to fool Father Pissaro the Second.

After he left my mother ran up to Grandma's room. She knocked and knocked but she couldn't get in. Grandma had locked her door again.

This morning, before I left for school, my mother said, 'I

think it's pretty funny that a boy who won't wear rubbers when it's pouring out suddenly carries an old raincoat around with him every day.'

'I like my raincoat,' I said. 'It's comfortable.' I wasn't about to explain the real reason I took it to school.

'You have a new jacket,' Mom said. 'I'd like to see you wear it once or twice before it's outgrown.'

'Maybe I'll wear the jacket tomorrow.'

'Maybe you'll wear it today!' Mom held the jacket and shook it at me. 'Put it on, Tony, and leave that old raincoat home. It doesn't look nice for school. Besides, it's sunny out.'

'Oh ... okay.' If I made a big scene she might get suspicious.

So I wore the new jacket to school and worried all day about what might happen. But nothing happened. Maybe it's a question of mind over matter.

One Friday in November, right after second period, I met Joel in the boys' room. He was up on the sinks singing, 'There was a girl in our town – her name was Nancy Brown ...' When he saw me he yelled, 'Hey Tony ... watch this!' So I stood there and watched as Joel ran up the row of sinks, then down it. By that time he had quite an audience and of course nobody could wash his hands. I wished my mother could have seen the Angel. As Joel sang his voice cracked. Everybody cheered. When the second bell rang Joel jumped down from the sinks and went to his class.

That day at lunch Joel was in front of me on line in the cafeteria. He still buys his milk and apple every day. Always the same routine. But this time I saw him take his apple, inspect it for bruises like usual, then stick it into his brown lunch bag. He only paid for his milk. I really got mad when I saw that.

After five days of watching Joel do this I wanted to shout at the cashier, 'Hey, this guy's stealing apples!' I'd yank it out of his lunch bag and shove it in the cashier's face. 'You see,' I'd say. 'You see how stupid you are – even if you are in ninth grade! He's been doing it for a week – stealing an apple a day for a week – and you haven't even noticed!'

Then I figured the cashier would look up at me and say, 'Please tell me what to do.' And I'd tell her in this deep voice, 'Call the principal, stupid!' Then the principal would pat me on the back and tell me, 'What we need is more young men like you, Mr Miglione. Honest – brave – unafraid young men!'

But Joel would never speak to me again. Marty Endo and Scott Gold would call me Snitch. So what did I do about the whole situation? Nothing! As usual.

I paid the cashier and carried my tray of meatloaf and mashed potatoes to our regular table. I sat down between Joel and Marty Endo. As I began to eat I got an awful pain. *Wow!* It nearly doubled me over.

'What's the matter?' Joel asked.

'I don't know,' I said. 'I got a pain in my stomach.'

'You want to go to the nurse?'

'No, I think it's going away.' After a few minutes it disappeared and I ate some of my lunch but I didn't enjoy it.

The pain came back that night after dinner and I went to my room to rest. That's when I discovered I could see Lisa's room from my room. I don't know why I never thought of it before. I guess I've been so busy pulling down my shades to make sure she can't see me it never entered my mind that I could see her. With all my lights turned off and with her lights turned on, I can see everything she's doing. And what she was doing was getting undressed. I forgot about my pain and concentrated on my window.

Then Again, Maybe I Won't

There was no school on Veterans Day. Just as we were finishing breakfast Grandma walked into the kitchen. She was dressed in black. All three of us stopped eating. This was the first time she'd come out of her room since Maxine started running things. Grandma handed my mother a note. First my mother read it to herself. Then she jumped up and hugged Grandma.

'Oh Mama ... you remembered!' My mother read us the note:

I'm ready to go to the cemetery.

I thought we wouldn't go this year. Somehow I figured that we've changed so much since coming to Rosemont we'd be able to skip the cemetery deal. But no, we were going. We go every year on Veterans Day, to bring flowers to Vinnie's grave. He's buried in Perth Amboy, which wasn't a bad trip from Jersey City.

From Rosemont it takes forever. We were all squeezed into the car. Me, my mother and my father in the front. Grandma, Ralph, Angie and the baby in the back. My mother kept turning around to talk to Ralph and Angie.

'If only Vinnie could see her. He'd be so proud! If only he knew he had such an adorable little niece.' My mother sniffled and I knew what was coming. Every year she devotes the whole day to talking and crying and saying *if only* about Vinnie. I always feel like an outsider on Veterans Day.

On the way to Perth Amboy Angie had to feed the baby. Halfway through her bottle Vicki spit up. It landed on Ralph. So Ralph passed Vicki to Grandma while Angie tried to clean off his jacket. After Vicki finished her bottle she started to cry. My mother said she must have gas. So Grandma passed Vicki to my mother in the front seat so she could try to burp her.

When Vicki cries her face turns bright red and she looks like she's going to explode. Finally Angie handed my mother a pacifier for Vicki to suck. I'm glad we don't have a baby at home. Two hours in the car is enough.

When we got to Perth Amboy my father tried to find the same florist as last year. My mother argued with him about that.

'What's the difference? One florist is as good as another.'

But my father said, 'I remember him. He was a nice guy. He went out of his way to be nice.'

'So you'll waste the whole day looking for him!' my mother snapped.

This went on for twenty minutes. Finally my father found the florist he was looking for. We all got out of the car to stretch our legs. My mother and Angie talked on and on about what kind of flowers to buy this year. Grandma kept pointing to yellow chrysanthemums but my mother said they reminded her of football games and that she preferred something all white, in a graveyard container.

We piled back into the car with me holding this huge arrangement of flowers. Last year it was only a third as big.

When we got to the cemetery I carried the flowers to Vinnie's grave and stuck the container into the ground. I stepped back and brushed off my hands. My mother bent down and sort of fluffed out the flowers. Then she cried. 'Oh Vinnie ... Vinnie ... I miss you so much,' she said. She covered her face with her hands.

Grandma kneeled and kissed the grave. She does that every year. It makes me feel awful. I hate it. Why can't I feel the way they do? Why can't I remember things about Vinnie and cry too? My father just stared at the grave and rocked back and forth on his feet. Angie held the baby close and whispered to her. She's telling Vicki about Vinnie, I thought. About how he died for his country and all that. About how brave he was and how he understood everything my father did in the basement in Jersey City.

Does Vinnie know about us now? Does he know that we live in a big white house and that we drove here in a new green hardtop instead of the old truck? Does he know that Grandma has her own colour TV because she's not allowed to cook anymore? Does he know about our boss, Maxine? And if he knows, what does he think? Is he laughing at us? Is he laughing and saying, 'Hey, what happened to you guys since you visited me last year?'

Ted Gibbons organized our Junior Youth Group basketball team. He said anybody who wants to play *can* play. He told us he remembers what it's like to try out for a team and not make it. So we wound up having two teams. Only two guys in our Youth Group didn't want to play and one of them agreed to be Ted's assistant coach and the other one said he'd like to be our sports reporter.

Ted meets with us every Friday afternoon at our junior high. We don't have any after-school activities on Friday so Ted got permission from the principal for us to use the gym. Ted's moustache is getting thicker. He touches it a lot as if he's checking to make sure it's still there. He's worked out a whole schedule of games for us. We're going to play every Friday night during January and February. Eight games in all against teams from other churches and temples. Since we have two teams Ted said we'll alternate and change over at every halftime. That way we'll all have a chance to play.

We started our practice right before Thanksgiving. I'm the best foul shooter. And I'm fast too. I think Ted is pretty impressed. I just wish I was taller. Because when somebody like Marty Endo guards me I can't shoot at all. I can't even see!

When I'm playing basketball I don't think of anything else. Not Lisa or school work or my family. I concentrate on the ball and getting it into the basket. Basketball makes me

eel good. I wish we didn't have two teams. I wish I could be
there all the time.

The whole family was invited for Thanksgiving. My three
aunts and uncles and my cousin Ginger from Weehawken.
Ginger belongs to my mother's sister Rosemary. We call her
Aunt Rose. Aunt Rose is married to Uncle Lou. Uncle Lou's
Jewish and my mother doesn't approve of him. It has nothing
to do with him being Jewish she says. It's just that he isn't
right for Aunt Rose, which is pretty funny because they've
been married for fifteen years.

This was the family's first visit to Rosemont and my
mother was really doing it up big. She hired another lady to
help Maxine in the kitchen so Maxine wouldn't get all tired
out what with cooking the turkey and all. Grandma refused
to join us. She hasn't left her room since Veterans Day.

My mother begged, 'Please, Mama ... just this once!
It's Thanksgiving. Give me some pleasure, Mama! Get
dressed and come downstairs. *Mama* ... will you please turn
off that television set and come down for dinner!' But
Grandma wouldn't budge.

Angie brought Vicki in a car bed. She was supposed to
sleep in it all afternoon but nobody told *her* that because she
screamed a lot. So we played Pass the Baby. All my aunts
and uncles got to hold her and make silly faces at her until
my mother came up with the brilliant solution of leaving
Vicki upstairs with Grandma while we ate.

Angie took the baby to Grandma's room and then even
if she was screaming we couldn't hear her. A very important
thing to remember about babies is that if you can't hear them
they're not so bad.

My relatives were really impressed with Rosemont and
our house. Uncle Lou kept telling Ginger, 'Now you can
say you have rich relatives, baby. *Really* rich relatives!'

And Aunt Rose said, 'When Ginger gets older Tony can

fix her up on dates and she can sleep over here.'

'Oh, can I, Aunt Carmella?' Ginger asked.

My mother nodded and smiled.

I thought, I'll never fix you up Ginger, because you're dumb and ugly and I don't like you anyway!

Uncle Lou said, 'Rose thinks of everything, doesn't she? Why should Ginger go out with a poor boy if she can go out with a rich one, right?'

So I said, 'What's so great about being rich? Money isn't everything, you know.'

They all laughed. Even Ralph and Angie laughed. Ralph said, 'Listen, Big Shot ... wait until *you* have to pay for baby shoes!'

How does he know so much about baby shoes? I wondered. Vicki doesn't even wear shoes yet! Ralph is different lately. He isn't The Wizard any more. He's just like an old guy with a wife and kid. Would he be like this if we were still in Jersey City? Is it being a father that changed him?

Finally we sat down to dinner. I've never eaten so much in my life. For dessert we had a choice of three pies – pumpkin, apple or lemon meringue. I chose lemon meringue because I knew Angie baked it and Maxine baked the other two.

After dinner the family went upstairs one at a time, to visit with Grandma.

When Aunt Rose came downstairs she said, 'Mama's lucky to be able to spend her last years in such luxury.'

'And with her own colour TV,' Ginger said.

Later they all decided the reason Grandma 'took to her room' was plain old age. I could have told them the truth but I'd have got in a lot of trouble.

My father offered Ralph and my uncles cigars. He laughed as he told them each one cost $1.00. When they all lit up, Aunt Rose asked Ginger to recite for us. Ginger's been doing that ever since I can remember. You'd think by now she'd know how dumb she sounds. You'd think she'd be too embarrassed to stand up in front of a bunch of relatives and

…y her stupid poems. But no! She jumped right up and …arted.

She had some new poems this year. Two about Thanksgiving, …aturally, and one about *love* by Elizabeth Barrett Browning. …hen she recited that one she closed her eyes. How I wished …oel could have heard her!

When Ginger was through I heard Aunt Rose telling my …other that Ginger wears a bra already, which reminded me …f Lisa. Soon it will be dark outside and I'll be able to watch …er from my window. When I feel my neck turn red hot I …now I better think about basketball in a hurry.

…orky's real name is Kathryn Thomas. I found out because a …irl in my formroom named Marian passed me a note. It said:

…. T. thinks T. M. is super!

… knew who T. M. was … me. But I didn't know who K. T. …as. And I really didn't care. So I crumpled up the note and …hrew it away. I made a disgusted face at Marian. That …fternoon I got another note. This one said:

…y real name is Kathryn Thomas. Love, Corky

… crumpled up that note too. I wished she'd leave me alone. …he's a real pain!

Ever since that day Marian runs over to me every morning …nd says, 'Hi Tony. How's Corky?'

Corky is always stationed right near us so she doesn't …niss a thing.

I answer Marian with a straight face. 'I don't know,' I …ay. 'Why don't you ask her yourself?'

Then Corky and Marian giggle like crazy until Mrs O'Leary …ooks up and tells them to settle down.

Marty Endo told me that Corky offered to do his maths …omework for a week if he arranged for me to wind up …itting next to her at our Junior Youth Group meetings.

Marty wouldn't do it. Why should he? He's great at maths.

The more Corky bothers me the more I think about Lisa. I wish it was Lisa who passed me notes and wanted to sit next to me.

This morning, in maths class, I wasn't thinking about Lisa. I was concentrating on a problem in my book and Miss Tobin called on me. She asked me to go up to the board and show the class how I worked it out.

Just as I finished writing the figures on the board I started to get hard. Mind over matter ... mind over matter, I told myself. But still it went up. I kept my back to the class and prayed for it to go down.

Miss Tobin said, 'That's an interesting way to solve the problem, Tony.'

For a minute I thought she meant my *real* problem, but then I realized she was talking about the *maths* problem.

'Could you explain your reasoning to the class, Tony?'

I started talking but I didn't turn around. I could just picture facing the class. Everybody would laugh and point to my pants. I wished I was wearing my raincoat.

'We'd hear better if you'd turn around,' Miss Tobin said.

What could I do? Pretend to be sick and run out of the room? Maybe. Or just refuse to turn around? No. Ask to go to the bathroom? No ...

'Tony ...' Miss Tobin said.

'Yes?'

'We're waiting for you to explain the problem.'

'Oh. Okay, Miss Tobin.'

I was holding my maths book in my left hand and a piece of chalk in my right. I turned sideways, keeping my book in front of my pants. I explained my answer as fast as I could and Miss Tobin didn't ask me any questions. She said, 'Thank you, Tony. You can sit down now.'

I walked back to my seat still holding the maths book close to me. But I didn't have to worry. By then it was down.

From now on I'm going to make sure I always have a

stack of books with me. Books are a lot better than my old raincoat!

One afternoon after Thanksgiving vacation Joel came over. My mother was in Queens with Angie and Vicki as usual and Grandma was locked in her room. So was Maxine. She has this strict rule about how she has to have an afternoon nap every day, so she'll be fresh as a daisy for supper, she says. My mother says, of course that's only fair. So we're not supposed to disturb Maxine between three and four-thirty.

While I was pouring two glasses of milk Joel asked if he could use the phone.

'Sure,' I said. I didn't pay any attention until I heard him ask for Denton F. Buchanan. I thought, oh no! He's at it again.

He dialled two more times, going through his whole routine, before he called back and said, 'This is Denton F. Buchanan. Have there been any calls for me?'

I said, 'Same old tricks!'

Joel said, 'Why don't you try it?'

'No. I don't think so.'

'Come on, Tony! Make up the name yourself.'

'I don't know, Joel. I could get in trouble.'

'For what? Nobody's going to know. Come on ... think up a good name. You're not chicken are you?'

'No.'

'Well then ... go ahead.'

'Oh ... all right.' I concentrated until I came up with a name. 'How's Peter Ira Grinch?' I asked.

'Peter Ira Grinch? That's a nutty name.'

'I suppose ... but it has good initials,' I said.

'P. I. G. Hey, yeah! I like that,' Joel said.

'How do I do it?'

'Just dial a number. Make sure it's not long distance though.'

I picked up the phone, clearing my throat several times

as I dialled seven digits and waited. It rang twice before a lady answered.

'Hello,' she said.

'Uh ... hello. May I please speak to uh ... Peter Ira Grinch.'

'What number you calling?'

I repeated the number I dialled.

'You got the right number but nobody's here by that name.'

I hung up.

'You did fine,' Joel said.

'I did?'

'Sure. Now call back.'

I dialled.

This time she answered right away. 'Hello.'

'Peter Ira Grinch, please.'

'Look kid ...' How did she know I was a kid? 'I told you ... you got the *wrong number*!'

I hung up without saying anything. I told Joel, 'She doesn't like me.'

'She doesn't have to like you,' Joel said. 'She doesn't even know you. Go ahead, Tony ... one more time.'

My hand shook as I dialled. It didn't even ring once.

'Hello,' she said. You could tell she was mad.

'Peter Ira Grinch, please.'

'Listen, you lousy kids,' she screamed. 'I'm fed up with you and your lousy phone calls. I'm gonna call the cops! You hear me? *The cops*. They'll find you and lock you up where you belong!' She slammed the phone down.

'She said she's going to call the cops,' I told Joel.

He laughed. 'She's not calling anybody. Go on ... call one more time.'

'I can't.'

'What do you mean you can't? You've got to call and say you're Peter Ira Grinch. Otherwise it was all for nothing.'

'I can't,' I said again. 'Don't you know they can trace calls? Don't you know that, Joel?'

'You've got to call her again, Tony!'

I got a stomach pain then. A bad one. 'I can't ... I can't because I'm sick!' I said, holding my stomach. 'You might as well go home Joel – I mean it, I'm really sick!' I rushed to the bathroom.

When my mother came home I was still in the bathroom and my stomach was killing me. My mother said nobody can have that much gas and that she was going to take me to the doctor.

She made a lot of phone calls to find out which doctor to see on Long Island. Finally she decided on the one Diane Hoober recommended. My mother thinks everything the Hoobers do is perfect. I wanted to tell her the truth about Joel. I wanted to see how her face would look then, but the more I thought about telling her the more my stomach hurt.

The doctor's name was Frank Holland. He has grey hair and a big nose. He asked my mother to wait in the outer office while he checked me. I had to lie down on his examining table with most of my clothes off while he pushed and prodded at my belly. I was supposed to tell him if it hurt in any special place. It didn't.

'I think we'd better do a test on you, Tony,' Dr Holland said. 'Come back tomorrow morning at eight. Don't eat after six o'clock tonight. And no breakfast in the morning.'

'What kind of test?' I asked.

'Oh ... I'm going to have a look inside you. It won't hurt. I promise.'

I couldn't sleep at all that night. I was worried about the test and about what might be wrong with me. I hope I don't need an operation. I'm really scared about somebody cutting into me.

The next morning my mother took me back to Dr Holland's office. He was right about the test. It didn't hurt. But he forgot to tell me I'd have to drink a glass of this horrible stuff called barium. It tasted like chocolate flavoured chalk. Dr

Holland explained that when I drank the barium and stood in front of his machine, he could see inside me.

Being a doctor must be really neat. Maybe I'll go to medical school so I can look inside people too. Then again, maybe I won't. Doctors have to do a lot messier stuff than that and I don't even like dissecting frogs in biology.

After the test, Dr Holland said I should get dressed and come into his office. He talked to me from behind his desk. I noticed he doodled on a prescription pad – dog and cat faces mostly. I sat in a chair to his left and I was pretty nervous. My hands were sweating like crazy.

'Well, Tony,' he said, 'there's nothing for you to worry about. Everything is going to be fine. Your test was normal.'

'I don't need an operation?' I asked.

'No, nothing like that,' Dr Holland said.

'Then what? I mean, why do I get so many pains?'

'Well ... I think you're pretty tense, Tony. And when a person gets tense about things his insides tighten up and that can cause pain.'

I rubbed my hands on my pants.

'You know, it's nothing to be ashamed of,' Dr Holland said. 'We all face some problems. It's just a question of learning how to handle those problems.'

'Really? That's what it really is?'

'Yes. Some people call it nervous stomach.'

'Oh that. I knew a kid in Jersey City with nervous stomach. He was a creep.'

'Well ... we hold things inside of us that might be better out in the open. Don't push yourself, Tony. Try to relax and unwind.'

'I am relaxed,' I said.

'Maybe now ... but not always. In any event I'm going to prescribe some pills for you. One tablet twice a day for two weeks. After that, only when you need them. When you get pains or diarrhoea.'

Dr Holland handed me the prescription.

As I stood up to leave he said, 'What about girls?'

I sat back down. 'Girls?' I asked.

'Yes. Do you think about them a lot?'

'Not much,' I mumbled, looking down.

'It's perfectly normal you know.'

'Oh sure. I know.'

'Do you like a special one?'

'Kind of,' I said.

'Does she know?' he asked.

'No.'

'Maybe you'd feel better if you told her.'

I could just see myself telling Lisa that! I shook my head at Dr Holland.

He gave me a small laugh. 'Well, you'll be just fine, Tony. There's no real problem here.' He stood up and patted me on the back. Then he opened the door to his waiting room and called in my mother. I read a magazine while she talked to the doctor.

Everybody was nice to me at home that day – even Maxine. She made my favourite kind of chicken for supper. While we were eating it my mother told us that the stores were decorated for Christmas already. And that since this was to be our first Rosemont Christmas she wanted it to be extra special.

'Make me a list of what you want, Tony,' my mother said.

'I thought I was supposed to mail that list to Santa,' I said.

My mother laughed. 'Listen to him!' Then she said, 'Not so many years ago you did write to Santa!'

'I'll tell you one thing,' my father said. 'This is going to be the first Christmas I've ever had where I don't have to worry about the bills. This year we can afford to splurge!'

'I really don't know what I want,' I said. 'But I'll think about it.'

Later I took my pill and got ready for bed. I kneeled in front of my window until ten o'clock but Lisa's room stayed dark. When I got into bed I thought, if I had binoculars I could see her really good – up close – her face and everything. I knew what to put on my Christmas list.

That night I dreamed about Lisa. My dream went on and on. It started out at the football game where Lisa put her arm around me. Only in my dream she didn't stop there. And Corky was in it too. She was sitting on the football field and Lisa kept saying, 'You see, Corky ... here's what to do ... to do ... to do ...'

I woke up suddenly. It was morning. I felt wet and my pyjamas were sticky. Oh God! There is something wrong with me. *Really wrong.* Dr Holland doesn't know what he's talking about! I am *so* sick. This proves it.

Wait a minute. Wait just a minute. Maybe I had a wet dream. Yeah ... I'll bet that's it. How about that? I thought they'd be different though. I thought a lot more stuff would come out. And anyway, I wasn't sure I'd ever have one. At least not yet.

What am I supposed to do? Maybe I should stay in bed all day. But then my mother might call the doctor and he'd probably tell her the truth. I better get up. But what about my pyjamas? I guess the first thing to do is get undressed. Okay ... I will.

I threw my pyjamas into the hamper in my bathroom. I soaked a washcloth and threw that in too. Then I mixed up all the dirty clothes so everything would feel damp, not just my pyjamas.

When I went back into my room I sat down on my bed. There was a spot on my sheet. I touched it. It was damp! Oh no – does that stuff stain? I grabbed some tissues and wiped it up.

Will Maxine know? I suppose I could change my sheet ... but that would look worse, wouldn't it? Then she might think I wet my bed like a little kid. No ... leave the sheet on and check it first thing after school to make sure nothing shows up.

I had an awful day. I couldn't concentrate on my school work and I got yelled at in English class for not paying attention. How could I pay attention? I kept thinking that when I get home the whole family's going to be there. Mom and Pop, Grandma, Ralph and Angie, Vicki, Maxine, even cousin Ginger! They'll all know about me. Maxine will show them the sheet and my mother will say, 'I don't buy the best sheets for you to mess up, Anthony!'

I'll say, 'It was an accident Mom ... a mistake ... it won't happen again.'

And Ralph will say, 'If you hadn't been thinking about that girl this never would have happened.'

Then Pop will say, 'I expected great things from you, Tony ... and this is what I get!'

After school I rushed home. Nobody was waiting for me. My mother wasn't even home. What a relief! I ran up to my room, closed the door behind me and pulled down my bedspread and blanket. The sheets were changed! There were striped ones on my bed this morning and now they were plain blue. Does that mean Maxine knows? Did she tell my mother? Or ... wait a minute ... is this the day the sheets get changed every week? I can't remember! I don't think I'll ever be able to look at Maxine again.

Then Again, Maybe I Won't

Finally, I handed my mother my Christmas list. That night, after supper, I heard her tell my father, 'Tony wants binoculars.'

'Binoculars?' Pop asked.

'That's what it says here.' My mother waved my list at him. 'It's the only thing he's asked for.'

'What's he going to do with binoculars?' my father asked.

All this time I was sitting on the floor leaning up against

a chair, reading a book about Wilt the Stilt. Did they think I couldn't hear or what? I didn't look up from my book. I pretended to be absorbed in my reading.

'Tony ...' my mother said. 'What are you going to do with binoculars?'

I didn't answer.

My mother repeated her question. 'I said what are you going to do with binoculars?'

This time I looked at her. 'What? Oh, binoculars ...' I had my answer carefully planned. I knew they'd ask why I wanted them, but I had to be really casual about it or they might get suspicious. 'Watch birds,' I said.

'Birds?' my mother asked.

'Yes,' I told her. 'This spring. I want to find out all I can about birds.'

My mother smiled. 'It all goes to show,' she told my father, 'if you take a boy out of the city and put him close to nature he'll become a better person.'

I wouldn't exactly say Rosemont is close to nature but I didn't argue with my mother. I knew I'd be getting my binoculars.

I had another dream about Lisa. This time I was hiding in her closet while she was getting ready for bed. When I came out she didn't scream. She was glad to see me, like she knew I was there all along. Corky was in this dream too. She was dressed up like a cheerleader and all through the best part of the dream Corky jumped around and shouted cheers.

The next night when I started upstairs to do my homework my mother said, 'Vic ... go on up with him.'

Now why did she say that? Why does she want him to come upstairs with me? That means something. Maybe they know about me. Maybe I talk in my sleep!

My father followed me up the stairs. When we got to the top he said, 'Tony ... I'd like to have a talk with you. Just for a minute ... okay?'

I looked down. My mother was standing at the bottom of the stairs, smiling. 'Sure Pop,' I mumbled.

'In private, Tony,' my father said. 'In your room.'

We walked to my room and when we were both inside Pop closed the door.

He knows! I'm sure he knows about me. I always knew he could read my mind. This proves it. Wait a minute ... maybe it's just going to be a talk about how I'm doing in school. Or what I want to be or something easy like that. I hope so. I really do. 'Did I do something wrong, Pop?' I asked.

'No, no,' Pop said. 'Nothing like that. I just thought we'd have a little talk. You know ... kind of man to man.'

Oh-oh ... here it comes! I was right the first time. What'll I say? Nothing. I won't say a word. I'll let him say it. I sat down on my bed. Pop pulled my desk chair over and sat close to me. He looked around for a while, rubbing his hands together, almost like he was praying.

'Uh Tony ...' he finally said.

'Yes, Pop?'

'Uh ... well ... now that you're in seventh grade there are things you should know about.' While he was talking Pop cracked each of his knuckles.

'Yes, Pop?'

'Oh ... I don't know ... maybe Ralph should be the one to talk to you. He's a lot closer to your age.' Pop stopped talking and looked around my room. Then he coughed a little and started again. 'You see Tony ... there are things you should know about girls and about babies and about ... look Tony, do you know anything?'

He doesn't know about my dreams, I thought. This has nothing to do with what I've been thinking about. He really doesn't know. He's more scared than I am.

'Tony ... I asked you, do you know anything?'

'Sure Pop,' I said.

'You do? You know about babies ... how they're made?'

'Sure Pop. Since third grade.'

My father looked like he couldn't believe it. 'Since third grade?'

'Sure Pop. Big Joe told me all about it.'

'You're positive you have the right information?'

'Sure Pop.'

'Do you know other things too, Tony?'

'Sure Pop. A lot.'

My father looked relieved. 'Well,' he said, 'the important thing to remember is that I'm here to answer all your questions.'

'Okay Pop. I'll remember.'

He rubbed his hands again. 'I don't know. Tony ... I feel like I should say more. Your mother thinks there's a lot for you to learn, but I don't know what to tell you. I never told Vinnie or Ralph anything. I don't even know how Vinnie learned. From his friends I guess. And Vinnie told Ralph. So I'm not too experienced when it comes to discussing the subject. But listen Tony ... man to man ... you can always come to me.'

'Okay Pop.' I got up and stretched. My father stood up and put his arm around me.

'Hey Tony ... how about a quick game of chess?'

'Okay Pop ... I guess I can do my homework later.'

When we were downstairs my mother gave Pop a look that said, *Well?* And he gave her one back that said, *Everything's taken care of.*

The next day my father handed me a book called *Basic Facts About Sex.* He said I should read it in my spare time and if I have any questions I should come to him. There's a whole section on wet dreams and another on masturbation. Maybe they do know about me after all! My stomach jumped around so bad I had to take a pill.

We got ready for our first Christmas in Rosemont. First we bought a live tree. Not a little one – a big floor-to-ceiling

182

one. We bought it at the high school field, where the Boy
Scouts hold their annual sale. I've always wanted a real
Christmas tree. In Jersey City we had a little white one that
sat on top of the corner table. It looked nice but it didn't have
that great smell. Frankie's family had a live tree every year
and sometimes I used to just sit in his living room and sniff
it for an hour.

My mother bought a million tree ornaments at
Bloomingdale's, including tinsel so wide we had to wrap
it around the tree instead of just hanging it from branches.

My father, being an ex-electrician, lit up the outside of our
house with a lot of tiny bulbs in the bushes. They twinkle on
and off. He set up spotlights to show off our front door too.

Maxine was in charge of the door. She covered it with gold
foil to match the twinkles. Over the foil is a huge wreath.
I have to admit, the house looks good.

My mother tried to get Grandma to come downstairs to
see our tree. Once a week Mom insists she leave her room so
Maxine can clean it and air it out. But instead of coming
downstairs for an hour, Grandma locked herself up in my
bathroom.

I told my mother, 'Grandma's not looking so good.'

And my mother said, 'How can she look good when she
never gets fresh air?'

So I said, 'Maybe she'd get some fresh air if you'd let her
go back to doing the cooking.'

'How would that look to the neighbours?' my mother
asked, 'like she's the maid or something!'

And I said, 'Who cares about the neighbours!'

'Grandma's worked hard all her life,' my mother said.
'Now it's time for her to take it easy and enjoy herself.'

'She doesn't act like she's enjoying it,' I argued.

'Of course she is! Doesn't she love that colour TV?'

'How do I know?' I said.

'Well, she watches it all day doesn't she?' My mother bent
over to pick a piece of lint off the carpet.

'That doesn't mean she likes it,' I said. 'She just hasn't got anything better to do.'

'What do you want her to do, Anthony? Play golf with Diane Hoober!'

Oh-oh. She was getting mad now. But so was I. I shouted, 'Maybe I want her to cook!'

'That's enough, Anthony!' my mother said. 'Maxine will hear you and get insulted.'

'Maxine is a lousy cook,' I mumbled. That isn't true but I felt like saying it. I was taking Dr Holland's advice – about when you feel like saying something, say it!

'Watch your mouth, Anthony!' my mother said very low, making each word sink in. 'It's growing faster than the rest of you.'

Joel asked me to go Christmas shopping with him. I told him okay, because I have a lot of allowance saved up and I want to buy something nice for everybody in our family. Now I'm sorry I said I'd go with him. Suppose he steals something?

I feel like calling him to say, 'Forget it, I can't go.' But then he'll want to know why and what will I say?

When Joel called for me I was in the bathroom. My stomach hurt. But in a little while the pain went away and we went downtown together. Once we got to the store I followed Joel around like a detective.

Every time he put his hands in his pockets I was there to make sure he hadn't taken anything. Once we were loaded down with shopping bags I really had a hard time. I paid more attention to Joel than to my shopping list. I was surprised to see that he paid for everything. Maybe Joel never really stole those batteries. Maybe it was all my imagination. It could have been a mistake! But what about the apples at lunch? He steals one every day and that's not my imagination.

I helped Joel pick out his present for Lisa. We decided on this stretch sweater that the saleslady said fits like a second skin. Joel chose the colour – green. I liked the orange one better.

The day before Christmas a piano arrived at our house. A baby grand. Six men delivered it. It was my father's gift to the whole family, but my mother had gone along with him to pick it out, so I was really the only one surprised.

When it was all set up in front of the living room windows my mother got tears in her eyes and said, 'It's absolutely gorgeous! I've always wanted a piano. Oh Vic . . . I'm so happy!' With that she threw her arms around my father's neck and kissed him. I don't like them to act that way in front of me.

'Do you like it, Tony?' my father asked, untangling himself from my mother.

'It's really neat,' I said. 'But nobody here plays the piano.'

'Not yet,' my mother said, putting an arm around my shoulder.

I knew what was coming. Piano lessons for me. Sometimes I wish we didn't have so much money. How can I tell them I don't want piano lessons? How can I tell them I can't even clap my hands in time to music. I don't even sing in the shower – I'm *that* bad!

On Christmas morning we waited for Ralph, Angie and Vicki to arrive before we opened anything. Here's what I got: Two V-neck cashmere sweaters – the kind Joel wears – one from my parents and the other from Angie and Ralph, a set of encyclopedias and *super deluxe* extra powerful binoculars! The card said:

For our son the bird watcher . . .
with all our love
Mom and Pop

We gathered upstairs in Grandma's room to watch her open her presents. She got a robe and slippers from my mother and father – a robe and slippers from Ralph and Angie – and a silver toothbrush from me. I bought it in the department they call 'For the Woman Who Has everything.' Grandma doesn't have everything of course, but at least this was something different. The only time she smiled was when she opened the silver toothbrush. So I was glad I gave it to her.

That night I kneeled by my window and waited. Lisa's lights were on and her shades were up as usual. I don't think she ever bothers pulling them down. Finally she came into her room. My hands were really shaking. I couldn't even hold my binoculars steady. The view was great. Just great! It was like she was standing right in front of me. I could even see the expression on her face. She was smiling. She has a terrific smile. The first thing she did was try on the green stretch sweater. She turned around and around in front of her mirror. She doesn't have to worry. She's beautiful from every angle. I wanted to tell her that. I watched until her lights went out. I love her, I think.

The next day Mrs Hoober rang our bell and I thought, she knows! She knows I've got binoculars and that I watched Lisa last night. She's going to tell my parents and they'll take away my binoculars and tell me I've got a dirty mind. They'll move me to another bedroom so I can't see her any more. Maybe I'll even have to spend six weeks in the Juvenile Detention Center. If I do, I hope Lisa will come on visiting day.

But I was all wrong. Mrs Hoober only wanted to give us some candies from England and wish us a Merry Christmas. When she left she called to my mother.

'Don't forget, lunch at the club in two weeks ... Friday. See you then, Carol.'

'Carol! Who's Carol?' I asked when Mrs Hoober was gone.

My mother laughed. 'Oh, that's what Diane calls me. She says Carmella's too hard to remember.'

'Just like Millicent! Just like their maid!'

'What's the difference, Tony?'

'Your name is not Carol!' I yelled. My mother just stared at me. 'Why don't you tell her if she can't remember your name then you don't want to be her friend!'

I wanted my mother to yell back at me, but she didn't. She turned to my father and spoke very slow. 'I don't know,' she said. 'You raise them with kid gloves and then they walk all over you. What's the point?' She repeated 'What's the point?' over and over as she left the room.

I ran upstairs and locked myself into the bathroom. I knew I'd get sick now. And it would be my mother's fault. She'd be sorry!

In a few minutes my father knocked on the door and called, 'You all right, Tony?'

'I'm okay,' I muttered.

'I'd like to talk to you.'

'I have nothing to say.'

'Come on, Tony ... open up the door.'

I unlocked it and said, 'It's open.' Then I turned on the water and splashed my face. When I was through my father handed me a towel.

'A name's not so important, Tony,' my father said. 'What's inside you is what counts. But not a name. It's just like Tony instead of Anthony. What's the difference if Mrs Hoober wants to call your mother Carol and she doesn't mind? It's not going to change her. You hurt her, Tony. She's very upset about you.'

'I'm sorry,' I said. I felt like I did on Veterans Day when I stood over Vinnie's grave ... guilty!

The next week I started my piano lessons. The teacher is Miss Orenberg and she comes to the house every Thursday from four till quarter to five. She has bad breath, which I reported to my mother after the first lesson.

'Maybe she ate something she shouldn't have,' my mother said. 'Diane Hoober says she's an excellent teacher. Lisa took lessons from her for years.'

But Miss Orenberg smelled the same the following week. When I told my mother she said she'd see what she could do. After that my mother greeted Miss Orenberg at the door with Chlorophyll candies. 'Take one,' she'd say. 'It'll refresh you for Tony's lesson.'

After the fourth lesson Miss Orenberg asked me did I practise much. I told her about fifteen minutes a day. Miss Orenberg said she found that hard to believe. And I told her if she didn't believe me she could ask my mother because it was true. Then she said I wasn't progressing as fast as she had hoped I would. And I said that was because I wasn't musically inclined and I really didn't want piano lessons in the first place. I wanted to add that I didn't like her, or her breath or the way she talked, but I didn't.

That night I told my mother that I was never going to learn to play the piano and there was nothing she could do about it and that if she made me take any more lessons my pains were going to get worse! And why didn't she ask Dr Holland if it was good for me to have to take piano lessons when I didn't want to at all!

The next day Pop said, 'Tony ... your mother and I have decided that if you don't want to take piano lessons you don't have to.'

'Really?' I asked. 'You really mean it?' I looked at my mother. She didn't answer me but she nodded her head a little.

Pop said, 'We're not going to force you to do something you hate. I just wish you'd remember that we only want you to have every opportunity we couldn't give your brothers.'

I wanted to say to let me alone and stop trying to shove everything that Ralph and Vinnie didn't have down my throat! But I couldn't say it because that would have hurt their feelings and they weren't trying to be mean. But sometimes they're so full of bull they make me sick.

Then Again, Maybe I Won't

My parents joined the Newcomers Club at church. They went to a couple of parties and said they met a lot of nice people. But they still haven't been invited to the Hoobers' house and I think my mother would rather go there than all the other places put together.

Father Pissaro the Second visits Grandma every week. I go to confession once a month, same as in Jersey City. I've thought a lot about what to confess. For a while I thought I should tell him about Lisa. But I decided that watching her at night isn't really a sin. As long as it doesn't hurt anyone what's so wrong about it?

There are a couple of things I'd like to talk over with somebody. Not with Joel though and not with Marty Endo or Scott Gold either. Whenever we have a discussion it always turns into a big joke. Maybe if we still lived in Jersey City I'd ask Ralph. But I'm not sure about that either. He acts so old lately. My father said to ask *him* if I have questions but I know he's hoping I never have any. I'm thinking about going to Ted Gibbons ... to ask him if he ever had dreams like me and then find out what he did about them.

Ted is really proud of our Youth Group. And especially our basketball team. We've only lost one game so far and even though he tells us he doesn't care who wins, because it's how you play the game that counts, I can tell he's pleased.

This coming Friday night we're playing the First Methodist Youth Group. They're the only other team in the league that's lost just one game. Ted said he's going to bring a date to this game – some girl he really likes a lot.

I'm getting used to Corky. She doesn't bother me the way she used to. She still spends a lot of time giggling but she's turned into a pretty good cheerleader. She doesn't look anything like Lisa but she sure can yell loud! For a while she tried to sit next to me in church every Sunday but now I make sure I'm between my mother and my father so she leaves me alone.

On Friday night my father and Ralph came to see the big game. My team got to start. I was really in good form. I scored six points in foul shots alone. At the end of the first half we were leading by two points. The Methodist guys were pretty good.

In the second half Marty Endo's team took over and we dropped two points behind. Three minutes before the end of the game Marty tripped on his shoelace and fell flat on his face. Time out was called and we all ran onto the court. Marty was out cold. His mother and father were at the game and they came flying down from the stand. His mother got really upset when she saw him stretched out on the floor and she started to cry, 'Oh my God ... oh my God!' It's a good thing Marty didn't hear her – he'd have been furious!

When Marty came to he didn't know what had happened. But when he tried to stand up he said he felt dizzy and nauseous and he had a big bump on his head. Ted said it could be a concussion so Mr and Mrs Endo decided to take Marty straight to the hospital.

With only three minutes left to play and our team down two points Ted called me. 'Go on in, Tony. Do your stuff.'

Corky squealed when she saw me running in and started cheering like crazy. I didn't even have a chance to get nervous. Because I wasn't on the court for twenty seconds when this big guy from First Methodist gave me an elbow in the stomach. The referee blew his whistle and called a personal foul.

It was very quiet. Everybody was watching me. I thought about Ted and about Marty and how much we'd all like to win this game. Then I aimed and threw the ball, nice and easy, the way Ted said to do it when you're under pressure. Right in the basket! The crowd started yelling and some of the guys patted me on the backside. We were only one point behind.

First Methodist had the ball. They were stalling, passing

it back and forth, when Gregg Kusiv jumped up and intercepted. Now it was our ball. When we got within shooting distance of our basket Gregg passed the ball to me. I dribbled around but I couldn't shoot – I was being guarded by the biggest guy on their team. I wanted to make a basket so bad! I wanted to be the big hero! But I had no chance – so I passed it to Jim Quinn and he put it in just as the whistle blew to end the game.

WE WON! WE WON! Our whole Youth Group ran onto the court and we all jumped around and hugged each other. When Ted stepped out Corky led us in a cheer just for him. Then I saw this blonde girl come rushing at Ted. She threw her arms around him and gave him a big kiss and we all stopped cheering to watch Ted and his girlfriend and that's when it hit me. The girl was Lisa! My Lisa, standing there kissing Ted ... right in public ... for everyone to see. Ted and his moustache! It wasn't fair. She should have been kissing me! I'm the one who won the game. Well, I did ... didn't I? Who knows what would have happened if Marty hadn't tripped over his shoelace and knocked himself out. *Who knows?*

While I was thinking about that Corky asked me to go out for ice cream with her and some other kids from our Youth Group. But all of a sudden I didn't feel like celebrating anything. So I told her, 'Some other time maybe.'

And she said, 'Oh Tony!' and I knew she was really disappointed but I didn't care much.

I went home with my father and Ralph and even though they kept saying how great I played I didn't want to hear it.

I called up Mrs Endo to see how Marty was and she said he was very groggy but that the doctor promised he'd be okay in two days. I said I was glad to hear that. Then I told my family how tired I was from the big game and I went up to my room and fell asleep.

I tried not to think about Lisa. I didn't feel like having any dreams. I just wanted to sleep and forget about everything.

But I dreamed about her and Ted and the things they probably do when they're alone and I knew I'd never ask Ted any of the questions I was thinking about asking him.

Towards the end of February Frankie Bollino called. I couldn't believe it at first.

'Hey Frankie! Is it really you?' I asked.

'None other,' Frankie said.

I asked him about my old paper route, which he reported was doing fine – about the old basketball game, which they were still playing – about junior high, which he said wasn't so bad – and about the weather, which was dumb because it was the same as in Rosemont, except we get more snow than Jersey City.

After that I didn't have anything else to say but Frankie did. 'Why don't you come back to see us some time?'

I said, 'Why don't you come see me?'

Then we both laughed until Frankie said, 'Okay. When?'

'When what?' I asked.

'When should I come see you?'

I said, 'Are you serious?'

He said, 'Sure.'

I said, 'Hey, that's great! Why don't you come on Saturday and stay overnight?'

He said, 'Swell.'

'Wait a second while I tell my parents,' I said. I put down the phone and ran into the other room.

'Guess who's on the phone?' I asked my mother and father. 'It's Frankie Bollino! I invited him to stay overnight this Saturday.'

My father said, 'I'll pick him up in New York ... at the station. That'll save him a train ride out here.'

'Thanks, Pop,' I called, already on my way back to the phone. I picked up the receiver and said, 'Hey Frankie ... it's all arranged. My father'll pick you up at the station in New York, Saturday.'

'What time?' Frankie asked.

'Oh ... whatever time you say.'

'How about eight?'

'In the morning?'

'Too early?' Frankie asked.

'Yeah ... better make it around ten.'

'Okay Tony. See you then.'

'Right,' I said and hung up.

I really felt good. I wondered why I haven't thought about calling Frankie. I'm sure glad he called me. I went into the living room. 'How about that?' I said. 'Good old Frankie Bollino.'

'You've got plenty of friends in Rosemont,' my mother said. 'I don't see why you have to start up with him.'

'What's that supposed to mean?' I asked.

'I've got nothing against Frankie,' she said. 'It's just that Jersey City is a long way off and you can't see each other very often so you might as well concentrate on your new friends.'

But my father said, 'There's no friend like an old friend! Right, Tony?'

To be honest I have to admit that I hardly ever think about Frankie and the other guys anymore. I don't really miss them. Still, I'm looking forward to Frankie's visit.

I rode into the city with my father on Saturday morning. Frankie was already there, waiting at the station. He was carrying an airline bag. He recognized our car right away and ran straight over. 'Hey, old pal!' he hollered.

'Hey Frankie!'

We sat in the back on the way home to Rosemont and when my father pulled into our driveway, Frankie let out a low whistle and said, 'Wow! You sure have come a long way!'

'Never mind the house,' I said, embarrassed. 'Come on in.'

My mother was waiting for us. 'Hello Frank.'

Frank dropped his airline bag on the floor and said, 'Hiya

Mrs Miglione.' He kept looking around at the house saying 'Wow!' and shaking his head.

'Well, it's nice to see you, Frank,' my mother said. I knew what she was thinking. That he didn't shake hands like certain other persons we know.

'My mother says to tell you she sends regards and when are you coming back to Jersey City for a visit,' Frankie said.

'Oh, well ... I've been busy,' my mother said. 'You know Ralph and Angie had a baby ... and I've been helping out.'

'This is some place!' Frankie said.

'Come on ... cut it out, will you!' I said, giving Frankie an elbow in the ribs. 'It's just a house.'

Later I asked him how Mrs Gorsky was and he told me she says I was the best paper boy she ever had. And that she misses me a lot.

'That's crazy!' I told Frankie. 'She hated me.'

'Well, now she hates *me*,' Frankie said. 'Say ... where's your grandmother? Doesn't she live with you anymore?'

'Oh sure,' I said. 'But she stays in her room most of the time. She ... she doesn't feel too well.' I don't think I'll ever tell anyone the truth about Grandma. I'm too ashamed.

Maxine made my favourite chicken for supper. Did she give me a special look when she served it? I'm not sure. I try to stay out of her way these days. I always bend my head when she comes into the dining room so she can't look me in the eye. I can't tell if she knows about me or not. My sheets don't get changed every time I have a dream but it seems to me Maxine smiles a lot more than she used to – and always when I'm around.

'*Wow!*' Frankie said. 'This is just great food, Mrs Miglione.'

'Thank you, Frank. We'll have to tell Maxine how much you enjoyed it. She does all the cooking.'

'You know,' Frank said for about the millionth time, 'this is really some place you have here.' He drank half a glass of milk. 'My mother said I should be sure to notice all the little things so I can tell her all about it.'

After supper Joel called and invited me and Frankie over. My father announced that he and my mother were going to a movie and that we could come along if we wanted to.

'What are you going to see?' I asked.

'*The Last Stranger*,' my mother said.

'What's it about?' I asked.

'Love.'

I looked at Frankie. 'No thanks,' I said. 'We'll go to Joel's.'

I think Frankie was even more impressed with Joel's house than mine. It's bigger and of course there are spotlights to show off the pool in the backyard.

Frankie couldn't believe the Hoobers' bedroom. He said, 'Wait till I tell my mother about this!'

I thought maybe I'd be able to see Lisa, but she was already out on a date. She goes out just about every Saturday night and sometimes on Fridays too. I know because I waited up for her once or twice but she's been coming in later and later. And she doesn't go out only with Ted. I can tell by the different cars that pick her up. Now I only get to see her four or five times a week.

We went into Joel's room where he showed Frankie his paperback collection. Frankie said it's even better than Big Joe's.

After that Joel asked, 'You guys want some beer?'

'What ... are you kidding!' I said.

'No, I mean it. Didn't you ever drink beer?' Joel said.

'You know I didn't,' I told him.

Frankie said, 'Me neither. But I'll try it ... if Tony does too.'

So we followed Joel down to the recreation room where there's a really fancy bar with barstools and everything. We started with one can. Joel had some first, then passed it to me. I choked and passed it to Frankie. We had another can when we polished off that one and then Joel asked us did we want to taste something even better.

Frankie said anything would be better than that. So Joel got out four bottles and lined them up on top of the bar. Scotch, rye, vodka and brandy. He said we'd have to drink from the bottles because if we messed up any glasses his father would know we'd been fooling around.

We started with the scotch, which burned my throat. Then the vodka, which Joel said has no taste at all and should be gulped because it would make us feel good really fast. Then the rye, which burned my throat some more. After that Joel passed around the brandy because he said that was for after dinner.

That's when Frankie fell off the barstool and started to laugh. Wow! I never heard such a crazy laugh. I mean, he just stretched out on the floor and laughed like a nut!

'Who's your friend?' Joel asked me.

'I dunno. I never saw him,' I said. It was hard to get the words out.

'Me neither. Mussbe some drunk!'

'Yeah. Mussbe.' I got off my barstool and sat down on the floor next to Frankie. 'Hey Misser ... you some drunk or what?'

Frankie just laughed, so I started laughing too. But when I lay down on the floor the whole room started spinning – around and around and around. I couldn't make it stop for anything.

'Hey Joel ... the room's going round. Commere and see.'

So Joel stretched out next to us and he said, 'Yeah ... sure is. All aroun ... all aroun and aroun and aroun ... like a merry-go-roun.'

'I tole you,' I said. 'Din I tell you? Whole room's goin roun!'

'Yeah,' Joel said. 'You tole me. Know what?'

'What?' I said.

'I don feel so good.'

'Me neither.'

'Les go outside ... get some air.'

196

Since Frankie was still laughing me and Joel had to lift him up and drag him over to the back door. We went outside with no coats or anything.

'Oh nice.' Joel said. 'Thas so nice.'

'Real nice,' I said. 'Good clean air.'

'Know what?' Frankie said. 'Is cold out here.'

'Yeah,' I said. 'Nice cold clean air.'

'Know what?' Joel said. 'I think I'm gonna be sick.'

'No kiddin?' I said. 'Me too.'

'Les be sick together,' Joel said.

'Sure, les be sick in the bushes,' I said.

Joel said, 'Yeah. The bushes is a good place to be sick. Is good for the bushes ... like fertilizer.'

All three of us were sick together. When we finished I grabbed Frankie and pulled him home by the sleeve. Was it cold out!

When we got to the front of my house Frankie said, 'Wait one more minute, Tony.'

I was freezing and feeling pretty bad besides. 'What now?' I groaned.

Frankie laughed and said, 'I'm gonna fertilize your bushes too.'

Well, we made it into bed and we weren't sick again but the next morning I told Frankie he looked green and he told me that if I thought *he* looked green I should just see me. So we staggered to the mirror together and discovered we were both kind of green. Only it didn't feel as funny as it sounded. Besides my colour, my head felt like six hammers were trying to split it open at once.

Since it was Maxine's day off nobody bothered us about getting up and having breakfast. We finally managed to get dressed around noon. Then we had to sneak next door for our jackets.

Frankie left late in the afternoon after telling me and my parents what a great time he'd had. Privately he told me what a terrific town Rosemont was and he sure wished his father could strike it rich too.

At the front door my mother took a good look at us and said, 'You sure you're all right, Frank?'

Frankie said, 'Sure thing, Mrs Miglione.'

'I don't know,' she said, shaking her head. 'You both look like you're coming down with something.'

The following Saturday I had to put on my best sports jacket and tie because me and my father were going to lunch with J. W. Fullerbach. I hate ties. They choke me. I have trouble swallowing my food when I'm wearing one.

Why do I have to waste a sunny Saturday anyway? Why can't I stay home and loaf around – or play ball – or even go to a movie? Because J. W. Fullerbach wants to meet me, Pop says. Why should *he* want to meet *me*? I can't figure it out.

When I was all ready my mother inspected me. She even looked inside my ears and checked my fingernails about twenty times. I offered to take off my shoes and socks so she could look at my toenails too but she didn't think that was very funny.

'You'll remember to shake hands and say *sir*!' she reminded me.

'How could I forget that?' I asked.

We drove into the city and met Mr Fullerbach at his club. I expected him to be very big, with silver hair and powerful hands. But he turned out to be short and pudgy. My father is much taller and looks more like J. W. Fullerbach as I'd imagined him than J. W. Fullerbach really looks himself. Besides being three-quarters bald, Mr Fullerbach has a twitch in his right eye. I tried to hide my surprise at his appearance. I shook hands and said, 'I'm very happy to meet you, *sir*,' in best Rosemont style.

'So this is the youngest Miglione! Right, Vic?'

'That's him, J. W.' my father said.

'Well, Tony,' Mr Fullerbach said. 'Your father's a very smart man. But you know that, don't you?' He put an arm around my father's shoulder. 'Did you know since your father sold me the rights to his electrical cartridges we've moved up seventeen points on the market?'

I smiled.

'What do you think of that, Tony?' Mr Fullerbach asked.

'It's very good,' I said, 'sir.'

'Yes, it's good all right!' Mr Fullerbach laughed. 'Right, Vic?'

'Right, J.W.'

When we sat down to lunch I didn't know what to order because the menu was all in French. But Mr Fullerbach told the waiter to bring three steaks medium rare, so I didn't have to worry. If you ask me my father was just as relieved as I was.

Mr Fullerbach attacked his food. He washed every mouthful down with water. His glass was refilled four times just during the steak. We had vanilla ice cream for dessert. Mr Fullerbach didn't ask us if we wanted it, he just ordered. I'd have preferred chocolate chip mint, but I ate my vanilla. Mr Fullerbach reached over and patted my hand. 'Some day, Tony ... some day I hope you'll join the company too. After college of course.'

'Of course,' I said, 'sir.'

'Yes, that will be nice. You'll join us just like your brother Ralph.' He waved his spoon at me. 'I haven't got any sons of my own you know.'

Ralph! I thought. What's he talking about? What does he mean about Ralph joining the company? That's crazy! I couldn't wait for lunch to be over. I wanted to be alone with my father. I wouldn't dare come right out and ask about Ralph in front of Mr Fullerbach. But after lunch they each smoked a whole cigar and had two brandies. I couldn't even look at the brandy. Just the smell was enough to remind me of last week and Joel's party. I excused myself and went to the men's room.

Finally Mr Fullerbach said goodbye and we thanked him for the delicious lunch and at last I was alone with my father on the expressway back to Rosemont.

'What did he mean about Ralph?' I asked.

'Ralph is going into the business.'

'How can he do that? He's a teacher! What about his job?'

'Oh, he'll finish out the school year and start over the summer.' My father never took his eyes off the road.

Why? *Why?* I wanted to scream. Ralph isn't even scientific. Everybody knows that! I wanted to grab the steering wheel and pull up the emergency brake and stop the car with a huge jerk. I wanted to yell at my father, *Go ahead and tell me the truth. Ralph's selling out.* SAY IT ... SAY IT!

I managed to avoid Ralph for a month. I said I was too busy to go to Queens on Sundays – I had homework to do. When I heard Ralph was going to drop over I'd drop out – to the library, to Joel's, to the movies.

Then I found out Ralph and Angie were looking for a house in Rosemont – that the apartment in Queens was getting crowded – that Vicki needed a room of her own. I knew I wasn't going to be able to get away with pretending my brother didn't exist. The next time he came over I decided to stay home.

'Hi Kid,' Ralph said, trying to box me. 'Long-time-no-see!'

'I've been busy,' I said, stepping away from him.

'Did you hear we're looking for a house?' Ralph asked, picking up Vicki and holding her up to the ceiling.

'I heard.'

'Did you hear I'm going in with Pop?' Now he shook Vicki up and down trying to make her laugh.

'I heard.' Vicki didn't laugh. She started to cry.

'Well, Kid ... you don't sound very glad.' Ralph put
Vickie back in her infant seat. 'You'll be able to see us every
day if you want to ... like the old days!'

Who cares? I wanted to yell. Who cares about seeing you
every day! I felt like grabbing Ralph and shaking him. I
wanted to ask him where was The Wizard. To yell, Hey
Ralph ... you stink! You're a sellout. You've gone soft – just
like Mom – just like Pop – just like Angie!

Instead I said, 'Excuse me please.' And I ran upstairs to
the bathroom.

I had awful pains.

On my way up the stairs I heard Ralph ask, 'What's with
the Kid?'

A year ago he wouldn't have had to ask. He'd have known!

In the bathroom I considered leaving Rosemont to make
my own way in the world. I could probably go to Jersey
City and get my paper route back. But that was dumb! I'd
never do it. It was just a thought. Anyway, I don't want to
live in Jersey City again.

When I calmed down enough to unlock the bathroom
door I went down the hall to Grandma's room. I haven't
been in there for at least two weeks. Sometimes I forget she
even lives with us. I stood there for a while, thinking that
me and Grandma have a lot in common. We're both outsiders
in our own home.

I knocked on the door and called, 'Grandma.' When
Grandma opened it and saw me she turned off her TV. Then
she sat down in her chair and held her hands out to me. I
went to her. I started to cry. I kneeled down and buried my
head in her lap. She stroked my hair. For a minute I felt
like a little kid again. Grandma used to hold me like that
when I fell down or when I was scared.

Then Again, Maybe I Won't

It didn't snow once in March. I was hoping it would. Joel got a toboggan for his birthday and he said the next time it snows we can try it out at the country club. Their golf course has plenty of hills. Now it looks like we'll have to wait until next year.

I keep remembering last March and all that rain. My mother sent my winter jacket to the cleaner early this year. She got me something new called an in-between coat to wear instead.

After school me and Joel, Marty Endo and Scott Gold started hanging out at The Bon Sweete Shop. If the weather is too bad for bikes we can walk. We always sit at the same table and always have the same waitress. She has this wild red hair and she chews gum. Her name is Bernice. She doesn't like us – you can tell. But she has to wait on us just the same. She stands there with her hands on her hips, cracking her gum and asks, 'What you kids gonna put away today?'

Usually we have milkshakes. Sometimes Marty Endo has a hamburger *and* a milkshake. He has this thing about hamburgers. I mean, he really loves them! First he smells the meat. Then when he's done smelling it he eats it, making these little noises the whole time. He calls them his happy noises.

One reason Bernice doesn't like us is we're sloppy. Somebody always spills something on the floor. The other reason is the tip. Joel thought up this idea of leaving Bernice's tip in the bottom of a milkshake glass. Every day we put it in a different glass, so she has to hunt for it. One day we didn't have any change except pennies. So we chipped in ten pennies apiece and put them in the bottom of Joel's chocolate milkshake glass which wasn't quite empty. Bernice really hollered when she saw it. By that time we were paying the cashier and getting ready to leave.

Bernice ran over to us and grabbed me by the collar. She's pretty big and I had to look way up to see her face.

'You lousy little kids! I oughta tan your hides! I oughta ...'

'Get your hands off my friend!' Joel said. 'Or I'll call the manager.' He sounded like he meant it – no fooling around.

Bernice growled, 'You'd like that wouldn't you! You'd like to see me get fired! What do you little rich kids know about earning a living? You think it's funny to make me fish around for a few lousy pennies? Well, let me tell you something. I *need* that money. And there's no place you can stick it that I won't reach in to get it! Your crummy forty pennies buys me a loaf of bread. Did you ever think of that!'

All this time Bernice still had me by the collar and I thought I was going to strangle. But as soon as she finished her speech she let me go. We got out of The Bon Sweete Shop in a hurry.

After that we never sat at a table in Bernice's section and we left our tip on the table – not in a milkshake glass. None of us ever mentioned the incident, but I know I thought about Bernice buying that bread with our pennies for a long time.

One afternoon I needed some notebook paper so I stopped into the corner store next to The Bon Sweete Shop. Joel was with me. I decided as long as I was in the store I needed a new ballpoint pen too. My old one leaks on my fingers and smudges a lot. The pens were displayed in a mug, practically in front of the cash register. While I was deciding what colour pen to buy Joel picked two out of the mug and put them in his pocket. I think he took one ballpoint and one felt tip. They each cost 49 cents. Joel didn't look at me. He didn't look at anybody. He just smiled his crooked smile and kind of hummed a little tune.

I was furious. I mean really furious! I wanted to punch Joel in the nose. I wanted to mess up his angel face – to see the blood ooze out of his nostrils and trickle down his chin. I wanted to look him in the eye and say, 'I've had it with you, Joel! You stink! Who do you think you're fooling? You think I'm afraid to tell the manager, don't you! Well, I'm not!' Then I'd beckon with my finger and call, 'Sir ... sir ...'

'Yes, young man?' the manager would say, running towards me. By that time I'd have Joel by the back of his collar the way Bernice had me that day. 'I've caught one of those shoplifting kids, sir,' I'd say. 'If you'll check his pockets you'll find two pens. A blue ballpoint and a black felt tip.' The manager would check and pull out the pens. Then he'd call the police. The police would arrest Joel and drag him off to the Juvenile Detention Center. My picture would make the front page of the *Rosemont Weekly*.

Soon after I would be beaten up in the boy's room and left bleeding on the cold floor. My attackers would never be caught and I would live in fear forever.

When we left the store Joel was still smiling but I was doubled over with pain. I must have caused quite a commotion. I think I fell onto the sidewalk clutching my stomach and a lot of people gathered around me.

Joel was the one who phoned my mother from the corner store. My mother rushed me to Dr Holland's office. He admitted me to the North Shore Hospital.

I ended up in the children's ward and was the second oldest person there. The oldest was a boy of fifteen who had his leg in traction and told me he'd be like that for two months and that he'd never ski again as long as he lived. He told me this from his bed across the room. At that time I was flat on my back being fed intravenously through a vein in my foot, which didn't hurt but wasn't exactly fun either.

Of course this wasn't the first thing that happened. What I remember first is my mother bending over my hospital bed moaning, 'Tony ... Tony ...' the way she says, 'Vinnie

... Vinnie ...' on Veterans Day. So right away I figured I was dying.

The first two days my mother stayed with me all the time. Then Dr Holland suggested she come only during regular visiting hours so the hospital routine wouldn't be upset.

I have three doctors. Dr Holland, who promised me I'm not going to die yet; a specialist named Dr Riley, who's in charge of my intestines; and a psychiatrist named Dr Fogel, who says that I'm not crazy, because when I heard he was a shrink I thought I was. And I wasn't the only one. My mother nearly had a fit.

She said, 'There's nothing wrong with Tony's mind. He's not crazy. And I don't want any psychiatrist asking him a lot of questions. They're the ones that make you crazy with their crazy questions.'

My father said, 'Carmella, Dr Fogel is going to help Tony with his problems.' He was much calmer than my mother.

'What problems? A thirteen-year-old boy doesn't have any problems! These doctors just want your money, Vic. In Jersey City this would never have happened. He's got some gas pains. That's all.'

'Mom!' Ralph said. 'You're making matters worse by discussing this in front of Tony.'

My mother looked at me. 'So now I'm crazy too!' She gave a funny laugh that sounded more like a hiccup. 'Maybe I need Dr Fogel,' she said.

'I like him,' I told her. 'And I'm not crazy!'

'Of course you're not,' my mother said. 'What a thing to say. Don't even think about it.' With that she got up off the foot of my bed and made a face at my father and brother like it was their fault I mentioned such a terrible thing.

I stayed in the hospital ten days. I slept an awful lot. Probably because they fed me so many pills. A lot of tests were done on me too. Sometimes they lasted all morning. I had to drink barium again. My insides were X-rayed. I had four separate blood tests – two from my arms and two from my fingers. I wasn't allowed to eat anything but soft, mushy foods like boiled eggs and Jello.

Mom, Pop and Ralph came to see me every day. Angie came every other day. I received eleven pairs of pyjamas. One pair from my Aunt Rose and Uncle Lou. One pair from my twin uncles and aunts. Two pairs from Mrs Hoober. Two pairs from Angie and Ralph. Four pairs from my mother and one pair from Marty Endo and Scott Gold.

I got six books, four games and two bunches of flowers – one from my formroom class with a card everybody signed – and one from my Youth Group. I also got a pair of knitted bedroom slippers from Grandma – they itched my feet. And a photo album from Maxine. Maybe she thought I could put my X-rays in it. Joel sent me a card and included a pen in the envelope. I think it was the felt tip one he stole. Corky wrote me a letter.

Dear Tony,
I am very sorry to hear that you're sick. I hope you'll be better soon. I really mean that. I miss you a lot. Formroom isn't any fun when you're absent. I really mean that, even if you don't care about me. Because even if you don't I still care about you. And I mean, REALLY! Because I think you're swell. And that's the truth.

I hope when you get better you'll come to a party I'm planning. I don't know when it will be. Maybe not until the summer. But I'm planning it anyway. Except I wouldn't even have it if you weren't better or if you won't come. Because I think you're the nicest boy I know and that's the truth. So please get well soon and I really mean that.
Love and things,
Corky
(Kathryn Thomas)

I didn't tear up her letter. Maybe some day I'll feel like reading it again.

The best visitor of all came on the sixth day – Lisa. I couldn't believe it when I saw her walk in. First I thought she was there to see somebody else. But she came right over to my bed. She ruffled my hair and pulled up a chair.

She said, 'Joel couldn't come because he's too young. You have to be at least fourteen. So I'm here in his place. He sent you this ...'

She handed me a brown bag and I took it. Inside was a paperback book full of clips and underlinings.

'He's been working on it just for you.' Lisa smiled. 'But I think you'd better hide it ... maybe under your pillow or something ... Here, let me ...' she said, bending over and slipping the book under my pillow. She was so close I could smell her. She smelled really nice ... like spring.

Right then was the perfect time for me to tell Lisa that I love her. That I've been watching her since Thanksgiving. That I'm really older than she thinks because I started school three years late since my real family are gypsies who roam the world. I was adopted by the Migliones who brought me to Rosemont. And even though we're the same age (almost) I've had so much experience – much more than her – that we'd be perfect together. When I get out of the hospital we can run off and never be seen again. We'll live on some deserted island and all we'll wear is flowers.

I must have dozed off while I was thinking these things because when I woke up it was dark and Lisa was gone.

A few days later Dr Holland told me that all my tests were fine and that my pains were functional, meaning not caused by anything physically wrong. He was turning me over to Dr Fogel who could help me get well.

When I came home from the hospital it was spring vacation so I had the week off. On Tuesday I went to Dr Fogel's office. My mother didn't come in with me. She dropped me off outside and said she'd be back in an hour.

I only saw Dr Fogel once in the hospital, but he seemed pretty nice. And I wasn't scared about my appointment because he told me when I come to his office we'll just talk.

His nurse took my name and showed me in. Dr Fogel was sitting behind his desk. 'Hello Tony,' he said. I wondered if I was supposed to lie down on his couch. In the movies that's what people do.

So I asked, 'Where should I sit?'

He said, 'Any place you're comfortable.'

I chose the chair next to his desk and waited for him to start. He smiled at me.

'I'm glad I'm out of the hospital,' I said. 'I don't like being sick.'

'Nobody does,' Dr Fogel said.

'Yeah ... well, I really got mad at this guy I know because he took some pens from the store and he didn't pay and I didn't know what to do. And I'll tell you something ... it's not the first time either. I mean, maybe I should report him. When I don't know what to do I get sick sometimes.'

Dr Fogel nodded.

'And then there's my mother and father ... well, especially my mother. She really burns me up lately. You know what she did to Grandma?'

Dr Fogel shook his head.

'Well ... she won't let her cook anymore and that's what Grandma loved to do. She's always cooked for us. So now my mother won't let her and Grandma stays up in her room all the time and she's miserable. Only she can't tell me how miserable she is because she can't talk – because she had cancer of the larynx ... You know what?'

Dr Fogel shook his head again.

'Sometimes I think about getting cancer. One time I thought my father had it and I got really scared. But the thing is ... my mother wasn't this bad in Jersey City. At least I don't think so. Or maybe she was and I was too dumb

to know it. That's where we used to live ... in Jersey City ...
She's really a phony. My mother is really a phony. That's
what I think. I'd love to tell her I think so.'

'Why don't you?' Dr Fogel asked.

'Oh ... then she'd start bawling ...'

'And how would you feel about that?'

'I'd feel really bad. I don't like to see her cry.'

Dr Fogel nodded and smiled.

'And I'll tell you something else. My brother is getting just
like her. Otherwise why would he go into the business?
What does he know about electrical cartridges?'

I got up then and walked around the room. There was a
checkerboard set up on one table and a deck of cards laid out
on another. I picked up a checker. 'Who plays?' I asked.

Dr Fogel said, 'Anyone who wants to. Do you feel like
a game?'

'No. I like chess.' That reminded me of Pop. I fiddled with
the checker some more and said, 'My father's really something.
He's a good one! He just goes along with everything. Nothing
bothers him. He's on top of the world. I don't know ... I
just can't figure him out.'

Dr Fogel grunted.

'What makes me mad is why should I care so much about
what they do? Any of them? Like Joel ...' I walked over
to the window and looked down. 'Why should I care if he
wants to steal a lot of junk?'

'But you do?' Dr Fogel asked.

'Yeah ... it really gets me!' I walked back to my chair
and sat down. 'Sometimes I think that people can see inside
me ... that they know what I'm thinking and everything.
I don't want anyone to know what I'm thinking. Like that
time Joel called me chicken. I didn't want to make that
phone call. I know they can trace phone calls. So why should
I care if Joel calls me chicken?'

'But you do?'

'Yeah ... I guess so. And another thing ... sometimes I

209

wish we still lived in Jersey City and other times I'm glad we don't. You know what? I like having plenty of money. Oh – I don't know what I want!'

I stood up then. So did Dr Fogel. He said, 'Well, Tony ... we've had a very good first session. I'll see you again next week.'

That's it? I used up the whole hour? I talked too much. I shouldn't have told him all those things. That was stupid. Next time I won't talk at all. Let him do all the talking.

When I got outside my mother was waiting in the car. I got in and she asked, 'How did it go?'

'Dr Fogel said it went good,' I told her.

'I hope so,' she said. 'He's very expensive.'

When vacation was over I went back to school. I didn't have many pains and everyone said I was looking great, especially Corky. People always say that when they know you've been in the hospital.

Then Again, Maybe I Won't

A funny thing happened to Vicki in the spring. She got better looking. I mean as far as babies go she isn't too bad. She looks more like those pictures you see in magazines than like a plucked chicken. She's much fatter than she used to be and she laughs a lot. Even I make funny faces at her to hear her laugh. Of course I don't go near her when she needs to be changed. Neither does my father or Ralph if he can help it. Vicki is around a lot because Angie's always out with the real estate lady looking for her house.

One sunny Saturday afternoon my mother got Vicki all wrapped up in her carriage and asked me to take her around the block for a walk.

'Me?' I said. 'You want *me* to take *her* for a walk? All by myself?'

210

'Why not?' my mother said. 'You're her uncle aren't you?'

'Well, yes. I mean sure ... but ...' I began. 'But I don't know anything about babies.'

'What do you have to know to take her for a walk? You just push the carriage.'

'Well,' I said. 'I don't know.'

'Come on, Tony,' my mother coaxed. 'I have to get to the store for an hour. And anyway, Maxine is here if you run into trouble.'

'Well,' I said. 'I'll try it.'

'There's nothing to it. Just push the carriage and she'll fall asleep.'

So I pushed – first back and forth in our driveway to get the feel of it. I felt pretty stupid. If I hadn't known Joel was at the dentist's office I might never have done it. I could just imagine what he would think of me pushing a baby around.

Me and Joel never talk about what happened at the corner store. I don't know if he knows I saw him take the pens or what. We act just like we did before I got sick. I asked Dr Fogel do I have to report Joel? And he said, 'That's up to you, Tony.' Dr Fogel never gives me any definite answers.

As it turned out I was mighty glad I decided to watch Vicki. Because as I was pushing her around who should back out of the Hoobers' driveway but Lisa, in her mother's car. I know she's practising up for her driver's test. I also know that the first time she backed out of the garage she did it without raising the garage door first and the car went halfway through the door. The Hoobers had to get a new garage door and Lisa wasn't allowed to go out on any dates that weekend which was good for me because it meant I got to watch her that Friday *and* Saturday night.

This time she backed out okay. When she saw me she slowed up and waved. 'Hi Tony. You have a real live baby in there?'

'Yeah,' I said. 'My niece, Vicki.'

Lisa stopped the car, jumped out and slammed the door

shut. She ran over to me, peeked into the carriage and said, 'Oh! She's adorable. I simply adore babies! I'm mad about them. I just love them!'

I got the message.

'Can I hold her?' Lisa asked.

'Well, I don't know. She's supposed to take a nap.'

'Well, can I push the carriage?'

This was really funny. Lisa asking me all these questions like I was in charge or something. If I'd known how she felt about babies I sure would have offered to take care of Vicki before this!

So I let Lisa push Vicki but I walked right alongside her. I knew I was growing because now I come up to Lisa's neck. I figure she's as tall as she's going to get and I'm just starting to grow so I'll wind up a lot bigger than her.

'Listen, Tony ...' Lisa said. 'If you've got something to do I don't mind watching the baby myself.'

'Oh no! I couldn't do that,' I said. 'I'm responsible for her.'

'Well, I'm a responsible person, Tony,' Lisa said, glancing sideways at me.

'No. I don't think that would be a good idea. Something might happen if I left you alone with her.'

Lisa stopped pushing and faced me. 'Listen, Tony ... I know you know all about the car and the garage door and all that, but I wouldn't dream of letting anything happen to the baby. It's all right! Really, I can take care of her myself.'

'No!' I said so loud I startled myself.

'Well, if that's the way you're going to be about it!'

'I'll just walk along with you,' I said. 'You can pretend it's just you and the baby if you want. After all, she is my niece!'

After that we didn't have much to say to each other. Lisa pushed and I walked behind her. I considered asking Lisa why she always gets undressed with the shades up but decided that would be stupid. My story about the gypsies would have to wait too. I didn't feel this was the right time.

We walked for an hour. Last week I told Dr Fogel about my binoculars and how I watch Lisa. I told him I've even seen her naked. I thought he'd be really surprised. But all he said was, 'How does that make you feel?' So I told him the truth. I told him that I like to watch her. That it makes me excited. Dr Fogel didn't tell me to stop doing it. And I'm glad. Because I don't know if I'd be able to. I haven't told him about my dreams yet. Sometimes I want to, but I just can't.

When we got back to my house Lisa thanked me very much for allowing her to help with Vicki and I said, 'Oh, that's okay.'

She told me she'd babysit if my sister-in-law ever needed her and she'd even do it for free because the baby is so adorable. I told her I'd keep that in mind.

After Lisa went home I bent down and whispered to Vicki, 'Thanks pal. You got me alone with Lisa. You're not so bad after all.'

My mother told me I'd done a fine job and she was proud of me.

The end of April Lisa got her driver's licence and her own Corvette – white with red leather seats. She was so excited she offered to take me and Joel for a ride.

As soon as we got out of town Lisa started doing about eighty miles an hour. I thought she was going to get us all killed.

Joel screamed, 'Hey Lisa ... slow down!'

Lisa laughed and her hair blew all over her face. By that time me and Joel, who were sharing a bucket seat, were hanging onto each other and making noises somewhere between laughing and crying. I closed my eyes so I wouldn't have to see the road. Lisa drove like a maniac. I vowed never to get into her car again. Not for anything! Should I be lucky enough to get out alive this time, that is.

Finally Lisa pulled off the road and came to a screeching halt. Me and Joel untangled ourselves and he started in on her.

'You're crazy, Lisa! I always thought so, but now I know it! Didn't you learn anything in Driver Ed?'

Lisa lit a cigarette and took a long puff.

Joel said to me, 'You see, she's got a death wish!'

'I do not!' Lisa said. 'I'm very fond of being alive.'

'Well, you'd never know it,' Joel hollered. 'You keep driving around like that and you're not going to make it to eighteen.'

'Don't be silly,' Lisa said. 'I was only trying her out. I have no intention of driving around like that all the time.' She turned to me. 'You weren't afraid, were you, Tony!'

'Well, not afraid exactly ... but I didn't like it.'

'Come off it, Tony. You were scared out of your mind,' Joel said.

'Okay ... I was,' I admitted. 'Sure I was scared – right out of my mind.'

Lisa laughed and kept puffing away.

'If you keep on smoking you won't have to worry about getting yourself killed in this car. You'll be dead of cancer,' Joel said.

'Will you listen to him!' Liza waved her cigarette around. 'All of a sudden he's my father! Just what I need! *Another George.*'

'My grandmother had cancer,' I told Lisa. 'Of the larynx. They had to take it out. Now she can't talk.'

Lisa looked me right in the eye. 'Is that true?' she asked.

'Yes,' I said. 'You can see her any time you want to. She lives with us.'

'How awful! Perfectly awful!' Lisa stubbed out her cigarette and threw it out of the car. 'She smoked, I suppose?'

'Oh yeah ... like a fiend!' I said. Actually Grandma never smoked at all. The doctors said it was just one of those freaky things.

But Lisa took her pack of cigarettes out of her bag and flung them out of the car. 'I'm never going to touch another weed. *Never!* Imagine losing your larynx!'

'While you're reforming,' Joel said, 'would you mind driving slower on the way home.'

She did. Only sixty miles an hour. But she drove up a one-way street the wrong way and almost got us killed anyhow.

I enjoy thinking that I'm responsible for Lisa giving up cigarettes even if there's nothing I can do about her driving.

The second week in May Lisa banged up her Corvette. What happened was she bumped into a tree. She told me and Joel she couldn't imagine how the tree got there. Lisa wasn't hurt but her car needs an new fender and she has to spend the next three Saturday nights at home.

Ralph and Angie are buying a house three blocks from us. 'Five bedrooms,' Angie said. And does Maxine have any friends who'd like to work for her? Maxine said she'd ask around.

'What are you going to do with five bedrooms?' I said. 'Rent them out?'

'Fill them up with kids!' Ralph said.

'We're expecting another one already,' Angie laughed, blushing. 'Didn't you guess?'

'No,' I said. 'I didn't guess.' But I thought how could I guess when you're still fat from having Vicki?

'Which is one of the reasons I'm going in with Pop,' Ralph said. 'Kids are pretty expensive. Especially when you want to give them everything.' Ralph and Angie gave each other a secret smile.

I thought, maybe that's the trouble. Maybe kids don't always want you to give them everything. I looked at Ralph. I can do that without hating him now. I can say okay, you're just ordinary, but I can't do anything about it. I'm trying to understand his feelings about wanting his kids to have everything. Maybe I'll be like that too. Then again, maybe

I won't. After all, I'm me. I'm not Ralph.

Well, at least I got through thinking about all that without getting pains. I'm learning how to handle myself. Dr Fogel will be glad when I tell him next week.

On 25 May me and Joel rode down to the Village Sports Store. Now that it's spring I need a new basketball net. Joel needs tennis balls for camp. He doesn't want to go back this summer, but he has no choice. 'I've been going to camp since I'm six,' he told me. 'I hate it.'

'So why not switch? Go to another camp?'

'They're all the same,' he said. 'At least here I know the guys already. I know what to expect.'

Lisa isn't going to be around for the summer either. She's going on a tour of the northwestern states and Canada. She'll be gone nine weeks. What am I going to do without her? I'll never be able to get to sleep!

When we got to the Village Sports Store we rested our bikes against the side of the building. Inside we browsed around. I saw a really neat fielder's mitt. It looked pretty expensive though.

Joel fiddled around with the tennis rackets. He tried out two of them pretending to have a volley with me. The reason we had to wait so long was the salesman couldn't get away from two Rosemont ladies.

One of them said, 'But Ginny, you know how I putt. Always to the right of the hole. So I need a putter that will send them left.'

The salesman said, 'It's your aim, Ma'am. You've got to aim more to the left of the cup.'

Then Ginny said, 'It has nothing to do with her aim. It's the way she's built.'

'I don't think so,' the salesman said. 'Build has nothing to do with it. It's all aim.'

Then the lady holding the putter said, 'Suppose I take it and just try it out. Then if I still put to the right I'll bring t back this afternoon. You can charge it to my husband's account.'

The salesman tried a smile but you could tell he was pretty burned up.

When he finally got rid of them he asked could he help us. Joel told him he was interested in a tennis racket but that he'd have to come back with his father for that. 'In the meantime I'll take two cans of good tennis balls,' Joel said.

The salesman showed him the two brands they carried and Joel picked what he wanted. He paid for them, counted his change and took the white bag with *Village Sports Store* written across it.

'Anything for you?' the salesman asked me.

'Yes,' I said. 'I need a new basketball net ... and I'd like to know how much that neat fielder's mitt costs too.'

'Which one?' he asked. 'They're all neat ... you'll have to point it out to me.'

'Okay,' I said, following him to the other end of the store where the mitts were displayed.

The salesman told me the mitt I liked was $37.50. I thought that was a lot of money for one fielder's mitt so I said I'd have to think about it. He told me to take my time thinking while he went to the stockroom for my basketball net. I walked back to the cash register where Joel was waiting. I wanted to know if he thought $37.50 was too much for a mitt. But I never asked him because he was smiling his crooked smile and humming some tune.

I thought, oh no! Please, Joel. I don't want to be sick again. I don't want to go back to the hospital. I know what you've done. I can tell by just looking at you. What'd you take this time, Joel? *What?*

This was no good. I had to calm down. I could feel my stomach tighten. I'd do what Dr Fogel taught me. I'd have a talk with myself inside my head. I know I'm tense. But I will be all right. I will *not* be sick.

'Let's go,' Joel said.

I could report him now. I could yell for the salesman and say, 'This guy stole something from your store.' I thought about doing that as I followed Joel outside. He got on his bike. Just as he was about to peddle off two men came running out of the store. One wore eyeglasses and a turtleneck. The other had red hair and freckles. They ran right up to Joel and the one with the glasses said, 'Okay son ... let's have the golf balls.'

They know, I thought. This is it. *This is really it.* He's swiped something and they know about it. Good going, Joel! *You idiot.*

'What golf balls?' Joel asked, looking innocent.

'Come on son ... I saw you take them,' red hair said.

'Saw me take what?' Joel asked.

I just stood there watching.

'Don't make this more difficult than it already is,' eyeglasses said. 'We've just installed closed circuit TV because of shoplifters. So we know you've got the golf balls.'

'I bought tennis balls,' Joel insisted. 'I bought two cans of tennis balls *and* I paid for them.'

Red hair grabbed the bag out of Joel's hand and opened it. He took out three packs of golf balls and held them up. 'Go ahead,' he called to the salesman who had waited on us. 'Make the call.'

'Oh, *those* golf balls,' Joel said, trying to laugh. But the laugh came out like a puppy's yelp. 'My father asked me to buy those for him. Here,' he said, fumbling around in his pocket and coming up with a ten dollar bill. 'I'll pay for them now. I just forgot, that's all.'

'Never mind,' red hair said. 'You should have thought about it before. It's too late now.'

'Tell them, Tony!' Joel shouted. 'Tell them I just forgot to pay!'

I didn't say anything.

'Tell them!' he screamed. 'You tell them or I'll never speak to you again!'

So don't, I thought. Who did he think he was, threatening me! I can get along without you, Joel. I just realized, I can get along fine without you!

'I hate you,' Joel whispered, looking at me. Then he turned away and began to cry. He bent over his handlebars and buried his head in his arms.

I couldn't stand another minute of it. I turned and started to walk my bike away. But the salesman called, 'Hey ... you forgot your net.'

'My net?'

'Yes, your basketball net.'

'Oh.'

'You want it anyway?' he asked.

'Sure,' I said. 'How much is it?'

'$2.62 including tax.'

I handed him the exact amount and he gave me my package. I put it in my basket and hopped on my bike.

Red hair and eyeglasses were walking Joel back into the store.

'Did you set him up, kid?' the salesman asked.

'I didn't have anything to do with it, sir,' I told him.

'Maybe not. I have no proof,' he said. 'But if I were you I'd be a lot more careful about who I run around with in the future.'

So when things finally caught up with Angel Face I had to be accused of setting him up. That's really something! Me – a criminal. Me – with my nervous stomach!

All these months of wondering what to do about Joel were over. Just like that! And not even because of me – because of a crummy closed circuit TV. I should feel relieved. I should feel happy, I told myself. But all the way home I thought ... Good old Joel ... that lousy creep ... fixed up a paperback just for me when I was in the hospital ... yeah, but if it hadn't been for him I might never have gotten sick in the first place ... he told Bernice to take her hands off me, didn't he ... sure he did ... what could she do to him ...

he's my best Rosemont friend ... at least he was ... well,
wasn't he ... what is a friend, anyway?

By the time I got home I figured Joel would be locked up in
jail. His father would get him a good lawyer though. I
wondered what my mother would think about Joel being
sent to the Juvenile Detention Center. I probably wouldn't
see him for years. Well, that's okay with me. I don't want to
see him. The way he screamed at me. The way he cried!

That night after dinner my father helped me put up my
new basketball net. As I watched him work I thought, he's
a lot older than most of my friends' fathers. After all, if
Vinnie was still alive he'd be twenty-eight. Pop's already
a grandfather. I don't know why I never thought about that
before.

He still doesn't know about Joel. Neither does my
mother. I decided to let them read it in the morning paper.
Let them be really shocked. I can just see the headline:

ROSEMONT BOY CAUGHT SHOPLIFTING
GETS TEN YEARS

When the net was fastened my father went into the house.
I stayed out and shot a few baskets. I practised dribbling
and foul shots too. Then I fell onto the grass and did pushups.

'Hi Tony.'

I looked up. I couldn't believe it – Joel! I jumped to my
feet. 'What are you doing home? I thought ... I thought ...'

'Yeah. Well, the owner of the store isn't pressing charges.'

'He's not?'

'Nope. He called the cops and my father. I got a long
lecture.'

'That's all?'

'Yeah. Since it's my first offence nobody wants me to
have a record.'

'Oh.'

'That's the way it's done in Rosemont.'

'Oh.'

'I'll be back in school tomorrow.'

'You will?'

'Yeah. But next year I've got to go away to school ... to some military academy.' Joel reached down for a blade of grass which he chewed on for a while. 'Can you see me in military school?'

I laughed but no sound came out. So I shook my head.

'Well, me neither,' Joel said. 'But that's how George Hoober deals with his problems. He puts them away some place. And right now I'm problem number one. You know ... anything so his golf game isn't messed up!' He picked up a stone and threw it in the direction of his house. 'I only did it for fun,' he said. 'To prove I could get away with anything.'

I just looked at him.

'I told them it wasn't a setup ... that you didn't have anything to do with it.'

Was he waiting for me to say thank you? I wasn't about to.

'Look Tony ... my father sent me over here to ask you not to say anything about what happened. He doesn't want it to get around.'

'I won't say anything. Why should I say anything now?'

'Well, thanks pal.' Joel pretended to tip his hat at me but he wasn't wearing one. 'See you around,' he called as he headed for home.

'Sure,' I muttered. 'See you around.'

The next day Mrs Hoober told my mother that Joel was going to military school in the fall because the young people of today need strong discipline and that this particular military academy was just about the best there was anywhere. And that of course Joel would get a much finer education than at Rosemont Junior or Senior High. My mother thought maybe I should go too.

'I want you to have the best possible education, Tony,' she said.

But my father looked at me and said, 'Let's leave the decision to Tony this time.'

I think he knows I'll be okay now – that I can face things.

'I want to stay at Rosemont Junior,' I told them.

I almost laughed. I almost laughed and said to my mother, 'If Mrs Hoober told you Joel was going to the Juvenile Detention Center would you ask me if I wanted to go too?' But I didn't say it. And I didn't get any pains either. Because it was funny. Funny and sad both.

Then Again, Maybe I Won't

Now it's 10 June. I'm riding around on my bike. I'm thinking about my birthday. That I'm going to be fourteen.

Fourteen years is a long time to have been around.

It's kind of old if you really think about it.

This afternoon they're going to break ground for our swimming pool. For the last three weeks my father's been spending all his spare time with the man from the Athena Pool Company. They've been drawing up plans – where to place the diving board – where to put the cabanas – what shape should the pool be – heated or not heated?

Our swimming pool.

The swimming pool of the Miglione family.

I pedal faster and faster till I'm almost out of breath.

You remember the Miglione family, don't you? They used to live in a two-family house in Jersey City. They used to wait on line for the bathroom.

I shift into low to get to the top of the hill. Suppose I wake up tomorrow morning and the money's all gone. Would I care? Would I?

I'm at the top of the hill now. I laugh out loud. I wonder if anybody hears me.

I put my feet up over the handlebars and coast all the way down. Faster and faster – scared I'll crash into the tree at the bottom, but not using my brakes.

I make it. I'm at the bottom of the hill now.

I had a funny dream last night. It wasn't about Lisa. It was about Corky, only she looked like Lisa. But still, I knew it was Corky. And I wasn't just looking at her either. It was a pretty good dream. I wonder what Corky will really look like when she's sixteen? I think I'll ask Dr Fogel about my dreams. Can too many of them hurt me?

I shift gears and pedal backwards.

I think what I'll do is – I'll go home and put my binoculars away on the top shelf of my closet – over in the corner – so they're hard to get.

Then again, maybe I won't.

Deenie

one

My mother named me Deenie because right before I was born she saw a movie about a beautiful girl named Wilmadeene, who everybody called Deenie for short. Ma says the first time she held me she knew right away that if she named me Deenie I would turn out the same way – beautiful, that is. I was only four hours old then. And it took me almost thirteen years to find out what *really* happened to the Deenie in the movie. She went crazy and wound up on the funny farm. Ma says I should just forget about that part of the story.

The reason I know about it is the movie was on TV last night and I saw it. Even Helen, who is my older sister, who never watches anything on TV, stayed up late to see the original Deenie. It was a great movie. I really liked it, especially the scenes between Deenie and Bud. He was this guy who was madly in love with her. It was all very romantic, even when she went crazy.

There's a boy named Buddy Brader in eighth grade and I think he's kind of nice. So it is possible that there might be a real-life Deenie and Bud some day, right here in Elizabeth, New Jersey.

This morning I wanted to sleep late. Everybody I know sleeps late on Saturdays but I couldn't because me and Ma had an appointment in New York.

My father drove us downtown in plenty of time to catch the nine-thirty bus. Before we got out of the car Ma said, 'Wish us luck, Frank. This could be the big day.'

'Just be yourself, Deenie,' Daddy told me. 'No matter what happens.'

'I'll try,' I said.

Daddy touched my cheek. Then he turned to Ma. 'Do you need any money?' he asked her.

'I've got enough,' she said. 'We're not doing any shopping.'

'Well then ... have a good time.'

Ma leaned over and kissed him.

The bus stops on the corner by Old Lady Murray's news-stand. Ma bought a magazine and a pack of gum from her. I try not to look at Old Lady Murray because she's so ugly she makes me want to vomit. She has a big bump on her back and she can't stand up straight. You can see the bump right through her clothes. Even in winter, when she wears an old black coat, you can see it. That's a fact. But today it was warm and sunny, just the way it always is in September when you're wishing it would hurry and get cold. And Old Lady Murray was wearing a plain cotton dress. I pretended to be window shopping so I wouldn't have to look her way.

I was happy when the New York bus finally came down the street. 'Hey Ma ...' I called. 'Here's the bus.'

As we got on, the bus driver greeted me with, 'Hi Beautiful!'

Ma gave him a big smile and said, 'Deenie's the beauty, Helen's the brain.'

The bus driver didn't say anything else because what does he know about our family? He was probably sorry he bothered with us in the first place. I hate it when Ma brags about me and Helen. One time Midge and Janet were over and Ma started in about Helen's brain and my face and I almost died! Later, I told her, 'Please don't do that again, Ma. You embarrassed me in front of my friends.' But Ma just laughed and said, 'I was only telling the truth, Deenie.'

Ma took our tickets from the bus driver and sat down in the second row of seats, next to the window. She dusted off the seat next to her with a tissue before she'd let me sit in it. Then she settled back and pretty soon she was dozing off. I looked out the window for a while but the view from

228

the New Jersey Turnpike's not so hot, so I started thinking instead.

My mother wants me to be a model, with my face on all the magazine covers. Ma says I'll make a lot of money and maybe get discovered for the movies too. A teenage model has to make it by the time she's seventeen if she's ever going to make it big. So the next four years will be very important to me. The thing that really scares me is I'm not sure I want to be a model. I would never tell that to Ma, but I've told Daddy. He says I don't have to be unless I want to.

Today is the third time this month that we're going to a modelling agency. The first one Aunt Rae read about in *TV Guide*. It was an ad that said, 'Be a model or just look like one.' When we got to that agency the lady in charge told my mother that I had a lot of potential and wouldn't Ma like to enroll me in a modelling course for only $250? They'd be able to teach me how to walk the right way and everything.

But Ma told the lady, 'My daughter already knows how to walk and with her face we don't need to pay anybody. She's the one who's going to get paid.'

After that Ma and Aunt Rae found out about some real modelling agencies. The kind that gets you paying jobs. We went to one two Saturdays ago. The lady there told Ma they were very interested in me, except for my posture, which wasn't great. Since then I've been walking around with books on my head. I hope that's helped, so Ma will leave me alone.

The bus stopped at the Port Authority building on Eighth Avenue. We rode the escalator down to the main level and walked outside to the corner where we took the crosstown bus. 'Once you get started modelling we'll be able to afford taxis,' Ma said.

'That'll be nice,' I told her. My feet were already

229

hurting. Ma says I should stop wearing sneakers. They make your feet spread so your regular shoes don't fit right any more.

When we got to the modelling agency there were two girls waiting to be interviewed ahead of me. I sat down next to one of them. She was by herself. I guess she was at least sixteen and very pretty.

She had her portfolio on her lap. My mother carries mine. It's like a loose-leaf notebook filled with photographs of me. Ma hired this guy to take a whole mess of pictures over the summer. In some of them I'm wearing wigs. I think I look kind of funny and much older than I really am.

'Are you a model?' I asked the girl.

'Yes,' she said. 'Are you?'

'I'm just getting started. Is it fun?'

'It's okay,' she said. 'It's a lot harder than most people think. You have to sit under hot lights for hours. Sometimes I get so bored I practically fall asleep.'

'I thought it would be more exciting than that,' I said.

'The money's pretty good,' she told me. 'That's why I do it. I hope I get this job. It could lead to a commercial.'

The receptionist called, 'Rachel Conrad . . .' and the girl next to me stood up.

'Good luck,' I said.

'Thanks. You too.'

When Rachel came out the receptionist called, 'Linda Levin . . .' and this very tall girl got up and went in.

'We're next, Deenie,' Ma said.

'I have to go to the bathroom,' I whispered.

'Now? You should have thought of that before.'

'I didn't have to go before.'

'Well, hurry up.'

When I get nervous I don't sweat or shake or anything but I always feel like I've got to go to the bathroom. I asked the receptionist where to go and when I came out Ma said,

'It's our turn ... I better put some drops in your eyes before we go in. They're a little bloodshot.' She opened her bag.

'Not now, Ma!' I told her, glancing at the receptionist.

'Deenie Fenner ...' she called.

Me and Ma stood up and the receptionist showed us into a small office. The walls were covered with pictures of beautiful girls. A lady was sitting behind a big glass-topped desk. 'Are you Deenie?' she asked.

'Yes,' I answered.

She held out her hand. 'I'm Mrs Allison.'

My mother reached over and shook hands with her. 'I'm Thelma Fenner, Deenie's mother.'

Mrs Allison smiled at me. She had a space between her two front teeth. 'So you want to be a model ...' she said.

'Yes.'

Ma said, 'I have her portfolio right here, Mrs Allison.' She handed it to her.

Mrs Allison opened it up to the first page. 'What a sweet baby,' she said.

I felt my face turn red. I wish Ma would get rid of that picture.

'That's Deenie when she was sixteen months old,' Ma said. 'She's won a national contest and had her picture in all the magazines, advertising baby food.'

'Have you worked as a model since then, Deenie?' Mrs Allison asked.

'No,' I told her. 'My father didn't want me to at least until I started junior high. I'm in seventh grade now.'

'Modelling *is* hard work,' Mrs Allison said. 'I don't blame your father.' She flipped through my portfolio.

I wiggled my toes around inside my shoes. The big toe on my left foot hurt bad. I think I cut my toenails wrong again. They're always getting ingrown and infected.

When Mrs Allison was through looking at my pictures

she zipped up my portfolio and said, 'You're a pretty girl, Deenie.'

'Thank you,' I said.

'Let's see you walk around the room.'

I glanced at Ma but she just smiled at me. I got up and walked across the room. The worst part of these interviews is having people stare at you while you walk around. I feel like a real klunk. When I finished crossing the room I stood in front of Mrs Allison's desk and turned around in a slow circle, the way Ma taught me.

Mrs Allison stood up and walked around her desk. She put her hands on my shoulders. 'Relax Deenie,' she said. 'You're too stiff.' She moved my head back and forth and kind of rearranged my shoulders. 'Now, try walking this way. You'll be more comfortable.'

I crossed the room again. I saw Mrs Allison make some notes on her pad. Then I stood in front of her and waited.

Mrs Allison looked at me without saying anything, and I was sure if I stood there for one more minute I would have to go to the bathroom again. I shifted from one foot to the other while I waited for her to say something.

Finally she said, 'I don't know, Deenie. There's something about the way you move that's not quite right. But your face is very lovely and you do photograph well. Let me think about you for a while. I'll be in touch.'

Mrs Allison stood up then and held her hand out to me. I shook it this time while Ma grabbed my portfolio off her desk.

'Thank you for coming, Mrs Fenner,' Mrs Allison told Ma. 'And for bringing Deenie.'

My mother nodded and took my arm, leading me out of the office. All the way down in the elevator Ma held on to my arm and she didn't say anything, not one word. When we were on the street she steered me into a lunchroom. We sat opposite each other, in a booth. Ma ordered a

eeseburger for each of us and when the waitress was gone
said, 'I'm sorry, Ma.'

'It looked like you slouched on purpose, Deenie.'

'I didn't, Ma. Honest. Why would I do that? I tried as
rd as I could.' Tears came to my eyes.

'Don't give me that, Deenie. You heard Mrs Allison say
ere's something funny about the way you move.'

'Please Ma ... please believe me ... I didn't do it on
irpose.'

My mother didn't say anything for a minute. I took a
p of water. Finally, Ma said, 'Deenie, God gave you a
autiful face. Now He wouldn't have done that if He
idn't intended for you to put it to good use.'

'I know it, Ma.'

'I hope so. Because I'm not going through this again.
ext time we have an appointment you'll have to try
arder.'

'But Mrs Allison didn't say *no* to us, Ma. She said she'd
iink about me, remember?'

'That means *no*, Deenie. So we'll have to try another
gency.'

'Can't we wait a little while? Maybe until next year?'

'Don't be silly,' Ma said. 'We don't want to waste time
hen you're ready now.' She reached out and patted my
and. 'I know this is hard for you, Deenie, but some day
ou'll thank me. You'll see.'

When the waitress brought our lunch I didn't feel like
ating anything, but one thing that makes Ma really mad
; seeing good food go to waste.

two

That night I soaked my foot for an hour. My big toe was killing me. Midge called to ask how I made out at the modelling agency.

'It was okay,' I said.

'Me and Janet went to Woolworth's. She tried on orange lipstick and brown eyeshadow.'

'Did she get caught?'

'Of course not.'

When we go to Woolworth's Janet's the best at trying on junk without buying. You're not supposed to do that but Janet always gets away with it. The one time I tried on some nail polish the saleslady caught me and I had to buy the whole bottle.

'*And* we saw Harvey Grabowsky,' Midge said.

'You did?'

'Yes. We followed him all around the store.'

'Did he say anything?'

'He never even noticed.'

'Oh.'

Harvey is the best looking guy in ninth grade. He's also on the football team and President of his class. Harvey has never said one word to me. I guess he doesn't talk to seventh-grade girls at all.

As soon as I hung up the phone rang again. It was Janet.

'We followed Harvey Grabowsky in Woolworth's,' she said.

'I know. I just talked to Midge.'

'Did she tell you what he bought?'

'No . . . what?'

'Three ballpoint pens and a roll of Scotch tape. And once I stood right next to him and touched his shirt sleeve!

I just knew I'd miss out on something great by going to New York.

Monday morning I got up early so I wouldn't have to rush. I wanted to make sure I looked my best because of cheerleading tryouts that afternoon. Most times I don't even think about the way I look but on special occasions, like today, being good looking really comes in handy. Not that a person has any choice about it. I'm just lucky.

The only girl I know who's not trying out for cheerleading is Midge. She would rather be *on* the football team. No kidding, she's tough! And she's the biggest kid in seventh grade, boys and girls included. When she gets to ninth grade if they don't let her try out for football she's going to court to sue the school for sexual discrimination. I used to think that meant something else but now I know the truth. In fifth grade we had a gym teacher who never gave the girls a chance to shoot baskets. I wish I had known about sexual discrimination then.

Me and Janet have been practising our cheers in her garage for two weeks. My mother doesn't know anything about it. She'd kill me. A lot of the games are on Saturdays and if I make the squad she won't be able to drag me around to any more modelling agencies. I'm counting on Daddy to make Ma understand ... I'd really like to be a cheerleader *and* a famous model. If only getting to be a model wasn't so much trouble. It would be fun to see my face in some magazine, if it could get there without my going through all those dumb interviews!

By the time I got down to the kitchen Ma had my orange juice ready and an egg in to boil. Daddy is never around in the morning. He leaves the house before the rest of us get up. He's got a gas station on Rahway Avenue and he opens for business at six-thirty.

'You look special this morning,' Ma told me.

'I do?'

'Yes, you do.

'Thanks Ma.'

'Drink all your juice. Vitamin C is very important.'

'I'm drinking it.'

My mother makes sure I have breakfast every single day. She's really fussy about what I eat. She leaves Helen alone but watches me like a hawk. She thinks if she's in charge of my diet I'll never get pimples or oily hair. I hope she's right. Helen has a little of both and so does her best friend. Myra Woodruff. Aunt Rae says they're in the awkward stage.

As soon as I cracked my egg Helen walked into the kitchen. She doesn't talk in the morning. And she doesn't eat breakfast either. She just sucks on an orange and drinks coffee.

A car horn tooted outside. It was Myra's father who gives Helen a ride to the high school. She took one gulp of coffee and ran out the front door.

I meet Midge at her corner every morning. We catch the bus together. Her father's our family dentist but he didn't put Helen's braces on. He sent her to an orthodontist for that. She's through with her braces now and Daddy's glad because braces are very expensive. He used up his whole savings account paying for them. I know because I heard Ma tell that to Aunt Rae. Helen's teeth look pretty good. They're very straight and she's always brushing them.

Our town doesn't have school buses, except for the one that picks up the handicapped kids. They come to our school from all over because we have a Special Class. Gena Courtney, who lives on my street, takes that bus. We were in first grade together until her accident. She was hit by a delivery truck. Now she wears braces on her legs and she's blind in one eye. I always feel funny when I pass her house – like I should stop and say hello – but then I think I better not, because I wouldn't know how to act or anything.

We get student discount tickets to use on the public bus. Janet gets on a few stops after me and Midge, so we always save her a seat. When she got on this morning she came running back to where we were and as soon as she sat down she opened her purse and pulled out a raw chicken's foot. She poked me and Midge with it – so naturally we screamed because who'd want to be touched by that! So the old grouch bus driver yelled, 'Shut up back there or I'll put you off!' Janet put her chicken's foot away.

'Why are you carrying that thing around with you, anyway?' Midge asked her.

'For good luck,' Janet said.

'A *rabbit's* foot means good luck, stupid,' I told her.

'I can't carry one of those around,' Janet said. 'Rabbits aren't kosher. And I need something to bring me good luck this afternoon. I'm so nervous about tryouts I'm sick to my stomach.'

'Does your father know you swiped a chicken's foot?' Midge asked.

'I didn't swipe it. He gave it to me.'

Janet's father is a butcher and his store is right near Daddy's gas station. There are Hebrew letters on the window. Janet says they're just to let people know that he's a kosher butcher. One time me and Midge called for Janet at her father's store. Mr Kayser had just gotten in a whole batch of dead turkeys. They were the ugliest things I'd ever seen. They weren't packaged nice like in the supermarket. They just looked like dead birds with feathers and everything. But the worst part was when Mr Kayser reached inside one and pulled out this disgusting mess of gutsy stuff and some of it was purple! Me and Midge

237

thought we'd vomit right on the sawdust but Janet just laughed and laughed.

We got to school just as the last bell rang. We said goodbye until lunchtime and headed for our formrooms. Mine's on the second floor. Susan Minton was waiting at my desk. She's always hanging around me. She says a lot of people think we look alike. I can't see it at all but whatever way I wear my hair Susan wears hers. And today she had her shirt buttoned up the back, the way I wore mine last Friday.

'I can't wait for this afternoon, Deenie,' Susan said, while I put my books in my desk. 'Aren't you excited about tryouts?'

'Not especially,' I said. I would never tell her the truth.

'Everybody thinks you're going to make the squad.'

'That's silly,' I said.

'But everybody thinks so anyway.'

I can't stand Susan and the way she talks. One time I complained about her at home and Ma said it's just that Susan looks up to me and I should feel flattered. But I don't. She's such a pain! And I don't think it's a compliment that she's always copying me either. I wish she wasn't in my form.

All morning I thought about cheerleading tryouts and I went over my cheers and jumps a thousand times in my mind, so I didn't hear Mr Fabrini when he called on me in English and he said I should stop dreaming about what I was going to eat for lunch and start paying attention.

Some days I bring my lunch from home and other days I buy it. It all depends on what Ma's got in the refrigerator. Today there wasn't anything good so I stood on line to buy the school lunch.

Midge usually gets to the cafeteria before me and Janet so she saves us a place. She brings the same lunch every day –

two hard-boiled eggs. But all she eats is the white part – the yolks wind up in the garbage.

Harvey Grabowsky always sits at one special table over in the corner. Nobody would dare sit there unless Harvey said it was okay. And he never waits on line for his lunch either. He's got a bunch of girls who do everything for him. Those girls are really stupid! I would never stand on line for the privilege of bringing Harvey Grabowsky his lunch. I wouldn't even do it for Buddy Brader, unless he asked me very nicely and had a good reason, like a broken leg or something.

When I carried my lunch over to where Midge and Janet were sitting I saw Buddy and two of his friends were at the next table. As I sat down he called, 'Hey Deenie . . .'

I said, 'Oh, hi Buddy,' and I shook my hair the way Deenie in the movie did when she talked to her Bud. Then I felt my face get hot so I looked away and started to eat. But it's hard to swallow when there's somebody staring at you and I'm pretty sure Buddy Brader was staring at me all through lunch.

three

At three o'clock I ran for the Girls' Room and so did everybody else. It was mobbed with all the kids who were going to tryouts. I didn't bother forcing my way close to the mirror. I went downstairs and when I passed the Special Class they were lining up to leave so I looked the other way. They give me a creepy feeling. I'm always scared Gena Courtney will see me and say something and I won't know what to say back.

I met Janet outside the auditorium. We waited a few minutes to make sure we wouldn't be the first ones going in. Then we walked down the aisle and found two seats in the middle of the fourth row.

The three judges were already there: Mrs Rappoport, Mr Delfone and Mrs Anderson. Mrs Rappoport is the girls' gym teacher. She really likes us – you can tell by the way she talks – she never raises her voice. And she doesn't make a big thing out of how clean our sneakers are either.

Mr Delfone is the boys' gym teacher and Mrs Anderson is the vice-principal of our school. As far as I know her only job is deciding what to do with kids who are discipline problems because if you make trouble you get sent to Mrs Anderson's office and sometimes you have to sit on the bench outside for a long time.

At three-fifteen Mrs Rappoport stood up and said, 'We're ready to begin now. Remember, girls, we'd love to choose every one of you but we can only pick one seventh grader, two eighth graders and three girls from ninth grade, so if you don't make it, don't feel too badly. There are so many other activities at Adams Junior High.'

Me and Janet squeezed hands. Hers felt cold and clammy. I pressed my legs tight together hoping I wouldn't get so nervous that I'd have to leave to go to the bathroom.

Mrs Rappoport said, 'We're going to call on you alphabetically and you can each do one cheer. After this round we'll decide on fifteen finalists.'

I looked around the auditorium. That meant most of us wouldn't even make the finals.

The first girl called was Alice Applebaum, a ninth grader. She went up on to the stage and did the same cheer I was going to do, spelling out the school name, first very slow, then faster, and finally very fast, with a big jump and a *Yea Team* at the end. She was really good and I was sure she would make it.

Four girls went before Mrs Rappoport called, 'Wilmadeene Fenner.' I stood up thinking this was almost as bad as at the modelling agency. Janet whispered, 'Good luck, Deenie,' and we squeezed hands again.

I ran to the front of the auditorium because that's what Alice Applebaum did and I figured she knew the ropes. I went up the stairs and out on to the stage. I didn't look at the judges or the other girls because I knew if I did I'd never be able to go through with it. I just stood there clearing my throat like an idiot and then I began.

A ... D ... A ... M ... S
A. D. A. M. S
ADAMS
Adams Adams
Junior High
Yea team!

I jumped as high as I could but my head didn't come close to touching my feet like Alice Applebaum's did. Still, I thought I'd done okay and when I passed Susan Minton on the way back to my seat she whispered, 'You were great, Deenie.' For once I was glad she thought so.

About forty minutes later Mrs Rappoport announced the fifteen finalists and Janet made it but I didn't. I pretended I was really happy for her. We hugged and everything before she said, 'I was sure it would be you, Deenie.'

I couldn't even answer her because I knew if I did I'd start crying so I just shook my head and tried to smile. I sat there all through the finals, not wanting to, but what would Janet think if I walked out on her?

I was hoping that Janet wouldn't make it. I wanted the other seventh grader who made the finals to win. Then me and Janet could be unhappy together.

But when Mrs Rappoport announced the judges' decision Janet was the seventh grader they picked and I had to act like I was really happy for her all over again.

She said, 'I have to call my mother right away. Oh Deenie . . . I'm so excited! I wish we both could have made it.'

I managed to say, 'Sure.'

Janet went to the phone booth outside the auditorium and while she was telling her mother the good news I knocked on the door and said I couldn't wait because I had to meet Helen at my father's gas station which was a big lie, but I couldn't face riding home on the bus with Janet.

four

I took the bus to Daddy's gas station, knowing that Helen
wouldn't be there because on Mondays and Wednesdays
she works at the library after school. Daddy wasn't out
front so I dumped my books on the counter inside and
looked in the garage. He was working away underneath a
station wagon. The second I saw him I started to cry. I
knew I would. I'd been holding it in so long it felt good. I
ran to him sobbing, 'Oh Daddy . . .'

He slid out from under the wagon and said, 'Deenie . . .
what is it?' When he stood up I grabbed hold of him and
buried my face in his uniform. It smelled nice, like
gasoline. I cried hard.

After a minute Daddy held me away. 'Deenie, what's
wrong?'

'I didn't make the cheerleading squad.' I could hardly
get the words out.

Daddy sighed and said, 'Is that why you're so
upset?'

I nodded. 'They chose Janet instead of me.'

Daddy smoothed my hair. 'Well, there'll be other times
for you to try.'

'No there won't. This is it!'

'So you'll find another activity.'

He sounded like Mrs Rappoport. When I was all cried
out Daddy gave me the key to the Ladies' Room and told
me to wash my face and he'd drive me home.

'Please don't tell Ma I was trying out. She'd probably
kill me.'

'I won't say a word to anyone,' Daddy said. 'Now go and
fix yourself up.'

I walked outside and around the back to the Ladies'
Room. I splashed some water on my face.

'That's much better,' Daddy said, when I came back. I hung the key on the wall and grabbed my books off the counter. Daddy and I walked outside together.

'I have to tell Joe to close up for me,' Daddy said, unlocking our car.

'I'll wait here.' I got in and slouched way down in my seat. I didn't want Joe to see that I'd been crying. Joe Roscow has worked for Daddy since June when he finished high school, and from the first day Helen met him she's been hanging around the gas station. He's only going to be here for one year because he's saving his money to go to Forest Ranger School in Oregon. I don't know what Helen sees in him except that he's friendly and he wipes everybody's windshield without them having to ask, which Daddy says makes for good business.

When we got home Ma and Aunt Rae were in the kitchen. Aunt Rae's not my real aunt. We just call her that because she and Ma have been best friends for years. Her kids are all grown and married and it makes me feel funny to think that Daddy and Ma could have kids that old too. Ma says she and Daddy wanted babies in the worst way but it took fourteen years for God to bless them.

Ma was surprised to see Daddy home so early. She said, 'Frank ... what's the matter?'

My father told her, 'Deenie dropped by so I decided I might as well drive her home and let Joe close up.'

'I'd better get supper started then. As soon as Helen comes home we can eat. Why don't you stay, Rae?'

Aunt Rae said, 'Thanks Thelma, I think I will.'

Aunt Rae's face reminds me of an owl. Even when I was a little kid I thought so, but I never told her. Not that there's anything wrong with looking like an owl. It's just that Aunt Rae might not think that's a compliment.

'How come you're so quiet today, Deenie?' Aunt Rae asked.

244

'I don't know.'

'You look like you've been crying,' she said. 'Thelma, doesn't she look like she's been crying?'

Ma squinted at me. 'Deenie, what's wrong with your eyes? They're all bloodshot.'

'Nothing, Ma.'

'You're sure?'

'Yes, Ma.'

'You better let me put some drops in them.'

'I don't want drops, Ma!'

'Thelma . . .' Daddy put his hands on Ma's shoulder. 'She's okay. Just let her be.'

Aunt Rae said, 'Well . . . we've got some news to cheer you up, Dennie. You have an appointment to see the head of one of the top modelling agencies in New York.'

'I do?' I asked Ma.

'Thanks to Aunt Rae,' Ma said. 'She sent your picture in without telling us. Today they called to say they want to see you.'

'They do?'

'A week from Friday, at two o'clock,' Aunt Rae said.

'But that's when I have French.'

'So you'll take the afternoon off,' Ma said.

'I can't. I can't miss French. I'll never be able to make it up.'

'Deenie . . .' Ma said. 'I don't think you understand. This is a very important interview.'

'I don't care,' I said. 'I'm not going to miss French.'

Aunt Rae stood up. 'I just remembered I have leftover chicken in the refrigerator. I think I'll go home for supper after all.'

When she was gone Ma said, 'That wasn't a very nice way to act in front of Aunt Rae.'

'I'm sorry.'

'I hope so,' Ma told me. 'Because Aunt Rae is very good to you.'

'I said I'm sorry!'

'I heard Janet made cheerleading,' Helen said at supper.

'Yes,' I told her.

'Well . . . don't feel too bad . . . I didn't make it either and I tried out all three years I was at Adams.'

'Who says I care one way or the other?' I took a sip of milk.

'Deenie has more important things to think about than cheerleading,' Ma said.

'But she tried out,' Helen told Ma.

Ma put her pork chop down. 'That was a waste of time, Deenie. Suppose you had been picked? You would have had to tell them you couldn't do it. You can't give up all that time. You'll be working soon.' She reached for the salt.

'I didn't try hard, Ma. I just did it to keep Janet company.' I glanced at Daddy but he kept on eating.

'Cheerleading's a big thing at Adams,' Helen told Ma. 'Practically all the seventh grade girls try out. Don't you remember how much I wanted to make it then?'

'With your brain you don't need to jump around yelling cheers!' Ma said.

Daddy finished his applesauce. 'I can understand why the girls try out,' he said. 'It makes them feel important to be on the cheerleading team.'

'Squad,' Helen said. 'They don't call it team. They call it squad.'

'Same difference,' Daddy said.

'As if Deenie needed to be a cheerleader to feel important. Just wait until her picture's on the cover of some magazine.' Ma waved her fork at me. 'I want you in bed by eight every night thi. week, Deenie.'

246

'But Ma ...'

'You heard me. I don't want to take you on this interview with circles under your eyes. And you've got to practise walking an hour a day. Remember the last time ... what that woman said?'

'Okay ... okay ...'

'Did you hear about Janet?' I asked Midge the next morning.

'Naturally. She called as soon as she got home. She was really excited.'

'She did just great,' I said. 'I knew the second she finished her cheer she'd make it. Did she tell you how I messed up?'

'No, what happened?' Midge asked.

'Oh, I flubbed my words and practically fell over backwards doing my jump. It was a riot! I almost cracked up right on the stage.' I laughed as hard as I could.

'Janet didn't tell me that.'

'I guess she didn't notice because she was nervous herself. But it was *so* funny. Anyway, I couldn't have accepted even if they'd picked me. You know I have all these interviews coming up. I really just tried out to keep Janet company.'

Midge didn't answer that because the bus came along then. We saved Janet a seat as usual, but when we got to her stop she wasn't waiting and we made it to school just as the first bell rang so we had to go straight to our formrooms. I wondered if Janet was sick. She seemed fine yesterday. Or maybe she was so excited she couldn't sleep last night and missed the bus.

Susan Minton was waiting by my desk in the formroom. 'I looked for you yesterday, after tryouts.'

'I had to go somewhere,' I said.

'Oh. I wanted to tell you what an awful mistake the judges made. They should have picked you. I just can't understand it.'

'Forget about it, will you, Susan!'

'Sure Deenie . . . if you want me to. It's just that everybody thinks you should have made it. I mean, Janet's okay and all, but she isn't anything special.'

'I said, just forget it! Janet's one of my best friends.'

'I know it,' Susan said. 'And you must be really happy for her.'

'That's a fact.' I took a book out of my desk and prentended to read.

I didn't see Janet until lunchtime. She was waiting for me in the cafeteria. I said, 'Hi . . . I thought you were sick or something.'

'Oh no. Alice Applebaum called last night to say her mother drives her to school three days a week and since she lives near me she offered me a ride. Especially since we'll be practising together and all that.'

'Oh.'

'We're getting our sweaters and skirts this afternoon.'

'That's nice.'

'Deenie . . . I wish we both could have made the squad.'

'Look,' I told her, 'even if I had made it I'd have to quit because my mother's lined up a lot of interviews for me and I just wouldn't have time for modelling and cheerleading too.'

'You know something? I think I made the squad because I had that chicken's foot in my purse. It really brought me good luck!' Janet opened her purse and pulled it out.

'You still have it?'

'Yes . . . but now I'm giving it to you. If you carry it on your next interview it'll bring *you* good luck!'

248

Janet handed it to me. I didn't want to touch it but I didn't want to insult her either. So I took some napkins, wrapped it up, and stuck it in my purse.

five

I have gym on Tuesdays and Thursdays right after lunch. I
like having it then because it makes the afternoon go fast
since there's only one period left after gym and that's when
I have French.

Our French teacher, Madame Hoffman, won't let us
speak one word of English while we're in her room. And
that means not one! On the first day of school I had to go
to the Girls' Room and Madame Hoffman wouldn't let me
out of her class until I could say, 'May I please be excused?'
in French. I almost died because by the time I learned to say
it I wasn't sure I would make it to the Girls' Room in
time. And the boys were all laughing at me too. I'm taking
Spanish next year.

Midge and Janet aren't in my gym class but Susan
Minton is. Whenever we have to take a partner she's always
right there grabbing for my hand. This year we have
modern dance. Starting in February we'll have sports. Then
we won't have to take partners so often.

I was so busy thinking about how to get out of being
Susan's partner that I didn't even care that the Creeping
Crud was getting changed next to me. Her real name is
Barbara Curtis but I named her the Creeping Crud because
she's got this disgusting rash all over her. It's supposed to
be some kind of allergy but who wants to take the chance of
finding out by touching her? It could be leprosy or
something like that! When we have to take partners in gym
she's always the one who's left over and Mrs Rappoport
says, 'Barbara, would you like to be my partner?'

I guess that's what would have happened today if I
hadn't been so pokey getting dressed. But by the time I
made it to the gym everyone had a partner, even Susan
Minton. And since somebody was absent there was an even

number of us today. So I wound up with Barbara Curtis and I had to do my warm-up exercises next to her, which wouldn't have been all that bad except when we were through Mrs Rappoport said, 'Okay, girls . . . now join hands with your partner and we'll practise our polka-step around the gym.'

I kept my hands behind my back until the music began.

'It's not catching,' Barbara said. 'It's just eczema.'

'I know that,' I told her.

'You act like you're scared to touch me.'

'Don't be silly,' I said and I grabbed her hand. It felt very rough, like sandpaper.

'And hop, step together, close . . .' Mrs Rappoport repeated as she clapped to the music. 'That's it . . . one, two, three . . . and hop, two, three . . . now spin your partner . . . very nice . . .'

When the bell rang I let go of Barbara's hand and ran for the row of sinks where I washed myself all over and lathered my hands at least six times.

At the end of the day, right before dismissal, Miss Greenleaf, my formroom teacher, called me up to her desk and handed me a note. It said:

Please send Deenie Fenner to see me in the gym after school. Thank you.

Eileen Rappoport

It must be about cheerleading, I thought. Somebody must have quit and I'm going to be her replacement. Janet was right – her chicken's foot did bring me good luck!

Midge was waiting for me in the hall downstairs but I told her I had to see Mrs Rappoport.

'What do you have to see her about?' Midge asked.

'I'm not sure,' I said. I didn't want to tell her the good news yet.

251

'Should I wait?'

'If you want . . . and if I'm going to be long then I'll come tell you and you can go home without me.'

I ran down to the gym and said, 'Hi, Mrs Rappoport. You wanted to see me?'

'Oh, yes Deenie. I'd like to talk to you about something.'

I smiled.

Mrs Rappoport ran her hand through her hair which is bright reddish-orange. She said, 'I noticed it yesterday, when you were trying out for cheerleading, and again today during gym class.'

What was she talking about? Maybe it didn't have anything to do with cheerleading after all.

'What is it?' I asked, thinking it might have something to do with Susan Minton – about her wanting to be my friend and me not being very nice to her. Or did Mrs Rappoport notice that I didn't want to hold hands with the Creeping Crud? Maybe I was going to get a lecture about that.

'I want you to bend over and touch your hands to your toes, Deenie.'

I did what Mrs Rappoport told me, all the time trying to figure out what touching my hands to my toes had to do with Susan Minton or the Creeping Crud unless this was how Mrs Rappoport punished kids who weren't nice to other people instead of sending them to Mrs Anderson's office to sit on the bench.

Mrs Rappoport circled around me a few times. Then she said, 'Okay Deenie . . . you can stand up again. This time I'd like you to walk across the room slowly.'

As soon as she said that I knew it wasn't Susan Minton or Barbara Curtis that Mrs Rappoport wanted to see me about. And it didn't have anything to do with cheerleading either. Which is why I suddenly shouted, 'It's my posture, isn't it? That's why I didn't make cheerleading. That's why I didn't even make the finals!'

'That has something to do with it, Deenie,' Mrs Rappoport said. 'Do you know your skirt is longer on one side than the other . . . and it was the same way yesterday, during tryouts.'

'I told my mother about that but she says it's because I slouch. What should I do . . . walk with books on my head for ever?'

'No, nothing like that. There could be some exercises that might help, though. I'll be in touch with your parents about it. We'll talk more another time. You run along now . . . and thanks for stopping by.'

Midge was waiting for me outside. 'That didn't take very long,' she said. 'What'd Mrs Rappoport want?'

'Something about my posture,' I told her.

'What about it?'

'I'm not sure. Do you think I have bad posture?'

'I never noticed. Let me see you walk.'

I walked a few feet and turned around. 'Well . . . did you notice anything?'

'Nope. You look just the same as always.'

'My mother's going to kill me. She'll say I'm slouching on purpose.'

'So don't tell her.'

'Don't worry . . . I won't. But Mrs Rappoport's going to call. She said she'd be in touch with my parents.'

'Maybe she'll write them a letter.'

'Maybe . . . but either way my mother's going to be plenty sore. You can't be a model if you don't have good posture.'

'So you can be something else.'

'Try and tell that to my mother!' I opened my purse, pulled out the chicken's foot and dumped it into the trash can on the corner.

six

Every night after supper Helen takes off for Myra Woodruff's house. They do their homework together. I can't believe my sister has that much studying to do. Nobody expects much from my schoolwork so I get by with hardly ever cracking a book as long as I don't bring home any D's or F's.

Ma says Helen is excused from helping with the dishes because she works at the library twice a week and she baby-sits every weekend, so she needs all the studying time she can get. I'm *never* excused from helping in the kitchen. Ma usually does the washing and I dry everything and if, God forbid, I put something away that's just a teensy bit wet I never hear the end of it. My mother's very fussy about the kitchen. Well, she's fussy about the whole house. She spends hours and hours cleaning the place. She says our floors are so clean you could eat off them, not that anybody is thinking about doing that, but you could. One thing I'm sure of is I don't want to spend my life cleaning some house like Ma. Sometimes I think Helen's lucky. She'll be a doctor or lawyer or engineer and she'll never have to do those things. But if I don't make it as a model, then what?

The phone rang just as I was putting away the last pot. I hollered, 'I'll get it,' and ran to the front hall.

It was Mrs Rappoport. I recognized her voice right away and she knew mine too because she said, 'Hello Deenie. May I speak to your mother or your father please.'

I thought about which one I should call to the phone and decided on Daddy. If Mrs Rappoport was going to discuss my posture Ma might get upset.

'Who is it?' Daddy asked, when I told him there was a phone call.

'It's Mrs Rappoport, my gym teacher,' I said, covering the mouthpiece with my hand.

I stood right next to my father while he said, 'Hello, this is Frank Fenner.'

After that he didn't say anything except a couple of 'uh huhs' and one 'yes, I see'. He motioned for me to go away so I went back to the kitchen, wondering exactly what Mrs Rappoport was telling him.

'Who was on the phone?' Ma asked.

'Mrs Rappoport, my gym teacher.'

'What does she want?'

'I'm not sure,' I said.

Ma sprinkled some cleanser into the sink. 'Did you do something wrong?'

'No Ma . . . nothing like that.'

She rinsed the sink clean. 'Then why is she calling here?'

'I don't know.'

'Well,' Ma said, putting down the dish towel. 'I better find out.'

Daddy was hanging up when we got to the hall.

'What was that all about?' Ma asked him.

'When was the last time Deenie had a check-up at Dr Moravia's office?' Daddy said.

'In April,' Ma told him. 'She had to have one before junior high. Why?'

Daddy looked at me. I don't think he wanted to say anything else but he did. 'It seems that Mrs Rappoport thinks we should take her for another one.'

'What for?' Ma asked, turning towards me. 'Deenie, do you feel sick? Is there something you haven't told me?'

'No, Ma,' I said. 'I think it's my posture. That's all.'

'That's right,' Daddy said. 'Mrs Rappoport noticed it and thinks we should look into the situation. There might be some exercises that Dr Moravia could recommend.'

255

'You're talking in circles,' Ma said.

Daddy gave her a sharp look which meant he wasn't going to discuss it in front of me.

Ma said, 'Deenie, you promised to practise standing very straight and tall.'

'I tried,' I said.

'I don't think so,' Ma told me. 'I think you've got other things on your mind so you forget what's really important!'

'Thelma ...' Daddy began.

'Frank, that girl has got to learn ...'

'I don't want to talk about it any more,' I called, racing up the stairs.

I got undressed and stood in front of my mirror. Helen doesn't have a full-length mirror in her room but I let her use mine whenever she wants to see her whole self, which is practically never. I turned around and around, trying to see myself from all angles. There wasn't anything wrong with my posture! I wasn't round-shouldered and my stomach didn't stick out either. So what was Mrs Rappoport so excited about that she had to call my parents?

The next afternoon, when I got home from school, Ma said, 'We have to be at Dr Moravia's office by four. Aunt Rae's coming to pick us up in a few minutes. Go and wash your hands and face and make sure your underwear's clean with no rips.'

'Oh Ma! Who cares about my underwear?'

'I do,' Ma said. 'So get going.'

'Okay,' I told her, heading upstairs.

I don't mind Dr Moravia as long as I don't need a shot or that tine test which he always says will feel like a little mosquito bite, when it really feels more like a big bee sting. But I had that in April. So probably he'll give Ma a prescription for some vitamins and tell her to stop worrying because I'm just going through the awkward stage. Or maybe I'm going to get my period again. I had it once, last June. The booklet I sent for says when you start out it might be a long time before you get regular, like Helen. So maybe that's why my posture's funny. Except I never heard of bad posture as a symptom of getting your period. But if that's what it is then Ma can't be mad at me, so I hope it is.

My mother doesn't drive. Aunt Rae takes her every place she has to go. Or else she goes by bus. But since Aunt Rae has nothing better to do she doesn't mind driving Ma around. Especially since she has a new car. It's bright blue and Aunt Rae takes such good care of it I wouldn't dare spit my gum in the ashtray like I do when I ride with Daddy.

When we got to Dr Moravia's office there were three kids ahead of me. Ma's always saying the best place to pick up germs is waiting at the doctor's office. By now I know better than to sit near anybody who's coughing or looking sick.

At my last check-up Dr Moravia filled in a bunch of forms for junior high. I got weighed, measured and had my blood pressure taken first. Then Dr Moravia looked into my eyes, up my nose and down my throat. He also listened to my heart.

This time when he called me into his office he told Ma to wait outside with Aunt Rae, instead of coming in with me.

'How's everything, Deenie?' Dr Moravia asked.

'Just fine,' I told him.

'Good . . . good . . . let's see how much you've grown. Step on to the scale please.'

'You've gained a half pound since last April and you're an inch taller,' Dr Moravia said, when he was done weighing and measuring me.

'Do you think I'm going to be huge?' I asked.

He laughed a little. 'You're going to be just right.'

'My mother wants me to be a model so it won't hurt if I get really tall.'

Dr Moravia smiled. 'Now Deenie . . . I'd like you to

bend over and touch your hands to your toes.'

'My gym teacher made me do the same thing.'

Dr Moravia pressed his hand against my side.

'I really try to stand up straight,' I said.

'It has nothing to do with that,' he told me. 'You can come up now, Deenie.'

'It's not my posture?' I asked, straightening my clothes.

'No. It's your spine, I think. But I'm going to send you over to see a friend of mine just to make sure. His name is Dr Griffith.'

'What's he going to do?'

'Oh, just take some X-rays and look you over.'

'You think something's broken?' I asked.

'No. But something might be growing the wrong way.'

'What do you mean?'

'Well, I can't say for sure, but Dr Griffith is a specialist – an orthopaedist – and he'll be able to find out exactly what the trouble is.'

'Do you think it's something bad?'

'Nothing that can't be fixed,' Dr Moravia said, opening the door to his office and calling my mother. 'Deenie, you can sit in the waiting room now. Your mother will be out in a minute.'

I sat down next to Aunt Rae. She was reading a magazine called *Today's Health*. She closed it as soon as she saw me and asked, 'What did he say?'

'I'm not sure,' I told her. 'Something about my spine.'

'Your spine?' Aunt Rae said.

'Yes ... why ... is that bad?'

'I don't know,' Aunt Rae told me. 'You're sure he said your spine?'

'Yes ... I think so.' He did, didn't he? Now I was getting all mixed up. Or did he say my *tine*? Maybe my tine test came out wrong. But if that was so why didn't he give me another one back in April?

In a few minutes Ma came out of Dr Moravia's office, clutching a piece of paper. 'What's that?' I asked. 'Is it a prescription? Did you remind him I can't swallow pills?'

'It's nothing,' Ma said. 'It's just a doctor's name and address.'

'Oh ... Dr Griffith ... right? He's a friend of Dr Moravia's. Did you know that?'

Ma didn't answer me. She just said, 'Let's go.'

When we were in the car I asked, 'Well ... what'd he tell you?'

'Nothing definite,' Ma said. 'We have to see Dr Griffith first.'

'But it's not my fault. He told you that, didn't he?'

Ma acted like she didn't hear me.

Aunt Rae said, 'Who wants to stop for a soda?'

Ma heard that because she said, 'Let's go home. We'll have something there.'

I said, 'Ma, didn't Dr Moravia tell you that it's not my fault?' I wanted to get that straight right away.

'Yes,' Ma said. 'Yes, he did tell me that.'

'Good! Now you can't be mad at me.'

'But I don't believe him,' Ma said.

'Then you do think it's my fault?'

'I didn't say that.'

'Then what?'

'I mean ... doctors make mistakes all the time.'

seven

Dr Griffith's nurse called Wednesday night, saying that
someone had cancelled an appointment for Thursday
morning and that Ma should bring me in at nine-thirty.

I phoned Midge to tell her I wouldn't be at the bus stop
because of an important appointment.

'Another interview?' she asked.

'No, a doctor's appointment.'

'Why? What's wrong?'

'I don't know . . . remember that business about my
posture?'

'Yes.'

'Well . . . this doctor I have to see is an orthopaedist.'

'That's a bone specialist.'

'How do you know?'

'Because last year, when I broke my arm, I had to go to
an orthopaedist.'

'Dr Griffith?' I asked.

'No, Dr Littel. He was nice.'

'I wish I was going to him. At least you could tell me
what he's like.' .

'Don't worry. It probably won't even hurt.'

'I hope not. I'll let you know on Friday.'

'Okay. Bye.'

What really surprised me on Thursday morning was that
Daddy didn't go to the gas station. Instead of Aunt Rae
driving us to Dr Griffith's office, Daddy was going to take
us himself, which is what gave me the idea that there was
something really bad wrong with me because why else did
Helen actually talk to me at breakfast? For somebody who
was so sick I felt fine. I felt just like always. So I decided
I must have one of those weird diseases where you

never know anything's wrong with you until the end.

Dr Griffith's office is in the Medical Arts Building on West Jersey Street. We parked in the lot behind the building and took the elevator up to the third floor. The waiting room was full of people and most of them had some kind of cast on their arms or legs.

We sat in the waiting room until ten after ten when the nurse called my name. Daddy and Ma stood up with me and the nurse showed us into a little office where another nurse told us to sit down. Then she asked us a lot of questions which Daddy answered, things like our address and phone number and what kind of medical insurance we have. When she got to that question Daddy took some cards out of his wallet and showed her the numbers on them. She must have been a good typist because as Daddy answered her questions she typed everything out on yellow forms, without ever looking down at her fingers.

After that the first nurse came back and told my parents they could go sit in the waiting room and she would call them when the doctor was ready to talk. She took me into an examining room and told me to take off all my clothes except my underpants. Then she handed me this white paper thing made like a bathrobe. 'Tie it in the back, please. The doctor will be with you in a few minutes.' She left the room and closed the door behind her.

I didn't like the idea of getting undressed, but I did. The paper robe was so big I had to wrap it around myself twice. And when I walked it dragged all over the floor.

I waited for the doctor for twenty whole minutes. I know because I watched a big clock on the wall. It jumped every minute, same as the clocks in school. I checked everything in the room, wondering what Dr Griffith would do to me, if he ever showed up. There was a table of instruments but none of them looked too scary. A few looked like different sized scissors. I didn't see any needles or knives, and was I glad! The stool I was sitting on turned around and around and I spent some time twirling on it until I got dizzy. Then I read all the diplomas on the wall. I found out Dr Griffith's first name is Harold. I also found out where he went to college, where he went to medical school and what year he got out of the army. There was an old fashioned picture of a football team too. I wondered if one of those funny looking guys was Dr Griffith.

Finally the door opened and this huge man walked in. He was wearing a white coat so I knew he was Dr Griffith. Another nurse was with him. She had a pin on her uniform saying MISS VERNON. 'Deenie ... this is Dr Griffith,' she told me.

Dr Griffith closed the folder he'd been reading and put it down on the instrument table. 'Hello there,' he said. 'Let's see what Dr Moravia's talking about. Come over here please, Deenie.'

Dr Griffith is about twice as big as Dr Moravia and I've always thought Dr Moravia is pretty big himself. Dr Griffith looks like a giant. I don't see how he fits through doorways, he's so tall. I didn't move. I just sat there on my twirl-around stool and looked at him.

'Come on, Deenie. I'm not going to hurt you.'

'What are you going to do?'

'Just have a look,' Dr Griffith said.

'Really?' I asked, glancing at Miss Vernon. I couldn't tell anything from her expression. She was busy checking her fingernails.

'I promise,' Dr Griffith said.

I stood up and walked over to him. His hands looked big enough to squash a person right in half. He turned me away from him and untied my paper robe. Then he put his hands on my back. They were freezing cold. I tried to think of

262

other things. I asked him, 'Were you ever a football player?'

'A long time ago,' Dr Griffith said, pressing on my back. 'When I was in high school.'

'I thought so. You're in that picture aren't you?' I asked him, pointing to the wall.

'Yes. Third row, seventh from the left. Would you put your hand down at your side please?'

'Oh, I'm sorry,' I told him.

'That's better.'

'Were you a good football player?'

'I was fair,' he said. 'Are you interested in football?'

'I'm not sure. I don't know much about it yet. I wanted to be a cheerleader, but I didn't make the squad.'

He didn't say anything about that. I thought he would. I thought he'd say, 'Well, you can try again next year' or something like that. Instead he said, 'Bend over and touch your toes with your hands, Deenie.'

'Why does everybody keep asking me to do that?'

'It's a good way for us to see if your hips are even,' Dr Griffith said.

'Suppose they're not?'

'If one is higher than the other it might indicate the problem.'

'Oh,' I said, wondering what that meant.

Dr Griffith pushed at my side. Then he told me to sit down on the turn-around stool and he looked me over from every angle.

'Now Deenie, lie down on the table please,' Dr Griffith said.

I climbed up on to the examining table. Miss Vernon stood next to me and smiled.

'Legs out straight please,' Dr Griffith said.

'Are you going to hurt me?' I asked. 'I'm not scared but I'd rather know in advance.'

'I'm just going to measure you,' Dr Griffith said. I didn't

believe him so I was really surprised when he held a tape
measure to my right hip and measured me from there to my
ankle. Then he went around to my other side and did the
same thing.

'Do I measure okay?' I asked.

'Um . . .' Dr Griffith said, as he jotted something down
in his folder. 'Now, one more thing, Deenie. Come down off
the table and stand up straight.'

I jumped down from the table and stood as straight as I
could. That's when Dr Griffith did the craziest thing – he
came from behind, put his hands on the sides of my face
and lifted me right off the floor.

'Put me down!' I said. 'I don't like that!'

'Sorry,' Dr Griffith told me, 'but it's important.' He
lowered me to the floor and moved me from side to side.

When he was done Miss Vernon asked, 'That wasn't so
bad, was it, Deenie?'

I knew then that Dr Griffith must be through examining
me.

'Okay,' Miss Veron said. 'Follow me and I'll show you to
the X-ray room.'

She led me down the hall until we came to a room
marked X-ray. Another nurse was waiting for me there. She
said, 'Hello Deenie, I'm Mrs Hall, the X-ray technician,
and I'm going to take some pictures of you. You won't feel
a thing, so just relax.'

Mrs Hall arranged me into certain positions and she was
right, I didn't feel anything. It was just like having a regular
picture taken. First she took X-rays of me standing up and
then lying down on the table and bending to the side. Each
time she got me ready she left the room to stand behind a
door with a glass window in it and she'd say, 'Take a deep
breath now . . . and hold it until I tell you to breathe again.'

All I heard was a little buzzer noise and then she'd say,
'Okay . . . relax.'

264

When she was done with me I got dressed and Miss Vernon came back to take me into an office with a nice orange rug. Daddy and Ma joined me there.

'How'd it go, Deenie?' Daddy asked.

'It didn't hurt,' I told him.

Dr Griffith opened the door and told us to make ourselves comfortable. He was carrying the same folder and when he sat down at his desk he spread it out in front of him. Finally he said, 'Well now . . . Dr Moravia was right. Deenie has adolescent idiopathic scoliosis.'

All I understood of that was adolescent and something that sounded like idiotic.

'What does that mean?' Daddy asked.

'It means she has a structural curvature of the spine which has a strong tendency to progress rapidly during the adolescent growth spurt. Let me show you something,' Dr Griffith said, taking an X-ray out of the folder. He stuck it up on some kind of screen on the wall and when he turned a switch it all lit up and the X-ray looked like a skeleton. He tapped a pencil to the X-ray. 'You see here . . .' he said. 'This is Deenie's spine. It demonstrates the curve and confirms my clinical diagnosis.'

'I don't understand,' Ma said. 'Why Deenie . . . of all people?'

'I can't answer that, Mrs Fenner. But there is a strong familial tendency.'

Ma shook her head. 'No one in my family has ever had anything like this. My family's always been very healthy.'

'I can't think of anyone either,' Daddy said.

'The important thing now is Deenie,' Dr Griffith said. 'Not who's to blame for her condition.'

'Am I going to die?' I asked.

'Deenie!' Ma said.

But I didn't care that she didn't like my question. So I asked it again. 'Well, am I?'

'Eventually we're all going to die,' Dr Griffith said. 'But not of scoliosis. I can promise you that.'

'Then what's the difference if I have it?'

'We have to correct the curve,' Dr Griffith said.

Daddy asked, 'What do you suggest, Doctor?'

'I suggest you see a scoliosis specialist,' Dr Griffith told him. 'I can recommend a good man to you.'

'Another doctor?' I asked.

'Yes.'

'But I don't want to see another doctor! Can't you just fix it up yourself?'

'No,' Dr Griffith said. 'I don't handle scoliosis cases.'

'What can be done for her?' Daddy asked.

'There are two choices,' Dr Griffith told him. 'Surgery or a brace.'

I stood up. 'Suppose I don't want either one,' I said in a very loud voice.

'We have to correct the curve,' Dr Griffith said again.

I was tired of listening to the same old line. So I asked him, 'Who says we have to correct it? Why not just leave it alone?'

'It has to be corrected for cosmetic reasons,' Dr Griffith told me.

'Cosmetic?' Ma said, before I had a chance to ask about it. 'What do you mean?'

'If the curve isn't corrected it will result in a spinal deformity,' Dr Griffith said.

'You're not telling us that Deenie's going to be deformed, are you?' Daddy asked, while Ma started whispering 'Oh my God,' over and over again.

'I'm saying her condition has to be corrected in order to prevent such a deformity,' Dr Griffith said. 'The sooner the better.'

In the car, on the way home, Ma told Daddy, 'Your cousin

266

Belle had something wrong with her back ... remember?'

'That was different,' Daddy said. 'She had a slipped disc.'

'But I'll bet that's where this came from.'

'I don't think so,' Daddy said.

'Because you don't want to think so!' Ma told him.

I wanted them to stop acting like babies and start helping me. I expected Daddy to explain everything on the way home – all that stuff Dr Griffith had been talking about – that I didn't understand. Instead, he and Ma argued about whose fault it was that I have something wrong with my spine until we pulled into our driveway. It was almost as if they'd forgotten I was there.

eight

As soon as Daddy unlocked the front door I ran upstairs.

'Deenie . . .' Ma called. 'Where are you going?'

'To my room.'

'Come have a snack with us.'

'I'm not hungry.' I closed my bedroom door and took the S volume of my encyclopedia down from the shelf. If Daddy wasn't going to explain anything to me then I'd have to find out about it myself.

I looked up scoliosis. It said: *Skoh lih OH sihs, means a side-to-side curve or bend of the normally straight spine or backbone. Scoliosis may occur in any part of the spine. It may be single (curved like a C) or double (curved like an S). Scoliosis starts in childhood or the teens. It has a strong familial tendency. Treatment includes exercises, braces or surgery.*

I copied all of that down in my notebook. I didn't understand the whole thing but I got the general idea. The next thing I looked up was spine. There was half a column, none of it very interesting. But under related articles it said *hunchback*. So I slammed the book closed and reached for *H.* I copied down everything: *Hunchback is a severe rounded or sharp prominence of the upper part of the back. Because this part of the back sticks out like a big hump, the condition is sometimes called humpback. Hunchback is caused by any condition that deforms the bones of the upper part of the spine. Hunchback involves the portion of the spine to which the ribs are connected. The hump results when the front part of the spinal bones collapses, spreading the back part.*

The last part didn't make much sense but the rest of it was a good description of Old Lady Murray!

That night, when I was ready for bed, I read over what

I'd written a few times before I made up my mind. I would have an operation! I'd let the doctors fix me up. So what if I missed a few weeks of school. It would still be better than wearing a brace or winding up like Old Lady Murray.

I ran downstairs to tell Daddy and Ma about my decision, but the kitchen door was closed and I could hear them talking. I stood next to the door and listened.

Ma said, 'No one's cutting Deenie open!'

'Thelma,' Daddy told her, 'he didn't say they'd have to operate.'

'I don't care what they say,' Ma answered. 'Nobody's cutting Deenie open. Doctors make mistakes all the time.'

'Stop fooling yourself!' Daddy said. 'The doctors are right about Deenie.'

'Even if they are I'm not letting them operate. Suppose they make a mistake while she's on the table? They could cut the wrong thing and she'll wind up a cripple. Is that what you want?'

'They probably won't have to operate. We'll see what Dr Kliner says. After all, he's a specialist.'

Ma started crying. 'My beautiful baby . . . my beautiful, beautiful baby.'

'Carrying on like this isn't going to help Deenie,' Daddy said.

'Oh Frank! I had such plans for her,' Ma said. 'I can't believe this is really happening.'

I turned away from the kitchen door and ran back to my room. As soon as I got into bed I started touching myself. I have this special place and when I rub it I get a very nice feeling. I don't know what it's called or if anyone else has it but when I have trouble falling asleep, touching my special place helps a lot.

The next day, in the cafeteria, I told Janet and Midge, 'I'm going to have an operation.'

'What?' Janet spat out a piece of ham. 'I don't believe it!'

'Is that why you went to the orthopaedist?' Midge asked.

I looked around to make sure no one else could hear, especially Buddy Brader, who was at the next table. Midge and Janet put their heads near mine and I talked very softly. 'I wouldn't want this to get around,' I said.

'Don't worry.'

'Our lips are sealed.'

'Well . . .' I looked around one more time but Buddy wasn't listening. He was fooling around with his friends. 'I have a crooked spine,' I whispered. 'And they have to operate to straighten it out.'

'No kidding!' Janet said.

'So it wasn't your posture?' Midge asked.

'No.'

'When are you going to the hospital?' Janet said.

'I don't know yet. I have to see one more doctor but I think it will be soon.'

'Which hospital?' Midge asked. 'General?'

'I don't know that either.'

'I hope we can visit you,' Janet said.

'You better!'

'But you have to be fourteen to visit patients,' Midge said.

'So? We can look fourteen,' Janet said. 'I'll just fix my hair like this . . .' She pulled all her hair up on top of her head. 'And I'll make an old-looking face like this . . .' Janet looked so silly me and Midge couldn't help laughing at her.

'Listen . . .' I told them, giving Midge a friendly punch in the arm, 'I like pink roses best!'

That night Janet called. 'Can you come downtown with me and Midge tomorrow?'

'To shop?'

'No . . . for lunch and a movie.'

'Hang on . . . I have to ask.' I put the phone down and went into the kitchen. Ma was finishing up the dishes. She said yes, I could go downtown with my friends.

We took the bus at ten-thirty so we'd have enough time to go exploring in Woolworth's before lunch, but at the last minute Janet and Midge decided to get off in front of Drummond's Department Store instead.

'Why are we getting off here?' I asked.

'To go shopping . . .' Midge said.

'But you said we weren't going to shop. I only brought $3.50 with me.'

'Don't worry,' Midge said.

Janet grabbed my arm. 'Come on Deenie!' She pulled me through the revolving door and into the store. Then Midge took my other arm and both of them led me to the elevator. 'Fourth floor, please,' Midge told the operator.

'What's going on?' I asked.

'You'll see in a minute,' Janet said.

I tried to think of what could be on the fourth floor. 'Shoes?' I asked.

'Nope,' Janet said, starting to laugh.

The elevator door opened and we stepped out.

'Tell me what's happening!' I said.

'Soon . . . soon . . .'

We walked across the floor to a small department called JUNIOR LINGERIE. There was a salesgirl behind the counter and Janet told her, 'We'd like to see something beautiful in a nightgown.'

'What size?' the salesgirl asked.

'For her,' Midge said, pointing at me.

I opened my mouth but before I could say anything Midge said, 'It's for the hospital . . . after your operation . . .'

'So you look pretty when we come to visit,' Janet added.

'I . . . I mean I . . . I don't . . .' I began.

'Don't say a word,' Janet said. 'That's what friends are for.' She turned to the salesgirl. 'She's having an operation . . . not that you'd know it to look at her, but she is.'

'Oh, I'm sorry,' the salesgirl said.

'She's going to be fine when it's over,' Janet told her.

'I'm sure she will,' the salesgirl said. 'What colour do you like?' she asked me.

'Ummm . . . pink,' I said. 'Either that or lavender.'

We looked through a pile of nighties before we found one made of two layers of the softest nylon. The top layer was pink and the underneath was purple so when you moved it around it had a sort of lavender look to it.

'That's perfect!' Janet said, holding it up to me.

'What do you think, Deenie?' Midge asked.

'It's beautiful!' I said. 'But it's $12·95.'

'Never mind about that,' Midge told me. 'We're charging it. As long as it's what you really want we don't care what it costs.'

'I love it!' I said, thinking that maybe Buddy Brader would visit me too.

'We'll take it,' Janet said. 'And we'd like it gift-wrapped because it's a present.'

When we were outside again I hugged Janet and Midge and told them, 'No girl could have better friends!'

Next we went to lunch but they wouldn't let me pay for anything even though I kept saying, 'But I have $3·50.'

'Save it,' Midge said. 'Everything's on us.'

'You're the guest of honour,' Janet said. 'And guess what movie we're taking you to see?'

'I don't know.'

'The one at the Rialto . . . it's X-rated.'

I started to laugh. 'But how can we get in? You have to be eighteen, at least.'

'We can pass for that with no trouble,' Janet told me.

'Just concentrate on looking old.'

But besides looking old you also had to prove you were at least eighteen and since we couldn't the lady in the booth wouldn't sell us tickets so we settled for the movie down the street which was called *Massachusetts General* and from the pictures outside we knew it was about a hospital.

There were two cartoons before the main picture and by that time we needed more popcorn so Midge went out to the lobby to buy it. When she came back she whispered, 'I just saw Buddy Brader and Steve Hildrick.'

'Where are they sitting?' I asked.

'I don't know. I saw them buying candy.'

'Did they see you?' Janet said.

'Sure,' Midge told her. 'I said hello to them.'

'Did they ask who you were with?' I said.

'No. They didn't say anything.'

I turned around in my seat but I couldn't find them anywhere.

'Are they by themselves or with a whole bunch of guys?' Janet asked.

'I don't know!' Midge said. 'What's the difference anyway?'

'None,' Janet told her.

I turned around again. Were they sitting near by? Could they see us? I should have worn a clean sweater.

The picture started. The first scene was of this young doctor making out with a nurse. You knew it was a nurse because she still had on her white hat. Naturally we all laughed. The next scene showed a gory operation. I could still hear Ma saying, 'Nobody's going to cut Deenie open.'

Midge leaned across Janet and said, 'Maybe you shouldn't watch this part, Deenie.'

'It's all right,' I told her. 'My operation's not going to be like that.'

'They're not going to mess with Deenie's guts,' Janet

whispered. 'Just her spine . . . isn't that right?'

'That's right,' I said.

Somebody sat down in the seat next to me then. I glanced over because Ma's told me a million times never to let a strange man sit next to me in the movies. If one does I'm supposed to get up and change seats and if the man should follow me I'm supposed to call the usher and report him.

Only it wasn't a strange man sitting next to me this time. It was Buddy Brader. When I looked over at him he was staring right at me. And he was kind of smiling too.

I said, 'Oh, hi Buddy.'

Steve Hildrick was sitting next to him. So I whispered, 'Hi Steve.'

They acted like they were really surprised to see me.

I tried very hard to concentrate on the movie but it wasn't easy. Pretty soon Buddy Brader put his arm around my chair and when he did, Janet, who was on my other side, gave me a kick and started to laugh. So I looked over at Buddy as if to say, 'What do you think you're doing?' and that's when he took his arm off the back of the seat and put it on my shoulder! After a few minutes of that he leaned close and whispered, 'Why don't you change seats with Steve?'

Janet, who was leaning just as close on my other side, said, 'Go ahead, Dennie.' I guess that meant she wanted to sit next to Steve. So I stood up and moved over while Steve sat down between Buddy and Janet. He put his arm around her right away. Not the chair, but *her*.

This time Buddy didn't do that. He reached down for my hand instead. I never held hands with a boy before. At least, never like that, in a dark place where you don't have to hold hands because you need a partner for any special reason, like dancing or something.

It felt very nice too. Buddy's fingers were warm. I didn't

look at him once the whole time we were holding hands. But when the young doctor and nurse were going at it again he squeezed my fingers which made me look over at Janet to see if she noticed that I was holding hands, and I saw she and Steve were doing the same thing except he still had his other arm around her. Midge was still looking straight ahead at the movie.

Halfway through the picture I noticed that my hand was sweating. It was during the scene where the girl died on the operating table. You knew she was dead when the bleeps stopped and the lines didn't go up and down on the little machine any more. By then I really had to go to the bathroom. I've never been able to make it through a whole show. Even when I was little Ma had to take me out a couple of times whenever we saw a movie. So I whispered, 'Excuse me,' to Buddy and he let go of my hand. When he did he wiped his own off on his pants.

I went to the Ladies' Room and when I was done I stopped to have a look in the mirror. If only I'd known I was going to meet Buddy Brader I'd have washed my hair.

When I got back to my seat Buddy picked up my hand again. I was hoping he would.

As soon as the picture was over we all walked outside together and then Buddy and Steve said, 'See you around,' and they took off.

I thought Buddy would say something more to me. And I guess Janet was kind of disappointed too because she called after them, 'Okay ... see you around.'

Buddy and Steve turned and waved and me and Janet waved back.

Then the three of us walked to the bus stop. Midge didn't say a word all that time. When we got there she bought a pack of sugarless gum from Old Lady Murray but she didn't offer a piece to me or Janet.

I didn't look away from Old Lady Murray like usual.
Instead, I said 'Hello' to her, which I've never done before.
She said 'Hello' back and I could see her gold front tooth.
She was wearing a black sweater with a rip in one sleeve
and over that she had on a carpenter's apron with a million
pockets where she kept her change. I studied the bump on
her back and wondered if she always had it or if it grew
there when she got older.

Our bus came and we got on and found three seats
together. As soon as we sat down I told Janet how my hand
sweated in the movies and how Buddy wiped it off on his
pants and she told me that Steve let his hand rest over her
shoulder like maybe he was trying to feel something else,
but she didn't know what to do about it so she didn't do
anything.

Midge listened to us and then right when Janet was
telling me she's always liked Steve Hildrick secretly, Midge
said, 'I think it's cheap to let boys sit next to you in the
movies. Did you see how fast they got away as soon as we
were outside? They were just interested in what they could
get in the dark.'

'That's not so!' Janet said. 'You're just saying that
because there were only two of them.'

'I am not!' Midge told her.

'Suppose Harvey Grabowsky sat down next to you and
wanted to hold your hand,' Janet said. 'I'll bet anything
you'd let him.'

'Those measly eighth graders aren't Harvey Grabowsky!'
Midge practically shouted.

'You're just jealous!' Janet insisted.

'Jealous ... ha!'

I didn't say anything because I knew the truth. Midge
really was jealous and I didn't blame her. I held my
gift-wrapped nightie close. It was too bad that Midge
had helped plan such a nice day for me and now she was

going home feeling worse than anybody. I hope the next time we meet Buddy Brader in the movies he's got at least two friends with him and that one of them will like Midge!

nine

Monday night I couldn't finish my supper.

'You need all your vitamins,' Ma said. 'Especially now.'

'I just don't feel hungry,' I said.

'I cooked all afternoon,' Ma told me.

'I'm sorry . . .'

'Oh, leave her alone for once!' Helen said.

'Since when are you her mother?' Ma asked.

'If I was I wouldn't pick on her the night before she has to see another doctor!'

'Nobody's picking on Deenie,' Daddy said. 'Ma's only saying she needs her strength.'

'And you should mind your manners, Helen Fenner,' Ma said.

'Besides,' Daddy said, 'Deenie's not worried about seeing Dr Kliner.'

'Of course she's not,' Ma said. 'Why should she be worried? Nobody's going to do anything to her.'

'Can I be excused?' I asked.

Later, Helen came to my room with a piece of cake and a glass of milk. 'If I had scoliosis I'd want to talk about it.' She put the cake on my desk and handed me the milk. 'But Ma's told me a million times not to mention it to you.'

'There's nothing to talk about,' I told her. 'I'm having an operation and then I won't have scoliosis any more.'

'I've been reading up on it at the library,' Helen said, 'and I don't think you're going to need an operation.'

'You're wrong, Helen. I do need one. I already told Janet and Midge. You want to see something?' I went to my dresser and opened the bottom drawer where I'd hidden my new nightie. I pulled it out and held it up. 'Midge and

Janet gave it to me for when I go to the hospital.'

'It's beautiful,' Helen said, touching the material.

'Do you remember some cousin of Daddy's named Belle?' I asked.

'No.'

'Ma says I got my scoliosis from her.'

'She had it too?'

'No, but she had a bad back.'

'That probably doesn't have a thing to do with it.'

'That's what Daddy said, but Ma doesn't believe him.'

'Ma really burns me up sometimes!' Helen said. 'I wish Daddy would tell her off just once!'

On Tuesday morning I wasn't surprised that Daddy stayed home from work to drive me to my appointment. I expected him to. What did surprise me was that Dr Kliner's office is in New York and the building it's in looks more like an apartment house than an office. There was a black door with a brass knocker and when Daddy used it a nurse opened the door and said, 'Deenie Fenner?' How did she know I was me?

She showed us into a big living-room kind of place with lots of chairs and couches and tables and a fancy Chinese rug on the floor with fringe around the edges. There were tons of magazines but no music playing like in Dr Griffith's office. Here it was very quiet.

Pretty soon the nurse came back and said, 'This way, please.' We got up and followed her. She showed us into a smaller living room. It had a fireplace and everything. The ceiling must have been at least two stories high. Daddy and Ma looked at each other and finally Daddy said, 'Well, he's supposed to be the best.'

I sat down in a big, soft green chair near the desk and Daddy and Ma sat on the little couch in the corner. In a few minutes there was a knock at the door and before we said anything a doctor came into the room. He looked a lot like the one in the movie I saw on Saturday. He sat down at the desk and said, 'I'm Dr Stewart.'

'But we're supposed to see Dr Kliner,' Ma told him.

'You will,' Dr Stewart said. 'I just want to get some information.' He opened a folder that was just like the one Dr Griffith carried around with him. Then he started asking questions. Daddy and Ma answered all of them. I didn't pay much attention until he said, 'Is there a history of scoliosis in the family?'

'Not in mine,' Ma said, looking over at Daddy, who cleared his throat and told Dr Stewart, 'I did have a cousin with a bad back. She was operated on for a slipped disc.'

'That wouldn't have anything to do with this,' Dr Stewart said.

'Then where did it come from?' Ma said, more to herself than to Dr Stewart.

'It's just one of those things,' Dr Stewart told her. 'It could just as likely be from your family as your husband's. We'll probably never know.'

'Hello Deenie.' I hadn't heard Dr Kliner come in until he said that.

When I first looked at him I thought I might laugh. Because Dr Kliner looks exactly like Mr Clean, except he doesn't wear an earring. But his head is shiny bald – the whole thing – there's not one hair on his entire head.

He shook hands with Daddy and told him, 'I'm Henry Kliner.' I liked the way he said that. I've never heard a doctor call himself by his first name.

Dr Kliner leaned against the edge of the desk and looked at me. I could see his socks, which were white. The same kind we wear for gym. 'I've reviewed the X-rays,' he said. 'Now I want to have a look at Deenie.'

There were a lot of things going on I didn't get. How come Dr Kliner had my X-rays? And who was this Dr

Stewart who stayed in the room and wrote things in the folder? I decided I'd better set things straight right away. 'I've made up my mind,' I said. 'I'm having an operation.'

'Deenie!' Ma said.

'I mean it. I am. I'm not scared or anything!'

Dr Kliner asked, 'Who's the doctor here, you or me?'

'You are,' I told him.

'Okay then ... I want to examine you myself ... go into the next room and get undressed ... I'll be right in.'

I went into the next room and found one of those robes ready for me but this one was made of cloth instead of paper. It didn't fit any better than Dr Griffith's though. I was ready for Dr Kliner before he knocked at the door. 'Come in,' I called. Dr Stewart was with him.

'I'll bet you want me to bend over and touch my toes,' I said.

'That will do for a start,' Dr Kliner said.

We went through the same kind of examination that I had with Dr Griffith, only this time it didn't take as long. When he was done Dr Kliner told me I could get dressed and as soon as I came back to his office he said, 'There's no doubt ... Deenie has a classic case of adolescent idiopathic scoliosis.'

'Why do you use that idiot-something word?' I asked.

Dr Kliner smiled at me. 'Sit down, Deenie.' He motioned towards the soft green chair closest to his desk. 'I think you should know about your condition. First of all we don't know exactly what causes it. That's why it's called idiopathic scoliosis. Idiopathic means without known cause.'

'Oh,' I said. So at least it isn't my fault and it doesn't have anything to do with being dumb.

'There are some things we do know,' Dr Kliner said. 'Scoliosis tends to run in families and it occurs mainly in girls. As a matter of fact, eighty-five per cent of all adolescent scoliosis occurs in girls. And the structural curve, which is what you have, usually progresses rapidly during the adolescent growth spurt. Do you understand?' Dr Kliner asked.

'Yes, I think so,' I told him. 'But do I have a C or an S spine?'

For some reason this made both Dr Kliner and Dr Stewart laugh a little. Dr Stewart has dimples, one on each side. He's cute for somebody his age.

Dr Kliner said, 'Your curve is more like an S than a C. And where have you been getting all this information anyway?'

'From my encyclopedia,' I told him.

'I see,' he said.

'I want to get fixed up as soon as I can so when do I get my operation?' I asked.

'I doubt that you'll need an operation,' Dr Kliner said.

Ma sighed, 'Thank God!'

'But how can you fix me up without an operation?'

Dr Kliner said, 'With a Milwaukee Brace.'

'I'd rather have an operation!'

'You think you would, Deenie. But let me tell you something about that. You'd spend months on your back recovering from it and there could be complications. In cases like yours we don't operate without trying the Milwaukee Brace first.'

'But I don't want to wear a brace. I just can't! There must be some other way.'

'Deenie,' Ma said. 'It'll only take a little while and then you'll be better.'

'How long?' I asked.

Dr Kliner didn't say anything for a minute. So I asked him again. 'How long will I have to wear it?'

'About four years,' he said.

'Four years!' me and Ma said at the same time.

'Until you've finished your growth spurt,' Dr Kliner told us. 'When you're about seventeen.'

'But she can't,' Ma said. 'You don't understand, Dr Kliner. Deenie's going to be a model. She can't wear a brace for four years.'

Dr Kliner raised his voice a little. 'I think you don't understand, Mrs Fenner. And it's important that you do.'

Daddy said, 'Look, Doctor . . . just fix Deenie up. That's all we really care about.'

'We will, Mr Fenner. We'll get that spine straightened out.' Dr Kliner went into a whole discussion about wearing the brace until my spine finishes growing and getting measured for it as soon as possible, maybe even this morning. And that scoliosis is more common than most people think. Dr Stewart left the room then but Dr Kliner sat at his desk answering Daddy's questions.

I thought, if I have to wear this Milwaukee Brace thing, no one is going to know about it. It will just be my secret. I'll be like Midge when she first got braces on her teeth. She said she wasn't going to open her mouth until the braces came off. For a while she even talked without opening her mouth, like a ventriloquist.

Dr Kliner stood up and walked towards a closet. I figured he was going to get his coat because with the air-conditioning on his office was kind of cold. But he didn't. Instead he reached in and came out with this weird-looking thing which he carried over to me.

'This is a Milwaukee Brace, Deenie,' he said. 'Of course yours will be made especially for you but this is just about the way it will look.'

At first I didn't believe him. I thought maybe it was some kind of joke. But then I knew it wasn't. Dr Kliner really meant it.

Dr Stewart came back into the room smiling. He said, 'Well, we're all set. You can go right over to the hospital and I'll meet you there. We'll make a mould of Deenie today and in a few weeks her brace should be ready.'

I wanted to scream, *Forget it ... I'm never going to wear that thing. Everyone will know. Everyone!* But the words wouldn't come out.

ten

In the taxi, on the way to the hospital, Ma said, 'I don't see why Dr Kliner can't do it himself. That's what we're paying for, isn't it?'

'Dr Stewart makes all the moulds,' Daddy told her. 'I asked the nurse about it.'

At the hospital Daddy checked with some woman behind an information desk and then we went down a long hallway to a door marked PLASTER ROOM. 'This is it,' Daddy said, knocking. A nurse opened the door and Daddy told her I was Deenie Fenner and that Dr Stewart had called. The nurse smiled at me and said, 'We have five girls to mould today and you're number three.' Then she told Daddy and Ma they could wait outside and Dr Stewart would tell them when I was done.

Ma grabbed me, hugged me and cried a little. But Daddy said, 'Deenie's going to be just fine.'

I pulled away from Ma and buried my head in Daddy's jacket. I whispered, 'Don't go . . . I'm too scared.

Daddy kissed the top of my head and said, 'There's nothing to be afraid of. I promise. Just do whatever Dr Stewart tells you and it will all be over soon.' He lifted my chin so I had to look at him. 'Okay?' he asked.

'Okay,' I said.

The nurse closed the door to the plaster room as soon as I stepped inside. I didn't even have a chance to look around before she pointed to a door and said, 'You can change in there. Take off all your clothes, including your shoes and put on both of these, one over the other.' She handed me two things that looked like very big socks.

The dressing room turned out to be a supply closet and I thought for sure somebody would open the door while I was naked so I tried to keep my back pressed against it the whole time I was getting changed. The things I had to wear were like body stockings. They fit very close and after I had gotten into the first one I looked down and noticed that you could see everything right through it. By the time I pulled the second one over the first you couldn't see as much and I was glad. Not that I have a lot to see but I didn't want Dr Stewart to see anything.

I adjusted the body stockings so they stretched from my neck down to my thighs. Just as I finished the nurse knocked on the door and called, 'Ready, Deenie?'

'I guess so,' I told her, opening the closet.

When I came out I saw that Dr Stewart was already there and so was some other guy dressed in a white coat.

Dr Stewart said, 'Deenie, I'd like you to meet Dr Hubdu and Mrs Inverness, who will both be assisting me.'

Mrs Inverness was the nurse who gave me the body stockings and Dr Hubdu was from some other country. I could tell by his accent.

'Jump right up here, Deenie,' Mrs Inverness said.

I climbed on to an examining table.

'Now lie down . . . put your head back . . . just relax.'

Dr Stewart and Dr Hubdu were busy studying my X-ray, which was flashed on the same kind of screen I saw in Dr Griffith's office. They mentioned a lot of words like *lumbar* and *thoracic* and I didn't know what they were talking about.

I looked around the plaster room trying to figure out what was going to happen. The room wasn't very big. There was a counter with a sink, like in our kitchen. And right in the middle of the room was some kind of strange steel contraption with a rope hanging from a wheel on the ceiling.

In a minute Dr Stewart was measuring me again and calling out funny numbers and names to Dr Hubdu, who wrote everything down. The only words I got were *iliac crest* and *body firm*, whatever they meant.

'Okay, Deenie,' Mrs Inverness said. 'You can come off the table now.'

Dr Stewart sat down on a stool in front of the contraption with ropes. He motioned to me and I walked over to him. He held up some funny looking thing and said, 'This is a head halter.' While he was talking he slipped it on me. It was made of two strips of white material and some string. One section of material fitted under my chin and felt like a scarf was tied there. The other part fitted around the back of my head and felt like I was wearing a head-band.

As soon as that was on me Dr Stewart attached a little wooden bar to the rope coming from the ceiling and somehow he hooked my head-halter to that. I was sure he was going to pull on the rope and leave me hanging in mid-air but just as I was about to ask him what was going on he said, 'We call this *hanging the patient* but you aren't really going to hang, because your feet won't leave the ground.'

I was glad to hear that.

Mrs Inverness said, 'Hold on to the bar above your head, Deenie. With both hands please.'

I reached up and grabbed hold of the bar.

'That's it,' Mrs Inverness said. 'Very good. You hold that the whole time.'

Dr Hubdu was behind me adjusting another wooden bar which came just under my backside. Dr Stewart told me to lean against it. I did but I guess I didn't do it the right way because Dr Hubdu said, 'Squat a little, please. Now just rest yourself against the bar as though you were sitting on it. That's better.'

Dr Stewart said, 'Lean forward a little. Good ... just fine.'

287

Mrs Inverness ran a long piece of felt under my body stockings and down my back. Then Dr Stewart tied a strip of adhesive around my waist and attached each end to the wooden bar I was resting my rear end against.

After that he stood up and opened a small package of rubber gloves. I watched as he pulled them on. While he was doing that Mrs Inverness was busy at the sink in front of me. She was wetting strips of something. As soon as Dr Stewart sat on his stool again, Mrs Inverness handed him the wet strips and he began to wrap them around me. But after the first few he said, 'I'm not happy with this plaster, Nurse. Give me another roll please.' And he ripped off the strips.

As he waited for Mrs Inverness to wet some more he told me, 'When this dries it will become solid plaster. I have to wrap you tight in order to accentuate the hip line and chest. The brace will be made from this mould.'

I didn't say anything.

Mrs Inverness handed him some more strips and after he wrapped a couple of pieces around me he said, 'That's much better.' He wrapped me from my waist down to my hips and then from my waist up to my armpits. All this time Dr Hubdu stood behind me and I could feel his breath on my neck. 'Make sure her back is perfectly straight,' Dr Stewart told him.

'Yes sir,' Dr Hubdu answered. I got the feeling he was just learning about what was going on.

As Dr Stewart wrapped me up he smoothed the plaster with his hands. I didn't like it at all when he had to smooth out the strips across my chest.

'Head up, Deenie,' Dr Stewart said.

'Watch a point in front of you,' Mrs Inverness suggested.

Now both doctors were pressing on me, one at my back, the other at my front and I tried hard to stare at the handle of the cabinet over the sink.

'Stay just like that,' Dr Stewart said, as he moved his hands faster. 'We'll be finished in no time.'

'There are still some creases in the back, sir.' Dr Hubdu said.

'Smooth them out,' Dr Stewart said. 'We can't have any wrinkles.'

I thought about telling Dr Stewart that he was wrapping me too tight. That I really couldn't breathe any more. But that's when he said, 'Deenie's very cooperative, isn't she?'

And Dr Hubdu told him, 'She certainly is.'

I knew Daddy would be proud to hear that so I didn't say anything about feeling like a mummy.

A second later Dr Stewart ripped off his gloves and said, 'That's the worst of it, Deenie. In a minute the mould will be hard and we'll cut you out of it.'

'It's very tight,' I said. 'And it's starting to feel hot too.'

'That's the chemical reaction. It's changing into hard plaster now.'

'I'm glad I don't have to wear anything like this mould,' I told him.

'Some scoliosis patients are still put into casts,' Dr Stewart said. 'But your brace will be a lot different. You won't mind it at all once you're used to it.'

Soon Mrs Inverness tapped me and said, 'It's hard, doctor.'

Dr Stewart felt me himself. 'Good . . .' He whipped a ballpoint pen out of his pocket and drew little lines up and down my mould. Then he measured me again and Dr Hubdu wrote everything down, just like before. 'This will help the brace man,' Dr Stewart told me. 'Okay, Deenie . . . I'm going to cut it off you now. My saw makes a lot of noise but you won't feel a thing.'

His *saw*! I thought, he must be kidding!

But he wasn't. He had a regular power saw that made an awful noise and as he stood behind me running it along my back I was so scared that my teeth rattled. I tried hard not to move at all and prayed that Dr Stewart wo in't miss with his saw and slice me in half.

At last he turned it off. 'Scissors please, Mrs Inverness.' A few seconds after that, he said, 'Spreaders ...' I didn't know what he was doing back there but he kept pulling at me. Finally he said, 'There we go! Turn to the right, Deenie.'

I did and I was out of the plaster mould. Dr Stewart cut the tapes and took my head-halter off. I was free! That's when I looked down and discovered that I was only wearing one body stocking. Where was the other one? It must have stuck to the wet plaster and ripped right off. If they hadn't given me two of them I'd be naked! As it was I knew they could all see everything and I was so embarrassed I almost died. I tried covering my chest with my arms and bending over to hide my other half. I'm sure my face was purple and I felt like crying.

Mrs Inverness handed me a wet cloth and said, 'This will help wash the plaster off. You can go and change now.'

I ran for the supply closet. I didn't even realize the plaster had dripped on my legs and feet until then. But I didn't care. All I wanted was to get dressed and out of that room.

eleven

That night I took my new nightie out of my bottom drawer and tried it on. I stood in front of the mirror and moved just enough to make it turn from pink to purple to lavender. Buddy Brader would never get to see it now and nobody would bring me pink roses either. I took the nightie off and packed it back in the Drummond's Department Store box.

I went to the phone and called Midge. Her line was busy so I tried Janet's number but that was busy too. They were probably talking to each other. I waited for a few minutes before I dialled Midge again. The phone rang three times, then Midge answered.

'Hi . . .' I said, 'it's me.'

'Hi Deenie . . . me and Janet were just talking about you. How'd it go today?'

'I'm not having an operation.' My voice was barely a whisper.

'You're not? How come?'

'I don't need one after all.'

'Well, that's great news! Isn't it?'

'I suppose.'

'You sound funny. Is anything wrong?'

'No . . . I'm fine. I just called to tell you since I'm not having an operation I'll return the nightie. Listen . . . I have to run now . . . bye.' I hung up before Midge could say anything else.

I put the Drummond's box into a brown bag and carried it to school with me the next day. I knew it would be safe inside my locker. At lunch Janet said, 'We're really glad you don't need an operation, Deenie.'

I nodded.

'Were they wrong about your spine?' Midge asked.

'Not exactly.'

'But if it's crooked don't they have to do something?' Janet said.

'The doctors are trying to decide about that,' I told them.

'Me and Midge think you should keep the nightie anyway. Your birthday's in January so it can be a birthday present instead.'

'I really don't need it now,' I said. 'I'd rather return it ... if you don't mind.'

They looked at each other.

'It's okay with us,' Midge said. 'We just didn't want you to think you *had* to return it.'

After school the three of us went to Drummond's. The same salesgirl was behind the counter. I handed her the box.

'She's not having her operation,' Janet told her.

'So she doesn't need the nightie,' Midge said.

'Well ... aren't you lucky!' the salesgirl said to me, and she didn't even try to talk us into keeping the nightie or choosing something else in its place.

I tried to smile. I could tell that Janet and Midge knew something was wrong.

I stopped hanging around the cafeteria after lunch. I told Janet and Midge I had a lot of work to make up because I'd been absent so many times. As soon as I finished eating I went to the library where I sat with my books spread out on the table while I scribbled in my notebook or looked out the window.

One day, while I was sitting like that, somebody sneaked up from behind and covered my eyes with his hands.

'Guess who?' It was Buddy Brader. I'd know his voice anywhere.

'I give up,' I said.

He took his hands away and leaned up against the table. 'What're you doing in here, Deenie?'

'Make-up work,' I told him.

'I came in to watch the fish.' Mr Balfour, our librarian, keeps a big tank of tropical fish on the table in the corner and a lot of kids do wander into the library to watch them. 'You know something?' Buddy said, 'You didn't wave to me this morning.'

'I didn't.' Buddy waves to me every day when we pass each other in the hall, on the way to our first-period classes. 'I guess I didn't see you,' I told him.

'You turned away when I was walking by.'

'Well, I didn't mean to. I just have so many things on my mind.'

'Yeah?'

'I mean it ... really.'

'Not that it matters ... I only come in here to see the fish anyway.' He started to walk across the room. Then he stopped and turned for a minute. 'See you around,' he said. He must think I don't like him any more! I wish there was some way to let him know the truth.

All that week I kept hoping Dr Kliner would call to say everyone had made a terrible mistake. That there's nothing wrong with me after all and that I definitely don't have scoliosis. Every time the phone rang I jumped but it was never Dr Kliner. I touched my special place practically every night. It was the only way I could fall asleep and besides, it felt good.

We're starting a new programme in gym. Once a month we're going to have a discussion group with Mrs Rappoport. It sounds very interesting because Mrs Rappoport asked us each to write down a question and drop it into a box on her desk. The question could be about anything, she said, especially anything we need to know about sex. She told us not to put our names on the paper.

She doesn't want to know who's asking what. It's a good thing too, because I'd never have asked my question if I had to sign my name. I wrote:

Do normal people touch their bodies before they go to sleep and is it all right to do that?

On Tuesday, when we walked into the gym, Mrs Rappoport told us to sit in a circle so we could talk easily. The first questions she discussed were all about menstruation. But I already knew most everything from my booklet. After that she said, 'Okay, now I think we can move on to another subject. Here's an interesting question.' She read it to us. 'Do normal people touch their bodies before they go to sleep and is it all right to do that?'

I almost died! I glanced around, then smiled a little, because some of the other girls did, and hoped the expression on my face looked like I was trying to figure out who had asked such a thing.

Mrs Rappoport said, 'Can anyone help us with an answer?'

Susan Minton raised her hand.

'Yes, Susan . . .' Mrs Rappoport said.

'I wasn't the one who wrote the question but I've heard that boys who touch themselves too much go blind or get very bad pimples or their bodies can even grow deformed.'

'Has anyone else heard that?' Mrs Rappoport asked.

Five other girls raised their hands.

Could it possibly be true? I wondered. And if it was true about boys maybe it was about girls too. Maybe that's why my spine started growing crooked! Please God . . . don't let it be true, I prayed. I felt my face get hot and I had to go to the bathroom in the worst way but I didn't move a muscle. I hoped nobody could tell what I was thinking.

'Well . . .' Mrs Rappoport said, 'I can see you've got a

lot of misinformation. Does anyone here know the word for stimulating our genitals? Because that's what we're talking about, you know.'

It got very quiet in the gym. Nobody said anything for a long time. Then one girl spoke. 'I think it's called masturbation.' ·

'That's right,' Mrs Rappoport told us. 'And it's not a word you should be afraid of. Let's all say it.'

'Masturbation,' we said together.

'Okay,' Mrs Rappoport said. 'Now that you've said it let me try to explain. First of all, it's normal and harmless to masturbate.'

'You mean for boys ...' Susan Minton said.

'No, I mean for anyone ... male or female,' Mrs Rappoport told us. 'The myths that some of you have heard aren't true. Masturbation can't make you insane or deformed or even give you acne.'

I wanted to take a deep breath when she said that but I didn't. I just gulped and looked at the floor.

'Does everybody masturbate?' Barbara Curtis asked.

'Not necessarily,' Mrs Rappoport said. 'But it's very common for girls as well as boys, beginning with adolescence.'

Any minute I thought Mrs Rappoport would ask us to raise our hands if we masturbate and I wasn't sure I'd be able to tell the truth. I never knew there was a name for what I do. I just thought it was my own special good feeling. Now I wonder if all my friends do it too?

But Mrs Rappoport didn't ask us to tell her if we did or we didn't masturbate and I was glad. It's a very private subject. I wouldn't want to talk about it in front of the class. She said the important thing to remember is that it is normal and that it can't hurt us. 'Nobody ever went crazy from masturbating but a lot of young people make themselves sick from worrying about it.'

I couldn't help thinking about Buddy. Can he get that special feeling too? I'd like to find out how much Buddy really knows about girls. I hardly know anything about boys. I think we should have discussions every week. They're more important than modern dance!

That afternoon, when I got home from school, there was a note from Ma, saying she was at the A&P with Aunt Rae. I put my books down, poured myself a glass of milk and was just about to sneak a few chocolate cookies from Ma's secret hiding place, when the phone rang.

'Hello ...' I said.

'Mrs Fenner?'

'No ... she isn't in right now.'

'This is Dr Kliner's office calling ...'

When I heard that my heart started to beat very fast. 'Can I take a message?' I asked then had to clear my throat.

'Deenie's Milwaukee Brace is ready and the doctor suggests an appointment on Friday at ten o'clock.'

'This Friday?'

'That's right. And the doctor also suggests a change of clothes for Deenie ... a size or two larger than her regular things.'

'What for?' I asked.

'Because the brace takes up a certain amount of room and the girls can't get their regular clothes over it.'

'Oh.'

'Have Mrs Fenner call if she can't make it on Friday. I'll be here until six.'

'I'll tell her.'

'Thank you,' she sang and hung up, like she didn't even care about what she had just told me.

I didn't say anything to Ma about the phone call when she got back from the market. I thought about not telling anyone. But I knew if we didn't show up on Friday Dr Kliner's office would call to find out what happened and

hen Daddy and Ma would know about the first phone call
nd that would make me a liar. So I told them during
upper. It was already past six-thirty.

'Friday's fine with me,' Daddy said. 'I'll ask Joe to work
hat morning.'

I'd been chewing on the same piece of meat for a while
ut I couldn't swallow it so I held my napkin to my mouth
nd spat it out.

'What's wrong?' Ma asked.

'It was all fat,' I told her. I drank some water, then took
 big breath and spoke very fast. 'I'm supposed to bring
ome other clothes to Dr Kliner's office because mine won't
it over the brace.' I looked at the food on my plate and
noved some of it around with my fork.

'Don't worry about your clothes,' Ma said. 'You can get
ll new things ... can't she, Frank?'

'Sure,' Daddy said. 'Never mind about that.'

'But my jeans are all broken in the way I like them!'

'So you'll break in new jeans,' Daddy said. 'As many as
ou want.'

'And I never even wore my two new skirts and sweaters.
 was saving them for when it gets cold.' I could feel my
hroat tightening.

'Maybe we can take them back and get the next size,'
Ma said.

'You already shortened the skirts,' I said.

'So we won't return them,' Daddy said. 'It's not
mportant.'

'But it's a waste of money,' I told him.

'Never mind,' Daddy said again. 'All that matters is
;etting you well.'

'I am well!'

'You know what Daddy means,' Ma said.

Later, Helen came to my room carrying a navy skirt and
 striped shirt. 'You can wear these tomorrow,' she said.

'They're bigger than your things and they'll probably look better on you anyway.' She put them down on my bed. They still had tags on them.

twelve

The brace looks like the one Dr Kliner showed us three weeks ago. It's the ugliest thing I ever saw.

I'm going to take it off as soon as I get home. I swear, I won't wear it. And nobody can make me. Not ever! I felt like telling that to Dr Kliner but I didn't. I had to fight to keep from crying.

Just when I thought I was going to be okay Ma started. 'Oh, my God!' she cried. 'What did we ever do to deserve this?' She buried her face in a tissue and made sobbing noises that really got me sore. The louder she cried the madder I got until I shouted, 'Just stop it, Ma! Will you just stop it please!'

Dr Kliner said, 'You know, Mrs Fenner, you're making this very hard on your daughter.'

Ma opened the door and ran out of Dr Kliner's office.

Daddy hugged me and said, 'I'm proud of you, Deenie. You're stronger than your mother.'

I wanted to tell him I'm not. I hate just looking at the brace, never mind the thought of wearing it. But I was glad he thought I was strong so I kept pretending I really was.

'Why don't you see about your wife,' Dr Kliner said to Daddy. 'I'd like a minute alone with Deenie anyway.'

Daddy said, 'Of course, Doctor,' and he left the room.

Dr Kliner pushed a button on his desk and told me, 'Miss Harrigan will be here in a minute. She's going to help you with your brace. But before she comes I want to tell you something. Your mother's attitude towards your condition is fairly common. Usually when the mother feels that way it rubs off on the patient. I can tell you have your father's attitude and I'm glad. Because wearing the brace can be as easy or difficult as you make it. Do you understand what I'm saying?'

I nodded.

'Before you leave we're going to give you a booklet about scoliosis which explains the exercises you'll have to do every day.'

'I didn't know I'd have to do exercises. I thought I wouldn't be able to do anything like that.'

'Just the opposite,' Dr Kliner said. 'There's nothing you *can't* do.'

'You mean I should take gym in school?' That would mean changing in the locker room where all the girls would be able to see my brace.

'Positively. Gym is very important. So is swimming. Can you swim?'

'Yes, but how do I swim with the brace on?'

'That's the one activity you do without the brace. I'd like you to swim at least three days a week for half an hour at a time.'

There was a knock at the door and Dr Kliner called, 'Come in ... Deenie I'd like you to meet Iris Harrigan.'

'Hello, Deenie,' Miss Harrigan was very tall and really pretty. She reminded me of that girl I sat next to at the modelling agency, the one who wanted to be in commercials. She picked up my brace and said, 'Let's go change.'

I stood up and followed her into the same room where Dr Kliner had examined me.

'You can get undressed in the bathroom if you want,' Miss Harrigan said. 'But take this in with you. It goes over your bra and pants.' She handed me a piece of material.

'It looks like a boy's undershirt,' I told her.

'It is a kind of undershirt. You wear it under your brace. It prevents most skin irritations.'

'I have to wear an undershirt? Like a baby?'

'Well, it's strictly for comfort.'

'Then I don't *have* to wear it?' I asked.

'It's not a *must*. But you'll feel more comfortable.'

'I don't care about being comfortable,' I said. 'I don't want to wear that thing!'

'Okay then,' Miss Harrigan said. 'Try it without.'

'I will.' I went into the bathroom and locked the door. I took off my dress and folded it up. Then I unlocked the door and called, 'I'm ready . . .'

'Come on out,' Miss Harrigan said. She picked up the brace. 'I'm going to show you how to get into it now. The first time will be the hardest. After today it will be easier every time you do it.'

The brace is made mostly of metal but there are some white plastic parts too. Miss Harrigan explained that the reason the plastic is full of little holes is so the air can get through to my skin. There are two metal strips down the back of the brace and one down the front. But the worst thing is that the strips are attached to a metal collar.

Miss Harrigan helped me into the brace. 'It's too tight around my neck.' I tried to pull it away.

'It has to hold your neck in place,' Miss Harrigan said. 'The whole idea of the brace is to keep your spine in one position and your spine begins at the base of your neck.'

'It hurts!' I told her. 'Please take it off!'

'It doesn't hurt. There's nothing to hurt you at all. Let me adjust the straps for you.'

Miss Harrigan buckled and unbuckled the side straps until I told her I felt more comfortable. There were three more strips of metal on my brace that I didn't notice right away. Two are around my sides and one starts at the front of my neck, goes under my left arm, and winds up someplace in the back, near my head.

'It feels tight under my arms too,' I told her.

'You have to get used to that,' she said.

Besides the metal strips I had a whole section of white plastic around my middle and some kind of pad on part of my back.

'You'd be more comfortable if you'd wear the undershirt.'

'You said I didn't have to.'

'Why don't you take it home anyway, just in case you change your mind.'

'Maybe,' I told her. 'Right now I feel like I'm in a cage and no undershirt's going to change that! And suppose I grow? What happens then?'

'The brace is adjustable but if you outgrow it Dr Stewart will make another mould of you and you'll get a new brace.'

'I don't think I can live through this. I really don't!'

'I know it seems that way. But you will live through it. Lots of girls do.'

'That's easy for you to say. You don't have scoliosis.'

'That's true,' she said, like we were talking about the weather. 'But when you think of the alternatives, isn't wearing a brace better?'

'What do you mean? Better than an operation?'

'I mean better than growing up with a curved spine.'

'I don't know,' I said. 'I'm not sure about anything.'

Miss Harrigan walked over to a desk and opened the middle drawer. She took something out. 'I'm going to show you some pictures, Deenie. Then you can decide for yourself.'

She opened a booklet to some sketches of people with terrible looking bodies, all crooked and bent over.

'Here's an illustration of a person with scoliosis, a side-to-side curve of the spine.'

'Like me?'

'Yes, except you'll never look that way. Aren't you glad?'

'I'd kill myself if I did.'

'No you wouldn't. But we don't have to argue about it

302

because it's not going to happen.' She turned the page. There was a sketch of somebody who looked just like Old Lady Murray.

'I know someone like that!' I said.

'It's an illustration of kyphosis,' Miss Harrigan told me. 'A front-to-back curve of the spine.'

'Is that the same as hunchback?'

'Yes.'

It was hard to believe that I really and truly had something in common with Old Lady Murray.

When we left Dr Kliner's office I was wearing the brace with Helen's skirt and shirt over it. I was kind of scared that Ma would start crying again when she saw me. Instead she said, 'Well, that's not bad at all. You can hardly tell you're wearing it, Deenie.' I knew from the catch in her voice that she was just saying it and didn't mean a single word.

Daddy asked, 'How does it feel?'

'Like I'm in a cage,' I said.

As I was getting into the back seat of the car I whacked my head on the top of the door.

'Are you all right?' Ma asked.

'I don't know.'

'Let me see,' Daddy said, parting my hair. 'There's no blood,' he told us, as he rubbed my scalp.

'I guess I'm okay,' I said. 'I guess I just can't bend my head with this brace on.' As soon as I said that I started to cry. I cried the way I wanted to when I first saw the brace, loud and hard, until my throat hurt. Daddy didn't try to stop me. He just held me tight while he rocked back and forth, patting my head.

thirteen

The crying stopped as fast as it started. As soon as we got home I went up to my room and pulled off my clothes. I stood in front of my long mirror, inspecting the brace carefully from every angle. I was a disaster. I was as ugly as anything I'd ever seen. 'Damn you!' I shouted at my reflection. 'Damn you, crooked spine!'

I went to my desk and took out my scissors. Then I stood in front of the mirror again and hacked off one whole side of my hair. Right up to the ear. I watched as it fell to the floor. I'm crazy, I thought. I'm like the Deenie in the movie. When she went crazy the first thing she did was chop off her hair. I threw my scissors down, kicked the mirror and hurt my foot. That got me even more sore so I picked up the scissors and started cutting away at the rest of my hair. I cut and cut and cut until there was a big pile of hair on the floor and just a few loose strands hanging from my head. If I was going to be ugly I was going to be ugly all the way ... as ugly as anybody'd ever been before ... maybe even uglier.

Ma called from downstairs, 'Lunch Deenie ...' and for some dumb reason that made me laugh because all of a sudden I was hungry. No matter how bad things are people still get hungry. That's a fact.

When I walked into the kitchen Ma was bending over the sink. She said, 'We're going shopping first thing tomorrow. Aunt Rae said she'll drive us downtown so you can get some new things for school.'

Daddy sat at the table and stared at me.

'What do you say to that, Deenie?' Ma asked, turning around. 'Oh my God! Deenie ... what have you done to your hair?'

'I cut it.'

'Why . . . why did you do such a thing?'

'I felt like it.' I reached for my grilled cheese and tomato sandwich.

Ma put her hand across her mouth and shook her head.

I tried to eat my sandwich as if nothing was wrong. But I was used to bending over towards my food and with the brace on I couldn't bend at all. Not even my head. I couldn't really see my plate. I had to lift my sandwich straight up to my mouth. It was the same with my milk, which is probably why I spilled some of it down my front. Daddy jumped up to help me. He said, 'I think you'd be more comfortable if you pushed your chair away from the table. That way you can lean over and see your food.'

'I'm not hungry anyway!' I shouted, and in my hurry to get away from the table, I knocked over the chair. I went up the stairs as fast as I could, slammed my bedroom door and tried to flop down on my bed. But I couldn't even flop any more. So I cursed. I said every bad word I knew. Every single one. I yelled them as loud as I could and then I screamed them again, spelling each out loud. I expected Ma to really punish me for that. She can't stand to hear those words. Once, when I was a little kid, she washed my mouth out with soap just for saying the F word. And in those days I didn't even know what it meant.

Later that afternoon I was in the bathroom. Even a stupid ordinary thing like sitting on the toilet wasn't the same for me now. The brace made everything different. And wouldn't you know it – that was when my period decided to come – of all the dumb times!

I called, 'Ma . . . Ma . . . I need help!'

Helen came to the bathroom door. I didn't know she was home from school already. 'Ma's not here,' she said.

'Where is she?'

'Daddy says she walked over to the A&P.'

305

'But she never walks anywhere.'

'I guess she didn't want to leave you home alone. Daddy's downstairs ... do you want me to get him?'

'No.'

'Are you okay?'

'I just got my period and I can't get to the stuff.'

'I'll get it for you,' Helen said.

I sat on the toilet because I didn't know what else to do and in a minute Helen came in with the pads. I pulled my bathrobe tight around me. I didn't want her to see the brace yet.

She stood there looking at me.

I felt like a freak.

Finally she said, 'You cut your hair.'

I put my hand to my head to feel it. I'd forgotten about my hair. I thought Helen was looking at the brace.

She started to laugh then. 'It looks so funny,' she said.

'It just needs to be washed,' I told her. What right did she have to laugh at how I looked? 'Now could I please have the stuff?'

'Oh sure.' Helen handed it to me. 'Are you really going to wear it like that?'

'What?'

'Your hair.'

'Of course!'

'I could probably help straighten it out. It wouldn't be bad if I snipped off the strands that are hanging.'

'I like it this way!'

'Okay,' Helen said. 'Do you need any help with the pad?'

'No,' I told her. 'I can do it myself.'

'Okay,' Helen said again as she left.

But I found out I couldn't do it myself because I couldn't bend over to see what I was trying to do. Maybe if I'd been really experienced in wearing that stuff it would have been easier but this was only my second time. I dropped the pad by mistake and then had to figure out how to get it off the floor. Finally I did a knee bend, like Mrs Rappoport taught us in modern dance and I picked up the pad and started all over again.

When I came out of the bathroom Helen said, 'I thought you were planning to spend the night in there.'

'I had some trouble. It's not exactly the easiest thing to do when you're wearing a brace.'

'I'd have helped you.'

'I managed myself.'

'Well, cheer up,' Helen said. 'Janet and Midge are coming for supper and Ma's cooking your favourite ... eggplant parmigiana.'

fourteen

I love eggplant parmigiana but I don't see why Ma had to
invite Janet and Midge for supper. I'm not ready to face
them yet. I need time to think and time to get used to the
brace. I'm not even going to school on Monday. I'm
almost sure Ma won't make me. Maybe next week I'll feel
like seeing people but not now!

At five-thirty the doorbell rang, and in a minute Janet
and Midge were knocking at my bedroom door, calling
my name. I'd washed my hair and I was dressed in Helen's
clothes again but I didn't let her snip off any extra strands
of hair. When I opened my door Janet and Midge
both said 'Hi,' in very loud voices, like they'd been
practising.

Usually when we get together in my room we lounge
on my bed or the floor but this time we just stood there
and I could tell that Janet and Midge were being careful
not to look directly at me.

Finally Midge asked, 'How do you feel?'

'Fine,' I told her. 'I'm not sick.'

'That's good.'

Then Janet said, 'We didn't know they'd have to cut
off all your hair.'

'They didn't,' I said. 'I did it.'

'Yourself?' Janet asked.

'Yes.'

'How come?'

'Because I felt like it.'

'No kidding!' Midge said.

'That's a fact,' I told her.

'Well, it looks cool,' she said, glancing at Janet.

'Yeah, it's really different,' Janet said.

I turned and walked over to my bed. I sat down on

the edge. 'Aren't you going to say anything about the brace?'

They looked at each other again.

'If you don't say something soon I think I'm going to scream!'

'But your mother told us not to talk about it,' Janet said.

'Oh . . . I should have known that was it!' I wish Ma would stop pretending. Does she think it's going to disappear if nobody says anything.

'Anyway,' Midge said, 'it's not so bad. An operation would be a lot worse.'

'You can hardly notice this,' Janet said.

I stood up. 'You're both lying!' I shouted. 'You're supposed to be my friends!'

'What do you want us to say?' Midge asked.

'The truth!'

They looked at each other.

'Well . . .' I said.

'Oh Deenie!' Janet said. 'We don't know what to say or how to act or anything. We were going to make believe we didn't even notice.'

'And say that you looked swell, like always,' Midge said.

'But if you want to know the truth,' Janet said, 'it was a real shock, even though we knew the doctors would have to do something because you can't grow up with a crooked spine.'

'It's not called crooked spine. It's called scoliosis.' I reached for my notebook and opened it to the page I'd copied from my encyclopedia. 'You better read this,' I said, handing the notebook to Janet.

She and Midge sat on my bed and read it together. 'This is very interesting,' Midge told me.

'You don't know anything yet!' I said, and gave them a rundown on all the doctors I'd seen and how I had to be sawed out of my mould and everything. 'I'm thinking of becoming an orthopaedist myself.'

'But what about modelling?' Janet asked.

'I never wanted to be one anyway.'

'You didn't?'

'That's a fact.'

Ma called then. 'Deenie ... supper ...'

'Let's go,' I told them. 'I'm starving!'

As we headed down the stairs Janet said, 'You're really brave, Deenie. If I had to wear that thing I'd go to pieces. I'd never be able to live through it!'

That night when I got into bed I couldn't find a comfortable position. No matter which way I turned the brace bothered me. I wanted to take it off but I knew if I did I'd only have to wear it longer. I was sure I'd never fall asleep again.

The next morning Aunt Rae picked us up in her car. When she saw me she cried which made Ma start in all over again. I was getting pretty tired of the whole thing. After all, I was the one in the brace, but the way they acted you'd have thought it was them.

We went downtown to Drummond's Department Store and I thought of my beautful nightie. I wonder if anyone's bought it yet? We got off the elevator on the third floor – Junior Sportswear and Dresses. The saleslady started asking questions right away. 'What happened dear? Were you in an accident?'

Before I could say anything Aunt Rae told her, 'She's sick. She's got scoliosis.'

'I'm *not* sick,' I told Aunt Rae.

But Aunt Rae and the saleslady looked at each other as if to say I didn't know the truth and they did.

Meantime, Ma went through the racks pulling out things for me to try on. Size was a problem because the brace takes up a lot of room and everything I put on looked terrible. Besides, Ma and Aunt Rae were both talking non-stop about what kinds of clothes would hide the brace and pretty soon I did start to feel sick.

The saleslady kept taking things away and bringing them back in different sizes and after an hour of the same thing I couldn't stand it any more so I said, 'I don't want anything new. I like what I've got.'

'But what you've got doesn't fit, Deenie,' Ma said.

'So I'll wear Helen's old clothes. Just let's go home.'

'We're all trying to help you,' Ma said. 'But if you won't help yourself there isn't much we can do.'

'I just don't want to try any more on, that's all.'

Aunt Rae rushed back into the dressing room. 'I've found it,' she told me. 'The perfect dress.' Then, for no reason at all, she turned to the saleslady and said, 'Deenie's going to be a model, you know. Doesn't she have the most beautiful face?'

'Please Aunt Rae! I can't be a model now. You know that.'

'Of course you can. Where there's a will, there's a way. I'll think of something. Here ... try this on.' She handed me the dress. 'The high neck will hide the brace.'

'I don't like it,' I said, looking at the white ruffles on the sleeves. 'It's too babyish.'

'Try it anyway,' Ma said.

'No!'

'Deenie, you're being stubborn!' Ma said.

'I'm old enough to choose my own things. Don't you think I know what I like by now?'

The saleslady was shaking her head and listening to every word. I wanted to yell at her – to tell her to mind her own business and get lost.

I got back into my things and told Ma, 'I'm going to the Ladies' Room.'

Aunt Rae followed me there. 'You know, Deenie, your

mother would do anything for you. She's trying to make you feel better. It's not her fault this happened.'

'Well, it's not my fault either.'

Aunt Rae didn't answer that.

'It's not!' I said again. 'There isn't anything that anyone could have done about it. And if you don't believe me just ask the doctor!'

On Sunday night we were sitting around in the living room. Me and Ma were watching the end of 'The FBI' and Helen and Daddy were reading the papers. When the show was over I said, 'I'm not going to school tomorrow so can I stay up for the Sunday night movie?'

'Why aren't you going to school?' Ma asked.

'Because I'm not ready yet. I need more time to get used to wearing this thing.'

'I guess one more day won't matter,' Ma told me.

But Daddy said, 'Deenie's going to school, same as always.' He didn't even look up from the paper.

'But Frank,' Ma said, 'if she isn't ready . . .'

Daddy didn't let her finish. 'She isn't going to get any more ready sitting around the house feeling sorry for herself.'

'I'm not feeling sorry for myself!' I shouted, jumping to my feet.

Daddy looked up. 'Good . . . then there's no reason for you not to go to school.'

'Even if I'm sick?'

'You're not sick.'

'I think I'm coming down with something.'

'Frank,' Ma said, 'maybe it's the flu.'

'It's not the flu,' Daddy told her, 'and Deenie is going to school and that's that!'

'I never heard anything so mean!' I shouted.

'It's for your own good, Deenie.' Daddy stood up and reached for my hand but I pulled away and wouldn't let him touch me.

fifteen

On Monday I wore one of the smock shirts Ma bought for me on Saturday. Even though I told her I wasn't ever going to put on that stuff I was glad to have it.

'Hi,' Midge said when I got to the bus stop, 'I wasn't sure you'd be coming.'

'I had no choice,' I told her.

As soon as we got on the bus some lady asked me if I had been in a car accident. And later, when we were getting off at school, this boy I never saw before asked me what was wrong with my neck. I told them both the truth, that I have scoliosis and would have to wear a Milwaukee Brace for four years to straighten out my spine. Neither one paid much attention to what I was saying. If they weren't interested why did they ask me in the first place?

At school it was worse. Everybody wanted to know what was wrong including my formroom teacher who called me up to her desk and all the time I was explaining my condition to her she was patting me on the back.

Susan Minton practically glued herself to my desk and wouldn't leave until I told her the whole story. Then she said, 'Well, if I can do anything for you, anything at all, I'd be really happy to. I could carry your books around or help you up and down the stairs ...'

I told her I didn't need any help and that I was just the same as before but I could see she didn't believe me. When the bell rang Miss Greenleaf told her to sit down at her own desk. Before she did Susan said, 'I think your haircut is terrific. I'm going to cut mine the same way,' which proved to me that Susan Minton is as stupid as I've always thought.

I waited in the formroom until everyone else had left for

their first-period class because I didn't want to risk passing Buddy Brader in the hall. On Mondays and Wednesdays I have sewing first period, which is a terrible way to start the day. My sewing teacher, Miss Wabash, is about one hundred years old and very mean. She doesn't like me because I don't know anything about sewing. I wouldn't take it except the girls have no choice in seventh grade. We're required to have one year of sewing and another of cooking. At least the cooking teacher is nice. Janet has cooking this year and she says they have a lot of fun. When they clean up they always pretend they're doing a cleanser commercial for TV.

Midge is in my sewing class. We fooled around a lot the first week of school so Miss Wabash separated us. Now Midge's machine is right in front of Miss Wabash's desk and mine is all the way across the room.

The minute I sat down at my sewing machine I remembered that we were supposed to buy our patterns and material over the weekend. As Miss Wabash called the roll each of us had to go up to her desk to show her what we had selected. It had to be either a skirt or a jumper. I hoped that Miss Wabash would understand why I forgot to get mine.

'Wilmadeene Fenner ...' Miss Wabash called.

Practically all my teachers call me Deenie by now, but not Miss Wabash. She refuses because she says we have to get used to our given names. Midge found out that Miss Wabash's first name is Matilda. I'd love to call her that. It really suits her.

As I stood up I could feel everyone in the class staring at me. I went to Miss Wabash's desk and told her, 'I don't have my pattern or material yet.'

Miss Wabash didn't look at me. She seemed to be concentrating on something on her desk.

315

'What is the reason?' she asked.

'I was busy all weekend.'

'Doing what, may I ask?'

She still didn't look at me. I don't think she knew I was wearing my brace. Either that or she thought I always wore one.

I told her, 'I was busy getting my Milwaukee Brace.'

'Do you think that is a valid excuse?'

'I don't know,' I whispered.

'I do not think that is a valid excuse,' she said. 'Therefore I will have to give you a zero in this assignment. If you have your pattern and material on Wednesday morning I will erase the zero and give you a fifty. Do you understand, Wilmadeene?'

'Yes, Miss Wabash.'

'Good. Today you will practise seams on your muslin while the other girls cut their patterns. You may sit down now.'

I wanted to run out of the room. I looked at Midge and knew she was embarrassed for me. I sat down at my machine and sewed the most crooked seams I ever saw. More crooked than my spine because I couldn't bend over to see what I was doing.

Second period I have math and right after Miss Varnicka put our problems on the board she came over to my desk to see if she could help. 'I think you'd be more comfortable standing at a lectern,' she said. 'If you'd like to give it a try I'll ask the custodian to bring one from the auditorium.'

'I don't think so,' I said. I could just picture myself standing in the corner at a lectern while everyone watched.

'Well,' Miss Varnicka said, 'then how about if you move your chair way back and lean forward with your body . . . that way you'd be able to see what you're doing.'

'I'll try,' I said. I pushed my chair way back, then leaned over my desk, and it worked! I could see what I was doing again. It wasn't exactly comfortable and the kid behind me had to move his desk too, but it was better than before and much much better than standing alone at a lectern.

All morning I kept wondering what Buddy Brader would think when he saw me. Once he told me that he likes girls with long hair and that mine was just perfect. I won't be able to shake it at him any more. Why didn't I think of that on Friday?

I was in the cafeteria, on the hot lunch line, when Buddy spotted me. He came right over and pushed in. The girl behind him yelled, 'Hey . . .' But Buddy just said, 'Hey yourself!' and he didn't move.

Then he looked at me and said, 'I heard all about your spine.'

'Who told you?'

'A lot of kids.'

'I guess practically everyone knows.'

'Yeah, I guess so. Now I know what you meant when you said you had a lot on your mind. Does it hurt?'

'No, it's just a little uncomfortable.'

'You can take that thing off sometimes, can't you?'

'I'm supposed to wear it all the time,' I told him. 'Except for swimming.'

'You even have to sleep in it?'

'Yes,' I kind of smiled then, to show how brave I am.

The lady behind the lunch counter called, 'Move along kids.'

'No gravy,' I told her, but she dumped a quart of it on my meat anyway.

Buddy said, 'No gravy,' too and she didn't pay any attention to him either. But as she went to put the gravy on his plate he moved it away and the gravy landed on the

317

counter. 'That's what you should do,' Buddy told me. 'Otherwise you'll always wind up with it.'

The line was moving faster and I grabbed a roll and some Jell-O.

'I'm playing drums at the seventh-grade mixer,' Buddy said. 'You going?'

I was trying to dig out my lunch money to pay the cashier but I was having trouble holding my tray and getting into my purse at the same time. 'I don't know if I'm going,' I said to Buddy. I had to put my tray down so I could pay.

'You should go,' Buddy said. We walked across the cafeteria to where I always sit.

'Maybe,' I told him.

'You never heard me play drums.'

'I know,' I said.

'I'm good.'

'Well, maybe I will go ... it all depends ...'

'You should go.'

'Well, I probably will.' We were at my table and Midge was already there, peeling her eggs.

Buddy put his tray down and for a minute I wondered if he was going to eat with me instead of with his friends. He's never done that. But he didn't sit down. He reached over and put his hand on my head, kind of the way you'd pet a dog. 'You shouldn't have cut your hair,' he told me. 'It was nice long.'

I looked at Midge and she started choking on her eggs. She got up and ran to the fountain. 'I had to cut it,' I told Buddy, '... because of the brace.'

'I didn't know that,' he said. 'It'll grow again, won't it?'

'Sure,' I said. 'I think hair grows almost an inch a month or something like that.'

'Listen,' Buddy said, 'I've got to eat my lunch now. Don't forget the mixer ... I've got a solo and all.'

318

'I won't forget.'

He finally took his hand off my hair. I may never shampoo it again.

sixteen

That afternoon, when I got back to the formroom, Miss
Greenleaf told me that Mrs Anderson, the vice-principal,
wanted to see me after school. I couldn't imagine what I
had done wrong but I knew it must have been something
important to get called to the office.

I grabbed my books and sweater and went downstairs.
There were three boys sitting on the bench outside Mrs
Anderson's office and as I walked by they made noises at
me. I tried to ignore them as I knocked on her door.

'Come in,' Mrs Anderson called.

I opened the door. Mrs Anderson was smiling. I've
heard she always does, even when she's punishing kids.
Her desk was in front of a big window but she sat with her
back to it so she couldn't see the pigeon standing on the
ledge. Ma says pigeons are dirty birds with lots of germs
and I should stay away from them.

'Deenie Fenner?' Mrs Anderson asked.

'Yes,' I told her, holding my books tight against me.

'How did you do today?'

I didn't know exactly what she meant so I said, 'Fine,
thank you.'

'No trouble?'

I wondered if Miss Wabash reported me? Should I tell
Mrs Anderson it wasn't my fault I forgot the material?

Before I could make up my mind Mrs Anderson said,
'Now then, Deenie ... the reason I sent for you ...' She
fumbled with a mess of papers on her desk and I was
pretty sure she was looking for the note Miss Wabash must
have sent to her office. 'Oh, yes ... here it is,' Mrs
Anderson said, holding up some kind of printed sheet that
definitely wasn't a note from Miss Wabash. She waved it
at me. 'How do you get to school, Deenie?'

'I ride the bus,' I told her.

'Take this form home and have your parents fill it out.' She handed it to me. 'You're eligible for the special bus now. It would be much more convenient and it's free.'

'You mean the bus that picks up the . . .' I started to say *the handicapped kids* but I couldn't – because all of a sudden there was a big lump in my throat. I had to look out the window so Mrs Anderson wouldn't notice. Another pigeon was on the ledge and both of them were walking back and forth looking at me.

'It's on your street every morning at ten after eight,' Mrs Anderson said. 'Deenie . . . Deenie . . . are you listening to me?'

'Yes,' I said in a voice that didn't sound like mine.

'just have your parents fill in the form and return it to me.'

I barely managed to whisper, 'Okay,' before I turned and walked away.

I wanted to run off by myself but Janet and Midge were waiting for me outside. Janet was fooling around with Harvey Grabowsky. He kept grabbing her jacket and throwing it in the air and Janet was shrieking, 'Harvey . . . give it back!'

When Harvey saw me he asked, 'What happened to you?'

He *would* be the only one in school who didn't already know. 'I have scol . . .' I stopped in the middle. I didn't feel like explaining anything to anybody. Instead I looked straight at him and said, 'I jumped off the Empire State Building!' After I said it I felt better. I usually think up clever things to say when it's too late. From now on, when people ask me what's wrong, I'm going to give them answers like that. It's a lot smarter than telling the truth. Nobody even wants to hear the truth. 'I jumped right off the top!' I forced myself to laugh.

'Oh Deenie!' Janet said. 'Tell him the truth.'

'I just did.'

'Hey . . . that's a good story,' Harvey told me.

'Deenie . . .' Janet was annoyed now. She didn't like Harvey paying attention to me.

'Let's go,' I said. 'We'll miss our bus.'

'You go,' Janet said. 'I'm not ready yet.'

Me and Midge looked at each other, then walked away.

'He's not interested in her,' Midge said. 'He thinks she's a little kid.'

'She'll find out soon enough,' I told her.

We walked down the hill, past the church with all the statues, and around the corner. Old Lady Murray was fixing up her magazines as we got to the bus stop. I bought a roll of Life Savers from her. I stood closer than I ever had before. When she gave me my change I told her, 'I have scoliosis. That's why I'm wearing a brace.'

She didn't say anything.

'You have kyphosis, don't you?' She went back to stacking her magazines.

'I know you have kyphosis . . . that's what made your spine crooked.' Old Lady Murray didn't answer me. She started coughing. She had a terrible cough. Her face turned purple. I offered her a Life Saver but she brushed my hand away.

When she stopped coughing I said, 'Do you have any kids?'

'No.'

'Are you married?'

'No . . . I got nobody . . . no family at all.'

'But you have a mother and father . . . I mean, you did when you were small.'

'No.'

'But . . .' I almost called her *Old Lady Murray*. I caught myself in time and instead I said, 'But *Miss* Murray . . . everybody has a mother and a father.'

322

'Not me,' she said.

'Then where did you come from?'

'The stork,' she said, and started to laugh.

'Deenie!' Midge called. 'Here comes our bus!'

I wanted to explain to Old Lady Murray that I wasn't fooling around with her. That I was really interested in her family. But Midge called me again and Old Lady Murray wouldn't stop laughing.

'Why did you have to start in with her?' Midge asked. 'Everybody knows she's crazy!'

'I never heard that,' I said.

'Well she is. Besides, she smells bad. Didn't you notice?'

'She smells like sauerkraut,' I said.

'Worse than that!'

'So does Harvey Grabowsky's breath.'

'What do I care about his breath?' Midge said. 'Tell it to Janet.'

'I think I will. Tomorrow.'

When I got home Ma and Aunt Rae were doing each other's hair. I went straight up to my room and tore the Special Bus Information sheet into tiny pieces. I wasn't taking any chances. Suppose Ma decided I should go to school on that bus? I'd absolutely die first!

On Tuesday morning Susan Minton was waiting for me outside the formroom. She had a haircut just like mine. There were even a few long strands hanging in the back.

'How do you like it?' she asked.

'Did you do it yourself?'

'No. My mother took me to her beauty parlour and I told Miss Lorraine exactly what to do.'

'If you'd done it yourself it would look better.'

'Really?'

'That's a fact.'

I thought Susan looked very funny and I almost told her

so but that's when she said, 'We could be twins, Deenie. We really look alike now!'

'I suppose you wish you had a brace like mine too,' I said.

'I wouldn't mind,' Susan told me.

Miss Greenleaf shouted, 'Please sit down at your desks, girls. We're waiting for you!' I never got to tell Susan I think she's a mental case.

I spent most of the morning worrying about gym. I didn't want to change in front of all the girls. So right before lunch, on my way to the cafeteria, I stopped at the nurse's office. 'I don't think I should take gym this afternoon,' I told her. 'I've got my period.'

'How many days have you had it?' she asked.

'Since Friday.'

'Well, that's five days,' she said, counting on fingers. 'There shouldn't be any problem. Besides, exercise is the best thing for you. I never excuse girls from gym because of menstruation.'

'Oh.' I turned to leave.

'You're the Fenner girl, aren't you?' the nurse asked.

'Yes.'

'How are you managing with your brace?'

'Okay,' I told her.

'Good,' she said. 'Keep it up!'

I ran to the cafeteria, gobbled my lunch and hurried to the locker room.

Barbara Curtis is the only girl in my gym class who has a locker in my row. If I can change before she gets here I'll be safe, I thought. No one will have to see my brace. I took my sneakers out of the locker and set them on the bench, next to the gymsuit I'd been carrying with me. Ma fixed Helen's old one for me because mine doesn't fit over the brace. I kicked off my loafers and pushed them under the bench. Our gymsuits are one-piece so before I had to take off my skirt I was able to pull the gym suit up to my waist.

Then I had no choice. I couldn't finish until I took off my shirt. My heart was thumping very loud. I sneaked a look down the row of lockers but nobody was there. So I stood facing the wall and unbuttoned my shirt. I got out of it as fast as I could, pulled on my gymsuit and zipped up the front. I made it! I thought.

But when I turned around there was Barbara Curtis, standing in front of her locker, getting undressed. I'm sure she saw my brace, even though she had her back to me now. Her creeping crud was getting worse. It was all over her arms and legs . . . big red blotches and ugly hivey-looking things.

When Barbara turned around she caught me staring at her. I didn't say anything and neither did she. I sat down on the bench to put on my sneakers. I got my feet into them okay but I couldn't bend over to tie the laces.

'You want me to tie them?' Barbara asked.

'No,' I said.

'You'll trip over the laces.'

'I don't care.'

'I really don't mind tying them for you.'

'Oh . . . all right. If you want to.'

Barbara knelt in front of me and tied my shoes. I felt like the world's biggest jerk.

We walked into the gym together. When Mrs Rappoport saw me she didn't make a big thing out of my brace. She acted the same as always and I was glad. When she told us to choose partners me and Barbara looked at each other and grabbed hands.

seventeen

I've been wearing my brace two weeks and I've finally found a comfortable sleeping position, flat on my back. I never thought I'd be able to sleep that way but I guess if you're tired enough anything works. Besides, I've got a problem now. The stupid brace is making holes in my shirts. I've torn two new tops this week and Ma is really mad. She says we can't afford to keep buying things. I've told her over and over that it's not my fault. I don't even know how they get ripped. I think it has to do with the metal parts of the brace. But I've promised to be more careful anyway.

Daddy's joined the Y so I can go swimming. Midge belongs too and she's going to swim with me three days a week after school. The Y pool is heated which is nice. Dr Kliner told Daddy that I have to swim laps and not just fool around in the water. I wish I could swim like Midge because she's a regular fish. She can make it halfway across the pool without a breath. She's going to coach me so maybe we can make the Olympics together.

The best thing about swimming is getting out of my brace. I feel so free. But when the hour is up and I have to put it on again I could just cry! Sometimes I think I should throw it in the garbage and force the doctors to operate on me. But then I remember what Dr Kliner said about spending a long time in bed and I think of all the things I'd miss like the seventh-grade mixer, which is next Friday.

I wonder what would happen if I didn't wear the brace at all? Would I really turn out like Old Lady Murray? I wish there was a way I could find out for sure, without taking any chances.

Mrs Anderson sent for me again, this time in the morning.

'It's been two weeks and I haven't heard from you, Deenie.'

'You didn't say I had to come back.'

'But where's the form? I expected you to bring it in.'

'Oh that ...' I looked out the window but no pigeons were on the ledge. I tried to think of what to say so Mrs Anderson wouldn't be suspicious. 'My parents threw that form away I guess.'

'Did you explain it to them?'

'Oh yes ... but I told them I like riding the bus to school with my friends and they said that was fine with them so I suppose that's why they threw it away.'

'As long as they realize they could save money if you rode the special bus ...'

'It's not that expensive. I get student discount tickets.' Could she tell I was lying?

'I've been talking to some of your teachers, Deenie ...'

Is Miss Wabash after me again? I wondered.

'And they tell me you seem to be managing very well in spite of your handicap.'

How could she sit there and say such a thing to me! Did she honestly think I was handicapped? Is that what everybody thinks? Don't they know I'm going to be fine in four years – but Gena Courtney and those kids are *always* going to be the way they are now!

When I got home from school Ma and Aunt Rae were waiting for me at the front door. I hoped that didn't mean Mrs Anderson had called.

'We have good news for you, Deenie,' Aunt Rae said.

'What?' I asked, praying it wasn't about the special bus.

'Remember that modelling agency where we had to break the appointment ...'

'Oh, not that again ...'

'Listen to Aunt Rae,' Ma said.

'I told you I'd fix everything,' Aunt Rae said. 'I talked to the head of the agency himself, Dennie ... and he told me that seventeen isn't too late to start out at all. So we can stop worrying. He'll be happy to see you when you're out of the brace.'

'But I don't even know if I want to be a model!'

'Of course you do!' Aunt Rae said. 'Isn't that what we've always planned?' She turned to Ma. 'Thelma ... what's wrong with her?'

'She's just upset,' Ma told Aunt Rae. 'She's not used to the brace yet.'

'You wouldn't let her waste that face, would you?' Aunt Rae asked Ma.

'I'm not just a face!' I shouted. 'I'm a person too. Did either one of you ever think of that?' I ran past them and up to my room.

Ma yelled after me. 'Don't be ungrateful, Deenie! Aunt Rae was only trying to help.'

'Ha! I'll bet you'd both like to trade me in for some girl with a straight spine!' I shouted downstairs. 'Then you wouldn't have to wait four years!' I slammed my door shut.

ighteen

Me and Midge have been discussing the seventh-grade mixer. She doesn't want to go and I know why. It's not just that she can't dance. It's mostly because she's a giant compared to the seventh-grade boys. I don't want to go either but on the other hand I don't want to miss it, especially because of Buddy Brader. I think Midge will go to the mixer with me if I promise that we'll just sit around and laugh but definitely not dance.

Janet keeps telling us that all seventh-grade boys are babies and it's a waste of time to go but I'm betting she'll change her mind at the last second. Steve Hildrick is the leader of the eighth-grade band and Janet knows it. Just because she's always hanging around Harvey Grabowsky doesn't mean she isn't interested in Steve too.

On Thursday afternoon Miss Greenleaf reminded us about the mixer. 'It's a good way to make new friends,' she said. 'After all, you come from four different elementary schools. Please make sure you wear clean clothes tomorrow ... I want to be proud of my form.'

On Friday morning I knew I was right about Janet changing her mind. She wore a new outfit to school.

'How come you're all dressed up?' I asked her.

'I've decided to keep you and Midge company this afternoon,' she said.

'Gee Janet ... that's swell of you,' Midge said.

'I agree,' Janet told her. 'But I may have to pretend I don't know the two of you. You both look awful!'

Me and Midge decided to wear jeans to the mixer to prove we aren't really interested but I didn't think I looked that bad. My hair is beginning to grow. It covers my ears now and I had on a very nice turtleneck with my jeans.

Turtlenecks do the best job of hiding my brace. Ma took two of my shirts back to the store yesterday and complained about the way they rip. The manager gave he new ones in their place. I'm sure he wouldn't have done that if he'd known about the brace. I'm glad he did thoug or I wouldn't have this purple top.

The rest of the day went so slow I thought it would neve be three o'clock. I didn't see Buddy at all and I wondered if he was absent. If he was I wouldn't stay at the mixer. I' tell Midge my stomach hurt and go home myself.

When the last bell finally rang and Miss Greenleaf dismissed us all the girls ran to the Girls' Room, just like th afternoon of cheerleading tryouts. Barbara Curtis was already in front of the mirror, brushing her hair. She mad room for me. 'I like your turtleneck,' she said. 'It's a nice shade of purple.'

'Thanks.' I looked into the mirror and turned halfway around. You could still tell I was wearing the brace. I gues there's just no way to hide it.

Me and Barbara walked to the gym together. I told her I wasn't going to dance with anybody and she said she wasn't going to either. So I said she could sit with me and Midge and just watch. Barbara said that was fine with her.

Janet and Midge were waiting for me outside the gym. They didn't know Barbara so I introduced them.

'You're in my English class,' Barbara told Janet.

'I am?' Janet asked.

'Yes. You sit in the front row and I'm two rows behind

'No kidding! Who do you hang around with?'

'I'm new here,' Barbara said. 'We moved in over the summer.'

'I didn't know that,' I said. 'I thought you were from Lincoln.' That's an elementary school in another part of town.

'No, I'm from Chicago,' Barbara said. 'My father was

ansferred here.' She started scratching her arms. You
ould hardly see her creeping crud today because she was
earing long sleeves and high socks. Of course if you knew
here to look, like me, you could always find it – on the back
f her neck and in between her fingers.

'Do you have poison ivy?' Janet asked her.

'No, it's just my allergy,' Barbara said.

'You shouldn't scratch like that,' Midge told her. 'It'll
nly make it worse.'

'I can't help it,' Barbara said. 'When I get nervous I itch.'

'When I get nervous I have to go to the bathroom,' I said.

'I'd rather do that,' Barbara told me. 'You can always find
 bathroom and be done with it. I'm never done!'

The four of us went into the gym together. I thought
here would be decorations or something. But it looked
ist like always. A lot of kids were already there and most
f the boys were racing around like idiots, which made me
hink Janet is right about them being a bunch of babies.
Mr Delfone and Mrs Rappoport were trying to calm
verybody down and get things organized. All in all it didn't
eem like much of a mixer to me.

Then the eighth grade band arrived and everybody
heered. I was really happy to see that Buddy wasn't absent.
t took three boys to carry in his whole drum set. I called,
Hi Buddy. I'm here!'

He called back, 'Hi Deenie. I'm busy now.' He dusted off
is drums while the boy with the guitar tightened his strings
nd Steve Hildrick played chords on the piano.

When they first started to play the band didn't sound
ery good and nobody danced. After a while they improved.
Still, nobody danced, but the boys did stop playing touch
ootball. Finally, Mr Delfone said we had to get up and
lance. The band played the Alley Cat and most of the kids
ot on line, including Janet, but me and Barbara and Midge
tayed where we were.

Janet's a very good dancer and she knows it so she practically led the Alley Cat. I noticed how she made sure she was dancing right up close to the band so Steve couldn't miss her, even if he wanted to. Sometimes I think Janet i getting to be a terrible flirt!

I love to dance. Last night I practised in front of my full length mirror to see how I'd look dancing in my brace. An I found out I look terrible. So I'm not going to dance for the next four years, except secretly, to make sure I don't forget how.

After the Alley Cat they played the Mexican Hat Danc and the hora and I began to wish I hadn't come to the mixe Watching other people have a good time isn't any fun at all. For the first time in my life I felt like a real outsider.

Then Mrs Rappoport told everyone to take partners an the band played the Gorilla. Danny Welker, who is this little freckled-faced kid who looks like he belongs in fourt grade, walked over to us. I've known him since kindergarten. He taught me every curse I know.

He said, 'Come on Deenie. Let's go dance.'

'I don't feel like it,' I told him.

'Then what'd you come for?'

'To watch,' I said, looking away from Danny. I saw Jane dancing with this creepy guy from my math class. His nam is Peter and he has eyes like a rat and ears that stick out. Janet will dance with anybody! 'Why don't you go dance with Susan Minton,' I said to Danny.

'She's an ass,' he told me, grabbing my arm. 'Come on. You're wasting the music.'

I pulled away from him. 'I told you, Danny ... I'm no dancing!'

He said all his curses at me, then looked at Barbara. 'I'l take you,' he said, pulling her up by the arms.

Barbara turned red and started scratching her neck.

'He's harmless,' I told her. 'Go dance.'

Danny practically dragged Barbara out to the middle of the floor and when he started dancing the Gorilla he really looked like one.

I turned to Midge, wondering if she was thinking that nobody'd asked her to dance. Did she care or was she used to it by now? I couldn't tell from her face.

At four-thirty Buddy played his solo and everyone stopped dancing and gathered around his drums. I stood as close to him as I could but he played so loud I had to move back just a little or I might have gone deaf. You could tell how hard Buddy was concentrating because he had his eyes closed and his hair was hanging in his face. He was even sweating. All of that made him look especially cute and I liked him better than ever. When he was done we all clapped for him and then the band took a break while Mrs Rappoport and Mr Delfone served pretzels and drinks.

I stood next to Buddy at the refreshment table. 'You were really good,' I said.

'I told you, didn't I?'

'I came just to hear you play!'

'I believe it,' Buddy said. 'I didn't see you dance once. Don't you know how?'

'Of course I do. I love to dance!'

'So how come you didn't? I saw Janet dancing the whole time.'

'She doesn't care who she dances with,' I told him. 'And I do.'

'Yeah?'

'That's a fact.'

'Would you have danced with me?'

'Well ... sure.'

'Let's go dance then.'

'But there's no music.'

'Not in here,' Buddy said.

'Then where?'

'Come with me.'

He took my hand and led me to the door of the locker room but Buddy opened the door and pulled me in so fast I had no time to do anything about it. It was very dark. 'Suppose somebody sees us?' I asked.

'Who cares?' Buddy put his arms around me and held me tight. 'I thought you said you know how to dance,' he said as he swayed back and forth.

'I do, but it's hard without the music,' I told him.

'Just make believe you hear it.'

'I'm trying,' I whispered, finding it hard to get the words out. I wanted to dance with Buddy. I wanted to in the worst way but all I could think of was my brace and I hated it more than ever. With all the people in the world why did I have to be born with a crooked spine! I pushed Buddy away from me.

'What's wrong?' he asked. 'You chicken?'

'No,' I said. 'Not exactly.'

'Then what, Deenie?' He got my back against the wall and put his arms out on either side of me so I couldn't get away. Then he put his face near mine. He's going to kiss me, I thought. He's going to kiss me and I don't know what to do.

Then he *was* kissing me but instead of enjoying it all I could picture was Mrs Rappoport catching us and sending me to Mrs Anderson's office. She'd call Ma, tell her I was making out in the locker room and I'd be in big trouble!

Soon Buddy came up for a breath. 'You *are* chicken,' he said. 'You don't kiss back.'

I didn't know I wasn't kissing him back. I never even thought about it.

'I'm not chicken,' I told him.

'That's good,' he said, moving one hand down from my shoulder to my chest. I know he was trying to feel me, same as Steve tried to feel Janet that day in the movies. I also knew that Buddy wasn't feeling anything but my brace, which only made everything worse, so I broke away from him and ran to the door.

'I have to go back to the gym,' I called. 'My friends are waiting.'

I opened the locker room door. Everyone was getting ready to leave. The mixer was over.

'Where were you?' Midge asked, when she saw me. 'I've looked everywhere! My mother's waiting for us outside.'

'I'm sorry,' I told her. I'd forgotten Mrs Otonis was going to pick us up at five o'clock. 'I didn't know it was so late. Where's Janet?' I asked.

'Already in the car.'

I looked around for Buddy. I wanted to say goodbye but I didn't see him anywhere. So I went outside with Midge and got into her mother's car. On the way home Mrs Otonis asked us all about the mixer and me and Janet told her it was really great but Midge didn't say anything at all.

nineteen

Barbara Curtis is a big liar! I knew it on Saturday
morning as soon as I woke up. Her creeping crud *is*
catching! I've got it on my back and chest. It itched all
night and spoiled my dream about Buddy.

I called down to the kitchen, 'Ma . . . come up here quick!
I've got something all over me!'

'What is it?' Ma asked, rushing up the stairs.

'Look . . .' I showed her my creeping crud.

She inspected it. 'I'll call Dr Moravia,' she said.

I followed her to the phone and listened as she explained
it to him.

When Ma hung up I asked, 'What did he say?'

'That I should take you to Dr Nelson.'

'Who's he?'

'A dermatologist.'

'What's that?'

'A doctor who specializes in skin conditions.'

'I don't want to see another doctor! Can't we just use
calamine or something?'

'No, we have to take care of it. You don't want it to
spread to your face do you?'

I thought about Barbara. She didn't have the creeping
crud on her face but it *was* on her neck. 'No,' I told Ma. 'I
don't want it on my face.'

'All right then. Get dressed. Dr Moravia said he'll make
an appointment for us to see Dr Nelson.'

At noon Aunt Rae came over and drove us downtown
to Dr Nelson's office. His nurse told me to get undressed.
She handed me a sheet to wrap around myself. Ma stayed in
the room with me the whole time.

When Dr Nelson came in I decided right away that I
didn't like him. He wasn't friendly like Dr Kliner. He didn't

even say hello to me. He just turned on a bright light and held a magnifying glass to my creeping crud.

'I caught it from Barbara Curtis, this girl in my gym class,' I told him.

'I don't think so,' he said.

'She's the only one I know who's got it.'

'What you have isn't contagious.'

'It's not?'

Dr Nelson didn't answer me. He touched my rash and looked at it some more. Then he sat down at his desk and wrote out some prescriptions which he handed to Ma.

'If it's not catching then what is it?' I asked.

'An irritation from your brace. You shouldn't wear it next to your skin. You need a soft shirt under it.'

'Not one of those things I saw in Dr Kliner's office?' I said.

'I don't know what you saw but you'll have to wear an undershirt to protect your skin from now on.'

'Oh no! I'm not wearing any undershirt!'

'Deenie . . .' Ma said. 'You'll do whatever the doctor tells you.'

'And that means a soft undershirt,' Dr Nelson said again. 'I'm also prescribing a cortisone cream to rub in three times a day and a solution to put into your bath water. Soak for half an hour a day until the rash clears up. Call me if it doesn't improve in a week,' he told Ma as he stood up.

As soon as he left the room Ma said, 'Get dressed, Deenie, and we'll stop by the drugstore on our way home.'

An undershirt! I thought as I got into my clothes. How can I go to school in an undershirt?

That night Ma ran my tub and dumped in one package of the powder Dr Nelson prescribed. 'I'm setting the oven so I know when half an hour's up,' Ma said. 'I'll call you. Soak until then.'

I got out of my brace and into the tub. At first I was

337

bored just lying there. Usually I take showers and get in and out as fast as possible. But the hot water was very relaxing and soon I began to enjoy it. I reached down and touched my special place with the washcloth. I rubbed and rubbed until I got that good feeling.

There are still a lot of things I don't understand about sex. I think Helen has a book somewhere in her room. I'm going to look for it.

When Ma called that my time was up I got out of the tub, dried off and put on the undershirt before my brace. I think what I'll do is wear my bra under it. I'm certainly not going to school without a bra.

I tiptoed into Helen's room. She's never home anymore. And when she is home she's always locked up in her room. I think something's wrong with her. She got two B's on her report card and that's never happened before. Ma was plenty sore too!

I opened Helen's desk drawers one by one. I didn't see the book I was looking for but I did find a piece of notebook paper that said:

Mrs Joseph Roscow
Helen and Joe Roscow
Joseph and Helen Roscow
Helen Marie Roscow
Helen Fenner Roscow
Mr and Mrs Joseph P. Roscow

At first I didn't know what all those names meant. Then it hit me. Helen was writing about Joe, from Daddy's gas station, and herself. Helen was in love!

Not long after that Ma found out about Helen too. Because one night after supper Daddy went back to the station to do his books and Helen was there with Joe, while she was supposed to be studying at Myra Woodruff's house.

338

I don't know exactly what happened but Daddy drove Helen home and she wasn't allowed out at night for the next two weeks, except to do her baby-sitting.

Helen cried a lot those two weeks. I heard her every night.

Then one afternoon Helen came home and started screaming at Ma. 'How could you? How could you be so mean?'

'It's not what you think,' Ma told her.

I wondered what was going on? I thought, maybe Helen and Joe want to get married and Ma won't let them.

'You *made* Daddy fire him just because we liked each other!' Helen shouted.

'That's not so,' Ma told Helen. 'Daddy had to let him go because we need the extra money. You can ask him yourself.'

'You're lying!' Helen yelled. 'You did it because you don't want us together. Admit it ... admit it, why don't you? You don't need the money.'

'Yes we do!' Ma said. 'I'll discuss it with you when you calm down.'

'I'm calm now,' Helen hollered.

Ma raised her voice too and I felt very uncomfortable. I wanted to leave the room but I didn't want to miss the argument. So I sat in my chair and listened.

'We have doctors' bills to pay,' Ma shouted. 'And we're going to have more of them. Until I can find some work Daddy's going to manage without help at the station.'

Doctors' bills, I thought. Ma must be talking about *my* doctors! I'll bet my brace cost a fortune. I didn't think of that before. I'm the reason Daddy had to fire Joe. Helen is going to hate me!

'You didn't approve of him anyway,' Helen told Ma.

'I don't want you throwing away your life,' Ma said.

'I wasn't throwing away my life! I just wanted to be with him. Is that so wrong? I'm sixteen, Ma! I'm not a baby!'

'He wasn't right for you,' Ma said.

'How do you know? Who are you to say what's right for me? It wouldn't bother you if a boy liked Deenie would it?'

Why did she say that? I wondered.

'That's different,' Ma said.

'What's different about it?' Helen asked. 'I'm human too.'

'God gave you a special brain,' Ma told her. 'And he wouldn't have done that if he hadn't intended for you to put it to good use.'

She's telling Helen the same thing she told me about my face!

'Oh Ma . . . you're impossible! God didn't give me a special brain. You made that up. And you almost convinced me, Ma . . . you almost did.' Helen was really crying now. Tears ran down her face and everything but she didn't stop. She said, 'I used to tell myself it didn't matter if I wasn't pretty like Deenie because I have a special brain and Deenie's is just ordinary . . . but that didn't help, Ma . . . it didn't help at all . . . because it's not true! None of it's true . . . don't you see . . . you can't make us be what you want . . .' Helen was sobbing so loud she couldn't talk anymore.

I didn't know what to do. I was hoping Helen and Ma had forgotten I was in the room. I wished I could vanish. I never knew Helen thought about me being pretty. I always thought it was just the opposite . . . that she was better than *me* because she was so smart. I feel funny knowing about Helen.

'If you think I'm going to sit by and watch you waste your

life on a stupid boy with dirty fingernails you have a lot to learn, Helen Fenner!' Ma said.

'He's not stupid!' Helen cried. 'He's going to be a Forest Ranger and he writes poems . . . did you know that? Do you know anything about him?'

Ma's not being fair, I thought. Joe does write poems. I know because I found one inside Helen's maths book last Wednesday. I couldn't tell that to Ma though. Then Helen would know I'd been snooping, so instead I said, 'Everybody gets dirty fingernails from working in a gas station . . . even Daddy!'

'Be quiet, Deenie!' Ma yelled. 'This has nothing to do with you.'

'It does too! You just said Daddy fired Joe because of doctors' bills and I'm the one who's always seeing doctors!'

Helen turned around and looked at me. Then she did the craziest thing. She ran to me and hugged me and cried into my shoulder. 'It's not your fault, Deenie . . . don't let them make you believe that . . . it's really not your fault.'

I started crying too. Helen doesn't hate me, I thought. She should, but she doesn't. We both cried so hard our noses ran but neither one of us let go of the other to get a tissue. And right through it all Ma kept talking. 'I wanted better for you,' she said. 'Better than what I had myself. That's what I've always planned for my girls . . . is that so wrong?'

twenty

I finally told Barbara Curtis about my undershirt. I got tired of rushing to the Girls' Room every time I had gym. And that's what I've been doing – taking off my undershirt and stuffing it in my bag.

As soon as I told Barbara I felt better. She said one time the rash between her fingers was so bad she had to wear white socks on her hands at night, to keep from scratching in her sleep. She asked me what kind of cream I'm using and I described it to her. She said it sounds a lot like hers. I think my rash is getting better because it doesn't itch anymore.

I'm glad Barbara's not a liar after all. She's a nice kid. I think I must have been really weird to not like her just because of her creeping crud. Janet and Midge like her too. Janet invited her to a party she's having in two weeks. She's also invited Harvey Grabowsky which is the dumbest thing I've ever heard. I know he isn't going to come.

I dropped another question into Mrs Rappoport's box. I wrote:

What does it feel like to have sexual intercourse?

The other night, when I'd finished my exercises, I went to Helen's room and asked if I could borrow her sex book.

'I lent it to Myra,' she said. 'You can read it when she gives it back.'

'But I need it now,' I said.

'What for?'

Because ...'

'You have a question?'

I nodded.

'Maybe I can help you.'

'I have a lot of questions,' I told her.

'Go on . . .'

'Well . . .'

'If you're going to be shy about it I can't help you.'

'All right,' I said. 'What does it feel like to have sexual intercourse?' As soon as I said it I was sorry because Helen turned colours. 'You told *me* not to be shy!' I said.

'I don't know the answer.'

'Oh, come on, Helen.'

'I really don't know,' Helen said. 'And now that Joe's gone I'll probably never find out!'

Joe left town without telling Helen. I think that was really rotten of him. Maybe he didn't love her after all. I hope Helen finds somebody else to love soon, because I can see how lonely she is without Joe. I also hope Mrs Rappoport can help me with my questions and that Myra hurries with the sex book.

I got a letter from Dr Kliner inviting me to a scoliosis clinic at his office, where all of his patients get together to talk about wearing their braces. I think I'll ask the other girls how they sit at their desks and if they get rashes too and if they all sleep flat on their backs and rip their clothes and worry about people looking at them wherever they go? And I'm going to tell them how I answer people who ask me what's wrong. I'll bet I'm the only one who's ever said, 'I jumped off the Empire State Building!' The most important thing I have to find out is how smart you have to be to become an orthopaedist because I've been thinking I might really like to be one.

This afternoon, on my way to French, I didn't look away when I passed the Special Class. I saw Gena Courtney working at the blackboard. I wonder if she thinks of herself as a handicapped person or just a regular girl, like me.

twenty-one

I'm not going to wear the brace to Janet's party. It can't hurt to take it off for a few hours. I do it three times a week when I go swimming, and I want Buddy Brader to see me without it. I want him to hold me the way he did in the locker room, without feeling all that metal.

I got dressed in one of the outfits I bought to start junior high – a skirt and sweater that doesn't fit over the brace. I wasn't sure how Daddy and Ma would take it but I had the feeling they'd let me go because I haven't been complaining about the brace and I haven't asked to skip school again.

I went downstairs. 'I'm ready to go to Janet's,' I told Daddy.

He looked at me. 'Where's your brace?'

'I'll put it on as soon as I come home.'

'You can't go without it.'

'Please Daddy . . . this is very important to me.'

'No,' he said. 'If I let you go without it now you'll want to leave it off every time you're going somewhere special.'

'No, I won't. I promise . . . just this once!'

'Go upstairs and change.'

'But Daddy . . .'

'Oh, let her go, Frank,' Ma said. 'She looks so pretty.'

Daddy slammed the book he was reading and shouted at Ma. 'We've been through this before, Thelma.' Then he turned to me and I thought he was going to yell but when he spoke his voice was back to normal. 'The day I found out about your brace I promised myself I'd be firm,' he said. 'That's why I made you go to school when you wanted to stay home. And now I'm telling you . . . no matter how much it hurts . . . you wear the brace or you don't go.'

'But Daddy . . .'

'I know . . . I know,' he said. 'It's hard for me too, Deenie.'

344

I ran up to my room and kicked the door shut. My father wasn't going to change his mind – even if I screamed and cried he wasn't going to change it. I knew that. I didn't want to miss Janet's party. I didn't want to miss a lot of things that would be happening in the next four years. But just tonight I wanted to be like everyone else.

Suppose I wore the brace to the party and as soon as I got there I changed? That way Daddy wouldn't know anything because my friends won't tell on me. And I'll never do it again. I swear this is the first and last time!

I changed into the brace and my regular clothes but I packed the outfit I'd been wearing into a shopping bag. Then I went downstairs.

Daddy drove me to Janet's house and when we got there he leaned over and kissed the top of my head. 'I'm glad you changed your mind, Deenie. I knew you wouldn't let me down.'

I felt bad about fooling him. I grabbed my shopping bag and opened the car door.

'Have a good time,' Daddy said.

'I will,' I told him, as I got out of the car.

The front door of Janet's house was open and as I walked in I could hear all the noise coming from her basement. I thought about going straight up to Janet's room to change before anybody saw me. Then I thought about my father and how he trusts me. I've never really lied to him and I don't think he's ever lied to me. I put my shopping bag down in the corner of the living room and went downstairs. Maybe I'd change later.

Janet has this great basement with flowers painted all over the concrete floor and posters decorating every pole. Midge and Barbara were already there. So was Buddy Brader.

'Hey, Deenie,' he said, when he saw me. 'What took you so long? I thought you weren't coming.'

'Well, I'm here now,' I said.

Mr Kayser served us a ton of food. There was a dish with rows and rows of turkey and roast beef. I guess he gets it cheap because he's a butcher. Janet said she promised her mother we'd play nice, decent games like charades even though none of us wanted to. Naturally Harvey Grabowsky didn't show up. I guess Janet finally realized he wasn't going to and she settled for Steve Hildrick instead. When she put on the record player they started dancing and I saw her press up against him.

Later Buddy grabbed my hand and led me into the part of the basement where Janet's mother does the laundry. It was dark and kind of damp in there and it smelled like Clorox. Buddy said, 'Couldn't you take off your brace for a little while?'

I thought about the shopping bag I'd left upstairs. 'No,' I told Buddy. 'I have to wear it all the time.'

'Oh well . . .' Buddy said. This time when he kissed me I concentrated on kissing him back. I hoped I was doing it right.

Daddy called for me at eleven-thirty and as I got into the car he asked what was in the shopping bag. I told him, 'Something I thought I might need for the party . . . that I didn't need after all.'